COWBOY BOOTS
FOR CHRISTMAS (COWBOY NOT INCLUDED)

CAROLYN BROWN

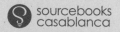
sourcebooks
casablanca

Published by Sourcebooks Casablanca, an imprint of Sourcebooks, Inc.
P.O. Box 4410, Naperville, Illinois 60567-4410
(630) 961-3900
Fax: (630) 961-2168
www.sourcebooks.com

Printed and bound in Canada.
MBP 10 9 8 7 6 5 4 3 2 1

To Cathy Genna,
with appreciation for all you do for romance authors!

Chapter 1

THE THIRD TIME IS NOT ALWAYS THE CHARM.

Twice now, Finn O'Donnell had told the government he wasn't interested in anything that the FBI, CIA, or any of the other alphabet agencies dangled at him like a carrot on a long stick in front of a donkey. All Finn wanted to do was watch his cattle grow fat on Salt Draw Ranch and be left alone with his dog, Shotgun.

So that black SUV coming down his lane could turn around and go on back to wherever the hell it came from. They didn't have enough carrots in the world to make him leave his new home in Burnt Boot, Texas, and pick up his sniper rifle again. He leaned against the porch post, and with arms crossed over his broad chest, he waited.

The yellow hair on Shotgun's back stood up like a punk rocker's, and a low growl rumbled out of his throat. The dog took a step forward and Finn stuck a boot out to touch his leg. That's all it took for the dog to heel even when his body quivered in anticipation of attacking something, like the wheels of that fancy SUV.

"Easy, boy. We can tell them to go to hell a third time easy as we did the first two." He pushed mirrored sunglasses up a notch and tipped his black cowboy hat down to block the sun from his eyes.

Dead grass and gravel crunched under the wheels of the black vehicle when it stopped in front of the low-slung, ranch-style house. Shotgun whined, but until Finn moved his boot, the dog wouldn't bail off the porch and go after the intruders.

"Not yet. We'll hear them out and then you can take a bite from the ass of their Italian suits as they get back in their van," Finn said softly.

An identical vehicle turned down the lane and parked right behind the first one. This was something new. Maybe since he'd moved to Burnt Boot on his own ranch and wasn't a part of his folks' operation in central Texas, they thought they'd best send out a whole committee to persuade him. Finn looked out over the tops of the sunglasses but the SUV windows were tinted and he couldn't see a damn thing.

"Looks like they've brought an extra van just for you, Shotgun. You want to join the army, old boy? You'll have to do boot camp and learn to sniff out bombs and herd camels instead of cows. And boot camp involves more than chasing rabbits when I'm doing my evening run."

He removed his black felt cowboy hat with stains around the leather band, raked his dark hair back from his forehead, and resettled the hat on his head at an angle to shade his eyes better. Were they waiting for Christmas? If so, they were a little early because that was four weeks away.

He pulled his denim jacket tighter across his broad expanse of a chest and leaned on the porch post, his boot still touching Shotgun's front leg. The entire O'Donnell family had chipped in the day after Thanksgiving to help him move from Comfort, Texas, to Burnt Boot. His herd woke up in holding pens and by nightfall they were grazing on the grass growing on Salt Draw three hundred miles away. His sister, two brothers, and a dozen cousins would put him in a straitjacket if he let the brass out there in those vans talk him back into the army after that move.

Then the door of the van flew open and a woman stepped out. He thought he was seeing things. Surely that couldn't be his Callie.

Callie Brewster had listened to the man in the front seat of the SUV tell her all the reasons why she and her nephew should be in the Witness Protection Program. Now he was repeating himself and she didn't want to hear any more, so she threw open the door the minute the vehicle stopped moving.

He said something about not getting out of the SUV until they'd talked to Finn, but she'd made up her mind. She stomped the legs of her jeans down over her boots and started across the yard. She damn sure didn't need anyone to talk for her or before her either.

She didn't need anyone to protect her. She could take the eyes out of a rattlesnake with any weapon the army slapped in her hands. She'd kept up her skills at the shooting range in Corpus Christi and kept in shape. But she did need someone to watch her back, and Finn O'Donnell had proven time and time again that he could damn sure do that.

From a distance he still looked the same. Broad shoulders, sculpted abs, biceps that stretched the sleeves of any shirt on the market, thighs that testified he was used to hard work, and hands that could be either soft or tough depending on what was needed. Yes, that was her Finn: the man she'd had a crush on for three years, though she'd never said a word about it. They were partners, sniper and spotter, and were closer than a husband and wife in lots of ways. But partners didn't act on crushes and they damn sure didn't get involved with each other, not when they had to do the jobs that Finn and Callie were called upon to do.

She threw back the hood of her jacket and put her sunglasses in her pocket. The moment he lowered his sunglasses and recognized her, he started her way, meeting her in the middle of the yard in a bear hug that brought her feet off the ground.

"God, I've missed you so much," he said.

Heart pounding, pulse racing, she was slow to let go when he set her firmly back on the ground.

"Lala?" she asked.

His wife damn sure wouldn't appreciate him showing so much affection to his old partner. Any minute now Callie expected her to come out of the house, maybe with a grenade in her hands.

He held her by her shoulders. "Lala isn't here, Callie. That's a story for another day. I can't believe you're right here in front of me. I've thought of you every day since I came home. What in the hell are you doing in Burnt Boot, Texas?"

Her aqua eyes locked with his crystal-clear blue ones and held for what seemed like an eternity. There was no Lala and he was glad to see her. She had known this was the right decision.

"I need a place to stay." Her voice was an octave too

high but, hell on wheels, Finn O'Donnell had hugged her. She'd almost had a damn fangirl moment.

He stepped back and looked toward the two vans. Three doors opened as if they'd been synchronized. A kid, who reminded Finn of a young colt that hadn't quite grown into his spindly legs, jumped from the van. Shotgun ran out to the boy, put his paws on his shoulders, and the two of them fell to the ground for a wrestling game.

"Remember me talking about my nephew, Martin?"

"He need a place to stay, too?" Finn asked.

She nodded and for the first time she had doubts about the whole thing.

"You brought government men. I guess this is serious?"

Another nod. "It is."

"Then I expect we'd best go in the house and talk about it." He draped an arm around her shoulders. "Okay if Martin stays outside with Shotgun? Old dog has missed kids since we've been in Burnt Boot. You haven't changed a bit in two years. You still as sassy as ever?"

"Callie?" the boy called out.

"You can stay outside if you stay in the yard."

"Yes, ma'am."

"Well? Are you still a pistol?" Finn asked as they took the three steps up to the porch.

"Damn straight, O'Donnell," she answered.

Callie's breath tightened in her chest. She could think it was fear of leaving Martin alone, but if she was totally honest with herself, it was the way Finn had hugged her and still kept an arm thrown loosely over her shoulders.

Old feelings surfaced that she thought she'd buried long ago, and now there was no Lala in the picture. Sweet Jesus, could she trust herself to walk into a situation like this?

Finn stood back to let Callie go inside first. "I've got a pot of coffee brewing and sweet tea in the refrigerator. Excuse the mess. I'm not even unpacked yet. I'd hoped that these men who brought you here wouldn't be able to ever find me again, but I guess Big Brother has his ways. Might as well come on in the kitchen."

Three men filed ahead of him and stopped inside an enormous great room housing a living room with a huge stone fireplace on the east end, a big dining room, and a country kitchen. Finn led the way to the kitchen area and motioned toward a round table flanked by six chairs. He hated to take his arm away from Callie, for fear she would vanish into the cold winter air, and he had so much to tell her about what had happened since they'd said good-bye in Afghanistan two years ago. Lord, he'd fantasized about Callie right up until Lala came into his life, but he remembered how much he wanted to kiss her full lips and how his hands itched to brush her long, dark hair away from her face. He'd dreamed about waking up to those big aqua-colored eyes staring at him in the morning. And now she was right there in his kitchen.

"Have a seat," he said.

"Need some help?" Callie asked.

"I got it covered." He opened three cabinet doors before he located the coffee cups and then glanced back over his shoulder. "Coffee for everyone?"

Three men nodded.

"Black just like always, Callie?"

"I haven't changed a bit," she said.

He carried cups to the table, then drew his chair close enough that his knee touched hers. "Okay, Callie, let's hear that story."

Otis picked up his coffee and said, "She needs to go into Witness Protection. She and the boy both. I'm Otis, by the way, and these are Special Agents Jones and Smith."

Finn shot a look across the table. "I know Jones and Smith. Pleased to make your acquaintance, Otis, but I asked her to tell me, not you."

Callie's hand shook as she picked up the coffee cup and took a sip. When she set it down, he covered her hand with his, squeezing gently. "Take your time. There's no hurry."

"My sister was killed in a car wreck a couple of weeks before I got out of the service two years ago. I came home to a six-year-old nephew in foster care. I convinced the authorities to let me have him. Last week he witnessed a murder in the alley behind our apartment complex. They want to put us in the WITSEC program but I refused."

"Go on," Finn said.

"Even though he's only eight, he got a good long look at the man who did the killing, and they are going to let him testify when it comes time," Callie said.

"Are you willing to let this be a safe house for her?" Otis asked.

Finn turned to face Otis. "I owe this woman my life more times than I can count. If she wants to stay here, she damn sure can stay. We were more than partners and she was more than my spotter. She was my best friend, so does that answer your question?"

"Thank you, Finn," she said.

He cocked his head to one side. "Callie, this is a ranch. If I remember right, you joined the army because you hated every damn thing there was about ranchin'. Are you sure you want to live here?"

"Guess I've found out there's worse things in the world than the cows, hay haulin', and calvin' season," she said. "I'm not askin' for a handout here, Finn. I'm willing to work. I'll work outside. I'll work inside cleaning and cooking or both if you'll give me and Martin room and board. And it doesn't matter if I like it, Finn. I'll do it until the trial is over, then we'll be out of your hair." She inhaled deeply. "I can ride a horse or a four-wheeler. I can pull a calf or drive anything that's got wheels and fix most anything that's got an engine. I'll work cheap and, in exchange, Martin and I get to live here without fear until the trial is over, probably in early February."

"That's putting a lot of faith in one man," Otis said.

"Not this man," Agent Smith said seriously. "I'd trust him with my life. Hell, I'd trust him with the life of the president of the United States. I've tried to hire him to do just that but he turned us down, twice."

Finn hated to unpack, do laundry, and most of all cook, and she'd offered to work inside or outside.

Finn O'Donnell, cats, dogs, and baby rabbits are one thing, but people are not strays. You don't train them. You don't get them well and turn them loose. Be careful, his inner voice warned.

"Have you gotten any better at frying a chicken?

Is your gravy still lumpy and your biscuits tough?" Finn grinned.

"Chicken will melt in your mouth and my biscuits and gravy are fine, thank you," she answered.

He hugged her close to his side, almost toppling her out of the chair. "Don't you lie to me, Brewster. I remember your burnt fried chicken, and your biscuits could have been used as weapons of mass destruction."

She pushed away from him. "Don't you talk to me in that tone, O'Donnell. We were both drunk when we fried that chicken and we did it together and you were as much to blame for it as I was. I've learned to cook in the past two years. Raisin' a kid means making dinner every night whether I want to or not."

His heart kicked in an extra beat. He hadn't felt so alive since he left Afghanistan and surely not since he'd heard what a fool he'd been when he fell for Lala. "Okay, we'll try it until after the holidays. I wouldn't want to spoil Christmas for Shotgun and it looks like he's done took to that kid."

Callie laughed until she snorted, held her hand out, and said, "Shake on it. I understand it's all for your dog, not for me or my nephew. Your crazy sense of humor hasn't changed a damn bit, Finn O'Donnell. Thank God for that."

Chapter 2

"WE WERE LIVING IN A FURNISHED APARTMENT." CALLIE shrugged when she caught Finn looking at the bags the federal boys unloaded on the porch before they left.

"What'd you do for a paycheck?" he asked.

"I worked as a trainer in a gym and taught women's self-defense classes," she answered. "The army didn't give me a lot of marketable skills for the outside world."

The muscles in his arms flexed against the knit of his long-sleeved Western shirt when he picked up one of the duffel bags and threw it over his shoulder like a bag of cattle feed. Then he stooped, grabbed the other one, and hefted it up on the other shoulder.

"You want to get the door for me and call the kid into the house? I'll show you where your rooms are," he said.

"Hey, Martin, a little help here," she yelled over her shoulder as she opened the door.

The boy came in a dead run with the dog right behind him. "Yes, ma'am. Wow, Callie! I bet Finn could pick you up."

Callie could feel the heat coming up the back of her neck, but she couldn't stop it. Soldiers didn't blush. They were mean and tough and could take out snakes, spiders, and even enemy combatants. But a visual of her hanging over Finn's back with her butt so close to his lips that he could kiss it—well, hell's bells, that would make the devil himself blush.

"I don't imagine she weighs as much as this bag," Finn said. "What'd you pack in here, Martin? Rocks?"

The boy picked up one of the smaller zippered bags and managed to hoist it up on his shoulder like Finn, but it came close to bowing his legs. "No, sir, but Callie put books in that one. This one is heavy, too."

"I bet it is, son. Just keep a tight hold on it and follow me. I'll show you where to unload it," Finn said.

The cold wind whipped around and came at them from the north, cooling Callie's scarlet cheeks considerably. "That wind feels like it's comin' off snow or ice. Martin and I can share a room. Couldn't afford a two-bedroom place. Mostly I just slept on the sofa and let him have the bedroom anyway."

The dog shot into the house before the door shut behind her and flopped down on the rug in front of the cold fireplace, put a paw over his nose, and promptly went to sleep.

"No need for that. This is a big house. This wing has three bedrooms and a huge bathroom. Y'all can have your choice of rooms, but I bet Martin is going to like this one." He slid the bags off his shoulders at the doorway of one of the bedrooms.

"Which one is yours?" Callie dropped a bulging suitcase in the hallway.

He turned her shoulders toward the living room and pointed. "There's another wing off the living room. I chose a bedroom in that area because it has a fireplace. It shares a flue with the one in the living room. Actually, Shotgun chose it when we first got here. We had a fireplace in my bedroom at the ranch in Comfort and he recognized it as a place to warm

his bones after working all day out in the cold,"
Finn answered.

The deep Southern drawl in his voice still affected
her the same way it had back when she first met him.
She didn't know the story, but Lala was a complete idiot
not to be living on the ranch with him.

Martin let go of the bag on his shoulder, and it fell to
the hardwood floor with a loud thump. "Are you serious? Is this really my room? I'm afraid to shut my eyes
because it might not be here when I open them again."

Callie peeked around Finn's shoulder to see Martin
jump over all three bags and spin around in the bedroom,
trying to see everything at once. "If I don't get nothin'
else for Christmas, this will be the best one I ever had
in my whole life. Can I invite friends over? There's two
bunk beds, so I can have three friends, right?"

Callie heard him talking but her mind was on Finn's
hand on her shoulder. She felt safe for the first time since
the murder, but it went much deeper than that. Finn had
always sent a wave of heat through her body. She'd just
managed it better in Afghanistan.

"Callie!" Martin said loudly.

"Sorry, kiddo, I was gathering wool," she said.

"I asked if I can unpack my bag right now."

"Yes, you may," Callie said.

Finn leaned over and whispered, sending shivers up
her spine. "I figured he'd like this room. We need to talk."

"He's begged for bunk beds since he was big enough
to know what they were," she said softly.

Martin kicked off his shoes, climbed up to a top bunk,
and sat cross-legged. "It's my dream room. Can I read
them books? I bet there's some good stories in them.

Can Shotgun come in here with me and sleep on one of the beds? Can I have friends spend the night?"

Before he could ask another million questions, Callie laid a hand on his shoulder. "Give Finn time to think and give yourself time to breathe. Yes, I'm sure you can read the books if you are careful with them. We'll talk about the dog and friends later on, but right now you get settled in while Finn and I have an adult conversation. Okay?"

Martin smiled. "Yes, ma'am."

Finn led the way into the living room and sat down on the sofa, patting the cushion beside him and motioning for her. "Callie, I mean it, I'm really glad to see you. Not just to have a hand or a cook. I missed you. I tried to get in touch, but the phone number you gave me was disconnected."

"I tried to call you for a whole month after I got things straightened out with Martin. I figured you were married to Lala by then, but I wanted to know you'd made it home safe," she said. "How did you wind up here? And how long have you been here? The neat freak Finn I knew wouldn't still have unpacked boxes after even a week."

He reached over and ran the back of his hand down her cheek, sending another round of flutters to her heart. "I've been here two days, Callie. I know that's you sitting there, but I keep thinking you'll vanish if I don't keep touching you. We've got two years of catching up to do. Am I right in thinking there is no boyfriend, since you came here?"

"You are very right." She held his hand to her cheek a few seconds longer before letting go. "Now tell me how you ended up in this little place."

"The lady who owned this property, Verdie, sold it to me, lock, stock, and barrel. She wanted out of town before any more cold weather set in. I'm not sure what I bought in the house. I've spent two days in the barn and on the property counting cows," he said.

"But it's miles from Austin."

"Comfort. I lived in Comfort, Texas, not too far from Austin. I looked for a place there, but nothing fit. Crazy to think of a ranch fitting like a pair of cowboy boots, but this place did. When Verdie said she wanted to sell it as it stood, it seemed like a dream come true. And now you are here for a few weeks and it seems like old times, sitting here, almost like we were back in the tents after a mission."

"I missed that most of all," she said.

"Hey, Callie, when is supper? Do I have time to read a little while?" Martin yelled from his room.

"He's afraid to come out here for fear he'll wake up and this will be a dream," Callie said and then raised her voice. "Go ahead and read."

"Speaking of supper, we should probably go to the store and lay in staples. It's closed tomorrow," he said. "I make a pretty mean ham and cheese sandwich and I do know how to open a can of tomato soup to go with it, but I'm not even sure there's enough ham for three sandwiches."

"I'll make supper, Finn. I think I can do better than soup and sandwiches if you'll show me where things are located."

He chuckled. "Your guess is good as mine. I've been living on frozen pizza and sandwiches for two days."

He stood up and held out his hand. "Trust me, there's

nothing in the refrigerator. The freezer is full, but everything is frozen. The pantry isn't too shabby, but pickin's are slim on staples."

She put her hand in his. "Then I suppose we should go to the store."

―⁓―

He pulled her up and held her hand just a minute longer than necessary. He could give her directions and the keys to the work truck, but he didn't want to let her out of his sight. He'd thought he was ready for solitude and to get away from the big O'Donnell extended family, but after two days he was downright lonesome. Old Shotgun listened well, but he didn't answer back with anything but a wagging tail.

Callie looked at the clock on the microwave. "When we get back, I could make supper while you do chores. He's a magpie and seldom ever shuts up, but if he could help in any way, Martin would probably love to go with you. But if you'd rather take care of things without him driving you crazy with a million questions, he can read in his room or I'll get him busy helping me."

"I'd love to take him with me and I'm sure it would make Shotgun happy. Want to tell him to get his coat on so we can go to the store now?"

His heart seized up the second she was out of his sight, so he followed her. "The old work truck is yours anytime you want to use it. Keys are hanging on a nail out in the utility room. I'll tell Gladys—she's the lady who owns the store—that you can charge on the ranch bill," he said.

Callie stopped at the bedroom door and knocked.

"Martin, we're going to the grocery store. Use a book-mark and get your coat."

"When we get back, if you're not too tired I expect I could use a hand this evening with the chores," Finn said, but his eyes were on Callie the whole time.

Martin climbed down the ladder at the end of the bed as quickly as his legs could get him to the floor. "I'm not too tired. You just tell me what you want me to do and I'll take care of it."

"I can always use an extra set of eyes to check on things for me," Finn said.

"I can do that. I like doin' ranch work. Are we going to church tomorrow?" Martin asked.

"You *want* to go to church?" Finn was amazed. "My mama had to drag me to church when I was your age."

"I like the music." Martin tied his shoes and grabbed his coat. "Someday I'm going to play a guitar and sing."

"Then, yes, we'll go to church if Callie wants to," Finn said.

"Thank you," Callie whispered. "For everything."

Finn led the way back to the kitchen, with Callie and Martin behind him. "You are more than welcome."

Her coat was still hanging on the back of the kitchen chair where she'd put it when she first came into the house. He picked it up and held it for her. The movement sent a whiff of her perfume wafting up to his nose, the scent triggering dozens of memories.

"I forgot to show your room to you. Want to see it now or when we get back?"

"Later," she said.

An old-time bell clanged when Finn opened the door into the country store. It was well stocked for a little country store. Cans of food lined up neatly on spotless shelves. A small but clean-looking meat counter at the back, and one of those old cash registers with a hundred buttons on it was centered on the checkout counter, which was cluttered with a candy bar display, a jar of lollipops, and a couple of newspapers dated two days before.

"Help you?" A head that went with the gravelly voice popped up from behind the butcher station. "Hey, Finn, I thought you'd be in before now."

"Hey, Miz Gladys, how are you this cold day?"

"Gettin' too damn old for this kind of hours, but what's a woman to do? Who you got there with you?" Gladys asked.

"This is Callie Brewster and her nephew, who lives with her. They are my new hired hands on Salt Draw. Can you make a note to let Callie charge on the ranch account, please, ma'am?"

"Of course I can. I'm Gladys Cleary. I'm glad to see he's hiring a crew." She wiped her hands on an over-sized white canvas apron that testified to the fact that she'd been working with a hindquarter of beef all day. She was a tall, lanky woman with just a touch of white in her black hair. High cheekbones and dark eyes said that she had some Native American blood, but the name Cleary definitely sounded Irish.

"We pay by the tenth of each month, right?" Finn asked.

"That's the way I do business with lots of folks around this area. I been doin' the same with Salt Draw for years. Long as it gets paid by the tenth, I'm okay with it. What do you need?" Gladys asked.

"Staples mainly. Looks like the pantry and freezer are both full, but the refrigerator is empty. Starting with butter, cheese, and mayonnaise," Callie said.

After the mega-sized supermarkets she was used to shopping in, the little store made her feel like she'd taken a step backward in time. The last time she'd been in a store like this was out around the Palo Duro Canyon area. She was five or six years old and her mother had taken her along into a small town on a Saturday for supplies when they'd gone to visit her grandparents.

Gladys tapped the counter beside the cash register. "First thing you'll need is a cart. And what's your name, son?"

"I'm Martin Brewster." He stepped forward and stuck out his hand.

Gladys shook it. "I'm pleased to make your acquaintance. Will you be going to school here?"

"Yes, ma'am. I suppose I will."

"I'll have to call Verdie later and tell her there's a boy living on the ranch. She'd like that," Gladys said. "I still have trouble believing Verdie is gone. She hung on to that ranch until the very end, hoping one of them grandkids of hers would want it. But kids these days, they want instant gratification and they want to live in the big cities where the fun is at. They don't want to work their fingers to the bone on a ranch."

Callie pushed the cart and Finn helped her fill the list she'd made on the way to the store.

Gladys talked nonstop. "She really got pissed at her grandkids when not a one of them offered to let her live with them or even near them. She checked herself into one of them fancy retirement homes in Dallas. Says she hopes she lives long enough to eat up every dime of the money. And if she don't, she's leavin' what's left to a ranch out in west Texas that takes in old jackasses that need a place to finish up their lives. She says they can put in a second home for aging donkeys right here in Burnt Boot. I hear from her nearly every day and she's not happy at that place. Been a month now and she's still not settled into it."

Callie put two gallons of milk into the cart. "What about her kids?"

Gladys tossed in a can of black pepper. "Had two boys. Both dead. One left three kids. The other one had four by three different women. Finn, have the Brennan women and the Gallagher gals come sniffin' around Salt Draw?"

"Who?" He picked up two packages of chocolate cookies and added them to the cart. "You mean the feuding families? Why would they come to Salt Draw?"

Callie laughed nervously.

"What's so funny?" Finn asked.

"Can I have bananas?" Martin asked.

Finn picked up a brown paper bag and filled it with bananas.

"Feuding families? Women? I'm wondering which one of us is going to be doing the protecting," she said.

"Feud? I thought Verdie was teasing." Finn's hand brushed Callie's as they both reached for the bread at the same time.

"I don't think so," Gladys said.

"Like the *Hatfields and McCoys*? Callie wouldn't let me watch it. She said it was too violent," Martin said.

"Something like that," Gladys said. "The Gallaghers

own the Wild Horse Ranch over to one side of my property. The Brennans own the River Bend over on the other side. Been feudin' since right after Moses led the people to the Promised Land, and they jump on any chance to fan the flames of the old feud. Besides, they both tried to buy Salt Draw from Verdie and she wouldn't sell to them. It'd be a feather in the feud cap if either one of them could get Finn to sell out to them, or better yet if they could get it with a marriage license. Y'all goin' to church tomorrow?"

"Thought we might," Callie said.

"Well, sit in the middle aisle. The Brennans sit on one side and the Gallaghers on the other. The middle is neutral and sittin' on either of their sides means you're takin' up with that bunch against the other one," Gladys said. "This store, church, and my sister-in-law Polly's beer joint are the only places they are even civil to each other. They each got their own private school on their ranches, so they don't send their kids to the little public school here in Burnt Boot."

"Good grief, they really are modern-day Hatfields and McCoys." Callie laughed.

"Oh, honey, they make the Hatfield and McCoy families look right tame. Story has it that, back in the twenties, times got real tough here in Burnt Boot. So old man Gallagher set up a moonshine still down close to the Red River. He was making a fair livin', keepin' his family alive and the bill paid here at the store. That was back when my husband's daddy had the store and the ranch. Anyway, the feds showed up one night and smashed up his still, carried him off to prison, and made him serve a year for bootleggin'. The Brennans were a religious lot, what with old Grandpa Brennan preachin' at church when the minister needed a fill-in." Gladys stopped beside the meat counter. "Don't suppose you need anything from here."

Callie nodded. "Everything is frozen at the house. Give me a pound of hamburger, and I'll make cowboy hash for supper."

"Will do," Gladys said and went on. "Now, the Gallaghers figured the Brennans ratted them out to the feds. And there's been a feud goin' on now for nigh on to a hundred years. The bootleggin' thing just kind of put the icin' on the cake. Story has it that they were already crossways with each other because right about the turn of the century Freddy Gallagher fell in love with Molly Brennan. Then the morning of the wedding, Freddy got cold feet and joined the army, leaving poor Molly in humiliation at the altar."

"Where do you sit in church?" Callie asked.

Gladys wrapped a pound of hamburger and put it in Callie's cart. "In the middle. Fiddle Creek, that's the name of my ranch, is right between their spreads. Both of them has tried to buy me out, but I'll leave my land to the coyotes before I'd let either of them have it. Don't get me wrong, I like both families, but I'm not being a part of their fight."

"Why wouldn't Verdie sell Salt Draw to them?" Finn added a five-pound bag of apples to the cart as Callie pushed it toward the checkout counter. They didn't always keep them in the little base store and Callie craved them worse than chocolate.

"Verdie hates the feud. She's a pistol on wheels, and me and her and Polly decided years ago that we wasn't going to get drug in the middle of the feud. We grew up together right here in Burnt Boot. It ain't been easy, what with Polly's cousin's kid marryin' into the Gallagher tribe and my cousin's son marryin' into the Brennans, but we all try to stay out of it best as we can."

"Why is this place named Burnt Boot?" Martin asked.

"Back in the days of the cattle drives old Hiram Cleary got tired of lookin' at the back end of cattle all day. He sat down right out there and pulled off his boot, threw it in the fire so he couldn't go no further, and built a store to sell stuff to the people comin' up the trail. He was an ancestor to my husband," Gladys answered.

"Wow!" Martin said.

They said good-bye to Gladys and put their supplies in the backseat of the truck. When Finn was returning the cart to the store, Callie heard a pitiful whine. She ignored it at first, but when she heard it a second time, she stooped down and looked under the truck.

A little yellow kitten with big eyes stared back at her. She held out a hand and it limped over to her, sniffed her fingers, and meowed pitifully. She gathered it up and went back toward the store. Gladys opened the door before she even arrived.

"It ain't mine and I don't want it," she said.

"I can't leave it in the parking lot. It'll get run over and killed. It's already hurt and limping," Callie said.

"You found it. It's all yours," Gladys said. "I got a whole barn full of cats and two that live in the house."

"Can we keep it, please, Callie, can we?" Martin bailed out of the backseat of the truck and ran toward her and the cat.

"We've got a big house and Shotgun likes cats, so I don't see why not," Finn answered.

Martin held out his arms and Callie handed the kitten over to him. He tucked it inside his coat and carried it to the truck where he hummed to it the whole way home.

The first snowflakes drifted out of the sky as they pulled up to the back door. Finn grabbed two sacks from the bed of the truck. Callie picked up two more bags and followed him into the house, with Martin bringing up the rear, walking slow so he wouldn't wake the sleeping kitten.

"Think it'll really snow or is it just teasing us?" she asked.

Finn unloaded bags and set the groceries on the bar. "I hope that all we get is a flake to the acre. What did you think of the store?"

"Do you believe what Gladys said about the feud?" Callie asked.

"Well, I only met Gladys once before. Verdie took me to the store and to the bar to introduce me to her and Polly. They mentioned the feud, but I thought it was a joke. You might want to put all this away so you'll know where it is, Callie."

"What's our mission in this, O'Donnell?" she asked.

The smile that covered his face brightened the room. "To make a success of this ranch, to be happy with our place here in Burnt Boot, and…" He paused.

"To stay out of the feud no matter how big it is," she finished for him. "We lived in tension, worry, and tight quarters with very little privacy in Afghanistan. This should be a piece of cake."

"I hope so." He hugged her loosely. "I'm glad you are

here. It got damn lonely with just me, Shotgun, and the television in the evenings."

Every nerve in her body tingled, just like she knew it would if they'd ever had a relationship. But that wasn't happening between partners, especially not a sniper and his spotter, and for sure not when Finn O'Donnell followed the rules without wavering. When Lala entered the picture, Callie had learned to be content with a close friendship.

The yellow kitten let out a downright pitiful meow. Martin came from a wooden rocker where he'd been treating it like a baby. "I think he's hungry, Callie. I'm sure glad you found it. Its leg is hurt and it would have been killed on the road. Come on back inside and grab a can of food and a little bag of kitten food."

Finn picked it up by the scruff of the neck and ran his hands down its legs and hip, then down its backbone. "Probably just bruised. I don't feel any broken bones. Have you introduced her to Shotgun? He was raised with cats all around him. He won't hurt it. We'll make it a bed beside the fire. Poor little thing will have to eat dog food and milk until we can get her some proper cat food next week."

"I picked up food before I left town," Callie said.

"Wow!" Martin whispered softly. "A ranch. A dog. A cat. All in one day. It's the best day ever, Callie."

Finn rubbed the kitten's ears and then handed it back to Martin. "You might want to pick out a girl name."

Martin dark hair flopped down over rich chocolate-colored eyes as he nodded emphatically. "I don't care if it's a boy or a girl. I'm just glad it gets to stay in a warm house."

Finn opened a cabinet door and removed a can of dog food. The minute he started the electric can opener, Shotgun came running from the rug in front of the fireplace. He picked up the dog's feed dish and shook out the can's contents. Then he chopped the dog food up, shoved a couple of tablespoons over to the side of the bowl, and set it down.

"Shotgun has been trained to eat with cats. Mama had a kitten not much bigger than that when the dog came to live with us. She trained him well. Put your cat beside the little portion and watch what happens," Finn said.

"But I bought her cat food," Callie said.

"She'll eat dog food. I promise."

Callie inhaled sharply and Finn draped an arm around her shoulders. "It's okay. I wouldn't let him kill the kitten."

Shotgun eyed the cat. The kitten kept a wary eye on the dog as she ate her part of the food.

"I'll be damned. Don't think I've ever seen anything like that," Callie said.

"The lion done laid down with the lamb, like they told us in church, Callie," Martin said. "Is it time to do chores, Finn?"

Finn moved to the side and laid a hand on Martin's shoulder. "It really is if we're going to get done by dark. Shotgun will watch after the cat."

"And I'll cook supper." Her shoulders were suddenly chilled without the warmth of his arm. She wished that she'd offered to help with the feeding that evening so she wouldn't have to let Finn out of her sight.

Chapter 3

FINN PULLED OUT A CHAIR FOR CALLIE BEFORE HE SAT down at the supper table. His big hands barely touched her shoulders and the whole room warmed by several degrees. When he'd settled into a chair he said, "I grew up in a house where the blessing was given before meals and we always took turns. Maybe Martin could take the first turn tonight."

Martin dropped his chin onto his chest and shut his eyes tightly. "Dear Lord, thank you for today because it's the best day of my life. Thank you for my favorite supper, cowboy hash, and for my very own room with bunk beds, and most of all, thank you for Finn and Shotgun lettin' us live here. And for the new baby kitten. In Jesus's name, amen."

Callie quickly wiped a tear and busied herself with unfolding a blue napkin with snowflakes scattered over it. When she had it smoothed out in her lap, Finn had already dipped deeply into the hash and was handing it to her. She spooned some onto her plate and handed it off to Martin.

"Snowflakes on the napkins. Maybe we'll have a white Christmas," Finn said.

"Do you want a white Christmas?" Callie asked.

"Do you like corn, Finn? Here, I'll start it around. I do and I really like it when Callie makes it like this with butter and that white cheese. Wait 'til you taste her chocolate cake over there. It's the bestest in the world."

Finn glanced over at the cake on the cabinet. "You really have learned to cook."

"She's a good cook, Finn. I can eat this stuffed in bread for breakfast. I did sometimes when she had to go to work early," Martin said.

"Thank you for fixing it for us. We'll be doing the dishes since you did the cooking," Finn said.

"Aw, man! I'd rather muck out stables than do dishes," Martin moaned.

"Well, if that's your choice, then you can muck out three stables tomorrow morning before church and I'll do the dishes. You big enough to lead the horses out and do a job like that?" Finn asked.

"Yes, sir. You got three horses on this place?"

Finn nodded. "I do."

"Can I ride sometime?"

Callie touched Finn's arm. "He loves horses, but he's only ridden the ponies at carnivals."

"No time like the present to learn."

Callie dabbed her mouth with the napkin and said, "I'll do the dishes and start straightening up that living room if you guys will get out of my way. I'm kind of possessive about my kitchen, never have liked to share it."

"Yes!" Martin pumped a fist into the air. "Can I take the cat to my room and read her a bedtime story?"

"'May I,' not 'can I.' And, yes, you may, but then you have to get your bath or shower or whatever is in the bathroom over there."

Finn caught her eye and their gaze held. "I'm going to help you with the dishes, Callie. Afterward, you need to decide which bedroom you want. You have two to choose from, and Martin has a choice of a shower or a bath. There's both."

Sparks sizzled right above them and fear struck a chord in her heart. It was too damn soon for her to be feeling like this. Sure, she'd had a major crush on him, maybe she'd have even fallen flat-out in love with him if circumstances had been different, but that was years ago. She had to get a grip on herself, her mind, and her heart.

"Thank you," she mumbled.

After supper was finished, Finn helped clear the table and dried the dishes as she washed them. She slipped the dishes into the drainboard; he scooped them up to wipe them dry. It seemed that more times than not, their hands touched, and sweet Jesus, the chemistry between them was hot.

"That really was a great meal. Now you need to unpack. Either bedroom is yours. One has twin beds. One has a queen size."

He led her back to the hallway by the hand. She could hear Martin talking to the cat, but the buzz in her head kept her from hearing the words. Not in her wildest dreams had she thought she and Martin would get a reception like this. Like Martin, she was almost afraid to go to sleep for fear that she'd wake up in a WITSEC program in some remote city so big that she couldn't find her way around.

"Bathroom." Finn opened a door.

She spun around and spontaneously hugged Finn, throwing both arms around his neck. "Hot damn, Finn! This is unbelievable. The women in our tent would have hunted down the terrorists on the deck of cards and killed them with nothing but their bare hands for a setup like this."

Finn's lips turned up at the corners. "Glad you like it. While Martin takes a shower or a bath, you can pick out your room."

She backed up a step and called out, "Hey, Martin, bring your pajamas and your toothbrush. You want a shower or a bath?"

"Shower. I don't want to leave the cat alone very long. She might get lonesome," he answered.

She adjusted the knobs to get the water just right. Martin's big brown eyes opened so wide, she could see the whites all around them when he crossed the hall. The bathroom was as big as the bedroom in their old apartment. A vanity stretched the length of one wall. Three mirrors hung above three separate sinks with plenty of storage underneath them. A huge claw-foot tub, a walk-in shower, and a toilet were on the other wall.

"Oh, Callie, this is huge. That tub looks like a swimming pool. Is one of them sinks all mine? I can put my toothbrush and toothpaste right there and my comb, and it'll be mine?"

"That's right. Choose the one you want, but you have to be responsible to keep the area all neat," she said.

Heat radiated from the small of her back when Finn laid a hand there to show her the two bedrooms.

"Do you help him take a shower still?" he asked.

She shook her head. "He's been taking care of himself for years. Long before I came on the scene." Her voice came out an octave higher than usual, but Martin was so intrigued with the bathroom he didn't notice.

"This one?" Finn opened a door into a room with twin beds and then led her across the hall to the room adjoining the bunk-bed room. "Or this one?"

"This one. A queen-sized bed all of my own. It's heaven," Callie said.

"I thought you might like it." He sat down in a gold velvet overstuffed rocking chair. "Tell me about your sister. You talked about her and I remember you telling me that you worried about your nephew. You were always sending money home to them, right?"

She sat down on the edge of the bed. "She didn't have a lick of sense when it came to men, but she was a good mother, Finn. Other than moving several times a year and never putting down roots for Martin, she adored that boy. When she had the car wreck and died, there was no family until I got home. It took a few weeks to get all the paperwork to go through so I could have him. Foster care turned him into a shy, frightened little boy, but kids are resilient. Now he's probably too outgoing, but it's better than before. My turn. What happened with Lala?"

"I asked her to marry me, but she gave me a song and dance about our cultures not mixing, so I brought a broken heart home with me and two weeks later got the news that she and her brother were killed by an IED on their way to the base. Last summer a friend with classified clearance told me their deaths had been staged because their cover had been blown at the base. They are really terrorist spies who are still alive and well to my knowledge. They don't have their pictures on the deck of cards, but they work for someone who does. It took me a long time to process the idea that I'd been played."

"I'm sorry, Finn."

"That's the past. Can't redo it. Can't undo it. Just got to put it in a box and bury the damn thing. I've still got some unpacking to do myself, so I'll leave you to get yours done," he said.

Emptiness set in the moment he left the room. A whirlwind of emotions had surrounded her since she stepped out of that van. Suddenly, she had no center of gravity. She flopped back on the bed and stared at the ceiling. Then she shifted her gaze to the nicest bedroom she'd ever had and the two bags on the floor inside the door where he'd brought them from the hallway. Maybe unpacking would make it all real and give her some sense of stability.

Finn laced his hands behind his head and watched the shadows move across the ceiling. The kid was a fast learner and took orders without fussing. He hefted a shovel full of wet hay pretty damn good for a scrawny little boy. By springtime, he'd be a pretty good hired hand, the way he'd taken to the work.

Callie could cook, so he wouldn't have to live on frozen pizza and soup out of a can. The living room was all cleared out. Boxes she thought were personal had been marked and lined up in the spare bedroom next to his. Blankets, pillows, and the rest had been put away. The house didn't seem nearly as empty that evening as it had the two days before.

But then how could a room, a house, even a whole base or a whole ranch be empty with Callie on it? She brought energy and warmth to every place she went. He'd been a fool not to act on the attraction he'd had for her that first year, but he'd vowed to follow orders. His had been a strange situation, what with having a woman for a spotter.

A picture of the first Christmas he and Callie spent in canvas tents stuck in his mind. She'd ordered a fake Christmas tree that was about six feet tall. They didn't have real decorations, and by the time the tree arrived what few were available on base had long since been sold out. The only thing left was one ornament—a real leather cowboy boot about three inches tall and stuffed full of tiny little fake presents. He'd bought the thing and they'd hung it on their tree.

"But you couldn't see it for all the paper." He chuckled.

They had colored birds, ornaments, and even icicles she'd drawn on copy paper to hang on the tree with jute twine. And then they'd created yards of paper chain to use for garland. It was the ugliest damn thing he'd ever seen, but she'd loved it. On Christmas morning she'd burned a candle that smelled like pine trees and snow all mixed up together and they'd opened their presents. She'd given him Rudolph antlers with red blinking lights, Rudolph socks, and a Frosty the Snowman mug full of instant coffee packets. He'd given her a long scarf with jingle bells hanging from the ends, a bottle of some kind of perfume that she'd mentioned liking, and a box of chocolates. She was still squealing over her presents when they got the news to suit up for a mission in ten minutes.

The Rudolph antlers and socks were packed in one of the boxes over there against the far wall. The mug was still in its wrapper with coffee inside and sitting on the end of his dresser.

A movement near the fireplace caught his eye, and he slowly reached for the pistol in his nightstand. Then Shotgun yawned loudly, whimpered, and ambled across the floor to lay his head on the other side of the bed.

"You want to make one last trip outside, do you?" Finn put the gun back into the nightstand and slung his feet out from under the covers.

Shotgun's tail thumped on the floor.

When he reached the living room, Callie was curled up on the end of the sofa with a quilt over her. He hurried across the cold floor and opened the door for the dog and then came back to the sofa to tuck his feet up under the edge of the quilt, his cold toes touching her warm ones and heating up far more than his feet.

"I should have put on socks. The floor feels like an ice-skating rink," he said.

She moved her feet over to warm his. "I took the chill off mine by the fire after I figured out the same thing."

"Mmmm, that feels wonderful." He wiggled his toes in closer to hers, and then something furry settled itself around their feet.

"Please tell me the cat is under there and a mouse hasn't joined us," he said.

"Her name is Angel and she likes me. And, honey, if that was a rat, I would be plastered to the ceiling," Callie said.

"I said mouse, not rat."

"There is no such thing as a mouse. They're all rats and they grow big as raccoons or sometimes as big as baby calves, depending on how much they scare me," she said.

Callie was so damn cute snuggled up in the curve of the sofa with her black hair flowing past her shoulders and the dim light putting highlights in her eyes. The book she'd laid to the side had a man with a lasso over his shoulder on the cover, and the title had the word "cowboy" in it.

"So you still read Western romance? Never quite understood that when you hate ranchin' so bad that you joined the army to get away from it." He pulled the quilt a little more his way.

"I like to read about cowboys. The ones in the books are like you, Finn. They're trustworthy and steady. But for the most part, men are men, whether they're in boots or flip-flops. My sister damn sure taught me by example that not many of them can be trusted as far as they can be thrown," she said.

"Trustworthy and steady…that's a pretty tall order to live up to," Finn said. "Why are you in the living room this late?"

"Nightmares again. I thought maybe the flickering fire would help calm my nerves. You ever get the nightmares?"

He stretched out, his legs plastered against hers all the way to the curve of her butt, where his toes rested. Even with two layers of flannel separating his skin from hers, it still put him into semi-arousal. "Of course I do. What we did scarred us, Callie. Nightmares are normal for us. I was remembering our Christmas over there in Afghanistan."

She smiled and the whole room warmed by several degrees. "That was a hoot, wasn't it? I still have the perfume bottle. It's empty, but I kept it to remind me of the good times, and the candy box holds my jewelry. When I look at them, the ugly stuff we had to live through kind of fades away and I remember that Christmas."

"And the argument? Do you remember it, too?"

"Oh, yes." She nodded. "I really was mad at the army for sending us out on that mission and I was right; the ham was all gone when we got back."

"Well, I was right, too. We took out the insurgents who were hell-bent on blowing up that girls' school. Those kids might not have celebrated Christmas in their world, but at least they woke up the next morning," he said.

"If you still remember that hellacious fight, then why did you let me and Martin stay? I'm surprised you didn't tell Otis to take me to Siberia," she said.

"I know you, Callie. You're a hard worker, and when you give your word, it's as good as gold. And you saved my life, so it's my turn to repay." He grinned.

She kicked backward and landed a soft blow to his shin. "You saved my hide, too, so don't give me that shit."

"Ouch! If you'd have missed, you could have killed the cat."

"I didn't hurt you, so stop whining," she said. "I really did try to find you, Finn."

"I lost my phone in an airport on the way home. I tried to find you, too, Callie. I figured you'd found some rich preppy guy and had a big wedding, settled down in a mansion, and started a brand-new life."

"I thought you'd convinced Lala to give up her lifestyle and move to the States with you at the last minute," she said. "I'm not a damn bit surprised that she's a spy or that she picked you out from the whole crew to get involved with."

"Why?"

"She picked out the best-lookin', hottest soldier on the base," she answered.

"You didn't say that over there."

"We were partners and it was frowned upon, and

besides, I didn't have the nerve to break the rules and then Lala was in the picture. I never did like that hussy. I knew she was trouble. I just thought it was a different kind of trouble than it was," she said.

"What kind was that?"

"I figured her for the type who was looking for a free ride to the States, not a spy," she said.

Finn leaned his head back on the sofa arm.

"Don't you go to sleep in that position, or you'll have a terrible crick in your neck tomorrow morning," she warned.

He slid one eye open and turned his head slightly. "There's Shotgun at the door. You going to let him in or do I have to run across the cold floor again?"

"It's your dog. My cat uses a litter pan," she said.

"You are a hard woman, Brewster."

"You knew that when you gave me a job." She laughed softly.

His Callie was soft and gentle, but she had sass and a bite. Not many people even got to see the soft side of her; more were subjected to the sassy woman who had had to stand her ground in a man's world.

———

Callie heard Martin moan. She quickly threw the quilt back, picked up the cat, and padded barefoot down the hallway.

"Everything all right?" Finn followed her, his arm around her waist.

"Shhh. Sometimes he has bad dreams about the shooting. The man chased him down the alley, threatening to kill him."

Shotgun ambled down the hallway and crawled up on the bunk at Martin's feet. His tail thumped a couple of times and then he curled it around his body and went to sleep. Callie set the kitten down in the hallway, expecting it to follow her up the hall or maybe even limp into her room, but it sniffed the air, then made its way to the bunk bed. It meowed pitifully until she picked it up and set it on the bed. It curled up in the curve of Shotgun's belly.

"Thank goodness, he's decided to sleep on a bottom bunk. The kitten couldn't get down from that top one," Finn said.

"The top one is his tree house. He told me so right after he said his prayers," Callie said.

Finn dropped a kiss on the top of her head. "Well, I've walked you to your tent, Brewster. Maybe we can get a good night's sleep without the bombs and the gunfire waking us up. Good night."

"Good night, Finn. See you in the morning."

"Hey, speaking of the service, I don't know about your fitness program, but I've picked out a five-mile path around the ranch for a run and moved my gym equipment into the old bunkhouse. It's not very warm, but then who wants heat when they're sweating? And I target practice once a week, not any particular day, but at least once a week."

"We work out every day?" she asked.

"Every weekday. I rest on Saturday and Sunday," he answered.

"What time?" she asked.

"Right after chores. Usually around eight."

"Sounds good to me. Martin will be in school by that time. Shootin' range?"

"Got an area picked out. You been keepin' up with practice?"

"Once a month, but it's been indoors."

"Looks like you might need some retraining. We'll start Monday after we get Martin enrolled in school," he said.

Chapter 4

THE LITTLE CHURCH WAS PACKED WHEN CALLIE, FINN, and Martin slipped inside. Gladys stood up and motioned for them to join her about midway down the middle section of seats. Callie could feel eyes assessing her, and then lo and behold if Martin didn't rush in ahead of her to plop down beside Gladys, leaving her to sit beside Finn in a space barely big enough for one person. It was a tight scrunch, and his entire left side was pressed against her right one. She could feel the texture of his jeans on her leg, the stiffness of his freshly ironed shirt through the fabric of her shirt.

Gladys leaned over the top of Martin's head and whispered, "Glad to see you. It's not always this crowded, but today is the beginning of the Christmas programs. Each Sunday is a special event. Whole community turns out in December. Come January though they won't care much for plain old preachin' every Sunday, and it will thin out a lot. That's Polly up there at the piano. Polly Cleary. We married brothers. Me and her and Verdie all grew up together here in Burnt Boot. I probably told you that, but when you get nearly eighty, you tend to repeat things."

"Polly is the one who owns the bar?" Callie asked.

Gladys nodded. "She was playin' the piano before her husband died and she had to take on the runnin' of the bar. Ain't nobody in town brave enough to tell Polly that she can't have a bar and play in church."

Finn's hand dropped from the back of the pew to rest on her upper arm. Did he not realize that in small towns and small churches that would brand him as a taken cowboy? Or maybe he did and he was sending a false message for the women to leave him alone. She glanced up to find him staring right into her eyes. He bent low to whisper, "Kind of a snug fit, ain't it?"

"You sure you want to send this message? There are some good-lookin' women in the church this morning."

"I'm not sending anything. I'm just trying to make some room for you so you don't wrinkle up that cute little skirt," he said.

The preacher pushed himself off the short deacon's bench, cleared his throat, and said, "Good morning and merry Christmas."

His deep, booming voice startled Callie. It didn't match the short, round, balding man wearing wire-rimmed glasses. His baby face looked like it could grow better pimples than whiskers, and his voice should be high and squeaky.

"Is he Brennan or Gallagher?" Callie whispered to Gladys.

"Neutral, but church is neutral, even if it is like the cold war," she answered.

The preacher went on, "We have four Sundays between now and Christmas. To keep us all reminded of the spirit of the holidays, we will have a special program each week, and tonight instead of the evening services we will be participating in the traditional Christmas tree decoration. The Brennan family will put up a tree in front of the general store, and the Gallaghers will put theirs up in front of the school. Refreshments will be served at both places, and everyone is invited to both or either. Today we are going to present the nativity in a musical worship service."

His words were a little fuzzy in Callie's ears. She couldn't think of anything but Finn's hand and the effect it had on her. No wonder they didn't want fraternization between sniper and spotter. She couldn't keep her mind on a simple church service with him touching her. They'd have blown every single mission if they'd been in a relationship over there in the sand.

Men began bringing in the props for a nativity scene as the preacher told the story. When the stage was set, he sat down and the choir behind him sang "What Child Is This?" A young couple, portraying Mary and Joseph, carried a baby from behind the choir. It wasn't a doll, but a real live child wrapped in blue blankets who cooed as they gently laid him in the manger of hay.

"Is that a real kid?" Callie whispered.

Gladys leaned toward her and said, "Yes, it is. This year the Gallaghers are presenting this service."

"Do they switch off with the Brennans?"

Gladys nodded. "That's right, and they never share it."

When the song ended, the preacher told about the wise men, the choir sang the traditional "We Three Kings" Christmas song, and three wise men wearing robes and crowns brought their gifts to put before the baby in the manger. "Silent Night" brought out the shepherds, and then a little boy did a good job of keeping time on his drum set when the choir broke into "The Little Drummer Boy."

"You reckon that boy will be in my school?" Martin asked.

She nodded. "He looks to be about your age."

"Keith Gallagher," Gladys said softly.

The service ended with the preacher raising his hands for everyone to stand. "We'll close our program with 'Do You Hear What I Hear.' It's on a special sheet right inside the hymnals. Don't hold back. Sing loud enough that even the courts of heaven can hear your voices."

Gladys stooped enough that Martin could share her music. Finn moved even closer to Callie, and they each held a side of the paper to keep it steady.

"Do you see what I see, a star, a star, dancing in the night," Callie sang, and she could imagine stars very easily while standing there with one of Finn's arms around her shoulders and sharing a music sheet with him.

"Do you hear what I hear, ringing in the sky," Finn's deep voice rang out, sending a whole different kind of shiver up her spine. He could easily have been a star in the music industry with a voice like that.

"He will bring us goodness and light," Martin's thin voice blended with the whole crowd. The way he was smiling as he sang, it was plain that he was happier than he'd ever been.

The last notes of the song drifted away, and quietness prevailed for a few seconds before everyone started talking at once. The preacher was already busy shaking hands with the people as they filed out. Those who'd played a part in the program disappeared through an opening behind the choir where they'd most likely shed their costumes.

A couple of men from the Gallagher side of the church cornered Finn when he stepped out into the aisle and were talking to him about Salt Draw and telling him that if he decided to sell they'd sure be interested in buying him out.

Gladys reached across Martin and touched Callie on the shoulder. "Don't think because Finn shared the song paper with you that they won't come after him."

"What?" Callie asked.

"The Brennan women and the Gallagher women won't let you stand in their way, darlin'. They'll be coming after Finn O'Donnell, probably starting real soon. Just thought you ought to be ready for the feud to get hot," Gladys said.

"Why?" Callie asked.

Gladys's old eyes sparkled. "He's new blood, and them dark, smolderin' looks and them blue eyes sure make it even better. He's a damn fine rancher, and they've already spit on their knuckles and started taking bets as to which clan will wind up with him. Betsy Gallagher is braggin' that she could have him cornered by Valentine's, but she's going to have to fight her way past Honey Brennan to get to him. Betsy is a scrapper, but Honey is meaner than a junkyard dog."

"Aren't there any other men in Burnt Boot?" Callie asked.

"Oh yeah, but he's a prize, and believe me, Salt Draw is a bigger one. They couldn't buy it from Verdie, but one of them could claim it through marriage."

"Just how rough will it get?" Callie said.

"Oh, darlin', it's like that fightin' stuff they do in cages. No rules and no whinin'. There's a feel in the air when the feud is gettin' fueled up for another round. It's been a while since it got real stinky but it's comin'. They're both just itchin' for the other side to start something. I forgot to ask, what happened to that kitten?" Gladys said.

"The kitten is Shotgun's new buddy. Its name is Angel."

She nodded. "It's a very good name for a Christmas girl cat."

Finn threw an arm loosely around Callie's shoulder and drew her close to his side. "I'd like you to meet Callie, my number one hand at the ranch. Declan has invited us to the River Bend Ranch for dinner, but I told him you have dinner in the oven waiting for us."

The cowboy tipped his hat toward her. His dark sapphire-blue eyes scanned her from her black high heels to a red skirt that just skimmed her knees, up past the black shirt and to her dark hair. "I'm right pleased to make your acquaintance. Y'all are welcome at River Bend Ranch any time. We'd be glad to take Martin into our private school if you want to enroll him there."

"Thank you, but I reckon he'll do just fine in the public school," Callie said.

Sandy hair, broad shoulders, a silver belt buckle that said he'd done some bull riding, and that full-body scan should have jump-started her hormones into overdrive, but the only person in the church who had an effect on Callie was standing beside her, their hands brushing with every step.

Martin tugged at her hand. "Can I go outside and wait? I might get to talk to that boy who had the drum."

"Sure you can. Just don't leave the church parking lot. We'll be out in a minute," Callie said.

A red-haired woman came from the other side of the church, weaving her way through people. She made it to the end about the same time that Callie and Finn took a couple of steps forward. She ignored Callie and smiled up at Finn. "Hello. I'm Betsy Gallagher. Wanted to introduce myself and tell you to drop by Wild Horse Ranch sometime to visit."

A tall, dark-haired woman with crystal-clear blue eyes pushed her way between Finn and Betsy. "I'm Honey Brennan, and you can ride with me over to River Bend to dinner. I'll see to it that you get home this evening by chore time."

Betsy tapped her on the shoulder and said, "You're a day late and a dollar short, Honey. He's going to Wild Horse today."

Honey's hands turned into fists and her eyes were barely slits. Betsy tilted her chin up, and her body language said that she dared the woman to take the first punch.

"Ladies, this is church," Gladys said. "Remember the rules."

"You'd better not cross me outside this place," Honey said.

"You'd do well to stay on your own shit farm and keep away from me," Betsy hissed.

"You'll pay for saying that about River Bend." Honey bowed up to her.

"Get out your big-girl panties and bring it on. I could take your sorry ass with one hand tied behind my back and a blindfold over my eyes," Betsy said.

"We'll see about that." Honey whipped around and marched out of the church.

Betsy laughed. "She's all bitch and no power. Don't pay no attention to her. That boy belong to you?" Betsy asked.

"He's my nephew," Callie answered.

"We've got a private school over on Wild Horse. We'll be glad to have him. Just bring him on over there and we'll get him enrolled in the morning."

"Thank you, but he's going to public school."

"What grade is he in?"

"Third."

"You'll be sorry. The third-grade teacher is old and outdated. She should have retired ten years ago, and the classes are so small that he'll have to be in her room."

"Small classes are a blessing, and older teachers are pretty wise," Callie said.

"Your loss." Betsy shrugged and looked back up at Finn. "I'll be over tomorrow morning with a pie, Finn. You got any particular kind that you like best? I'm hell on wheels when it comes to baking, and apple pie is my specialty."

"Nothing comes to mind," Finn said.

"You get the coffee ready, and I'll be there in the middle of the morning with a pie right out of the oven. And if you change your mind about that kid coming to Wild Horse school, just call the ranch number and let Granny know," Betsy said and moved away into a sea of people.

"Did that just happen?" Finn drew Callie closer to his side.

"Looks like that bit about protecting you might come into play pretty quick." Callie laughed nervously. "Kind of feels like we're back in the war between the feuding families over in Afghanistan, doesn't it?"

"I could work with that scenario better than this one," Finn said.

"Girl, you ain't big enough to protect him if they go to war over him," Gladys said.

"We're not getting into this feud, Gladys," Finn said sternly. "We'll keep to ourselves over on Salt Draw, and they can do whatever the hell it is that feuding families do."

"Good luck with that." Gladys chuckled.

———

Finn had tried his damnedest to pay attention to the Christmas program, but it hadn't been easy. The tension surrounding him felt like the stillness right before a tornado drops out of the sky and rips apart everything from outhouse to hog sheds. It partly came from sitting in church between two families who'd like to shoot each other if only the law would make homicide legal. But the other part came from within his heart. He couldn't keep his hands off Callie, and he was a grown man, not a sophomore in high school. He knew her well enough to know that she wouldn't take to smothering. She'd always needed her space, and yet, even now his hand was on the small of her back. This new chemistry between them was hotter than July in Texas, and he flat-out liked the way it felt.

He wove their way through the rest of the congregation, shook the preacher's hand, and was eager to get back to the safety of Salt Draw when he noticed a crowd of kids in the churchyard. When he rolled up on his tiptoes, he could see that Martin and the drummer boy had squared off with a whole group of other kids around them. Fists were up and their shoulders hunched forward in a stance that reminded him of a couple of young fighting roosters.

"Shit!" he mumbled.

"What?" Callie asked.

"Trouble," he spit out and took off for the middle of the parking lot with her right behind him.

"Martin Brewster," she yelled.

Finn didn't say a word until he was between the two boys with a hand on each of their heads. "This is Sunday. There'll be no fighting on the Lord's day. Why do you want to fight Martin anyway?"

"He's going to school over at River Bend. I heard my aunt Honey talkin' about invitin' him to join up with them, and that makes him my enemy," the blond-haired drummer boy said.

"Martin is going to public school," Callie said.

Keith dropped his fists and frowned. "He ain't got on boots, so he ain't a rancher. A cowboy wears boots, not them sissified shoes like he's wearin'."

"Well, you was wearin' a skirt awhile ago," Martin countered.

"Okay, boys. This is over," Finn said. "We're going home to have some dinner."

The Gallagher boy ran back to a group of his buddies, and Martin stomped all the way to the truck, where he fumed in the backseat. "Why'd you go and do that? I could have whipped his ass, Callie."

Callie turned around in the seat. "If I hear dirty words from you again, you'll be punished. And the first thing you learn in combat is to know your enemy. If he's smart, you be smarter. If he's strong, then you be stronger. And the last is that you are not fighting anyone on the churchyard."

Martin looked up and nodded seriously. "The next time he's a smart"—he paused but Callie knew it took a lot of willpower not to say a bad word—"aleck, I'll just drag him off the churchyard and whip his"—another pause—"hind end there. I'm glad I don't have to go to school with him."

"This is no way to make friends," Finn said as he crawled into the truck.

"I didn't make a friend. I made an enemy, and I will whip him next time he calls me a sissy just because I don't wear cowboy boots," Martin said.

"I guess we'd best go buy Martin some boots," Finn said.

Martin folded his arms across his chest. "Yes, sir, I need boots, but I can make it 'til Christmas. I plan on askin' Santa Claus for boots." He popped in his earbuds and stared out the window.

"His shoes are new and they're fine. I'm not wasting money on boots," Callie said.

"His shoes have neon green on them, and this is a country school where the boys wear cowboy boots," Finn argued.

"And once he testifies and that man is in prison, we'll move on to a city where those green shoes will fit right in, Finn. He doesn't need to be a follower. He has to learn to be himself and not mimic all the other kids," she said.

"Boots won't make him a follower. They'll just stop a lot of name-calling and fighting," Finn argued.

"My answer is no."

Finn started up the engine and drove out of the parking lot toward Salt Draw. He disagreed with her about the boots, so he'd have to find a way around her. One that made Callie think it was her idea all along.

Chapter 5

CALLIE PULLED THE SEAT BELT AROUND HER BODY AND propped an elbow on the console between her and Finn. Immediately he did the same, their arms touching, sending bursts of heat all the way to her shoulder.

"Didn't you love the Christmas tree over there beside the piano?" She tried to ease the tension in the air from the backseat.

"Y'all want a fake tree or a real one or no tree?" Finn asked.

Martin removed an earbud. "Did I hear something about a tree? I always wanted to go out in the woods and cut down a real tree."

"How about you?" Finn asked Callie. "We don't have a lot of decorations, but there appears to be plenty of cedar trees on Salt Draw if y'all are up for a hike through the property. If we find the right one, we could maybe get it put up before we go to town for the official lighting ceremony this evening."

Martin let out a whoop in the backseat of the truck. "Can it be a big one? Big enough to reach all the way to the ceiling when we put the star on the top?"

"If we can find one that big. I only have a small box of decorations, but I suppose there aren't any rules that say we have to fill it all up this year, is there?" Finn said.

"Heck no!" Martin said. "Will there be presents under it?"

"You believe in Santa?" Finn asked.

Callie poked Finn on the shoulder. "You remember what I told you over there in Afghanistan? If you don't believe, there won't be presents on Christmas morning. I believe in Santa, and you'd best be a believer if you want a new set of Rudolph antlers."

"What's that about antlers? Is that what you want, Finn?" Martin asked.

Finn smiled into the rearview mirror. "Ask Callie."

"I bought a set of antlers for him when we were over there in the war zone," Callie explained. "He had to believe or he wouldn't have gotten them. I imagine that he's lost them by now and needs a new set."

"I did not. I brought them to Salt Draw with me, and I wore them last year," Finn said.

"What do you want for Christmas, Callie?" Martin asked.

"A box of candy and a pair of warm socks and maybe some perfume," she said.

Finn's hand found hers and squeezed. "You're not hard to please."

"Not when it comes to presents. Presents are just an added bonus. If I have family all around me, then I'm a happy lady," she said.

"That's what she asks for every year," Martin said. "She's got an old empty box that she keeps her jewelry in and an empty perfume bottle that she sets on her dresser. I think someone important gave them to her, but she won't never tell me who it was."

Finn made a turn from the paved road and crossed the cattle guard under the sign that said Fiddle Creek, which was swinging between two tall metal posts. In a few minutes he'd parked the truck in the backyard and Callie bailed out without waiting for him to play the gentleman and open the door for her.

She hurried from truck to kitchen, grabbed a faded apron from a hook beside the pantry door, slipped the bib string over her head, and opened the oven without tying the waist strings.

"Man, this place smells good. I'm hungry enough to eat every bit of that roast all by myself." Martin came in right behind her, sniffing the air and rubbing his stomach.

Finn shook his head. "I don't think so. I'm getting my fair share of that food. My stomach was growling so loud right there at the end of the church service, I was afraid that baby Jesus would think it was a howling wolf and start crying."

"Martin, you get on back to your room and change your good clothes. Put on your old shoes if we're going to be stomping around in the woods." Callie kicked her high heels into the corner and reached around behind her waist to tie the apron.

"Let me do that," Finn said quickly.

Tying apron strings wasn't a big thing, but it felt so personal and intimate. Callie quickly moved toward the coffeepot, poured the last cup, and popped it into the microwave. "That will be hot in a minute."

"For me or you?" he asked.

"We'll share it, since it's the last cup."

The bell dinged and he took it out, offering it to her first. "You don't think that woman will really bring an apple pie over here tomorrow, do you? Truth is, I don't even like apple pie."

"I remember you bitchin' and moanin' about it when they served it instead of peach or cherry in the mess hall." She grinned. "And don't worry, she was just mouthin' to get ahead of Honey. Lord, who names their child 'Honey'?"

"It's probably a nickname," Finn said. "But I don't care what it is. I don't intend to be drawn into their feud. Verdie made it sound like a silly little thing, but those two were pretty serious this morning."

"Yep, they were. And it looks like you are going to be the match that lights the bonfire." Callie handed the cup to him.

He closed his hands around hers for a few seconds before taking the cup. "I think Gladys was teasing about the intensity of this whole thing. It was just a catfight, and it'll blow over."

Her fingers tingled long after he'd backed up and leaned against the counter. "I think Gladys was dead serious, but don't you worry, I'll keep those big mean old kitty cats from tearing you to shreds with their sharp claws."

"Whew!" he said. "I'm glad you came along when you did."

"I know, darlin'. Madam Fate sent me at just the right time."

Finn set the coffee down and took two steps forward. His arms went around her waist and hers went around his neck. She felt as if any minute she'd drown in his blue eyes when she looked up at his face. The tip of her tongue moistened her lips as his eyelashes slowly came to rest on his cheekbones. It would be their first kiss and already her chest was so tight, she couldn't breathe.

"Hey, is dinner on the table? Need me to set the table?" Martin yelled as he ran down the hall.

Callie quickly backed up, picked up a pot holder, and opened the oven door. She could feel Finn's eyes on her as he handed the boy the plates from the cabinet. She had to remind herself to breathe in and breathe out, or she would have fainted right there on the kitchen floor.

"Hey," she said, "since we won't have enough decorations for the tree, maybe we could each buy an ornament on Friday night when we get paid." If she said something, maybe normality would return and she'd quit feeling like her whole body was on fire.

Callie acted as a measuring stick and stood beside the first cedar tree. Finn shook his head. "Too small. It's not even as tall as you, so it's not five feet three inches."

"It's a foot taller than me," she argued. "That leaves room for the tree stand and the star without it bending at the ceiling."

"It's too skinny, and besides, when we cut it down, it won't be that tall," Martin said.

"And it's got a big hole in the branches right there," Finn pointed out.

So they trudged on another quarter mile through the brush and mesquite. She stole sidelong glances toward Finn as they searched for the right tree. It didn't matter if he wore fatigues or tight-fittin' jeans; he still had the cowboy walk that made women take a second look. Honey and Betsy would have gone after him even if there wasn't a feud or if he didn't own a prime piece of Burnt Boot land.

"I see it!" Martin yelled and ran on ahead with Shotgun at his heels.

Finn sat down and braced his back against a big pecan tree. "Why can't I buy that kid some boots?" he asked abruptly.

She cleared a space of pecans and sat down beside him. "I told you why, and I don't want to talk about it. We should pick up these pecans for our Christmas baking."

"There's probably a hundred bags of picked-out pecans in the freezer. Verdie said they had a bumper crop last year."

A snowflake floated down from the pale gray skies and rested on her cheek. He gently brushed it away with the tip of his forefinger. And then the whirr of blades cut through the cold wind whistling through the treetops.

She grabbed his hand. "Shhh, do you hear that?"

He went completely still, only his eyes moving to check the skies. "It's probably a medical helicopter going down to Dallas. We are safe, Callie."

She blinked several times. "Certain noises still make my heart race."

"The whirring of the blades. The rapid gunfire on television. The smell of any kind of fire might always send our minds back over there," he said.

"Don't I know it." She shivered.

He scooted closer to her, draped an arm around her shoulders, and drew her to his side. "They didn't tell us about this part when we signed up, but it is what it is."

"Are we talking about the war?" she asked.

"I think it's all tangled up together like one of those yarn balls my sister has when she knits," he said. "War.

Relationships. It's all a ball that has to be untangled a few inches at a time."

He tipped her chin up with his gloved fist, but that time she didn't have the chance to moisten her lips. His mouth claimed hers, and the whirlwind took them away to another world where there was no noise to startle either of them. She clung to him like a lifeline in an angry sea with choppy waves. When the kiss ended, she leaned against him, wanting more and yet knowing it was a bad idea.

"I've wanted to do that since you got out of that van. Hell, I wanted to do that in Afghanistan for a long time, but I was afraid you'd knock me on my ass." He chuckled.

"What is that noise?" She couldn't tell him that she would have pushed him into the nearest empty bunk, not knocked him on his ass.

"I reckon we've got a boy and a dog on their way back to tell us they've found the perfect tree," he explained.

Martin broke through a copse of mesquite and threw himself on the ground. "Y'all old people had to stop and rest, did you? Well, me and Shotgun done found our Christmas tree, and it's perfect. Hey, these are pecans. We got to come out here and pick these up so we can make lots of Christmas candy instead of just one pan full of fudge."

"Or you could pick them up and sell them," Finn said.

"They're a long way from the house." Callie was amazed that her words sounded normal with her heart about to jump right out of her chest.

"Shotgun can come with me. He'll protect me, won't you, boy?" Martin grabbed the dog's ears and kissed him on the nose. "Now y'all have to get up and help me cut down this perfect Christmas tree."

~~~

Martin picked leaves, spiderwebs, and even a bird's nest from his perfect tree as it lay stretched out over a good portion of the front porch. He hummed the song about the little drummer boy, coming in with "rum-pa-pum-pum" at the right places.

Callie opened the front door. "I'm going inside to make hot chocolate and get out some cookies. The wind is shifting around to the north. It's liable to get serious about snow before the night is done. How long will it take to get that thing ready for the house?"

"Just long enough for me and Shotgun to find some scrap wood and a couple of screws to make a stand for it," Finn said.

"Can't he stay here with me? I like it when he's close by." Martin's wide eyes said that he didn't feel safe alone.

"If he marks that tree, we'll have to live with the smell. We couldn't find another one that good before Christmas," Finn said.

Martin pointed to the other end of the porch. "You'll sit right there and watch me get all this stuff out of it, won't you, Shotgun? You won't go peeing on a Christmas tree when there's all them mesquite trees out there just waiting for you."

The big yellow dog flopped down and shut his eyes.

"See, he'll be just fine," Martin said.

The norther hit with a force when Finn was halfway to the barn. The temperature dropped at least fifteen degrees in five minutes, and a cold mist began to fall. If it kept up, there'd be a sheet of ice over everything come morning. That would mean giving the cattle extra feed and chopping through the ice on their watering troughs.

He zipped his work jacket up and held on to his cowboy hat. When he was in the barn, he stomped his feet to get warm. Screws and maybe a couple of pieces of wood would be in the tack room, so that's the direction he headed as he fussed at himself. A mama cat followed by three kittens scampered from one stack of hay to another. He made a mental note to feed them regularly and to tell Martin that they were there. In a week, he'd have the whole bunch of them tamed and named, with Shotgun protecting them.

A quick movement took his attention to a top shelf the minute he was in the tack room. Two mice were gray blurs as they ran from a hole in a box onto the rafter and out of sight.

"Here, kitty, kitty, kitty," he called out to the mama cat. "Until I can bring food to you, these mice will be supper."

He was still looking up when he realized the boxes were labeled with big lettering written in black marker. Evidently one housed an artificial Christmas tree.

He moaned out loud. "And I just stomped all over the ranch looking for a tree when all I had to do was come out here and tote this one in the house?"

The next one was marked *tree stand and skirt*. And the third one, *Christmas stuff.*

He pulled the last two off the shelf, checked to make sure there were no mouse holes, and headed back toward the house. With a real stand, they could keep the tree watered, and it wouldn't shrivel up and die within a week.

He'd barely cleared the door of the barn and started back to the house when he heard a noise behind him. He turned slowly, boxes still in his hand, to see a black-and-tan Chihuahua following him. When he stopped, the dog did; when he took a step, the dog did the same.

"Well shit fire!"

Good grief! Did the dog talk?

"Shut up, dog."

Finn raised his eyes slowly and saw a brightly colored parrot right above his head in the branches of an old scrub oak tree. It fluffed its wings and pranced up and down the mesquite limb. "Shut up, dog," it said again in a gruff voice.

The Chihuahua barked at it that time.

"Hot damn!" the bird squawked.

The Chihuahua wagged its tail.

"You two traveling together?" Finn asked.

He set the boxes down right there on the ice-covered grass and whistled softly. The dog wagged his tail, ducked its head shyly, and sniffed Finn's outstretched hand.

"Who are you and what are you doing on the ranch? Verdie didn't mention a dog, and I don't see her having a little guy like you around. I guess if Callie can bring in a stray, I can, too. It's a big house and a big ranch. I hope you aren't afraid of cats, but your friend there, I'm not too sure about him," he said.

Finn's feet slipped when he straightened up, but he got his balance before he took a tumble. Ice was so much worse than snow, and if the weatherman was right, the temperatures were going to stay below freezing for several days. It was going to be a cold tree-decorating party downtown that evening. Maybe they'd stay in after they'd decorated their tree.

He touched his lips. He'd far rather have one more kiss from Callie than go to town amongst all that feuding.

Martin looked up from the tree when Finn rounded the end of the porch. "I got it all cleaned out. I even rolled it over so I could make sure. And the only time Shotgun moved a muscle was when he got to quiverin' and yippin' a little while ago. I think he was chasin' that rabbit in his dreams. It sure did get cold when that wind hit, didn't it? What is that?"

"I expect it's a Chihuahua," Finn said.

"Can we keep it?" Martin's sudden intake of breath had nothing to do with the cold. He pulled off his ragged gloves, and the old dog licked his fingers.

The parrot flew down and landed in the cedar tree branches.

"Hot damn!" it said.

"And a bird, too? Wow, Finn. We sure are a lucky bunch here on Salt Draw. How are we going to get the bird inside the house? Callie is going to love it."

Finn looked over the tree. "Good job, Martin. The bird and dog seem to be traveling together. You think Angel will try to eat the bird if we let it in the house? Poor dog looks too old to be able to endure much of this weather. Shotgun, come over here and give us your opinion on this overgrown rat."

Shotgun got up and slowly made his way to the newcomer. They sniffed noses and circled each other a couple of times, then the big dog put a paw on the little guy's back and began giving him a bath.

"He likes him," Martin yelped. "Does that mean we get to keep him?"

"I guess it does. Open the door and we'll drag that tree in the house," Finn said.

"You got the stuff in those boxes?" Martin asked.

"I found a stand out there in the barn and something else, but I don't know what it is. Guess we'll have a surprise when we open it up," Finn answered.

Callie opened the door and took the boxes from Finn's hands, and then the two guys dragged their tree into the house. Shotgun dashed inside, with the new dog right on his heels. And the bird flew into the house like he owned the place.

"Shut up, dog." The bright-colored parrot lit on the curtain rod in the living room.

"Where did the dog and bird come from?" Callie asked as the bird lit on her shoulder and squawked, "Cat! Cat!"

"Guess it talks and it doesn't like cats." She moved slowly away from the door.

"They just appeared. They seem to be partners in crime though. The dog won't be a problem, but we'll have to get a birdcage for the parrot if he's going to stick around. Or else we'll be cleaning up after him all the time," Finn said.

"Cat! Cat! Run, dog, run!" the bird said.

Angel peeked out from around the corner of the kitchen, all the hair on her back standing straight up. She let out a pitiful meow and ran over to Shotgun for protection.

"I've got an idea." Finn hurried into the spare room in his wing of the house and drug out Shotgun's old kennel. He set it on the dining room table and opened the door.

The Chihuahua barked twice, and the bird lit on the curtain rod above the window looking out into the front yard. "Shut up, dog. Joe needs crackers," he said and then set about preening his pretty feathers.

"The dog talks to him," Callie said. "I wonder how long they've been out in the cold. Poor little things."

"It's misting. You know what that means?" Finn asked.

"Ice," she said. "The dog might have died if you hadn't found him. And parrots are tropical birds. He wouldn't have made it through the night. Wonder what their names are?"

"If no one claims them, we'll have to think about that, but the bird just told you his name. He said Joe needs crackers." Finn removed his coat and hung it on the rack inside the door. He held out his arm, and Joe lit on it and fluffed his feathers.

"Hot damn! Time to dance." Joe wiggled his head and body from side to side.

"I bet he'd really dance to music." Martin laughed.

"I'm going to ease him into the cage," Finn said.

It was easily said, but when he got close to the cage, the bird went crazy. "Run, dog, run. Cops. Prison. Run." He flapped his wings and flew around the room squawking about somebody killing him, dropping specks of crap on the table, on the floor, and even on Shotgun's back. The Chihuahua got all excited and started howling, and Angel screeched like someone was wringing her tail as she headed for safety under the kitchen table. Martin tried to talk the bird into lighting on his arm, but

Joe wasn't having any part of it. He finally lit on his curtain rod perch and gave Finn the old stink eye.

"Guess he don't like a cage." Callie grabbed paper towels to clean up the mess.

Callie was so cute in that red plaid flannel shirt and jeans that Finn wanted to forget about the damn bird, cuddle up with her on the sofa again, and hold her close as the embers crackled in the fireplace.

Callie finished the cleanup and whispered, "Let him alone until he calms down. Maybe we could get a leg ring and attach it to a perch in the window. Just go about your business like he's not there. Now, what's in the boxes?"

"Don't know, but they were marked *Christmas*, so I brought them inside. Hopefully, there really is a tree stand in that one." Finn shivered.

"Hot chocolate is ready. I've got it poured up, so go warm your hands and then we'll dig into them together," she said.

Martin shucked out of his coat and hung it on the lowest hook of the rack. Finn kicked off his boots and set them beside the door. Martin did the same with his shoes, which had seen better days, but then, they were his work gear, not those ugly neon-green things he would have to wear to school the next day. Maybe if the boy forgot to change shoes when they cleaned horse stables and he ruined the shoes, then Callie wouldn't fuss about new ones.

Martin dropped down on his knees and held his hand out to the new dog. "Look, he likes me. I think we should name him Pistol. That would go with Shotgun, wouldn't it?"

"Well, shit! Guns. Hit the ground, punk!" Joe hung upside down on the perch and shut his eyes.

Finn wrapped his cold hands around the mug of chocolate and sipped at it. "Tastes wonderful, and the dog does look like a Pistol, so we'll call him that until we see if someone claims him. Welcome to Salt Draw, Pistol and Joe."

Angel slithered out from under the kitchen table and walked sideways on her tiptoes toward the dog. It ignored her completely until she was just inches away and then it flopped down on its belly and wagged its tail. Angel sniffed its nose and then licked it up across the face.

"Looks like Shotgun and Angel think he needs a bath," Finn said.

"They're just making friends with him. He's sure enough different than Shotgun," Callie said, smiling. "I've always wanted pets, but an apartment isn't the place to have them."

"I don't reckon he'll be much good at herding cows, but he might be real good as an alarm system." Finn would have gathered up every stray in the county just to see her smile like that every day.

"How is a dog an alarm system?" Martin asked.

"Well, if someone comes around, I bet he lets the whole house know it."

"Sue the bastards." The bird flew down, lit on Martin's head, and deposited a dollop of bird crap on his back.

Callie grabbed another paper towel and wiped it away. "We've got to get him settled somewhere. I've got a necklace that might work for a chain, but we need a perch."

"I know." Martin got up slowly and motioned for them to follow him to the utility room. He pointed at a foldout clothes-drying rack made of dowel rods. "If we set that up in front of the window and put a chain on his leg, he could move from one end to the other. It looks like four rods all the same height, so he could even hop from one to the other if the chain wasn't too short."

"With newspaper under it to catch all the droppings," Finn said. "It just might work."

"Will you take care of keeping the newspaper changed?" Callie asked Martin.

"I sure will." Martin beamed.

Finn carried the rack to the living room with Martin and Joe right behind him. Callie went off to her bedroom to get the leg-irons.

They managed to get the chain around his leg, but then he figured out what was going on and threw a hissy fit. "Run, dog. Police. They're killin' me. Sue the bastards." Joe hopped from one rung to the other and back again.

"I think Joe has watched too much television." Finn laughed.

"Where's the remote? Damn police. Joe wants doughnuts." He went as far as the chain would let him and pecked at the edge of the curtains.

"One problem solved, now let's go back to the Christmas tree," Finn said.

"He's very vocal. I've never seen a bird that could say so many words." Callie sat down on the floor in front of the fireplace, and the new dog crawled up in her lap.

Finn joined her, thigh against hers, the sizzle there every single time. "I think he's taken to you."

She picked up the dog and held him up to her face. He promptly licked her from chin to forehead. "You do look like a Pistol. I like this little guy. The bird belongs to you guys. I don't even like canaries and parakeets, so I sure don't want a bird."

"Hot damn! Joe needs a cracker," the bird said.

"His name is Joe for sure," Callie said.

"Well, Mary!"

Callie laughed out loud. "I bet his owner is married to Mary. That should narrow down the list, right?"

Pistol wiggled out of her arms, sniffed the air, and followed his nose to the food bowl in the utility room. Angel romped along behind him, hackles up and meowing like someone had rocked on her tail.

"She wants him to play," Callie said.

"Either that or she's warning him not to eat all that food." Finn stole sideways glances at Callie. She'd aged little in the past two years, but there was a more mature look to her. Maybe instant motherhood did that to a woman. Whatever, it damn sure looked good on her.

Callie dragged one of the boxes over to her side and opened it carefully. "It's a red metal tree stand and a quilted tree skirt. Wonder why Verdie left these behind?"

Finn stood up and crossed the great room into the kitchen area. He put his empty cup in the dishwasher and settled in on the end of the sofa. "Maybe where she moved to doesn't have room for a big tree that requires water."

Callie ripped open the other box and said, "Look. It's a strand of those big old lights folks used to put on trees. And this used to be strung popcorn, but the string is so old that it's falling apart. This other thing is cranberries that have turned into raisins."

Finn patted the sofa beside him. "We could string popcorn and cranberries, but if we want to go to the Christmas tree lighting, we'll have to put that part of the decorating off until tomorrow evening. It's your choice."

"Popcorn. Popcorn. Joe wants popcorn." Joe made noises like corn popping in the microwave, complete with a ding like a timer going off.

"Please, can we go to town?" Martin begged. "I might meet some kids that like me, and tomorrow won't be so scary."

"We can string popcorn and cranberries another day," Callie said.

It was the right thing to let the boy meet other kids, but Finn's heart took a nosedive. He really would have rather stayed home with Callie than mix and mingle with people who didn't even like each other.

A couple of hours later, Finn stood back and looked at their tree. It looked kind of pitiful with one strand of lights and a couple of paper decorations that Martin made at the last minute.

"Oh, I forgot something. I'll be right back."

He was only gone a few minutes before he returned with a small boot in his hand. He handed it to Callie. "You can put it on the tree."

Her eyes widened at the sight of the small ornament. "You kept that thing all this time?"

"Of course. It was our only real ornament, remember? The last ornament the base store had to offer on Christmas Eve." His arm went around her shoulders. "You said it would have to be something like a damned old cowboy would buy."

He could tell by the instant sparkle in her eyes that she really did remember.

"Y'all had a Christmas tree together before this one?" Martin asked.

"Yes, we did." Callie nodded.

While she circled the tree four or five times, she told him about going to the base store and the boot being the only ornament left. She cocked her head this way and that way and finally came back to the front and gave the boot the most visible place on the tree—front and center.

"The crowning glory," she said. "Now it's time to eat supper and get bundled up to go see this Christmas tree thing they were talking about in church this morning."

"Gladys whispered to me that there was lots of refreshments, so we need to save room for them," Martin said.

"I've already had my dessert, out there under the pecan tree," Finn whispered for Callie's ears only.

Chapter 6

GLADYS WAS WATCHING AN OLD WESTERN MOVIE ON television when her phone rang. She grabbed it on the fourth ring and said, "Hello, Honey."

"Have you heard anything about the Christmas tree lighting?"

"After that catfight you and Betsy had in church this morning, I've been hearing plenty. There could be a problem at the lighting, but you'd best make sure nothing happens in my store."

"Betsy isn't getting away with putting me down in front of Finn like that. Even if I didn't want him, I'll have him now that she does. We're lighting our tree first. If they do something, they'll be damn sorry. Call Polly and see what she knows. And nothing will happen inside the store. They might try something like burning our tree, but they wouldn't dare do anything in the store," Honey said.

"You know I don't like spying," Gladys said.

"Yes, you do. It keeps you young." Honey laughed. "And besides, you know that we all consider you family."

"All the butterin' up in the world won't make me sell you Fiddle Creek," Gladys said.

"I've given up hope for that to ever happen, but I would like to know ahead of time if those hussies who'll back up Betsy are planning something evil. Please find out for me. I'll owe you big time," Honey pleaded.

"Yes, you will," Gladys said.

She didn't even put the phone back on the end table when Honey hung up but promptly hit the speed dial button for Polly. She heard all kinds of things in the bar, and she'd know if there was trouble brewing in the Gallagher court.

When Polly didn't answer, she left a message after the beep and went back to watching television. It was still several hours until tree lighting time, so she didn't have to rush right back to Honey. It would do her good to learn a little patience after the way she'd acted in church. For two cents, Gladys would stop being her spy, but then blood was thicker than water, and Honey's mama was Gladys's cousin's kid.

Polly had just lain down for a nap when her phone rang, sounding like a marching band coming right down the middle of her bed. She grabbed for it and came close to falling off the bed before she got her balance.

"This better damn sure be good," she growled.

"Miz Polly, darlin'," Betsy said sweetly. "Are we going to have trouble at the Christmas tree lighting tonight?"

"Don't you go sweet-talkin' me with the same mouth you used in church this mornin', Betsy Gallagher. I don't care if I do have a family member in your clan. I was about to take a Sunday afternoon nap, and I don't give a shit if the Brennans set fire to your Christmas tree."

"Oh, they are?" Betsy gasped.

"I said I didn't give a shit. I didn't say that I know if they are or aren't," Polly said. She shouldn't have answered the phone. She hadn't picked it up when Gladys called, and she was her best friend.

"But they're gettin' ready for war, aren't they?" Betsy asked.

"I damn sure would be. Y'all better load your guns, check your ammo supply, and count your cows."

"Would you call Gladys and find out what they're really doing? People talk in the store, and she hears things."

Polly sighed. "Okay, but only since I'm already awake, and I'll call you after we talk a spell. Don't be callin' me. I hate it when I'm trying to talk and those beeps cut off the words."

"I'll be waiting right here," Betsy said.

Polly pressed the button to end the conversation and immediately hit the speed dial for her sister-in-law. Lord, she wished that her cousin's son hadn't married into that wild bunch of Gallaghers. She felt like she was in bed with the devil every time she pumped Gladys for information.

"Why'd you take so long to call me back?" Gladys answered.

"I was tryin' to take a nap but I couldn't get to sleep," Polly said. "And then I got to thinkin' about that dustup in the church this morning. Do you think it was just the tip of the iceberg and they're about to get serious? It's been awhile since the feud has fired up real good."

"You know I hear things in the store just like you hear things in the bar. I believe they've just been lookin' for a reason to fan the fires. Well, I think the Brennans are fearful that the Gallaghers are going to sabotage the Christmas tree thing tonight. What do you reckon they'll do?"

"Hell if I know, but I'm damn sure going to be there because I overheard a Gallagher sayin' that if they set fire to their tree, then they'll retaliate," Polly said.

"I sure wish Verdie was here. She'll miss all the fun. She always thought we ought to make the Brennans and Gallaghers put both their trees on the churchyard since it's neutral territory."

Polly laughed. "Verdie tries to be a peacemaker, and there ain't been no peace in Burnt Boot for very long at a time."

"You're right. It's been goin' on too long now to ever expect an end. Wouldn't surprise me if the Brennans don't fire the first shot at this one after the way Betsy went after Finn this morning. Honey's been sayin' for two days that she was takin' him home for Sunday dinner. Betsy had to know and she stepped over the line."

That's all Polly needed to know. The Brennans were planning to start the war in retaliation. Well, they'd started a new episode in the past for a lot less, and once she reported to Betsy, Polly still had time for a nap before the ceremonies that evening.

―⁂―

Red satin tablecloths covered two long refreshment tables right inside the General Store doors. Candles burned brightly in the centerpieces, and two women kept busy helping the folks with hot chocolate, coffee, and spiced cider from silver carafes and red punch from a crystal punch bowl. Every square inch of both tables were filled with finger foods of all descriptions.

"It is a big spread," Callie said.

"It's pretty, ain't it?" Gladys said. "Try one of those

decorated Christmas cookies. Leah Brennan makes them, and she don't share her recipe."

"This is the Brennan party, then?" Callie asked.

"Yes, they always put their tree in front of my store, and the Gallaghers set theirs up over at the bar. You'll have to go to both, but don't forget to have a cookie. I heard that Honey has asked her to make a couple dozen in the morning to bring over to Salt Draw," Gladys whispered.

"They might have a bigger tree, but ours is prettier," Finn whispered so close behind Callie that his breath warmed her neck and shot all kinds of delicious little shivers down her backbone.

With his hand on her upper arm, he led her to the window to get a better look at the tree in the parking lot. It was covered with huge Christmas bulbs and gold tinsel that the north wind kept in constant movement.

"I agree," she said. "Where's Martin?"

Finn nodded toward the end of the table where Martin was talking to a little girl about his age. "He's fine."

"I'm going to get a cup of something hot. Can I get you one?" She wiggled free of his embrace and started toward the end of the table with the hot cider.

"Coffee, please," he said.

Honey passed her on the way. Callie caught the look in her eye and stopped in her tracks. Forget the coffee and cider; Finn might need her.

Honey looped her arm through his and pressed her body against his. She was dressed in a skintight red velvet dress that looked like it had been spray painted onto her skin. Callie took a couple of steps in that direction and heard her say, "Finn, I'm so glad to see you again. I've got a surprise for you tomorrow morning."

"And what is that?" he asked.

She kissed him on the cheek and whispered something Callie couldn't hear, but Finn's expression said that it was downright sinful. With those long red fingernails, the woman reminded Callie of a giant hawk with its claws out to pick up a helpless kitten.

"Finn," Callie yelled over the noise of a store full of people.

His eyes darted around until they found her. He walked away from Honey, his eyes never leaving Callie's. "Yes?"

"It's getting hot in here. Let's go on outside," she said.

"Oh, darlin', it will get much hotter before the week is out. That's a promise you can take to the bank." Honey laughed.

Finn laced his fingers with Callie's and motioned to Martin, who nodded. They were all three about to push the door open when suddenly the two lovely ladies serving refreshments started screaming, stomping, and carrying on like they were possessed or else going into seizures. They held their arms out to the sides and shivered from head to toe.

"Mouse," one of them finally gasped.

And sure enough, a little brown furry creature ran out the loose-fitting arm of her flowing shirt and jumped straight into the punch bowl. The other woman shook her arms so hard that they were nothing but a blur, and another mouse dropped out on the table and ran across the cookies and cupcakes.

Like a flying squirrel, the critter bailed off the table,

all four legs stretched to the sides and its tail straight as a ramrod. It landed about waist level on Honey's pretty red velvet dress, scurried upward, and came to rest on her head. She did a combination break dance and a series of clumsy acrobatic moves as she tried to swat the thing off her head without touching it.

In all the commotion of women screaming and men running to help poor Honey, someone grabbed the edge of the table holding the punch bowl with the first mouse doing laps around it and yanked. Coffee, hot chocolate, and punch went every which way, and the people who'd been trying to help Honey retreated to the back of the store.

Callie seriously considered climbing on the checkout counter, but one of the mice took off in that direction, so she made an abrupt turn and headed for the door. A kid who she recognized as Keith Gallagher brushed past her and made his way outside with the scrambling crowd. She watched him flee into the shadows between two cars and squat down. If he was the culprit in turning those mice loose in Gladys's store, he should be grounded for eternity plus three days. She shivered, not from the cold as much as from the fact that those damned mice were so close to her feet. She would have fainted dead if one of them had run up inside her clothing.

"What the hell just happened in here?" Gladys yelled. "I don't have mice in my store. The Gallaghers put someone up to this shit."

"I saw one of their brats running out of the store," Honey screamed. "I'll tar and feather the little bastard if I catch him."

Declan Brennan, bless his heart, attempted to salvage

the rest of the party. He turned on the microphone and said, "Looks like there was a little mishap with the refreshments inside, but it's time to light the Brennan family tree. We'd like to welcome everyone. We've done this for a hundred years right here in Burnt Boot, and we're glad you could join us." He picked up the plug and the long extension cord running electricity from the store and made a big show of connecting the two.

Callie was busy watching the kid in the shadows rather than the tree. He stood up and hurled what looked like a rolled newspaper toward the big fancy tree. The flame on the end sent her adrenaline into overload for a split second until she figured out it wasn't a stick of dynamite, but a whole package of firecrackers. She covered her ears when they went off, and everyone hit the ground or ran toward their cars.

"What the hell?" Finn pulled both Callie and Martin close to his sides. "Where's the shooter?"

"It's firecrackers," Callie yelled, but it sounded so much like machine-gun fire that her blood ran cold.

Gladys laid a hand on Callie's shoulder. "I was afraid something like this would happen. War has been declared."

"I guess everyone will go home now and the Gallaghers' party will be a bust," Callie said breathlessly.

"Oh no! We'll all go see what the Brennans can come up with on the spur of the moment. Paybacks are hell," Gladys said. "I wouldn't miss this for the world."

"What about the mess in your store?"

"The Brennans will clean it up. Let's go on over to the bar," Gladys said.

"Lord, I thought we'd really gotten between the

Hatfield and McCoy bunch there for a minute," Callie said.

"I know," Finn said. "It did sound like machine-gun fire when we were that close to it."

"Would you look at that tree?" Callie quickly changed the subject. Too much talk about guns and Martin would have a nightmare for sure.

"Do you think they'll have cookies, too?" Martin asked. "I never did get one, and I sure didn't want one after that mouse ran all over them."

Finn laid his hand over Callie's on the console. "I imagine they'll have something good to eat. They won't let the Brennans outdo them."

"He'll remember the mice more than the firecrackers," Finn said in a low voice as he gave Callie's hand a gentle squeeze.

The tree out in front of the bar was a foot or so taller than the one in front of the store. It sported a star on top instead of an angel, and it had lots of garland that would probably be blown away by the north wind before a week was out. But right then it was as pretty as the Brennans' tree.

The Gallaghers had set up a flatbed out in the middle of the pasture right beside the bar with upbeat holiday music coming through the big speakers. Several young folks were dancing to "Merry Christmas Baby," performed as a duet by Elvis Presley and Gretchen Wilson.

"May I have this dance?" Finn asked when they were out of the truck. "Maybe if everyone sees us dancing, those two women will think we're a couple."

Callie looped her arms around his neck, and Finn executed some very fine two-stepping. "That's not the way it works. They'll just put me in their crosshairs to get rid of the competition."

"Santa Claus," Martin gasped.

"Where?" Callie turned quickly.

Martin pointed toward the bar. Two little boys ran out with paper sacks in their hands and there was a flash of a red suit before the door slammed shut. "Can we go inside now, Callie? I really need to talk to him."

"Of course we can," Finn answered. "Are you going to sit on Santa's lap, Callie?"

"Only if he's wearing cowboy boots and has blue eyes," she flirted.

Santa Claus was set up at the end of the bar. Elves led folks of all ages through the candy cane–lined lane to sit on his knee and have their picture taken with him. Then, while other elves took them out another way to get a brown paper bag filled with fruit, nuts, and candy, a Gallagher with lots of computer savvy printed the picture and passed it off to an elf who took it to the guests.

Martin thought he was far too old to sit on Santa's knee, but he stood beside him and whispered in his ear, had his picture taken, and carried it close to his heart for the next half hour as they waited for the next tree to light up.

Finn looked at the picture and asked, "What did you tell Santa you wanted this year?"

"Can't tell. That's between me and Santa." Martin grinned.

Finn leaned down until his mouth was against Callie's ear and asked, "Are you going to get your picture taken with him?"

"He's not wearing cowboy boots, and his eyes are green," Callie said.

"And what would you ask for if you could sit on his knee?" Finn asked.

"That would be between me and Santa," she answered.

"Want to know what I asked for?" Betsy bumped Callie out of the way with a well-slung hip shot and looped her arms around Finn's neck.

He didn't have time to shake his head, nod, or even blink before she rolled up on her toes and kissed him right smack on the lips. When he pulled away and took a step backward, she laughed.

"Now I believe that Santa delivers," she said with a grin. "I sat on his lap and asked him to bring me a hot cowboy with a cute little ass and promised if he would I'd mark him with a kiss. Oh, hello, Cathy."

"That's Callie," she said coldly.

"Cathy. Callie. It doesn't matter. You're just the housekeeper." Betsy grinned and walked away.

"Where's a mouse when you need one?" Callie grumbled.

"Sorry about that," Finn said.

"Did it taste like apple pie?" Callie asked.

The scowl on his face answered her before he said, "Yes, and I don't like apple pie."

The flash of the camera kept lighting up the bar until Betsy announced that the lighting of the tree would be taking place in five minutes. "Santa will do the honors this year, but he'll be back in here for more pictures and to listen to more Christmas wishes right after the tree is lit. Let's go watch the most beautiful tree in Burnt Boot light up, folks."

Santa Claus adjusted his fake fat and stuffed belly before he waddled out the door with a whole crew behind him. Callie heard whispers of disappointment that the Brennans hadn't planned anything in retaliation for the earlier fiasco. After that little scene with Betsy, she was ready to join the Brennans' side. Then she remembered the way Honey had acted and decided she'd rather shoot the whole bunch of them— Gallaghers and Brennans both. What kind of people ruined Christmas, anyway?

Santa Claus crawled up on the flatbed trailer and raised his arms. The star on top of the tree weaved back and forth as the north wind picked up. The roar of a nearby train added its noise to the mixture.

"I didn't realize there was a train track anywhere near here," Callie said.

"First time I've heard one," Finn said.

"Train track?" Polly said behind them. "That's not a train. It's an airplane. There must be something big in the works here, like elves parachuting out of the sky."

Her comment went through the crowd faster than the speed of light, and everyone was looking up when Santa tapped on the microphone and said, "Ho, ho, ho! Time to light up the tree so here we go!"

He snapped the two cords together, and someone yelled from the back of the crowd, "Holy shit! That's not a plane or a train. It's a damn stampede."

The crowd started to panic for the second time that night, running toward their vehicles for safety when two big black trucks roared down the street right toward the cattle. The herd turned in front of the trucks and came hell-bent right into the parking lot. The big tree went down in a blur. It didn't even slow them down, and the flatbed was smack in the middle of their path.

Santa dropped to his knees and covered his head. For the most part the cattle split in two directions, but one rangy old bull tucked his front legs and landed on the flatbed with Santa, raised his tail, and dropped a load of fresh bullshit right there. Tired from the whole stampede, long silver icicles stuck to his winter coat and tail, he stopped beside Santa, hooked his horn in the white beard, and shook his big black head a couple of times. The beard fell over one eye like a punk rocker's long hair and frightened the old boy so badly that he stomped his way off the truck, leaving two ruined speakers behind.

"They've got Gallagher brands, but I bet that was two Brennan trucks that turned them," Gladys said. "Now the Gallaghers have to gather up their own cattle that ruined their part of Christmas. The Brennans didn't do too bad for a spur-of-the-minute stunt."

"Anybody hurt?" Polly yelled.

"No, but I'm layin' low the next few weeks. Looks like Burnt Boot is in for a war," a voice said at the back of the parking lot.

"Let's go home and get out of their fightin'. I came here thinkin' a little town like this would be peaceful, but this is the last time I want to see any of their feuding shit," Finn said.

"Now you know why that woman who sold Salt Draw wanted out of here," Callie said.

Chapter 7

Finn was in that state between dozing and sleep when he heard whining. When he opened his eyes, Shotgun was standing beside the bed, and he figured that the dog needed to make a trip outside. So he pulled on a pair of flannel pajama bottoms and a thermal shirt, shoved his feet down into his boots, and opened the door.

Shotgun didn't race out into the hall but did a semi-low crawl.

Joe made noises like gunfire from his perch, where he alternately preened his tail feathers and pranced from one end to the other, shooting imaginary police. Weren't birds supposed to sleep at night? Chickens tucked their heads under their wings and went to roost. Why didn't that damn bird do the same?

"Take cover, Finn. They're low. Don't move," Callie said in clipped words.

She was stretched out flat on her stomach with her hands over her head. "Maybe the ghillie suit will keep them from seeing us. Be still, Finn. Breathe easy. Don't look up."

Finn sat down beside her on the floor and gently touched her shoulder. He recognized the position. She was back in Afghanistan, and they were on a mission. She was wearing a camouflage ghillie suit, and they were covered in camo-netting. The enemy was flying low above them, and she was afraid they'd use thermal imaging to locate them.

She grabbed the place where he'd touched her and groaned. "I'm hit, Finn. Don't know how bad, but it hurts like a son of a bitch."

"Callie, wake up. It's Joe doin' the shootin'. I swear his owner must have watched cop shows nonstop." He shook her shoulder.

"Don't touch it," she gasped.

"Callie, it's a nightmare," he whispered.

Her eyes flew open and scanned the area. She touched her head and then her arms.

"Shhh," she said.

"You're on my ranch in Salt Draw." He pulled her up to a sitting position and shifted her into his lap. She was sweating bullets and shivering at the same time. He knew exactly what she'd been dreaming because he'd had the same nightmare too many times to count.

"Finn, I'm not going to die, am I?" she whispered.

"You are not hit. It was a bad dream."

"It was so real," she said.

He kissed her on the forehead and held her tighter. "I know. It was probably brought on by all the noise of the evening with the firecrackers and the stampede. I didn't want to go to sleep either."

She opened her eyes wider and scanned the room. "I haven't had one in almost a month. I thought they were done with."

She shivered again, and he grabbed the quilt and wrapped them both in it. "I'm not sure they'll ever be gone. We saw a hell of a lot of bad stuff, Callie. It's burned into our subconscious. Did you do the psych eval before they turned you loose?"

"It was required, and besides, they had to have it on

file before they'd let me have Martin. I hate this feeling. My insides are quivering and my heart is still racing."

"Just be still and watch the flames in the fireplace. That always helps me. That's why I chose the room I did." He gently massaged her tense shoulders. "Why were you on the sofa?"

"This is the second nightmare. The first one was right after I went to sleep. We were arguing about not getting to eat Christmas dinner, and then the bombs hit the base and there was blood everywhere. I woke up, crying because you had blood on you. I couldn't go back to sleep in that room, so I came out here," she said.

"Red punch pouring out over the floor and Christmas trees and firecrackers. It all went together to make a hell of a nightmare. Add that to Joe shooting up the whole living room with his gun noises, and it's pretty good fodder for a nightmare," he said.

"Hold me for a little while longer," she said.

"As long as you need me, Callie. I'm right here." He leaned his head forward and rested his chin on the top of her head.

"Call the coroner," Joe squawked.

―⁂―

Callie wasn't surprised when Martin showed up at the breakfast table clutching his stomach and saying he couldn't go to school. She'd suffered with the same symptoms too many times to count when she'd been his age. But staying home another day wouldn't help one bit.

"Time for the magic?" she asked.

He nodded.

Finn looked up from his morning coffee. "Magic?"

"Callie makes a magic cup of stuff that helps my stomach settle down when I'm afraid. Mama used to make it, but Callie does it better," Martin explained.

"What's in it?" Finn asked.

"A witch doesn't reveal her secrets, not even during the Christmas season," Callie said.

She poured half a cup of milk in a mug, added a package of hot chocolate mix, a few drops of almond extract, and enough liquid coffee creamer to fill the cup. She stirred it well, stuck it in the microwave for one minute, and pulled it out.

That and two pieces of cinnamon toast completed the magic breakfast guaranteed to heal any nervous tummy. It worked when she was a little girl having to start all over in a different school every time she turned around, and it worked when she was about to go on a mission over there in the sand.

Martin sipped it, ate a bite of the toast, and nodded. "You will go with me, won't you?"

"Of course I will. We have to fill out all the papers, but on Tuesday, you have to ride the bus," she answered.

"I'm really scared, Callie."

The lump in her throat got bigger instead of smaller. Finn reached out and ruffled Martin's hair. "I'm only a phone call away. I can be there in five minutes if you need me. There's always a teacher close by so if anything spooks you, just run to her and tell her to call Salt Draw. And in the evenings when you come home, you've got two dogs, a parrot that never shuts up, and a cat that will be waiting for you as well as me and Callie."

Martin nodded. "What do I do if somebody like that Keith boy picks a fight?"

"Bury the bastard in the backyard." Joe hung upside down on the perch like he was dead.

Finn ignored the bird and gave Martin's shoulder a gentle squeeze. "Here's what the rules were at my house when I was a boy: You are in trouble if you start a fight. You are not to throw the first punch or goad someone into throwing it. But if there's no way out and some kid hits you, then you do what you have to do. And then you tell the teacher to call Salt Draw. Callie will be sure to tell them her cell phone number and the ranch number."

"Okay, then let's get it over with, Callie. I've changed my mind about Christmas, though. What I really want is to never change schools again." Martin sighed.

The lump grew so big that it almost closed her throat completely off. When she was a kid, she and her sister both asked for that same thing for Christmas almost every single year.

"Well, I'd say that it all begins with today, and if you don't finish up that magic breakfast and get dressed, it can't come true," Finn said.

Martin gobbled down the rest of his toast and drained the cup of glorified hot chocolate before he ran off to his room to get dressed.

"Want me to go with y'all this morning? Might make him feel better," he asked.

Standing at the kitchen sink with her back to him, Callie barely nodded.

"Are you all right?" He pushed the chair back and crossed the floor in a few long strides, put his hands on her shoulders, and turned her around to face him. Tears rolled down her cheeks like a river in the springtime, dripped off her jaw onto the dark green sweatshirt she wore, and left dime-sized wet dots.

Finn drew her close to his chest and patted her back. "He'll be fine, Callie. He might have some arguments, but that's just new-school stuff."

"I know. I've been there," she sobbed.

"He'll make friends," Finn said. "This is Burnt Boot, and it's public school he's going to. The feuding families have their own private schools." He tipped her chin up and looked into her watery eyes. "We're all starting over here, but we'll be okay, Callie, I promise."

His lips found hers in a sweet, passionate kiss that sealed his promise, and she believed that they would be okay. But first they had to get past this day. She clung to him as long as she could and then spun around toward the sink to dry her face on a tea towel when she heard Martin's footsteps.

"I'm ready if you are, Callie," he said.

"Finn was just asking if we'd like him to go with us this first day," Callie said.

Martin raced the rest of the way across the floor and hugged Finn. "That would be great. You reckon you could come in the school with me, too, just so all the kids could see who you are?"

"I could do that," Finn said.

Martin looped his backpack over his shoulders and squared up his shoulders. "I'm ready. Move 'em out, cowboys."

Finn noticed that Martin was wearing his black work shoes when they got into the truck. They'd been cleaned up, but they showed signs of lots of wear and the laces were frayed. He didn't blame the kid. He would have gone barefoot before he wore those ugly shoes with lime-green soles. Looking at them was probably what gave him a stomachache that morning to begin with.

When they got out of the truck, playground noise rattled the naked limbs of the old oak trees circling the area as if they could protect the children of Burnt Boot. Cold north wind didn't faze the kids as they ran instead of walked and yelled instead of talked normally.

Warm air full of the smell of glue, kids, and fresh floor wax rushed out when Finn opened the big old-fashioned wooden door. The Christmas pictures taped to the windows and the smells that permeated from the hallways said that it was probably the same as other small Texas schools: maybe older than some but definitely not so different.

"Could I help y'all?" a lady asked.

"We're here to enroll a new student. I'm Callie Brewster," Callie said.

Finn could hear the nervousness in her voice, and he took her hand in his. "Callie and Martin here live on Salt Draw with me. I'm Finn O'Donnell."

"What grade are you in, Martin?"

"Third," he said shyly.

"I'll take you to the elementary wing. That way you won't have to go back out into the cold. I'm Gloria Dean, the first-grade teacher. I have a son in the third grade." She led them down a long hallway, through a double set of modern glass doors, and into another wing.

"What's his name?" Martin asked.

"Harry. He's got red hair and lots of freckles. You'll

meet him today. Right down there is the office. See that sign hanging out there over the door?"

"Yes, ma'am."

"You go on in there and talk to Miz Tamara. She'll get you all enrolled. I'll tell Harry that you're here. He'll be excited that the new student is a boy. There's only five, counting you, in the class. There are seven girls, making an even dozen now in the third grade."

Martin grabbed Callie's other hand in a death grip. "Can't you just homeschool me, Callie?"

The office door swung open before Callie could answer.

Tamara smiled brightly and motioned for them to come inside the office. "Come right on in here. We've been expecting to see y'all this morning. Gladys is my distant cousin and told me you'd be coming in. You can start classes today, but there will be some things like shot records that I'll need by the end of the week."

Callie pulled a manila folder from her big purse and handed it to Tamara. "This might cover it, but if it doesn't, just let me know, and I'll find the rest."

"Oh, I see that you've done this before," Tamara said. "Well, have a seat right there while I copy these off."

Callie briefly explained the situation with Martin and the upcoming trial. "Finn is providing a safe house, but we'd rather not make any of this public. We just want Martin to fit in with the kids here in Burnt Boot."

"We're so far back in the woods here, I don't see a problem, but we'll keep a watch. How's that?"

Finn nodded. "Thank you. Being a new kid in a small school is going to be tough enough without that business coming out."

A buzzing noise was followed by kids flooding the hallway out in front of the office. One little red-haired boy waved at Martin. Finn could have shouted when he saw that the child was wearing black athletic shoes and not cowboy boots.

"That must be Harry," Callie said.

"Seven girls," Martin moaned.

A few snowflakes fell on the truck windshield on the way back to Salt Draw. The temperature had dropped low enough that they scooted off as fast as they hit.

"Looks like we're in for a cold run this morning," Finn said.

Callie groaned. "It'll be like training camp all over again."

"Terrorists don't wait until the weather is perfect," he said.

"But we're civilians," she argued.

"It's up to you, Callie. I'm going. You can come with me or stay in the house. I've kept up with my training for two years, and it's not going to get any better. Verdie told me this part of Texas was in for a real stinker of a winter if she had it figured right. That's why she sold the ranch when she did. Said she didn't want to fall and freeze to death before anyone came around to figure out why she wasn't answering her phone."

"I'm fighting this rather than thinking about Martin in a new school," she said honestly.

He ran a palm up her arm. "He's going to be all right."

"I know that, but it might not be today."

"No, today is going to be tough even if it goes

well. Seven girls, for God's sake." He chuckled. "Stop worrying."

"What if…" she started.

He reached across the seat and put a finger on her lips. "'What if' just creates worry. Let's go run ten miles to loosen up our bodies and then work out for an hour. That'll take your mind off everything. You probably won't even make the first loop this morning, but when you get tired, you can turn around and come on back to the house. You'll have to build up to capacity in my makeshift gym to keep up with me, so if you can't do that this first day, it's okay."

She pushed his hand away. "Don't bait me, Finn."

"Don't be a wuss, Brewster." He parked the truck close to the back door. "I'll be ready to run in five minutes. I'm not waiting on you." He jogged around the truck and opened the door for her. When she bailed out, he grabbed her around the waist, spun her around to his chest, and laid one of the hottest kisses on her lips that she'd ever experienced.

"There now. That'll warm us both up while we run," he teased. "But I'm still not waiting for you."

"Wait, hell! O'Donnell, you'll have to catch me," she smarted off.

She ran through the house, jerked on her running gear, added a hooded sweatshirt to it, and was heading out the back door when she saw him a few feet ahead of her. She sprinted until she was beside him and he started the cadence.

"One mile," he called out the first line.

"No sweat," she came in behind him.

"Two mile—better yet," he said.

"Three miles—gotta run," she singsonged.

"Four miles—just for fun."

They both yelled the next lines: "Come on—let's go. We can go—through the snow. We can run—to the sun."

Then he started the countdown. "S-N."

She chimed in with, "I-P."

He yelled, "E-R."

And they both yelled, "Can you be—like me? Sniper, yes, sir."

By then they'd both found their pace, and their feet hit the ground at the same time on every step. It was exhilarating running outside again, pushing herself until she only thought about making the end of the line, but she wasn't expecting to find a damn rope hanging in a tree when she got there. Finn grabbed it and, using the knots for handholds, hauled his body up to the high limb of the cottonwood tree then, using the same rope, rappelled down the backside.

When his combat boots hit the ground, she jumped and grabbed the first knot, made her way up it, and did the same thing he did. He ran in place until she was ready. "Ready for the return trip?"

"I thought this was a loop."

"It is. This is the turnaround on the loop." He took off and she kept up.

"That's more than five miles," she said.

"Eight, actually. We did this much in training before breakfast," he reminded her. "One mile," he called out the beginning of the cadence.

"You're full of shit," she yelled.

"Two miles," he said.

"You're a slave driver."

"Three miles."

"You are going to hell for this."

He chuckled without even losing his breath. "Callie is a wuss."

"Callie is an S-P-O-T-T-E-R."

He stepped up the pace a notch, but neither snow-flakes in her eyes or sleet collecting on her jacket was going to let her fall behind. They hit the bunkhouse porch at the same time, and he held the door for her. Once inside, he tossed a bottle of water at her. She caught it in the air, twisted off the lid, and downed half of it before coming up for air. He pulled his jacket off, drank the whole bottle of water, and fell down on a floor mat.

She hated sit-ups every bit as bad as push-ups, but with her competitive spirit, she wasn't losing to Finn the very first day of workouts. She did the same one hundred that he did then flipped over on her stomach and did a hundred push-ups. When he popped up and headed for the weights, she was right behind him.

"You want to spot or go first?" he asked.

"I'll go first," she said. If she stopped even for a few minutes, she'd collapse. The only thing that kept her going was the idea of a long soaking bath in that big tub back at the house.

She did ten reps and then traded places with Finn. "We going to shoot after this, or is that after dinner?"

"I thought we'd wait until it's snowing harder to make it more fun." He grinned. "Did you bring a ghillie suit? We could play real war."

"Hell no! I don't care if I never see one of those things again," she said. "But rest assured, darlin', I can outshoot you even in blinding snow. All you had to do was pull the trigger. I had to do the work."

"But you've been practicing inside and I've kept up my skills in the weather." He finished his reps and sat up on the end of the bench.

She threw him a towel, and he wiped sweat from his face. He combed his wet dark hair back with his fingers and looked up at her. "So what's for dinner, darlin'?"

She slapped him with her towel. "Apple pie after that shitty comment."

"Joe wants apple pie." The bird pranced from one end of his rod to the other. Angel sat on the back of the sofa, watching his every move.

"I'm going to fry that foulmouthed fowl if he doesn't learn to shut up," Callie said.

"You are a wicked woman, but your kisses are straight from heaven. They're hot as hellfire, but nothing that passionate could come from anywhere but the courts of heaven."

"You are full of shit, Finn, but I like that pickup line real well. We're having a light dinner and a big supper on school nights. I don't think Martin eats enough in the school cafeteria, and he refuses to take his lunch with him."

"I'm not bitchin'. If you weren't here, honey, I'd be eating soup out of cans and bologna sandwiches," he answered.

"Don't call me by that bitch's name. You can call me anything but that."

He jumped up, squared his shoulders, and stood at stiff attention, then saluted. "Yes, ma'am. I bet I can beat you to the house."

"Not in your wildest dreams." She grabbed her jacket and was gone before he could bend over and pick his up from the floor. She barely slowed down enough to open the door when she reached the porch. She rushed inside and headed straight for the bathroom. He was only two steps behind her, but she turned on the hot water and didn't know whether he collapsed on the sofa or went straight for the shower in his end of the house.

"Kidney bean soup for dinner," she mumbled as she left her clothing on the floor and slid into the steaming hot bath. "Fried chicken and biscuits for supper. There's plenty of chocolate cake left over from yesterday and store-bought cookies in the jar for after-school snacks."

She leaned back in the tub, letting the warm water work the kinks out of her body. She hadn't had a workout like that since she'd been home. The gym seemed like a pansy cop-out after the paces Finn had just put her through, but he'd been right. It had damn sure taken her mind off Martin's first day at a new school. She waited until the water went lukewarm before she crawled out and wrapped a towel around her body. She peeked out the door to be sure Finn wasn't in sight and darted across the hallway to her room.

She'd barely gotten her jeans and shirt pulled on when she heard the crunch of tires out front. That put her into fast mode as she started to worry. Martin had gotten sick and they'd been away from the house phone, so Tamara had driven him home. Or, worse yet, that damn convict had connections on the outside and he'd sent someone to make sure Martin did not testify. She opened the top drawer in the dresser and pulled out a small locked safe. Two minutes later she was shoving a clip into a Glock Gen4 pistol and heading out toward the door.

The front door was wide open, and Finn was nowhere around. If someone was bringing Martin home, then the door wouldn't be hanging open. She pressed the gun against her leg. Then the screaming began and she put on the speed.

"You damn bitch. You've ruined my pie."

Holy shit! That was Betsy and she'd really brought Finn an apple pie. Where in the hell was he, anyway?

Callie threw open the storm door to see Finn, arms crossed over his chest, standing there like a statue in his thermal shirt, jeans, and boots while Honey and Betsy squared off for another match. Only this time it damn sure didn't look like it was going to be words only.

Good, she thought. *Maybe they'll snatch each other baldheaded and scratch each other's eyes plumb out.*

"Well, look what you did to my cookies!" Honey yelled.

Shotgun was making short order of the pie, and Pistol was gobbling down the cookies. Joe had set up a howl in the dining room squawking, "Cat. Cat. Run. Run," over and over.

Betsy threw the first punch, landing it square in Honey's right eye, and the fight was on. They pulled hair, screamed obscenities, and slapped or punched wherever they could find a place to hit.

"You going to put a stop to this?" she asked Finn.

He shook his head. "I'm going in the house. They can roll around in the snow until they freeze for all I care. I didn't know that Shotgun liked apple pie. Guess he does."

Pistol picked up the final cookie and carried it in the house. Shotgun slurped up the last bit of pie and paraded past them to his warm spot in front of the fire. Now Joe was screaming that he wanted a cracker.

"I don't want to deal with the undertaker or frozen dead bodies," she said. She aimed the gun at the mesquite tree nearest to the women and fired off six shots, sending bark flying everywhere.

They both jumped up and covered their heads with their hands. "Why in the hell are you shooting at us?" Honey screamed.

"If I was shooting at you, you'd be graveyard dead, woman. Get your sorry asses off this ranch, and don't come back or I might miss that 'squite tree next time and put a bullet in your boobs. I mean it, get out of here." She brought the gun up to aim right at Honey's big breasts.

"You going to let her talk like that to me?" Honey asked Finn.

"I'm not crossin' her," he answered.

"This ain't over," Betsy declared on her way to her truck.

Callie fired one more shot that landed two feet from the front tire of the truck. "You want to fight among yourselves, then get on with your sorry-assed feud, but when you step on Salt Draw, you leave your fightin' behind."

They spun out of the driveway and slipped and slid all the way out to the road in their hurry to get away. She jacked the magazine out of her gun and carried it to the kitchen table. Damned old bitches, anyway. Now she'd have to tear it down and clean it before she put it away.

"I've got to make a fast run to Gainesville for a load

of feed. You want to go or stay here and calm down?"
Finn asked.

"I'd best stay here. You'll be back in time for dinner,
right?"

"Joe wants a cracker," the bird yelled.

Pistol picked up the cookie he'd brought inside
and carried it to the newspaper under Joe's makeshift
tree house.

"I'll be damned. That dog saved a cookie for his
buddy. Guess I'd best help him get it up to the bird.
I'll run by Walmart for some parrot food. Anything you
need?" Finn said.

Leave it to a man to act like nothing had just happened. She'd fired her gun seven times and taken care
of the catfight over him. A thank-you would be nice; a
hug would be even better.

"Not a damned thing." She laid the gun down with
the clip right beside it.

He spun her around, wrapped his arms around her,
and hugged her tightly. "That was some fancy target
practice out there, Brewster. But I got to admit, I was
wonderin' just where we were going to bury two bodies
in this kind of weather and if the feud wouldn't get
worse when both sides thought the other one had killed
one of their own."

"Well, shit fire! If I'd thought of that, I wouldn't
have shot the tree, I'd have stopped them from sniffing
around you for good. And I'd have gotten away with
murder, Finn." She laughed. "But I don't reckon we'll
have any more problems with their damned old feud, not
on Salt Draw."

His lips found hers at the same time she uttered the

last word. The feud, the shooting, and all thought of the two feuding women left her mind immediately. She pressed her body tightly to his, wanting to keep the heat going, to take it further, but it ended and gave her something more to be angry about.

"I'll see you at dinnertime," he said.

All she could do was shake her head and then he was gone.

Leaving the gun on the table, she plopped down on the sofa, and Angel hopped up into her lap. Pistol was too chubby to get from floor to sofa so she had to help him, and soon he and Angel were both sound asleep. She rubbed Pistol's ears and then Angel's, giving them equal time.

Her phone rang and she pushed the two animals to the side, hurrying to the kitchen table, where she'd set her purse. Thousands of images ran through her head. Martin had a broken nose and two black eyes from fighting with some kid like Keith. Or Finn had fallen and broken a leg out there on the slippery grass.

She grabbed it and answered without even looking at the caller ID, only to hear it still ringing. "Well, shit!" she said.

The house phone and her cell phone had the same tone. She trotted across the kitchen and picked up the receiver from the old land line hanging on the wall in the utility room.

"Hello," she said.

"I just heard that you tried to kill Honey and Betsy." Gladys laughed.

"Like I told Honey, if I'd have wanted her dead, she would be stretched out on the undertaker's table. They were going at it in the front yard, and I gave them a little frozen tree bark bath is all," Callie said.

"Well, you might be interested to know that the sheriff is on the way to talk to you. Honey called him," Gladys said. "Looks like it's going to be a good day in the store. Nothing like the feud firin' up to bring in customers. Talk to you later."

The phone went dead and the doorbell rang at the same time.

She sighed as she padded to answer it. Sure enough there stood an officer with a box of doughnuts in his hand.

"Yes, sir?" she said.

"Mind if I come inside?" he asked. "It's pretty cold out here."

His voice was high-pitched, but it matched him to a tee. His round baby face was red from the cold and probably a dose of high blood pressure. There was definitely a spare tire around his middle, probably from too many sweets, too little exercise, and way too much sitting behind a desk.

She stood back and opened the door wide for him. He quickly removed his hat, revealing a narrow rim of light brown hair circling a bald head above it. His green eyes darted around the room when Joe yelled, "Cat. Cat. Run."

"It's the parrot," she said.

He unzipped his jacket and said, "Birds and me don't get along too good, and I'm allergic to cats."

"There's one of them around here, too, but she's skittish around strangers," she said. "Would you like a cup of coffee? There's some made."

"I'd love one. I got two doughnuts left in this box. We can share."

"No, thanks, but you're welcome to have one."

"Gun?" he said.

"It's registered and I have a permit to carry," she said quickly.

"Then I guess you really did shoot at them women?"

"No, I shot at a tree to scare them. They were rolling around in my front yard acting like a couple of idiots. I didn't feel like going out there in my bare feet and pulling them apart."

He grinned. "Last time I got in the middle of the feud, I got a bullet in my leg. So nowadays when I get a call to come up here, I take my time and have a few doughnuts before I leave Gainesville. If they kill each other, well, they shouldn't be feudin'. Let's have a cup of coffee and visit a spell and then I'll be on my way."

"And your report?"

"What report?" He grinned.

Chapter 8

"HEY, CALLIE." FINN PUSHED HIS WAY INSIDE THE house. "Is that kidney bean soup I smell? It's my favorite."

She turned around at the sink and nodded. "It's ready to dip up a bowl, and we've got hot biscuits to go with it."

"Now that's a treat. Give me two minutes to wash up. It's blowing like crazy out there and supposed to get worse. Could I get you to help me feed this afternoon? I promise we'll be finished by the time Martin gets home. Where did that box of doughnuts come from?"

"It's an empty box, so don't get your hopes up," she said.

"But where did it come from?"

"Remember the fight this morning?"

Joe chose that moment to imitate the noises he'd heard when Callie fired at the tree. "Cops! Cops! Hide!" he yelled in a deep voice.

He hung his coat on the back of a chair. "How could I forget it? Are you telling me that Honey or Betsy brought a peace offering?"

"No. Honey called the sheriff after the shooting. My gun was on the table, but we just moved it aside so he could eat his last two doughnuts. I think he was flirting with me." She laughed.

"He'd have to be stone-cold blind or crazy as bat shit

not to flirt with you," Finn said. "Now about helping me feed?"

"I hired on to do whatever you needed," she said.

"Whatever?" He wiggled his eyebrows. Even that silly gesture put her mind into the gutter. Need and want were two different things for both of them, and she still wasn't over being angry at having her morning ruined or by him stopping at one red-hot, scorching kiss either.

"Needed, not wanted. Wash your hands and let's eat dinner."

Feeding cows, driving a truck, and cutting loose hay bales all came back to Callie like riding a bicycle, but that didn't mean she enjoyed it. The wind got harsher as the day went on, and the skies got darker. If she was going to stay on the ranch, she'd have to buy a warmer coat next time they got into a bigger place than Burnt Boot because her jacket didn't do much to keep the warmth in or the cold out. Running in the snow in nothing more than a sweatshirt was one thing; working in it was quite another.

She had located a fairly new pair of broken-in work gloves in the console of the old truck, and they fit just fine so her fingers didn't go numb as she helped Finn toss hay out to the cattle. She'd worked on ranches from the time she was old enough to stick her hand under a hen's feathers and get the eggs until she signed on the dotted line and became the property of the U.S. Army for six years. She had dreamed every night of getting away from the smell of cow manure back then, and now here she was right back in the middle of it.

"Let me help with that," Finn yelled over the noise of bawling cows, wind, and the engine of the truck. He pulled a pair of clippers from his back pocket, snapped the wire loose, and kicked the hay bale away from the rusted tailgate.

A bit of a red flannel shirt peeked out from the mustard-colored work coat. Under that shirt was a broad chest of tight muscles, probably covered with a crop of soft chest hair. She fought back the desire to reach up under there and warm her cold hands.

"What are you thinking about? You look like you're in another world." He started around the truck with her right behind him.

"I guess I was." She got into the pickup quickly so that all the warm air wouldn't escape.

"One where there's no cows or hay to deal with?"

"I didn't like ranchin' when I was a kid, and my opinions about cows and hay haven't changed since I left it," she said.

"You go there to that other world very often?" he asked as Shotgun jumped into the truck from the driver's side and settled between them.

She wasn't about to confess that the world she'd been visiting had to do with chest hair and not with sand and broiling-hot sun or even cows and hay.

"More than I should," she answered honestly.

"At least Christmas on a ranch is a lot different than Afghanistan at Christmas, isn't it?"

"Here, it's really Christmas. Over there, it was like we were playacting, but we did have a pretty tree," she said.

He reached around Shotgun and squeezed her knee.

Denim and leather gloves separated skin from skin, or she was sure it would have left a red hand print on her leg. "That, honey, was the ugliest damn thing ever put up and called a Christmas tree. But I still smile every Christmas when I think about it."

"Yellow light," she said softly.

"Don't start that shit on me now, Callie."

"So you remember?"

"Of course, I remember. We all had to take those damn classes on sexual harassment. Red light meant back off six feet. Yellow light meant don't come any closer, and green light meant lock the door because we're about to start shucking out of our clothes."

"I don't think that's the way the instructor really explained it," she told him.

"It's the way I heard it. So why did you say yellow light right then?"

She gathered her thoughts as she looked straight ahead, knowing if she looked at his jawline, his lips, or even that damn black hat, she wouldn't be able to explain. "You know about my sister and the way she went from one boyfriend to another, each one not worth a damn. I'm afraid I'll turn out to be like her."

"Callie, you can kick that shit out of your head. You aren't anything like that. You are raisin' Martin, and you're a damn good mother to that kid."

"Maybe I just cover it up real good," she said.

"Bullshit. Whatever you think is written all over your face. You couldn't cover up anything," he said.

She damn sure had him buffaloed, but she wasn't going to 'fess up about the blistering-hot thoughts she'd had all afternoon.

Finn liked everything that had happened in his world since Callie showed up. He liked the way they worked together, her damn fine cooking, and the comfortable feeling between them. It had always been like that, from the first day they were sent out on a mission together. He'd about gone AWOL when they told him he'd be working with a female spotter, but she'd shown him that first time that she was solid as a rock.

A month ago, when he had driven through the cattle guard out by the road and through the arch onto Salt Draw Ranch, he knew that his soul had come home to roost. And now that Callie was there, he was more at peace than he'd been in two years, and he'd do anything to keep her around.

They finished up the chores and had just settled into the sofa with a cup of piping-hot coffee when Martin burst through the front door. Shotgun raised his head, jumped to his feet, and put his paws on Martin's chest. Pistol opened his big, bulging brown eyes and ambled over to Martin. Angel darted from under the sofa and sniffed the backpack on the floor as if a strange critter had come to threaten her position.

Joe said, "Cat. Cat. Run, dog, run."

"He doesn't need a bit of coaxing to talk, does he?" Callie asked.

"Well, dammit, Mary! Joe wants apples!" He rattled on as he pranced back and forth.

"Hey, Joe, how you doin', old man? I think they all missed me, Callie. Poor things had to stay home all day and wonder if I was comin' back." He kissed Shotgun right on the nose and got a big slurpy kiss up his cheek for his efforts. "I'll change out the newspaper soon as I get something to eat. I'm starving."

"So I don't see black eyes or a bloody nose. You must've got along all right." Finn patted Callie on the back as he talked.

"And I see your old work shoes on your feet," Callie fussed.

"Ahh, Callie, I couldn't wear them others to the first day of school. I like my teacher, but I don't like all them girls except for Olivia. She's okay because she's real smart, and me and her tied for the math test today. We was the only ones who made a hundred."

"Sounds to me like you had a pretty good day," Finn said.

"I did, and tomorrow I get to ride the bus with Adam and Ricky and Olivia. They're my new best friends. I'm going to put on my old jeans so me and Shotgun can go outside and play." Martin ran off to his room to change.

"Shotgun! Hit the dirt, scumbag," Joe yelled.

Chapter 9

CALLIE GRABBED THE BLANKET FROM HER BED AND trailed it behind her on the way to the porch. She wasn't in Afghanistan. She was on a ranch in north Texas. But it wouldn't be real until she was out of the house and could feel the cold against her skin, know that she was for sure on Finn's ranch, and discern the difference between nightmare and reality.

She tiptoed past Joe. His head was tucked under his wing, and for once he didn't start yelling or making gun noises. She'd gone for weeks without the dreams, and this was the second night of them in less than a week. Martin was doing well in school, making friends, and she and Finn settled into their routine. He was constantly hugging her or touching her hand or her shoulder, and there'd been a few more kisses, but mostly it was workouts in the morning, work on the ranch in the afternoon, entertain Martin in the evening. So why tonight?

A raccoon half the size of Shotgun ambled across the porch, down the steps, and out into the night. She checked for other wild varmints before she eased down in the corner, drew her knees up to her chest, and tucked the blanket in tightly around her body. Those were real snowflakes falling from the sky, and the landscape said she was in Texas. This was Salt Draw for sure, and the vivid pictures in her mind had been a nightmare.

A cow bawled in the distance, and a coyote howled

up to the north of the ranch. No cows and coyotes where she'd been stationed. She'd just sit there a little while longer to let her heart settle, and then hopefully when she went back to bed, she'd sleep peacefully until morning.

Shotgun cold-nosed Finn right on the cheek and his eyes snapped open. Slowly, his eyes adjusted to the darkness, and he could see the hackles on Shotgun's back standing straight up. A low growl came from Pistol over beside the fireplace, and Angel's eyes were trained on the window. A slight bump against the outside wall brought Finn to a sitting position.

He tiptoed across the room, peeked through the blinds, and saw a big raccoon making his way down the steps. "Just a coon, boy, and, no, I will not let you out to chase him."

Then he saw Callie slide down into the corner and roll up in a ball. He jammed his legs into a pair of flannel lounging pants, his bare feet down into cold boots, and his arms into the work jacket hanging on the bedpost. When he reached Callie, he sat down, pulled her into his lap, and wrapped his arms tightly around her.

Heart pounded against heart. Snow whirled around in a kaleidoscope of patterns under the dim moonlight. Words weren't necessary. Finn knew exactly why Callie was on the porch at three o'clock in the morning.

Shotgun made two passes through the yard, nose to the ground, before he gave up and came back to rest his head in Callie's lap. She pulled one hand free of the blanket and scratched his ears.

"Must've been a bad one," Finn finally said.

She nodded.

"Want to talk about it? Therapist says that talking helps. I'm a good listener."

"Therapist is full of shit."

"I'm still a good listener."

"You know without me talking," she said.

He hugged her closer. "I do, Callie, but if and when you want to talk, I'm here."

"I know, Finn, and I don't mean to be bitchy. What we did over there, just tell me it was for the greater good."

He tipped her chin up and his lips felt oh, so warm when they touched her cold mouth. "It was definitely for the greater good. That's the only way to think if we want to stay sane."

"Okay, then let's go inside where it's warm. I'm convinced now that I'm not over there on a mission." She pushed out of Finn's lap and went into the house.

Shotgun raced inside ahead of Finn and dropped like a chunk of lead in front of the fireplace beside Callie. One side of her face was in shadow, the other side dimly lit by the glow of the dying embers. Finn had seen her like that lots of times on midnight missions, but never had she looked as beautiful as she did right then.

He went to his room, kicked off his boots, changed damp pajama bottoms for a pair of jeans, tossed his coat over the back of a rocking chair, and dug a thermal shirt from a drawer. He padded barefoot back to the kitchen, where he made two cups of strong, hot tea in the microwave and carried them to the living room.

He sat down beside her and put a cup in her hands.

"Thanks," she mumbled.

"Drink it. It'll warm you from the inside," he said.

Finn scooted his feet toward the fireplace. "Remember when my cousin Sawyer sent me the whiskey in a mouthwash bottle?"

A smile played at the corners of her mouth and lifted his spirits. He knew how hard it was to shake off the nightmares.

"We saved it for just the right time," he said.

She nodded. "And after that Christmas, we figured since we'd missed the turkey, we might as well drink the whiskey."

"And you got drunk as a skunk. I swear you can't hold your liquor worth a damn," Finn said.

"That's because you let me drink the whole damn thing except for two shots," she said.

He moved closer so that his feet were against hers. "Well, you were the one bitching about not getting to eat the big turkey dinner, and I was being a gentleman, letting you have all you wanted so you'd be happy. I bet it was even frozen turkey and the gravy was that canned shit."

"You couldn't see past Lala in those days, cowboy. I didn't give a shit about the dinner itself. I just wanted to share it with you," she said.

"Why didn't you say something?" he asked.

"You were up in Lala's brown eyes," Callie said.

He set his half-empty cup on the coffee table and took hers from her hands and put it beside his. Then he laced his fingers in her hands and leaned in closer, gazing right into her eyes.

"Right now I only see Callie Brewster," he whispered.

"Good. I never did like Lala. I knew something wasn't right with that woman," she whispered.

His lips were still cool when they landed on hers. His hands moved up under her shirt to massage the tight muscles in her back. She groaned.

He backed off. "Did I hurt you?"

"God, no! It felt wonderful," she said. "Hold me, Finn. I don't want to go to bed alone."

He picked her up and carried her to the recliner, where he sat down with her in his lap and then pulled the lever. They faced each other, her body pressed against his, his face buried in her hair. "I'm right here, Callie. All night if you need me to be."

Sleep didn't come when he shut his eyes. Instead he got a picture of Callie lying beside him in the sand, camouflage covering everything but their eyes as they watched a truck approaching. Together they took out the target. Together they made it back to base in one piece. But it wasn't until time and experiences brought them both to Salt Draw that they were really together.

He'd barely shut his eyes when all hell broke loose. Joe started squawking about police and coroners. Pistol added his high-pitched barking, and poor old Shotgun went crazy, running from the window to the door, howling like a rabid coyote at the full moon. Callie's cussing over the top of it all came through loud and clear.

Finn jerked the lever and Callie was suddenly standing in the middle of the floor.

"What is going on out there? It sounds like Big Foot is on our porch," Callie said.

Finn threw the door open. "It's cattle and a lot of them. Looks like another stampede, only this time it stopped in our front yard."

She flipped on the porch light. Shotgun pawed at the

storm door, and Joe started yelling about crackers and cats, as if he couldn't figure out what he wanted.

"There's a big hindquarter pressed up against the door, and I can see a brand. Looks like these came from River Bend Ranch because there's an RBR right there in plain sight. I guess we call them, right?"

"The Gallaghers are getting back at the Brennans for ruining Santa Claus and their tree. Dammit, Callie. I thought we were through with this feud. Call the sheriff and get him out here before you call anyone else," Finn said. "Me and Shotgun will get them off the porch."

"Looks like more than a hundred of them, but how did they wind up in our yard?" Callie asked.

"I expect that Betsy is sending you and Honey a message," Finn said. "And to think I came to Burnt Boot for peace and quiet."

She found the sheriff's number in the old phone book on top of the refrigerator and poked the numbers into her cell phone.

"Sheriff Orville Newberry here," he answered.

"Hello, this is Callie Brewster out at Salt Draw. We've got cattle all over the ranch with the River Bend brand. They're even on our porch. I expect when we call the Brennans there's going to be a problem because they're going to blame the Gallaghers for turning their cattle loose," she said.

"Go on and call them. I'll be there right soon. And, Callie, it's nice to hear your voice again," the sheriff said.

With modern-day technology lending a helping hand to the gossip grapevine, news traveled faster than the speed of light, even at midnight on a cloudy night. The

Brennans, led by Honey and Declan, showed up at Salt Draw before Finn and Shotgun shooed the last cranky heifer off the porch.

They arrived on four-wheelers, with dogs that Shotgun did not like, to round up their cattle and take them back to River Bend Ranch. Honey was decked out in a cute little snug-fitting light blue jacket that matched her gloves and stocking hat, tight jeans, and cowboy boots.

"Does she go to bed with her hair done and makeup on?" Callie grumbled.

"Well, hello, Finn," Honey said sweetly as she parked her four-wheeler right up next to the porch. "Looks like somebody done cut the fence to our pasture of prize breeders and turned them loose on Salt Draw. You reckon your bodyguard did that? We called the sheriff on our way over here to tell him. I reckon he'll have a few questions for her. I suppose I would be willin' to drop all charges, which I do plan to file, since I'm sure you probably got at least one high-dollar breedin' from the best bull on River Bend Ranch while my herd was mingled up with yours."

"Callie didn't do any of this. She's been in the house all night," Finn said gruffly.

Callie never wanted to slap the shit out of someone so bad in her entire life, and right here at Christmas when folks were supposed to be nice and have kindness and love in their hearts.

"I'll drop the charges against her if you'll go out with me on Friday night," Honey said. "Little dinner at my place. Little movie afterward with some wine, and then we'd see where it leads."

"For one thing, you twit," Callie said, "you can file all the charges you want to, but there's got to be some proof for them to stick. I was either in this house all evening or on the porch and have witnesses to prove it."

"Guess that answers your question," Finn said. "I'm surprised you haven't gone gunnin' for the Gallaghers."

"That's exactly why we called the sheriff. Damn Gallaghers have gone too far this time," Declan said. "We're going to nail their asses to the wall and laugh when they have to spend time in prison for this. Honey, get back on your machine and help us. We'll be until daylight gettin' them all back in our pasture. Don't suppose you'd want to help us, Finn?"

"Ain't my feud or my problem. I didn't cut a fence, yours or mine. You get your herd back through and make sure ain't none of them carryin' my brand or the Salt Draw one, and I'll fix my own fence."

Sheriff Orville showed up at ten minutes past one while Honey and Declan were trying to herd one rangy old bull from behind the house toward the gap in the fence out near the road. He parked the car, sidestepped every cow pile between there and the house, and handed Callie a box of a dozen frosted doughnuts with sprinkles on the top.

"Most of the shops shut up in the middle of the afternoon, but Walmart stays open all night." He smiled. "You can have them for breakfast. Might be a little warmer inside for me to take down your report of what's happened here."

Honey skidded to a stop beside the porch, hopped off, and popped both hands on her hips. "Orville, I'm pressing rustling charges against Callie Brewster and

Betsy Gallagher both. Way I see it is that Betsy cut the fences and Callie intended to sell my cattle on the black market."

"Way I see it is that y'all are back in the middle of your feud, and Miz Callie ain't got a thing to do with it. You can press charges all night, but if you ain't got evidence to bring to court, you might as well spend your time primpin' and cussin'," Orville said. "You can come on down to the office tomorrow afternoon and give me your statement."

"You can come to the ranch," Honey said.

Orville crossed his arms above his doughnut belly. "I could, but I ain't. Last time I got in the middle of the feud, I got shot. I ain't goin' nowhere near them ranches unless it's life or death. This ain't. So you got something to say, you come to the office."

"I'll put these doughnuts inside. Thank you for them. It's late, Sheriff. Maybe we could tell you our side of the story tomorrow, too," Callie said.

"That'd be just fine, and it's Orville, ma'am." He tipped his hat and headed back to his car. In his haste, he stepped in a fresh pile of manure.

"Well, crap!" Callie said when he was in his vehicle.

Finn chuckled.

"What's so damn funny?" Callie asked.

"You're right. He is flirting. We can share the doughnuts with Martin tomorrow. You going to help me fix a fence?"

"Who says I'm sharing? And, yes, I'll hold the flashlight," she answered.

Martin was out the door and running toward the school bus before Callie realized he wasn't wearing his good shoes again that morning, but then she'd only had two hours of sleep after helping Finn with the cut fence. Thank goodness for Shotgun, who kept Salt Draw cattle at bay so they could get the barbed wire tightened enough to keep their cattle in and anyone else's out.

"Don't go out there. Danger. Danger. Danger," Joe fussed when Martin left.

"Why couldn't your owner have liked country music instead of cop shows?" Callie made a mental note to check Martin's shoes the next day. She'd paid good money for new shoes, and he'd picked them out himself, so be damned if they were going to sit in the closet until he outgrew them.

"Hey, I have to go into Gainesville for a load of feed. We can go right after our workout," Finn said.

"I thought we had a workout last night," she moaned.

"That was a mission. We still have PT." He grinned.

"Anyone tell you we're not in the military anymore?"

"Couple of times, but it didn't keep me from staying fit. I'm not forcing you to work out, Callie. You were up all night. Go on back to bed and catch a few hours of rest," he said.

"Hell if I will. I ate three of those doughnuts, one last night and two for breakfast. I'll be ready when you are," she said. "Will we have time to stop by a Western-wear store or a tractor supply where they sell work coats?"

"Sure. Does Martin need a new coat?"

"His will do until Christmas. It's a little short in the arms, but it will last a few more weeks."

Chapter 10

THE QUICK SHOWER HADN'T DONE NEARLY AS MUCH AS a soak in a tub of hot water to help her tight muscles from the workout that morning, but if she got into the tub, she would fall asleep and not wake up until evening.

So she trudged into her bedroom, pulled a vinyl bank bag from under a stack of underwear, and removed a hundred dollars. She filed it neatly in her wallet and put her jacket on before she slung her purse over her shoulder.

"That didn't take long," he said.

"The mission takes top priority."

"And that is?"

"Buying a coat so I don't freeze my ass off when we're feeding cows or fixing fence in the middle of the night because two women are fighting over you." She bent against the wind and took off in a jog toward the truck. She was halfway across the yard when her feet went out from under her, and strong arms caught her as she grasped for anything other than snowflakes to break her fall.

"Whoa, darlin'," Finn drawled.

One second she was about to land on the ice, the next he had pulled her up to a standing position and held her to his chest. She could feel his heart beating beneath all those tight chest muscles and hoped that he attributed the extra thump in hers to almost falling.

He traced her jawline with the back side of his fist, opening up his hand when he reached her lips to outline them with his calloused forefinger. She hung in limbo for his next move, wanting him to kiss her so bad that she moistened her lips with the tip of her tongue.

His blue eyes bored into hers, unblinking, going all dreamy and soft as thick dark lashes fluttered shut and rested on his high cheekbones. Then his lips met hers in a long, lingering, passionate kiss that made her knees go weaker than ever before. His big hand held her head firmly as he deepened the kiss.

Forget the damn coat. All he had to do was kiss her about every two hours and she could run through the snow naked as a newborn baby and not even feel the cold.

"Guess we'd best get going," he said hoarsely.

"Guess so," she whispered.

He kept a firm grip on her arm as he got her settled into the truck.

"You need some boots, too. Those sneakers ain't worth a damn in this kind of weather. At least let me buy you some rubber boots," he said.

"I have money, Finn. I can buy what I need, and right now these shoes work just fine," she told him. Dammit! She wanted to talk about that kiss, not boots and coats.

When he started the engine, the DJ's voice filled the truck. "It's only twenty-three days until Christmas, folks. Have you started your shopping? The weatherman is agreeing with my grandpa's almanac that this is going to be a tough winter, so drag out the horse-pulled carriage because some of the back roads could get too slick for cars and trucks. And now five of your favorite Christmas songs performed by your favorite country artists. At the end of the five for five, the fifth caller who can tell me all five singers in order will receive a ten-dollar gift certificate to Buster's Western Wear in Gainesville, Texas."

"Is that where we're going?" she asked.

"I have no idea. Only been to Gainesville a couple of times, and that was traveling through—not going into—town. I know where the feed store is, but we're on our own for shopping," he answered.

"Suzy Bogguss," she said.

"She's got a Western-wear store here?" Finn asked.

Callie pointed at the radio. "No, that's Suzy singing 'Two-Step 'Round the Christmas Tree.' I like this song, and we'd probably get a better deal at the tractor supply or a feed store. Most of them carry work coats."

———∿∿∿———

Callie moved her shoulders to the beat of the music and sang along with the lyrics, asking if you'd ever seen Santa in cowboy boots two-steppin' around the Christmas tree.

Finn chuckled. "When I was a little boy, Grandpa O'Donnell would dress up as Santa, but he always wore his cowboy boots. He'd grab Grandma after he'd handed out the presents, and they'd dance around the tree. She'd pretend to be embarrassed and say that Grandpa would be mad if she danced with another man even if it was Santa Claus."

"Tanya Tucker," Callie said when the next song started.

"'Christmas to Christmas,'" he said. "This is one of my mama's favorites."

Tanya sang about having someone to watch each Christmas come and go with, and then the lyrics continued with "love is always in season."

"Oh, hush," he muttered.

"You talkin' to me?" Callie asked.

"No, ma'am, I'm arguing with myself," he answered honestly.

"Do that often?"

"More than I like to admit."

"Well, I do every day. Be careful about answering that voice in your head. Some folks don't understand us, O'Donnell."

"So I'm O'Donnell instead of Finn?" he asked.

"We're complicated. We started out as partners, and we will never be able to get away from that. Then we were friends, and now I'm not sure what we are, but sometimes we'll always be O'Donnell and Brewster, like when we're doing our morning workout. Sometimes we'll be Callie and Finn. And sometimes…" She paused.

"We'll be darlin' but never honey?" He grinned.

"You understand perfectly, just like I knew you would." She nodded.

She'd been right. The feed store had a section of work clothing, and that's where she headed while he told the clerk what to load up in the big black truck parked right out there in front.

It didn't take her long to pick out a mustard-colored work coat and carry it back to where Finn had found the small boot section. "Looking at boots always reminds me of Christmas. That's when I got a new pair and got to relegate my old ones to the utility room for work boots. Unless they were too little, and then Mama polished them up and passed them on down to brothers, sisters, or cousins, in my case, since I was the youngest in the family."

He picked up a pair that looked about right for Martin and inspected them. "These look like some good sturdy boots that might last through two or three boys."

"I said no," she told him.

"A person gives what they want to give for Christmas, and I want Martin to have a pair of nice boots for Sunday. A rancher is known by his boots," Finn said.

"So is a cowboy." She made a beeline for the checkout counter.

"What's that supposed to mean?" He was only a step behind her. "I understand why you don't want to have a relationship with a cowboy, since that's what kind of men your sister was drawn to all the time, but what's wrong with Martin having boots?"

"What if Martin acts just like his father, who didn't stick around? I won't encourage him to be a cowboy."

Finn laid a hand on her shoulder. "It's not all genetics, Callie. Environment does play a role. And besides, he's just a little kid. A pair of new boots isn't going to make him fall in love or get a girl pregnant."

She laid the coat on the counter, and the cashier rang up the price. Callie handed her the hundred-dollar bill and she counted back less than three dollars in change.

"Don't bother with a bag. If you'll remove the price tags, I'll just wear it out of here," Callie said.

The lady snipped a couple of strings, tossed the tags in the trash, and handed Callie the sales receipt. "It really is cold out there. You looked about half-frozen when you came in here. Do they not have northers where you come from?"

"Not so much, and my last job just required that I get from car to office or from car to apartment. I didn't have to be out in it when the north wind decided to get serious," Callie answered.

"Well, that coat will keep you warm. You need gloves?"

"Not today," Callie said. The cheapest pair of leather-palm work gloves cost a hell of a lot more than two dollars and fifty-seven cents.

"Yes, she does. Those right there." Finn pointed at an expensive leather pair as he pulled out his wallet. "And give me a pair of the cheaper ones in a size small. Don't look at me like that. I'm just protecting my interests. If your fingers get frostbit, I won't even get any cookin' out of you. And I'm not taking Martin out in the weather another day without decent gloves."

"Take the cost of both pairs out of my Friday night paycheck," she said.

"Want a burger or a taco or maybe we could stop by the pizza bar on the way home?" he asked when they were in the truck.

"A big old greasy hamburger sounds great," she said.

"Remember the ones we used to grill on that little hibachi thing over in Afghanistan?"

"I'd shut my eyes and pretend we were eating them next to a lake in Texas rather than over there in that place," she said.

"Was it hard for you to fall back into civilian life?" Finn asked.

"Martin was a newborn baby when I joined the army," she answered.

"That's not what I asked," Finn said.

"I'm getting around to the answer," she told him. "He'd just finished kindergarten when my enlistment was up and he came to live with me. I don't think I ever had the time to adjust to civilian life. Everything was thrust upon me so fast that I just had to endure, not adjust. I missed the army. I might have considered reenlistment, but you were already gone, and I didn't want another partner. Besides, Martin needed me."

"You missed the friends you made. For the first time in your life you had good friends who had your back, Callie. That's what you really missed."

She couldn't tell him that the real reason she wanted to go back into the army was because she missed him and that the reason she didn't reenlist was because she knew he wouldn't be there.

"I started getting moody a couple of days ago. I think it's what my sister had. Do you think I'm bipolar or something, Finn?"

"Hell no! I get the same moods. It's got something to do with what we did and our jobs over there. Last year I went on a monthlong cattle drive. It was a trial run for that new Chisholm Trail reality show on television."

"You are part of *that* O'Donnell family?" She jerked her head around to stare at him. Yes, he did look like the boss on the trail drive. What was his name? It was strange sounding. "Dewar," she muttered.

"My cousin." Finn smiled. "By the time it was over, I figured out that I was just hunting for an escape, thinking that it would cure all my nightmares and somewhere out there was the perfect place where there was peace.

Took me awhile to realize that the peace has to come from within. It's not a place and no one else can bring it to you. You got to do that for yourself."

"And?" she asked.

"I decided to find a ranch that felt right. I looked at dozens, but when I drove down the lane at Salt Draw, it felt right. You know the rest," he answered. "I guess what I'm trying to say is that when you come up to that fence that separates you from the grass on the other side, you got to look around in your own pasture and realize that what you've got is just as good as what's between the fence and the road or the next ranch over."

"Then why are you still hanging on to your anger at Lala?" she asked bluntly.

He braked so hard that the truck slid several feet before it came to a halt. He turned around in the seat and stared at her for several seconds before he opened his mouth. "What makes you say that? I'm over her. It's been more than two years, for God's sake."

"You trying to convince me or you, O'Donnell?" she asked.

"That's not a fair question."

She shrugged. "You don't have to answer it, but you do need to face off with it and get the thing over with. I know you, and there's a little bit of something holding you back. I think it's Lala."

"It's not easy to know that I was played for a fool," he finally whispered.

"Guess we've both got a lot of baggage, don't we?" she said.

He eased his foot over to the gas pedal and started back down the curvy, twisting road toward Burnt Boot.

"Yes, we do, but O'Donnell and Brewster can take out the enemy together, can't they?"

A dozen deer stood in the pasture right across the fence. The big buck held his head proud and tall, antlers gathering snow as he watched over his harem.

"Isn't he majestic?" She turned around so she could keep an eye on him longer.

"Not as majestic as you look in that coat," he said.

"It's a work coat, for God's sake, Finn, and that's a horrible pickup line."

"Just stating facts. I always liked you in camo with just those pretty eyes of yours peeking out, but a rancher woman, now that's just about the sexiest thing I've seen you in," he said.

"Well, then I'll have to save my money and buy a pair of Carhartt coveralls. I bet you'd really go wild if I got all dressed up in them. But don't hold your breath. I still don't like ranchin'." She laughed.

He chuckled. "Don't hold me responsible for what might happen if you put on a pair of coveralls. Hot damn, Callie! That would be too much for my poor old heart to take."

"You mean you might kiss me again?"

"Oh, honey, all you'd need would be a pair of boots and I'd do more than kiss you," he teased.

"Finn O'Donnell, you are full of bullshit. We were going to stop and get something to eat, weren't we?"

"I figured we'd get a burger at Polly's place in Burnt Boot. She makes the biggest, greasiest ones I've ever eaten. If we unload the feed first, we could sit up to the bar and eat it, drink a couple of beers, and then pick Martin up at school. And we're past those deer. I was afraid there would be a stray fawn and you'd want to take him home and name him Bambi. The way you are about strays, you'd want to keep him in the house."

"Yes, I would. Poor little thing. I bet Angel would just love him," she said. "I have no doubt you would be the one bringing a stray fawn home, and you'd keep it in your room. So don't tell me I'm guilty of hauling strays to the farm when you're just as bad. Now drive on back to the barn, and I'll help unload this feed. I've got a brand-new coat, so I won't freeze to death. And with two of us working, we can go to Polly's faster. That burger and beer is sounding better every minute."

He pulled the truck right into the wide doors of the barn, got out, and tossed the bag with the two pairs of gloves in it at her. "I don't turn down any kind of help, and if I'd known you were going to offer, I'd have bought you a stocking hat to go with the gloves. And about that deer, you're probably right."

"Not a cowboy hat?" she asked.

"What about a hat?"

"If you were going to buy me a stocking hat, why not a cowboy hat?"

"You have to earn it. You have to tell me that you've changed your mind about ranchin' and cowboys to get a cowboy hat, darlin'."

"I'd like to go to Polly's for a burger, but Martin needs to learn to ride the bus every day," she said.

"Bus might have trouble turnin' around at the end of our lane," Finn said.

Our lane.

He said *our lane*, not *the lane* or *my lane*.

Chapter 11

A BRIGHT RED CARDINAL LIT ON THE WINDOWSILL AS Callie was cleaning up the kitchen after breakfast. Its feathers were brilliant against the white snow banked up against the glass, and its inquisitive little eye looked like someone had painted a perfect black circle around it.

"Angel, you want to see something pretty?" she whispered.

She reached down and set the cat on the windowsill. Angel made a funny noise down in her throat, something between a purr and a chortle.

"Pretty bird. Pretty bird." Joe whistled, and the cardinal chirped back at the noise.

Callie glanced over her shoulder to see Joe watching a different cardinal out on the front porch. She smiled and fussed at herself for even thinking that blasted parrot could see through walls.

The ringing of the phone startled her, but Angel didn't move. Callie picked up the receiver of the old wall phone and leaned against the doorjamb.

"Hello," she said.

"This is Verdie McElroy. Where is Finn?" Her voice had enough grain in it to suggest that she was a longtime smoker, yet nothing in the house gave testimony to that. No smoke smell, no ashtrays, not even a cigarette butt in the yard.

"He's out doing chores," Callie answered.

"Then you are Callie Brewster, right?"

"Yes, ma'am."

"See that chair right there beside you?"

"I do."

"Well, it's sittin' there so folks can sit down to put on their boots or take them off or sit down to visit on the phone. Have a seat and tell me about Salt Draw. I'm so homesick I've been crying, and this tough old bitch don't cry for nothing," Verdie said.

Callie pulled the chair over a few more inches.

"Cord will reach just fine without you scootin' it around," Verdie said.

Callie sat down. "What do you want to know about Salt Draw?"

"Everything. Start with the room where the bunk beds are. That's where Martin sleeps, ain't it? Don't get all worried. Burnt Boot is a little place and y'all are the new kids in town, so you are the topic for gossip until something else comes along. Gladys and Polly and I keep on top of things. We got to filter out what's shit and what's real. And after we talk about the ranch, we'll go on to the feud. I can't believe that damned Honey and Betsy are dragging you into their shit pile."

"Rooms first, right?" Callie laughed.

"That's right. Feud takes second place to my homesickness."

"Martin loves the bunkhouse room, and he's been trying to read the books. Some of them are above his pay grade, but he'll grow into them."

Verdie sighed. "The ranch needs kids, has for a long time. Now tell me about your bedroom. Do you like that one?"

"I do," Callie said.

"It was my sister's room. And mine was the other one on that wing. There were six boys and two girls who grew up in that house. The four youngest boys got the bunk room. Two of the older boys shared the other bedroom, and my sister got the third one. I came along when Mama had given up on having any more kids. The older boys had left home, but the younger ones were content in the bunk room, so when I got old enough to move from the nursery, I got the room with the twin beds. My sister was the next one up the sibling ladder and she was ten years older than me, so it wasn't long until I was the only one in that part of the house."

"Was it lonely?" Callie asked.

"Not a single day. I could read all the boy's books and I had my own, too. Television came into the house when I was a teenager, but it didn't amount to much there at first. Then I got married and Mama died that same week. Oscar was already working as foreman on the ranch, so we just moved from our little bitty cabin on the back forty in with Daddy. We raised our boys there," she said.

It didn't take much prompting to keep Verdie talking. Callie was able to stretch the cord to the kitchen bar and hold the receiver on her shoulder while she made a pot of chili.

"What are you doing? I hear you moving around," Verdie asked.

"Just putting together Finn's dinner. We have the big meal of the day in the evening, since Martin is in school," she answered.

"Why ain't you out there helpin' him?"

"I helped with the feeding. Now he's cleaning the tack room and working on that old green tractor, and I'm doing housework," she answered.

"And you were his partner when he was over there in the war?" Verdie changed subjects.

"I was."

"What are you now?"

Callie gasped. "I'm a hired hand."

"Are you slow-witted or blind?" Verdie asked.

"Pardon me?"

"You heard me. You got to be one of them things. That boy is damn fine-lookin' and he's a hardworkin' cowboy and you are livin' under the same roof with him. If I was your age, I'd be figuring out a way to get him to bed. God, I miss the ranch." The sigh would have been audible from Dallas even if they weren't connected with a phone.

"Next time you're in Burnt Boot, you are more than welcome to visit Salt Draw. We'll bust out a pitcher of sweet tea, and I'll make some cookies. And you can meet Angel and Pistol. Have you met Shotgun? Did Finn bring him along when he signed the papers?"

"Haven't met any of the animals. I heard that you rescued a cat at the general store. Are you serious about me visiting Salt Draw?" Verdie asked.

"Yes, ma'am, I am serious. I'd love to meet you."

"Cops! Cuff him, Mary!" Joe held up a foot and hopped along the perch on one leg.

"Who is Mary? And what about cops?" Verdie asked.

"It's this damned parrot that came with the Chihuahua." Callie went on to tell Verdie the story of the dog and the bird.

"Little black-and-tan older dog?" Verdie asked.

"Do you know who he belongs to?"

"Belonged to, not belongs. Old man Rawling died about two weeks ago. His family intended to have Pete and Joe put to sleep the day after the funeral, but they both vanished. Those two made their way from a couple a miles away to Salt Draw. You say they're in the house?"

"Finn brought the dog in and the bird followed him. He threw a squawkin' fit when we tried to put him in a cage, so we made a roost from an old folding clothes-drying rack," Callie answered.

"Dickie bought that crazy bird for his wife, Mary, about six years ago. He'd promised her that someday he'd take her to a tropical island, but then she got cancer and he couldn't take her, so he bought her the bird. She died about a year later," Verdie told her.

"That explains a lot. Now we know where they came from and that no one is coming to claim them. And, Verdie, I meant it when I said for you to come visit us," Callie said.

"Honey, I'd love to come for a visit, but when I do, we'll leave the sweet tea in the icebox and bust out some bourbon. You can go on and make cookies, though. My favorite is gingersnaps. I've got to go now. The damned old buzzer will ring in a few minutes, and we'll all shuffle down to the dining room to eat shit that is good for us. I don't know why in the hell I thought I'd be happy in a place like this. There's a real good recipe for gingersnaps up in the cabinet in a little wood box. And I'm guessin' that Angel is the cat and Shotgun is a dog?"

"I'll look for the recipe, and, yes, ma'am. Angel is the

cat I found at the store, and Shotgun came to the ranch with Finn."

"I figured that's the way it is. Now you go on and make them cookies. Finn likes them."

"He does?"

"Oh, yes. We sat right over there at the table and had them when I sold him the ranch. Bye now, and you have a good day. We'll talk about that damned feud another day," Verdie said.

Callie put the receiver back on the wall base and rolled her neck to get the kinks out. "Poor old darlin' is lonely. She lived in this house or on this ranch her whole life, and now she has nothing but a buzzer to regulate her life. I wonder if she ever had a cat in the house, Angel. What do you think? Do you smell the ghosts of cats past in here somewhere?"

Finn fished his cell phone out of his pocket and answered on the third ring. "Hello, Miz Verdie. How are things in the big city?"

"Boring as hell. I hear y'all got a couple of inches of snow up there and that there's more on the way toward the end of the week and it ain't goin' to melt off before the big one hits," she said.

"That's what they say. I'm working on this old John Deere tractor. How old is this sucker, anyway?"

"Well, let me think. My oldest son was still in diapers when we bought it, and I mean them kind of diapers that you wash and put on the line, not the kind you ball up and throw in the trash. He was born in 1954, so I'd say it's a 1955. Lord, we thought we'd died and gone straight to heaven when we got that thing with its double-barreled carburetor. It would fire right up in the wintertime no matter how cold it got. You get that live power shaft fixed, and she'll run another fifty years."

"I'm working on it." Finn backed up and sat down on a bale of hay. "The old mama barn cat has a litter. I just saw one peeking out at me."

"Crazy old cat ain't got a lick of sense. She'll throw a litter in the winter every year, and the funny thing is they usually survive better than the spring litter does. So tell me about this woman I hear you got in the house. Gladys says she's pretty sassy," Verdie said.

Poor old girl not only missed the ranch but Burnt Boot. Finn could well understand the way she must feel. If someone jerked him up by the roots and tried to plant him in a place as big as Dallas, he'd be climbing the walls within a week. He leaned back on the stack of hay and got ready for a long conversation.

"She was my spotter over in the war." He went on to explain the situation with WITSEC.

"They let women do that?"

"It don't happen real often, but she was very good at it," he answered.

"Well, shit! I knew I was born in the wrong time. I'd have made a damn fine sniper or spotter, either one. I can shoot the hair out of a billy goat's beard at a hundred yards." Verdie laughed.

"The way you ran this ranch single-handed, I don't doubt it," Finn said.

"Got a confession. The last ten years I leased most of the ranch, and I just took care of the hundred acres around the house there. Grew a few acres of hay and a big garden but only ran twenty head of cattle most of the time. I didn't have no idea how bad I'd miss them cantankerous old cows, but I guess in time I'll get used to this place. There's the buzzer that tells me they're puttin' our dinner on the table in the dining room, so I'll go on down there."

"You makin' friends?" Finn asked.

"Oh, sure I am. I sleep with a different man every night," she cackled.

"Verdie!"

"Don't fuss at me. I ain't got no cows, and they damn sure wouldn't let me haul my mama cat into this fancy-smancy place. A woman has to have an imagination, or she'd go crazy."

Finn laughed with her. "You take care of yourself, and you know that you're welcome here on Salt Draw anytime you want to come for a visit."

"Thank you, Finn. I might take you up on that sometime. I'd like to meet your Callie," she said. "Now the lady is knocking on my door, which means all those old worn-out cowboys who can't remember how to put their boots on will be waiting for me at my table. Bye now."

Finn put the phone back in his pocket and headed out across the pasture toward the house. "Hey, is that chili I smell?" He kicked off his boots at the back door, picked Callie up, and swung her in circles. "I'm so glad you're here, Callie. That sounds wonderful on a day like today. The heater can't keep up out there in the barn."

Callie set the whole pot on a trivet in the middle of the table while he removed his coat, gloves, and hat. "I told you I could help you with that tractor. I've worked on lots of old machinery. Betcha it's the power shaft. That might be the first year they came out with that feature so they didn't have it down as well as they did later on. One of my sister's boyfriends was a crackerjack mechanic, and he taught me a little about it."

Finn sat down at the table. "Did he teach you to shoot?"

"No, that I learned from my first boyfriend. His idea of a perfect date was target shooting." She dipped up a bowl of chili and handed it to him and scooted the bowl of saltines and the plate of corn bread his way.

"Callie, you are not like your sister," Finn said.

"What made you say that?"

"I can read your mind."

"What makes you think part of me isn't like her?"

"The cats," he answered.

She brought her head up, her aqua eyes locking with his blue ones. "What does that have to do with anything? And why is she in the barn during this weather? She might get cold. Bring her into the utility room, and I'll make her a bed in an old laundry basket."

"She has kittens out there, and they're too wild to catch." Finn's eyes twinkled.

"I can catch them with a bowl of warm milk. I'll set it down, and they'll come up to drink it," she said.

"Point proven," he said.

She went back to eating. "What are you talking about?"

"You take in strays."

"Lacy said it was a good thing elephants didn't grow in Texas, or I'd want to bring them inside during the winter." She smiled.

"Lacy was your sister? I don't think I ever heard her name before now."

"Yes, she was, and taking in strays isn't settling down, Finn," Callie said seriously.

"Folks who take in strays are putting down roots. Did your sister ever bring home homeless cats and dogs?"

Callie shook her head slowly. "And she didn't like it when I did. Said it just made leaving harder to do. When Mama died, I was sixteen. I lived with Lacy two years before I enlisted."

"Well, there you have it. You are a settler, not a runner. Plain and simple. Verdie called me this morning," Finn said.

"She called me too," Callie said.

"Maybe when it clears off, she'll come up to visit with Gladys and Polly, and we'll invite her for supper," he said.

Callie refilled his tea glass. "I bet she'd like that a lot."

Finn reached out and cupped Callie's cheeks in his hands. "I meant it, Callie. You are a settler."

"I hope so," she whispered.

He pushed the chair back after the second bowl of chili and a piece of chocolate cake. "Want to come out to the barn with me and see the mama cat and the kittens after dinner? I could sure use your opinion on that driveshaft, too."

"No! No! Cats in the house, dog," Joe said.

She grabbed his hand and held it against her cheek. "I swear he's going to show up on the table in alfredo sauce some night. I would love to go see the kittens, but I'll have more fun doing mechanic work. It's been a long time since I got to tear into a tractor."

He bookcased her cheeks in his calloused hands again and bent at the waist to fall into her gorgeous eyes gazing up into his. Not even Lala had captured his soul the way Callie had since she'd arrived at Salt Draw. No woman had ever made him feel so protective, yet so protected at the same time.

He shifted his gaze to her lips. He had to taste them, had to claim them for his own right then, or his heart was going to jump right out of his chest and die on the floor at the ends of her cute little toes.

Green light, please let it be a green light, he thought as her eyelids slid shut, heavy black lashes fanning out on slightly toasted skin, and her lips parted.

Chapter 12

"WELL, SHOOT!" MARTIN SAID WHEN THE ANCHORMAN on television said that Burnt Boot would be having school that morning. "Oh, man, I wanted to build a snowman."

"The snow isn't going anywhere, and the bus will be here in ten minutes, so go put on your coat," Callie said.

"Finn, will you help me build one over the weekend?" Martin asked.

"We're supposed to get at least three more inches tonight, and the temperature isn't supposed to raise enough to melt it off, so I expect we'll have enough by the weekend to build a decent one. If we built one today, it wouldn't hold together anyway, as dry as that stuff out there is," Finn said.

"Can we have snow ice cream?" Martin looked at Callie.

"You, young man, are procrastinating in hopes of missing the bus, but it's not happening. Coat. Hat. Gloves, and not those new ones that Finn bought you to work in either. The ones inside your coat pocket."

He looked at the floor and exhaled loudly. "Okay, I have to do it, but I don't have to like it. I could be a big help on the ranch today."

"You'll be a big help at school today. If they closed, then you'd just have to make it up later in the year. You might even have to go to school on Christmas day," Callie told him.

Martin slapped his hands over his eyes and headed toward his room. "Don't even talk like that."

Finn turned to Callie. "So what have you got in mind for after we do our workout?"

Joe made kissy noises and turned around to look out the window.

"I guess he watched something other than cop shows a few times." Finn laughed.

"I wish he would have listened to country music instead of watching anything. To answer your question, there's a ranch to be run and cookies to be made after our workout. I heard through the Verdie grapevine yesterday that the sexy cowboy who lives in this house likes gingersnaps."

"Sexy?" One dark eyebrow shot up.

"That's according to the grapevine," she said.

"I kind of like the grapevine then. You reckon you could put off the cookies until after lunch? I could sure use a driver this morning. Feeding would go a lot faster if you drove for me," he said.

"If you'd rather have a driver than cookies, that's what I'll do. I've got a new warm coat and gloves, remember?"

Martin dragged his backpack up the hallway, books clumping along the hardwood floor. "It's not fair that you get to go outside and help, Callie. I heard you talking about wearing your new coat. I'll be stuck inside that old school all day, and you get to go help feed. It's just not fair."

"He's a rancher for sure," Finn said.

"I bet Adam and Ricky won't even be there," Martin continued to fuss as he headed toward the door.

"And who are Adam and Ricky?" Callie asked. "I thought Harry was your best friend."

"He is when we're in class. But out on the playground, we join up with Adam and Ricky. They're both in second grade, but Ricky is a little bit older. They're Olivia's brothers, and if she ain't there, then math ain't no fun, because she and me, we're the team leaders because we always have the good grades. And if she ain't there, then the other team leader is Mindy, and she's just mean." Martin sighed.

"I'm not sure I understood all that," Callie said.

"Olivia and Ricky and Adam all live in the same house. If they don't have to come to school, then she don't either. They have foster parents," Martin explained.

Finn laid a hand on Martin's shoulder. "The bus is pulling up in the yard. Maybe your friends will all be there. What'd you say their names are? Amos and Raymond?"

Martin mumbled as he left, "Yesterday Olivia got called to the office, and she came back with her eyes all red and puffy like she'd been crying. I hope there ain't nothing wrong."

Callie changed into work jeans and her heaviest sweatshirt, then checked Martin's room before she put her coat on. The bed was made tightly, just like she'd shown him. He'd always liked to draw, and his newest creations drew her to the desk. There was a fair rendition of the ranch house with a Christmas tree shining through the window, snow on the ground, and those two four-legged things on the porch had to be Shotgun and Pistol. Another yellow figure was sitting in the window.

"Evidently animals aren't going to be as easy for you as houses and snow." She smiled.

She was toting her coat into the kitchen when Finn came out of his part of the house.

"Workout or feed first?" she asked.

"This first just to get me going for a workout." He bent her backward and gave her a Hollywood kiss.

"Well, I reckon that heated me up enough," she mumbled.

———~~~———

The cows were lined up around the feed trough like it was a Sunday buffet at the local café. Callie kept the truck running, but the heater only worked at about half speed. He was doubly lucky to have her in his life. Not only was the house in good shape, the meals on the table, and the laundry kept up, she was always ready to do real ranching work even if she didn't like it.

He swung the ax one final time, and an old bull lumbered toward the edge of the creek for a drink. He nodded at the bull and jogged back to the truck, tossed the ax into the back, and got inside in a hurry.

"Maybe we should have Christmas this week. Then we'd be guaranteed to get our white Christmas." He removed his gloves and stuck his hands on the heater vent. "This thing isn't throwing hardly any heat."

"You need to buy a new thermostat next time you're in town, and I'll put it on for you."

"Is there anything you don't do?"

"Define 'do.'" She put the truck in reverse, and the tires spun twice before she got turned around. "While you're thinking of a definition, I don't knit or crochet or do any of that needlework stuff, and although I don't mind gardening, I've got a black thumb when it comes to raisin' flowers. Roses wilt and die when I pass by them, and if you're depending on me to keep those flower beds all pretty next spring, you can fire me right now."

"I reckon I can do without flowers for a decent mechanic," he said.

The truck hit a hole and she yelped. "Holy shit! Looks like this thing needs shocks, too."

She'd barely gotten the words out when a hissing noise and a long, greasy slide send them straight into a grove of mesquite trees. "Dammit! We've got a flat."

"It don't require knitting or none of that crochet shit, so you can fix it," Finn teased.

She shook her head from side to side. "I don't think so, cowboy! Not even if you fire me. I can fix a tire but not when there's a big, strong handsome man who can do it."

He pulled on his gloves. "Flattery is the only thing that would make me get out in this cold wind."

~~~

Callie expected the rear passenger side of the truck to rise as he jacked it up to change the tire. At that point she'd planned to get out and help him take the blown tire off and put the new one on. The front end probably had another dent or two, but there wasn't any steam coming out, so they probably hadn't busted the radiator.

He tapped on her window, and she rolled it down an inch.

"Spare is flat. Shut it down. We'll have to walk to the house and come fix it later, or if you'd rather, I'll bring my truck back and get you. Either way, it's going to get cold."

"How far?" she asked.

"Half a mile at most. Maybe a little less. We should have saved our PT until after we'd done chores. You up for a second run?" he asked.

"I'm not going to just sit here and wait." She looked down at the shoes on her feet and wished to hell she hadn't been so stubborn about a pair of boots. Now she had to walk half a mile and maybe get frostbite on her toes by the time she got home.

He opened the door. "How about a nice little Thursday afternoon stroll, darlin'?"

She looped her arm in his and said in a sarcastic Southern twang, "Are you asking me on a date, Finn O'Donnell?"

"Can't fraternize with the partner, but it's a lovely day for a walk." He grinned.

"Walk, nothing, soldier. I'm going to jog."

As if on cue, the heavens opened up and snow began falling so hard that visibility was limited to five feet. By the time they'd gone twenty feet, Callie couldn't even see the truck when she looked over her shoulder.

"I could give you a piggyback ride," he said.

"If we can live through a sandstorm, I reckon we'll make it through a blizzard," she told him.

"Just follow the ruts."

"They're filling up fast," she said.

When they reached the backyard fence, her feet were numb and her fingers tingled. The glow of the lights coming from the kitchen window was the most beautiful sight she'd seen in years. Finn tried the gate, but it was frozen shut, so he climbed over and then reached up to help her when she made it to the top of the rails.

"Just a few more feet, Callie. Martin is going to get his snowman this weekend for sure the way this stuff is coming down."

"My feet are freezing."

"You are getting boots as soon as I can get to the store and buy them, and so is Martin. He needs them in weather like this, and you can argue with me until hell freezes over, but you both will be getting boots," Finn declared.

She didn't argue. Swallowing her pride was easy when she couldn't even feel her toes. She didn't wait for him to be a gentleman and open the door for her but rushed in ahead of him, sat down on the chair under the phone, and kicked off her shoes. Then she peeled off her wet socks and started rubbing her feet. A towel landed in her lap as Finn stomped the snow from his boots and jerked them off. She rubbed feeling back into her bright red feet before she looked up to see where the towel came from. Then the aroma of ginger mixed with something that smelled wonderfully like tacos or Mexican food hit her nose.

A short woman with short jet-black hair and brown eyes set in a bed of deep wrinkles poked her head around the door. "Y'all best go on and change clothes while I put this dinner on the table. Old truck finally give up the ghost, did it? It's been a good one, but the damned old bastard could have gotten you home before it quit. I hope y'all meant it when you said I could come for a visit. I put my things in the bedroom across the hall from the bunk room."

Callie stuck out her hand. "Hello, Verdie. That truck hasn't given up the ghost. I can put a new thermostat in it, and with a new tire, it'll be good for another ten years."

Verdie bypassed Callie's hand and hugged her tightly. "It's so good to be home. I can move my things if you want me to." Then she moved past Callie and hugged Finn. "Y'all are about frozen. You'd best get out of them wet clothes and get over there by the fire to get warmed up. I'll make a fresh pot of coffee."

"Thank you, Verdie, and you can stay in the room where you put your things. I hope it was clean, and you are very welcome to stay as long as you like. Is that taco soup I smell?" Callie said.

"I hope it's taco soup, because I'm cold and hungry, and that would sure taste good," Finn said.

Verdie swiped at her eyes with the tail of her apron and said, "I was hungry for it, but they don't serve anything that's got any flavor to it at the funny farm I was stupid enough to run off to. Y'all go on and change, and I'll put it all on the table. Oh, the school called a few minutes ago. They'll be letting out early. Bus drivers are afraid that they can't get through the back roads the way it's coming down out there. Glad I got here when I did."

"Did you drive?" Callie asked.

"Hell no! Didn't have anything to drive. Left my old truck here. I caught a ride to Gainesville with the daughter of a lady who lives in the funny farm. Then I paid a cab double fare to bring me on home."

When a timer bell dinged, she whipped around and picked up a pot holder. "Last of the cookies is ready. I ate most of the first dozen soon as they came out of the oven."

"Well, soon as I get into some dry clothes, I'm going to eat that dozen." Finn grinned.

Callie's feet tingled as she made her way to the bedroom where she rustled up a sweat suit and a pair of fluffy socks. She towel dried her dark hair and drew it up into a fresh ponytail. She was crossing the room when she realized that Joe hadn't said a word since she and Finn came into the house.

She glanced in his direction to find a crazy contraption sitting on two bars of the drying rack. It had a brightly colored apron tied around the top of it.

"Damn bird was driving me crazy. He needs to be covered at night and when he gets too noisy. I put a tomato cage over him and tied an old apron around it. He's sleeping like a baby," Verdie said. "That constant shit he spits out would drive a woman to drinkin'."

Before Callie could say thank you, the front door flew open. Martin ran across the floor without even wiping his feet and threw himself into her arms, sobbing like his heart was broken.

"Callie, you got to do something. They can't go to another of them foster places. I won't even ask for a Christmas present. I don't need no cowboy boots anyway. It's Olivia and her brothers. We've got to help them." The words came out in ragged gasps between sobs.

She drew him to the sofa and sat down with him right beside her. "Dry up the tears and tell me what's going on."

"That's the kids that the Laytons have, isn't it?" Verdie asked.

Martin wiped his eyes and stared at her.

"I'm Verdie. I used to own Salt Draw. I'm here for a visit. Now tell me what's happening to the children. They've been with the Layton family about six months."

Fresh tears washed down his face. "The mama is real sick, and she can't keep them no more, and Adam said that they liked it here and they don't want to leave, and Olivia was crying."

"What's goin' on in here?" Finn's big frame filled the hallway door.

"I'll work real hard if you can let them stay here. We got lots of room, and they're just little kids, so they won't eat much," Martin said.

"It's a little more complicated than that," Verdie said and went on to explain the situation to Finn. "But Polly used to work for the office that takes care of foster kids, so I'll call her and see what can be done. Right now all y'all need good warm food in your stomachs. And then we're going to talk about decorations for that tree in there. Something that big needs more foo-rah on it, and I know just where to find it."

Martin nodded and removed his coat, hung it on the rack, and kicked his shoes off beside the door.

Finn patted Callie on the back. "It'll be all right. Don't worry."

"Easier said than done," she said.

Chapter 13

NOTHING WAS AWKWARD, AND THAT MADE EVERY-thing awkward. One minute Callie and Finn were jogging home through the snow and then boom! They had a houseguest who wasn't really a visitor because she was part of the ranch even more than they were. Callie could count on the fingers of one hand the times she'd entertained an overnight guest, and not a single one of them had ever moved right into the kitchen and taken over the cooking.

She tried reading a book when she went to bed, but her mind wouldn't shut off. Next she tried visualizing a black dot and making it bigger like her therapist suggested. That didn't work, either. Finally, she got out of bed, wrapped the chenille bedspread around her like a cape, and tiptoed across the cold hardwood floor to the den.

Shotgun's tail thumped on the floor a couple of times, then he tucked his head under his paw and went back to sleep in front of the glowing fireplace with Pistol and Angel snuggled up against him. Callie settled into the corner of the sofa, tucked her feet up under the bedspread, and hoped the warmth of the fire mesmerized her right into sleep.

"You couldn't sleep either?" Finn's deep drawl came from the recliner in the shadows.

His voice startled her, but it didn't surprise her.

"It's been a crazy day, hasn't it? It keeps playing through my mind on a continuous loop."

"Verdie?" he whispered.

She heard his movements before she saw him shift from chair to sofa. The chair popped down, Shotgun raised his head to check out the noise, and then Finn was sitting next to her. The scent of masculine soap and shampoo filled the space between them and sent her senses into a spiral.

It was a full minute before she could get a hold on her emotions and answer. "Not so much Verdie as those poor children. She'll be gone back to her new place in a few days. Probably as soon as the weather clears up. I overheard her telling Martin while she was helping him with his English assignment that she had to visit with Gladys and Polly before she went home."

"The kids and even Verdie aren't kittens or a stray Chihuahua," he said.

"I know that, Finn."

He moved closer so he could wrap her in his arms. "But?"

She sighed. "But I've never seen Martin so upset. He's made friends here in Burnt Boot. It would be different if they were snatched away because their parents were moving, but this hits a raw nerve."

Finn slid farther down the sofa until they were touching, then reached out to take her hand in his. "He have trouble in foster care?"

"Not really, but Lacy was all he had, and then she was gone. She'd left a will of sorts saying she wanted to be cremated, and there was enough of a life insurance policy to make that happen. They let me leave two days early so I could get home, but Martin had to go into foster care until I could prove that I could take care of him."

"Proves my point, again."

She snuggled down into the curve of his shoulder. "What point?"

"You aren't a runner. They don't worry. They just go wherever the wind takes them."

"Verdie is a settler, too, Finn. She's not happy in her new world and is still hanging on to this one. We should ask her to stay until after Christmas. There's lots of room here, and she and Martin have struck up a granny-slash-grandkid relationship already. She told him to call her Granny Verdie. If his friends get taken away, it might help to have her here. Did you know that she read to him tonight? She's so happy to be back on the ranch. I hate to think of her down there in that place with no family," Callie said.

A week ago Finn had a dog. Period. Now there was a sassy parrot that never shut up.

"Kill the bastards and kiss the girl!" Joe said.

"Time for his tomato cage and apron," Callie said.

Finn hurried to the corner and slipped the wire cage down over the bird and tied the apron around it.

"Good night, Irene," the bird singsonged and then was quiet.

"Simple enough. Verdie is a genius for coming up with it." Finn settled back into his place beside Callie. "Now back to what we were talking about. I don't think Verdie will agree. She wanted to sell. Remember when you couldn't wait to join the army and then after a few days of basic you wondered what in the hell you had done? Then you went home for a visit after basic and couldn't wait to go back to the army. A visit is one thing; an extended stay is another thing altogether."

Callie looked up at him and nodded. "So you think she'll spend a few days here and be ready to leave. I don't think so, Finn. She's not a runner. I think she made a mistake when she sold the ranch."

He could hear her talking, but it was just noise. He cupped her face with his hands, and his lips found hers in a soft kiss that soon deepened in raw passion that yearned to be satisfied. One of his hands moved to her neck; the other to the small of her back to draw her even closer.

"Callie, where are you?" Martin's whisper cut through the darkness.

Finn quickly moved to the recliner, and Callie tucked the bedspread back around her body. His heart thumped in his chest and his breathing was still labored as he grabbed a throw to cover his lap.

"I'm right here, Martin," Callie called out softly. "On the sofa by the fire."

He curled up beside her and she wrapped the edge of the spread around him. "It was the dream again, Callie. I couldn't get back to sleep."

Like mother and child, Finn thought.

"That man was looking right at me, and he chased me. When I got to our apartment, the police sirens started and he ran the other way," Martin said.

"I'm right here. Shut your eyes. We'll rest awhile on the sofa. Shotgun is here, too. Nobody can get past him.

And you can't see him, but Pistol is curled up right at his back. Remember, he's our alarm dog."

"Granny Verdie made it past both of them. I like her just fine, but what if she'd been one of them bad people, and what if they're still looking for us? I wish Finn was in here. Nothing gets past him," Martin said.

"I'm right here in the recliner, son," Finn said.

"I'm glad. You know what I want for Christmas, Callie? I want Finn to always be here, because he'll keep us safe."

All the tension left his small body as he stretched out beside Callie and went back to sleep. She wiggled down and used the wide sofa arm for a pillow.

"Is he asleep?" Finn whispered.

"Out like a light. He thinks he's too big to crawl into bed with me, so when he has the nightmares, we sleep on the sofa the rest of the night."

"So you are the nightmare whisperer." He chuckled.

"What?"

"Like the horse whisperer. Only you banish nightmares with your presence. Damn, Callie! I wish I'd have known that two years ago. I would have looked you up and slept on the sofa with you," he said.

"You are full of bullshit." She giggled. "Go back to bed, or else pop up that footrest and go to sleep. We've got a long day ahead of us tomorrow. There must be six inches of snow out there by now. There are cattle to feed and a truck to tow home, and Verdie says we'll be putting up more decorations after we do chores."

She heard the recliner pop as it went back. Shotgun

moved away from the fire, checked on Finn, and then hopped up on the other end of the sofa.

She awoke early the next morning when sunrays had just begun to filter in through the mini-blinds, creating stripes of light across Finn's face. She'd seen him with scruff on his face when they went out on a mission, but that was before they'd shared kisses that tilted the world off its axis.

Pots and pans rattled in the kitchen, awakening Shotgun, who cocked an eye that way and growled deep in his throat. The hackles on his back stood up, and his ears laid back.

"It's just Verdie," Callie whispered.

Shotgun peeked over the arm of the sofa and caught a glimpse of the newcomer. His tail set up a drumbeat on the leather, and that woke Martin, who hopped up and grabbed the dog around the neck.

"Where's the other two?" Martin asked.

Pistol waddled in from the utility room, and Angel slunk down the hallway from Finn's bedroom.

"Here we are. One big old happy family. I wish my friends could be here with us this morning. I know that would make them so happy." Martin sighed.

Verdie yelled from the kitchen area of the great room, "Well, good morning. Looks like I missed the party, but I'm not bitchin' a bit. I slept like a baby. I called the school, and it's canceled for today. Weatherman says this will melt by Sunday and we got another front moving in on Monday. Biscuits and sausage gravy for breakfast this morning and an oven omelet to go with it. Y'all goin' to sleep all day, or are we going to make this house look like Christmas after chores are done?"

"Did Polly call?" Martin asked.

"Not yet, but the office where she worked don't even open until nine, and since this bad weather has hit, it might take her awhile longer to get ahold of her friends who work there."

Martin looked over Shotgun's big head at Finn and then back at Callie. "What? Did I do something wrong?"

"What are you talkin' about?" Callie asked.

"Y'all was talkin' to each other with your eyes."

"We were?" Finn asked.

Martin nodded. "Grown-ups do it all the time. They've got a secret language us kids can't understand. Can I help you with the chores this morning, Finn?"

"I'd appreciate a good hand. Dress warm and put on two pairs of socks." Finn stretched, flipped the lever on the side of the recliner, and sat up.

"We're burnin' daylight," Martin announced. "And I'm starving. Granny Verdie, you will tell me when Polly calls, even if it ain't good news."

"I'll be honest," Verdie said.

He took off for his room in a run, yelling back over his shoulder that Callie promised they could make snow ice cream if there was enough snow.

The coffeepot gurgled its last, and Verdie carried two full mugs to the living room. "Polly told me this morning over the phone that Beth Layton is sick, but they didn't tell the kids that she's only got a few weeks to live. Stage four liver cancer. And Arlan is taking her home to Kentucky, where their people are from, to live out her last days. He doesn't plan to come back to Texas."

"I hope someone around here is willing to step up

and take them in," Callie said. "Martin has never made friends like he has here."

"It's Christmas. Miracles do happen," Verdie said. "The biggest one is that I haven't killed that damn bird. Which reminds me, it's time to uncover him and let him start his perpetual speechifyin' again."

By the time Callie brushed her teeth and dressed in faded jeans, a clean sweatshirt, and a pair of socks, breakfast was waiting on the bar. Finn came from his end of the house just as she pulled four plates down from the cabinet. Verdie brought out orange juice and milk from the refrigerator.

"Y'all don't say the blessin' without me," Martin yelled.

"Wouldn't dream of it. It's your turn," Finn said.

"It's Verdie's turn," Martin said.

"Be my pleasure." She bowed her head. "Dear Lord, thank you for the life inside this old house and for this wonderful little family who is sharing it with me. Thank you for the good food and for the company. Amen."

"Amen," Joe said. "Now pass the biscuits, Mary."

When Callie raised her head, her eyes caught Finn's and, in that secret language that Martin had talked about, she told him that she'd been right—Verdie was a settler and she had come home.

"Okay, now dig in before it gets cold. Ain't nothing worse than cold gravy or eggs, neither one," Verdie said. "The decorations are up in the attic and you get up there through an opening in the nursery closet, so when you cowboys get done with chores, we'll send Finn to get them. They ain't been brought down since Patrick died twenty years ago, so there'll be some dust. I lost the desire to put them up and"—she leaned forward and lowered her voice—"there are spiders up there, and I do not go where there is a spider."

"They ain't all bad. Some of them eat other bugs," Martin said.

"That's all fine and good, but I don't like any of them." Verdie straightened up.

"I didn't think you'd be afraid of anything." Callie smiled.

"Spiders and snakes," Verdie said.

Martin shivered. "I understand about snakes. Callie is afraid of mice. What are you afraid of, Finn?"

"I'm not real fond of mountain lions. One cornered me when I was out huntin' wild hogs one time. I was about fifteen, and that big old cat with green eyes let me know he sure wasn't afraid of me," Finn answered.

"Will you take me huntin' for wild hogs sometime?" Martin asked.

"We'll see when you get old enough to get a huntin' license," Callie said quickly.

Martin dug into his breakfast. "I won't be afraid of mountain lions. Shotgun will protect me."

After breakfast, Callie found herself in the living room alone, warming her hands by the fire, when Finn came out of his bedroom. He crossed the room, pulled Callie close to his chest, and said, "I wanted to hold you all morning and tell you that I slept better in that recliner last night than I do in my big king-sized bed. I believe it's because you were right there and you kept the nightmares at bay."

"You're welcome." She rolled up on her toes and kissed him hard. Someday they were going to take the next step, but she had decided to be patient and enjoy the sweetness of kisses, hugs, and touches until that time.

———

"Okay, now they're gone and the kitchen is cleaned up. Let's talk," Verdie said.

"In here or the living room?" Callie asked.

Verdie pulled two glasses down from the cabinet. "The living room over drinks."

Callie raised an eyebrow. "It's only ten o'clock."

"Like the song says, it's five o'clock somewhere."

She set the glasses on the coffee table and went to the bookcase beside the fireplace. "This old house has lots of secrets, Callie. This morning I'm going to show you the first one. Patrick's daddy liked his liquor, so he built a safe place back during prohibition days."

She pulled a book from the case and threw a switch located behind it. The whole thing moved to the right three feet, and there was another bookcase, only this one would put some liquor stores to shame. "We'll have a shot of Jack Daniel's this morning. Mainly because I've been craving it, and those folks at the funny farm don't sanction drinking. They didn't bother to tell me that when I signed a six-month lease with them. It might have been in the small print, but, hell, I can't see that shit."

She poured a healthy two fingers in each glass and held it up to the sunlight. "Damn pretty, ain't it?"

Callie touched her glass to Verdie's and said, "Merry Christmas."

Verdie sipped, shut her eyes to enjoy every smoky bit of the flavor, and held it in her mouth awhile before she swallowed. Callie did the same. It had been a very long time since she'd had liquor. A beer once in a while, but the last time she'd had anything stronger was in Afghanistan when she and Finn finished off the last of what was in one of many mouthwash bottles smuggled in by Finn's cousin Sawyer.

When she opened her eyes, Verdie was in the recliner, a smile on her face and her feet propped up. "Tell me how the feud is going. I want to hear more about you shooting at those women, and then tell me all about any rumors you've heard."

"They were acting like hussies," Callie said.

"Run, dog. Hussies are coming," Joe said.

Verdie giggled. "He is entertaining, but is there nothing he can't repeat? Ignore him and enjoy your whiskey."

"Joe is spittin' dust. He needs a drink." He made noises like he was spitting.

Verdie shook her finger at him. "Shut up, bird. Now back to the whiskey. It's not to be thrown back like an old cowboy would in a Western movie but savored and sipped. It's time for us to talk. I like to cook for a family. Hated to make a mess for just me all those years, but I do like to fix and fuss around in the kitchen for a family. Way I figure it is I'm too damned old and my bones aren't strong as they used to be for me to get out there and do ranchin'. If I wasn't, I wouldn't have sold the place to Finn. But I can cook."

In one swift leap, Angel was in Verdie's lap. She turned around a couple of times and settled down for a nap.

"She likes you," Callie said.

"Always did like cats. Last house cat passed on right after Halloween. That kind of fixed it in my mind that it was time to get serious about selling Salt Draw. Got real lonely without nothing to talk to around here, and that damned old barn cat wouldn't have a thing to do with me."

"Verdie, you don't have to cook or do anything. You're a guest here," Callie said.

"No, I'm at home here, and I'll pull my weight, but if I'm overstepping my boundaries in the kitchen, then I'll dust or clean or do laundry, all of which I can do but I hate."

"You can cook all you want. No complaints from me," Callie said.

"Good. That'll leave you free in the mornings to help feed after y'all do that damned workout shit. I swear, the way you two look all fit, I don't know why you'd want to go run in this shit. Martin idolizes Finn, so it's good for him to help when he's here. Now let's talk about Finn. He was like a haunted lost soul when I sold him this ranch. He's more alive now. I think you did that," Verdie said.

"Sometimes I could just kick him in the butt," Callie said.

"'Ass,' darlin'. Women who drink Jack at ten in the morning don't kick butt, they kick ass. Why are you ready to put the boot to his ass?"

"I had a crush on him over there, but, oh, no, he had to fall for one of the translators who came to the base every day. I knew something was wrong with her, but I couldn't figure out what it was," Callie said.

Lord, why was she discussing this with a woman she'd only met the day before and talked to once on the phone? What was the matter with her? She could hold her liquor better than that.

"That's life. Things were like green fruit then and would have been bitter if you'd bit into it. Now the fruit is ripe and ready to be harvested. Just be sure you want it, because a serious relationship takes a lot of work and energy," Verdie told her.

"Sounds like the voice of experience," Callie said.

"It is, and we'll talk about my story another time. It's time for me to start dinner. Those boys are going to come in here starving in about an hour. What's on your list for the rest of the morning?"

Callie carried her glass to the kitchen. "Are there any mice up there in the attic?"

Verdie shook her head. "Not that I know about. Might be a spider or two, though."

"Those don't scare me. I'll bring down the Christmas boxes. Are they all marked, or do I open up each one? And, Verdie, I can't stand the idea of you being at the funny farm for Christmas, so please say you'll stay with us through the holidays."

Verdie poured another bit of whiskey in her glass and tossed it back. "That's the best damn Christmas present anyone ever gave me."

"A second shot of whiskey?" Callie asked.

"Hell no! The invitation to spend the holidays with y'all. We've got to go shopping soon as this weather clears up and buy presents to go under the tree. I'm getting that kid some boots. He can't do ranch work in them shoes. He'll catch pneumonia, and you need a pair, too." Verdie threw the switch to cover up the bar. "This is our secret. We wouldn't want the kids to know it's here."

"Kids?" Callie asked.

Verdie just smiled again and set about peeling

potatoes. "There's a rope on the trapdoor. Pull it and one of them fold-up ladders will come down for you."

The attic was a treasure trove of antiques. Fully floored, it was dusty, and the only place Callie could stand up straight was in the middle, but everything stored up there intrigued Callie.

What could Verdie have been thinking to leave all this family history? Callie would have loved to be able to say that cradle over there in the corner was where her great-grandfather had slept.

Using a rag she found draped over a rolltop steamer chest, she dusted off a sewing rocker and sat down.

"Roots," she said. "Mama and my sister were blessed with wings, but I have roots."

When she was old enough to ask questions about her father, her mother told her very little. Her exact words were burned onto Callie's brain: "I'll always love your father, Callie. He was my first love. We were going to get married and he got killed in a motorcycle wreck."

Sitting there with the old chair squeaking with every rocking movement, she wondered if maybe that's why her mama kept running away. She was simply looking for that first love feeling again.

"You okay up there?" Verdie's voice filtered up through the opening.

"I'm fine. I found a sewing rocker, and I'm just sitting here looking at all this stuff," she answered.

"That was my mama's chair. Woman didn't want arms on a chair when she was knitting. You find the Christmas stuff?"

"I did."

"I'll come about halfway up, and you can hand it to

me. Make sure there ain't no spiders on the boxes. Don't want to fall and break a hip when you've invited me to stick around for Christmas. Can't believe it's been sixty years since this nursery was even used. All of us kids plus my two sons slept in this baby bed," she said.

"Not your grandchildren?"

"My boys didn't like the ranch. Got off it soon as they could. Oldest one went straight into the army, married a girl from California, and settled out there when he'd finished twenty years. Raised his kids in California, and believe me, that bunch of grandkids damn sure don't want anything to do with this old place. I used to feel sorry for myself because they left Burnt Boot, but then I realized one of them could have married a Gallagher and one a Brennan, and my family would have been split down the middle for all eternity," she answered.

Callie picked up a lightweight box and handed it to Verdie, who'd come far enough up the ladder that Callie only had to stoop to put it in Verdie's hands.

"And the other son?"

"He went to college and became an engineer. Met a girl at the college who was from Florida and raised his kids down there. Never got to know any of my grandkids too well."

"I'm sorry. They've missed a lot," Callie said.

"So have I, but this Christmas I've got y'all, and I'm going to make the best of it," Verdie said. "Oh, there's the phone. Maybe it's Polly or Gladys with some news on the feud. Speakin' of which, us old-timers around here remember things pretty often by what was going on with the feud during that time of our lives. It's like our history clock in Burnt Boot. Be right back."

Callie sat down in the rocker again and let the peace settle around her like a worn, old, favorite coat in cold weather. She heard someone coming up the ladder and figured Verdie was bringing news about the children, but it was Finn's beautiful smile that popped up in the opening the next time.

"Hey, Verdie is on the phone and she just pointed in this direction. I got the feeling she's talking to Gladys, because they were talking about the store shelves getting scarce. Holy shit! What is all this stuff?" Finn stopped with just his head showing.

"History. I'd love to know more about it," she answered. "Come on up here and take a look. I bet some of it's been up here since before that rotten feud even started."

"Was it spiders that spook you? I can't remember if it was that or mice or snakes," he said.

"Snakes belong to Martin and spiders to Verdie. I killed a spider awhile ago. Don't know if it was a good one or a bad one, but now it's a dead one."

"I want you to get up slowly and come down the steps," he said.

"Why?"

"Because there's a rat the size of a possum over there beside that box marked *Christmas*," he said.

"That's not funny," she told him.

"I'm not kiddin', Callie. Just get up real easy and come down the steps. It's not moving right now, so it might run and hide when you start this way."

She followed his eyes to the biggest, ugliest rat she'd ever seen. He was right about the size, and it was glaring at her, teeth bared, not moving a muscle.

She froze. Plain and simple, she couldn't move a muscle. She couldn't breathe. She couldn't speak.

"Callie, I'm coming up to get you. Don't move. I think the thing is deaf," Finn whispered.

Move, hell! Her vocal cords had tightened up to the point that she couldn't even squeak. Which was a crappy word to enter her mind right then. Any minute that critter was going to run right at her, and she'd have a heart attack. Twenty-seven years old and dead because of a damned rat. And she hadn't even told Finn exactly how she felt about him.

He had just cleared the top of the steps and taken a step toward her when Verdie scrambled up the ladder. "Well, I'll be damned," she said with a giggle. "There's one of them rotten old rats that Patrick worked on when he started taxidermy classes. Ugly son of a bitch, ain't it? I bet you raked him out of the corner when you was fiddlin' with them boxes. Y'all come on down here for dinner. Me and Martin are already washed up and ready to eat."

"It's dead," Finn told Callie. "Did you hear Verdie? The thing is dead."

Verdie was gone, and Callie could hear Martin talking about the chores they'd done, but she still could not move.

"I'd carry you out of here, but I don't think we'd fit down the stairs, so you're going to have to move," Finn said. "You didn't act like this over there when we saw a rat, and there were lots of them."

"I had a gun on my leg and one in my boot and a knife in my belt," she whispered.

He chuckled. "It is pretty fierce-looking. Don't come

back up here without a gun and a knife, and I think you'll be all right."

She wrapped her arms around his neck and shivered from head to toe. "Hold me, Finn. I'm more scared right now than I was over there with bombs all around us. I'm not coming up here again. The past can stay in the past if it includes rats."

Chapter 14

"THIS PLACE LOOKS LIKE WE'RE EITHER MOVING IN OR moving out," Finn said when all the boxes were out of the attic and in the living room.

"We're" moving...not "I'm" moving... Callie's heart did one of those crazy twists that left her breathless.

"About ten of them are full of outside lights. The hooks stay up on the roof all year so it's not as tough a job as it could be and the sun is shining. But the lights ain't been up in years, so some of them might have gotten busted up. Last time I put them up, I remember Polly callin' to tell me the feud had fired up hotter'n a two-dollar pistol. There was talk that Naomi's son was seen at a movie theater with one of the Brennan girls, and all holy hell broke loose that year," Verdie said.

"And it's not snowing," Martin chimed in. "This box says it's for the tree. Can I open it, Granny Verdie?"

"It all belongs to Finn, so you'd best ask him," she answered.

He pulled a knife from his pocket and cut the tape loose. "Now see what you got in there, but remember that Angel is in the house, so don't hang any breakables too low on the branches."

Callie pointed at the tree. "I don't think it'll matter where we hang them."

There was Angel in the fork of a branch watching them from between the greenery. She tilted her head to one side and was completely hidden, as if she knew that Callie would be reaching in to take her away from her newfound safe spot.

"Come on, girl. You can't be in there. I know it's a nice little place to hide from those mean old dog boys, but you'll hurt your shoulder trying to get down." She talked to the cat as she laid her on the corner of the sofa on a soft throw. "See there. That's not nearly as scratchy as those cedar branches."

Verdie pulled the box over toward the sofa, sat down, and started removing tissue paper from around each ornament.

Callie took one look and inhaled deeply. "That is an antique. It should be in a museum, not on a tree where a cat might knock it off or a dog's tail might get to going too hard and send it flying."

Verdie handed it to her. "They're just things, Callie. If they get broken, then at least they were being enjoyed. Hang every one in the box on the tree, and then you boys need to get those boxes labeled *outside lights* and check them while we put all this stuff on the tree and out in the house," she said.

"What do you mean check the lights?" Martin asked.

"They're the kind like what is on the tree. If one is shot, then the whole string won't light up. So you plug them in, and if it don't light up, you start at one end and replace bulbs until you find the shot one," she explained. "Make sure every light is working before you get out there on the roof, and it'll make your job go faster. Plus it's warmer in the house."

Finn and Martin used the dining room and kitchen to stretch out the first strand of lights and both let out a whoop when it lit up. When they'd checked the rest of the lights and none of them had bad bulbs, they carefully carried out the first strand like it was a twenty-five-foot-long snake. Finn crawled up on a ladder and Martin fed the wire up to him while he snapped it into place.

While they were doing that, Callie took two glass ornaments from Verdie's hand and held them up to the light. "They're gorgeous."

"I think Mama called it mercury glass. They were her favorites," Verdie said.

"We really shouldn't be taking the chance of getting them broken. I'll cry if they get destroyed."

"If they get broke, at least I got to be here the last time they were used and I got to enjoy being with y'all. You want something worthwhile to worry about, I'll give it to you. Polly called this morning right after you went up to the attic," Verdie said.

Callie stopped halfway to the tree and looked over her shoulder. "And?"

"She got ahold of her contact, and it's like this. Nobody in this part of the state is willin' to take on three kids right here at the holidays. Some folks out in west Texas said they had room for one. Someone down near Corpus Christi says they'll take one, and another family in the middle of Fort Worth will take the third one, so they're not staying in Burnt Boot, and they aren't staying together," Verdie whispered.

"When?" Callie asked.

"The Laytons are plannin' to leave on Sunday morning, so the kids will be taken somewhere that day and then split up on Monday morning, I guess. Martin probably won't even see them again."

Callie hung the two ornaments and sat down in the recliner, put her hands over her eyes, and let the tears flow.

Verdie patted her on the shoulder. "Polly says she could probably put in a word if someone wanted them through the holidays around here, so they could finish out the semester at school and not be yanked up right here at the finish, but who's going to take on three orphans a couple of weeks before Christmas?"

Callie pinched her nose with her two fingers, but it didn't stop the headache. "You think they'd let me have them?"

"Don't know. You sure couldn't do it without talking to Finn first. Now let's get these decorations up. You and I will do some shopping on Monday and even have presents under the tree when Martin gets off the school bus. That might help a little bit," Verdie said.

"Come outside and see the front of the house," Martin yelled from the door. "Oh, oh, what is that? Is it a cookie jar shaped like Santa Claus?"

Verdie held it up. "Yes, it is, and it's guaranteed to stay on the cabinet and have magic cookies in it every day for your after-school snack."

Martin let out a whoop. "What's magic cookies?"

"It's not the cookies that are magic. It's the jar. It never runs out of cookies," Verdie answered.

"Hey, you hear that, Finn? We got magic in this place until after Christmas."

"Shut the door before you let all the warmth out, and we'll be out there in a few minutes. Got to get our jackets. Don't get chilled. We can always finish decorating tomorrow if we don't get it done today," Verdie said.

"I can't wait to see it all lit up." Martin's last two words were muffled through the door.

"See there, the decoratin' business is takin' his mind off it." Verdie set the cookie jar on the coffee table and pulled out a small nativity scene. "We used to put this on the mantel. I see that Finn hasn't put anything on it yet. What do you think? Mantel or foyer table?"

"Mantel," Callie said. "I'll put the cookie jar in the kitchen, and then we'll work on the mantel together."

Verdie handed the jar up to her. "I'll sit here and unpack. My old bones are like Pistol's. We like to settle in and get comfortable. You're like Angel, climbing trees to get a better look at the world. And them boys out there are like Shotgun, full of piss and vinegar. You can arrange the mantel while you tell me a story about that boot in the tree. I haven't ever seen a real leather boot ornament before. Aha, that brought a smile to your face. It must be a good one."

"It is, but first we've got to go brag on the outside lights."

"My coat is hanging on the back of the rocking chair in my room. Would you get it for me, please?" Verdie asked.

A pang of guilt hit Finn right in the gut when he realized snow was over the top of Martin's shoes. He should have fought harder to get the kid a pair of boots.

The guilt trip was cut short when he saw Callie's face. She looked as if she'd been crying, and only one thing could have caused that. Polly had called with bad news. He quickly went to her side and took her hands in his.

"I'm sorry."

"He's going to be devastated. Don't tell him now. It'll spoil his fun," she whispered.

"Dammit, Callie! I want to hold you and kiss you and make it all go away," he said.

"Me too. Maybe later."

Verdie pushed outside in an old coat not so very different from his grandmother's work coat. Callie was right; they couldn't let her go back to that impersonal place for the holidays. They had to invite her to stay on at the ranch and enjoy Christmas in Burnt Boot.

"Goin' up good and tight," Verdie said.

Martin clapped his hands in excitement. "It's going to be beautiful. Santa won't have a bit of a problem finding this place in the dark. With that big old roof and these lights, he'll think he's on a landing strip."

Verdie laid a hand on Martin's shoulder. "You got that right. When you get that strand up, you need to come inside for some hot chocolate and have some cookies. Your nose looks like it's about to freeze and fall plumb off. A boy would look just plain weird without a nose."

"Yes, ma'am. Now y'all got to come all the way to the back side of the house. We got a lot done." Martin took off in a run, oblivious of the snow packing around the hem of his jeans.

"Boy needs boots," Verdie mumbled right behind him.

Finn nodded. "I been tellin' this stubborn woman that ever since they got here."

"Don't say a word to me about boots or snow or strays," she said.

"I was fixin' to tell you how beautiful you look out here in the snow." Finn kissed her on the forehead in front of Verdie and Martin. Verdie winked. Martin made fake gagging noises.

She shook her head at him. "You were thinking about how right you were in the Western-wear store and how wrong I was. This isn't our first rodeo, Finn. I practically lived inside your head for a whole year, remember?"

He shivered. "Yes, darlin', I remember."

"I know his feet are cold, but I still don't want him to have cowboy boots." Her body had stiffened and her tone was colder than the snow.

"Callie, you aren't losing control, I promise," he whispered.

"I'm not a control freak," she said.

"Yes, you are, and with good reason, but it's okay to let go," Finn said.

"What are you two whispering about?" Martin yelled.

"Nothing," Callie said. "We're just talking about your Christmas presents."

"I hope it's cowboy boots. I want to grow up to be just like Finn."

"We'll talk about it later," Callie said.

Finn whispered for Callie's ears only, "And, honey, this is not the time or the place to pick a fight so you can get mad and run away."

She took a few steps toward the porch. "You could just write my weekly paycheck, and I'll…"

He crossed his arms over his chest. "You will what? Walk twenty miles to town? There's very little traffic out there on those twisty roads, so you wouldn't have much luck hitchhiking with a boy who doesn't even have proper boots. You are the most bullheaded, stubborn woman I've ever encountered."

She shook his arm from her shoulders and stormed into the house, slamming the door. He followed her, with Verdie and Martin right behind him. They stopped in the living room, but he followed her right into her bedroom, not giving a damn if he left bits of snow on the floor in his wake. He didn't even knock on the door but plowed right into her room.

Callie was standing in front of the window, staring out like a bird in a cage. He crossed the room in long strides, scooped her up, and sat down in the rocking chair with her.

"I'm scared," she said.

"I know. So am I."

"This is too perfect, Finn. There's a grenade somewhere, and the pin is pulled. It's just a matter of time until it all goes boom. I figured if I left now, it would be with good memories and not horrible ones. But I don't want to leave. Just thinking of walking away from you and Salt Draw, even Verdie and the animals, breaks my heart."

He tangled his fingers in her hair and held her head against his chest. "I'll help you work through the fear if you'll do the same for me."

She drew her head back, her aqua-colored eyes swimming in tears. "Don't bullshit me, O'Donnell. You'd face off with the devil."

He let go of her hair and bent just enough that their lips touched in a salty kiss. Her arms sent desire shooting through his body when they laced around his neck. The kiss deepened into more as she opened her mouth and let his tongue inside to make love to her mouth.

"Darlin', never doubt that my fears are every bit as big as yours, with commitment topping the list in big bold letters. Don't run away, Callie. I need you to stay," he whispered softly.

"I want to stay," she said just before he kissed her again. She drew away and laid her head back on his chest. "We should go. They'll be waiting."

"They know how to make hot chocolate, and we don't have to leave until you're ready," he said.

"I like it here. Can we stay forever?"

"We might get hungry."

"There's things other than food that will satisfy a body," she whispered.

"But if the body is weak, it doesn't perform too well, does it?" he chuckled.

"I'm not fighting any more today. I don't have it in me. But I do have to tell you this before we go out there and get lectured by Verdie. Martin's friends are going to be split up and sent to different homes on Sunday, and there doesn't seem to be a damn thing we can do about it. He's going to be so sad."

"Then let's go take our medicine from Verdie for fighting. Afterward we will make this place as happy as we can for him," Finn said.

"I always wanted a grandmother like her," Callie said, but she didn't make a move to get up from his lap.

With his boot heel, he set the rocker into motion. "I have two just like her. Love them both. They'll come see us in the spring, I'm sure. They didn't help with the move, and my grandfathers will have lots of advice for the ranch."

"You are a very lucky man," she said.

His strong arm shifted to hold her tighter. "Yes, Callie, I am."

A gentle knock on the door was followed by a low voice. "Callie, is it time for me to pack?"

"Is he crying?" Finn asked.

"Probably. I really have to go take care of this." She hurried to open the door.

"Hush, kid. He's not dead," Joe said as he flitted from one side of his clothes dryer perch to the other.

Martin looked up at her with tears streaming down his face.

Verdie was right behind him, arms crossed, her wrinkled face drawn up in a frown.

Callie dropped down on her knees and hugged Martin. "Finn and I had a fight. We do that sometimes, but we aren't leaving Salt Draw."

"For real?" Martin asked.

"For real, son." Finn laid a hand on Martin's shoulder and one on Callie's. "Arguments don't mean that you have to pack up and run away. It takes a strong person to work it out, but your aunt has that kind of strength."

Martin pushed away and dried his tears. "Callie is strong, ain't she, Finn?"

"Yes, she is. I'm sure hungry. Did you leave me any cookies?"

Martin nodded and pointed toward his toes. "And look."

Verdie pursed her lips and narrowed her eyes. "They was Patrick's old work boots. 'Bout worn out, but I reckon they'll do for a couple of weeks for him to do chores in. Could use a coat of polish later tonight, and he had to put two pair of socks on to fill up the toes. Patrick was a little man, only about five feet four inches, and he wore a small shoe. Bein' little didn't mean he wasn't a fighter."

"Thank you." Callie swallowed hard against the lump in her throat.

"Now, Martin, you go on to the kitchen and finish up your last cookie while I talk to Finn and Callie."

"Joe needs a cookie. Dog! Joe needs a cookie," the bird fussed as he sharpened his beak on the wood rod under his feet.

Martin's new boots sounded like size tens rather than the sixes they probably were as they clomped down the hallway.

Finn looped an arm around Callie's waist and waited. "Are we in big trouble?"

Verdie nodded seriously. "Yes, you are. First thing is, this ain't my place no more and it ain't my business to fuss at y'all, but I love that kid and I can't stand to see him cry. My dad gave me a bit of advice when our boys were little that I'm about to give y'all. You're going to argue, but it's your argument, not his. Don't let him see it, and don't go to bed angry with each other. We got enough of a feud goin' on all around us. We don't need one inside the walls of the house. Now let's go have some cookies."

Finn gave Callie a gentle squeeze. "Sounds like good advice to me."

Martin was standing right under the phone when it rang, and it startled him so badly that he knocked over the chair below it. It hit the floor with a thud, and he grabbed the receiver before Verdie came out of the hallway to answer it. If anyone could talk sense to Callie and Finn, it was Verdie, and he sure didn't want her to answer a telephone right then.

"Hello," he said cautiously.

"Could I please talk to Martin Brewster?"

"Who is this?" he whispered.

"It's me, Olivia. I have to talk low or Miz Beth will wake up. They're sending us away on Sunday, Martin, and they're going to split us up. We go to three different places, and that means we'll never see each other again. The last place we was at, there was a boy there and they did this to him and his sister. He didn't even know where she was anymore."

"Oh no!" Martin gasped.

"We're going to run away tonight."

"Do you know where Salt Draw is?"

"It's where the school bus gets you every morning. Down the road from us and then down a lane."

"It's all lit up for Christmas. You can see it from the road. I know you can. I'll leave my light on so you can come around behind the house and knock on my window. Y'all can stay out in the tack room. You won't freeze until we figure this out, Olivia. I'll help you," Martin said.

"I trust you, Martin. Will you watch for us?"

"I'll leave my curtains open. Tap on my window when you get here. Here comes Granny Verdie. I got to go."

Chapter 15

CALLIE KICKED AS MUCH SNOW FROM HER SHOES AS POS-
sible before she went inside the general store, then she
stomped a few more times on the big rug in front of the
door. "Glad I caught you before you closed up, Gladys.
Verdie says we need flour, sugar, and cooking oil."

"She called me and said to tell you to add baking soda to
that." Gladys tipped her head toward the back of the store.

Callie looked that way, and there was Betsy
Gallagher. Their cold gazes locked as Betsy made her
way right up into Callie's space, not stopping until they
were practically nose to nose.

"You are like a bitch in heat. You can't be satisfied
with one man hanging on you. Now you've got to go
and mess up my cousin's relationship with Orville. Ilene
has been in love with Orville since they were in school.
Do you want an ass whipping, woman?" Betsy's tone
got colder with each word.

"How in the hell did I do that? It was your damn feud
that brought him to my door to begin with."

"He brought you doughnuts. He's never brought
Ilene doughnuts," Betsy said.

"That doesn't mean a damn thing, so get out of my
face, and, darlin', you don't want to call me a bitch
again," Callie said.

Betsy leaned in until they were nose to nose. "I call
it like I see it."

Callie smiled.

"What's so funny…bitch?" Betsy drew out the last word.

"I think it's funny that the Gallaghers want the sheriff in their back pocket so bad that they send one of their own out to seduce the poor old guy. I'm not stupid," Callie whispered and rubbed her nose against Betsy's.

Betsy jumped back and swiped a hand across her nose. "Don't touch me."

"Oh, darlin', this relationship has gone too far for you to close me out now. Remember, I'm a bitch, and bitches rub noses with other bitches," Callie said.

Betsy's hand came up in a flash, but Callie was faster. She caught it midair and held it in a vise grip. When her left hand shot up, Callie caught it, too.

The woman shivered from head to toe and kicked Callie in the shin. "Are you a freakin' crazy bitch?" she yelled.

Callie kept a grip on her hands and nipped her on the arm, leaving faint teeth marks but no blood. "Bitches are lady dogs. They bite. You had enough, or you want to call me that again? Next time, I promise there will be blood and you will need rabies shots."

She shoved, and Betsy had to do a lot of fancy scrambling to keep from knocking down a display of canned peaches. When she finally got her balance, she stormed out of the store without looking back.

Gladys slapped the checkout counter and laughed so hard that she had to sit down. "I swear to God that was the funniest damn thing I've ever seen. If Honey wasn't so hell-bent on having Finn, the Brennans would invite you into their fold with open arms."

"I don't want to be a part of none of their shit. I just want to live my life and be left alone," Callie said.

"Then you come to the wrong part of Texas," Gladys said.

Callie steamed all the way home and didn't even feel the cold from truck to kitchen. She carried in the groceries and set them on the cabinet before she even noticed the doughnuts on the table.

"Shit!" she mumbled. "That's all I need today."

"That you, Callie?" Verdie yelled from her room.

"Yes, it is."

"I made part of the yeast dough into doughnuts. Just finished fryin' and glazin' them. They're on the table if you want one to warm up. Coffee is fresh." Verdie's voice got closer with each word.

"Well, hot damn!" Callie said.

"Heard you had a little dustup with Betsy down at the store." Verdie pulled out a chair and sat down at the end of the table. "Looks like they may make it a three-way feud."

Callie hung her coat over the back of a chair, picked up a doughnut, and bit into it. "Holy smoke, Verdie. These are to die for. Has Orville ever had one?"

"Hell, no! I didn't want him hangin' around my back door whinin' like a half-starved hound dog," Verdie answered.

"You hear that Ilene Gallagher is out after Orville?"

"Of course. There ain't much goes on in Burnt Boot that I don't know. Crazy thing is that she really likes him, but he's afraid to get tangled up in the feud. Did Gladys exaggerate, or did you really bite Betsy?"

"She did not exaggerate." Callie pulled out a chair and sat down.

"Why didn't you just knock the shit out of her?"

"Gladys wouldn't like us fightin' in her store."

"And this makes Betsy look like a fool, right?"

Callie reached for another doughnut. "Yes, ma'am."

Verdie had just finished reading a chapter to Martin that evening when Callie peeked into the room.

"Come right in and join us. Martin is a good kid. He lets me read to him when he's plenty old enough to read it for himself, but he knows it brings me pleasure." Verdie smiled.

Martin had been antsy all afternoon and evening, as if waiting for something. Callie couldn't put her finger on it, but something just flat-out wasn't right. His eyes darted from the window to the bunk beds, back to the window, and then to the closet, as if he was casing his own bedroom to rob it.

"Did I tell you that my feet didn't get all wet in them boots that Granny Verdie let me borrow? They're a little big, but, boy, they sure beat wadin' through snow in my shoes." Martin changed the subject quickly.

A hard pang of guilt slapped Callie in the ribs as she sat down on the bottom bunk of the extra set of beds. Cowboy boots wouldn't make him a bad person, and it was downright crazy to let him continue to work without something warm on his feet.

"I been thinkin' that with my first paycheck I'd buy me some of them rubber boots. Santa Claus knows I want cowboy boots for Christmas, and I won't have the money to buy them for a long time, but rubber boots don't cost so much and…" He paused for breath.

"Next time we get into Gainesville, I'll get you some rubber boots," Callie promised.

Finn stuck his head inside the door. "You want the plain old black ones or some with pink hearts on them?"

Martin did a fake gag. "Come on, Finn. You know boys don't wear pink ones with hearts on them. I want some black ones or red ones like firemen wear."

"So you might be a fireman?" Finn sat down on the bed next to Callie, legs touching from hips to knees, causing her thoughts to drift away from boots of any kind or fashion.

"Maybe a volunteer fireman right here in Burnt Boot, but my real job will be ranchin'," Martin said. "Finn, did you ever know of coyotes, the ones like are howling out there tonight, to attack people?"

"Never heard of it. Besides, you're in the house, and coyotes never break through windows to get into a house. They run from people," Finn said.

"I like it when we're all together in my room for just a little while," he said.

"Well, young man, it's time for us all to get into our own rooms so you can go to sleep. Good night, all y'all," Verdie said. "It's so good to be back home."

She headed off to her room, and Callie started toward the living room with Finn right behind her. She sat down on the end of the sofa and pulled her legs up under her, tucking a fluffy red throw tightly around them.

"He's up to something," she said.

"Yep." Finn sat down beside her and shifted her feet into his lap. Starting at her toes, he massaged one at a time. "Don't know if it's a ploy for cowboy boots, or if he's going to sneak out the window and go coyote hunting, but he's definitely up to something. Did you notice the way his eyes kept going to the window?"

"I did," she said. But thoughts of her young nephew were fading fast as Finn worked on her feet. "You could go into business. We could make more on foot massages than we can raisin' cattle. Big old steamin'-hot cowboy like you with those hands, wow, just wow."

One dark eyebrow jacked up toward the ceiling.

"Stop it. I wouldn't really want you to be touching another woman," she said.

"Jealous?"

"No, just protecting my interests. There's a major difference between jealousy and protecting one's property." She smiled.

The eyebrow went up another notch. "And I'm your property?"

"Shhh! Did you hear that?" Callie whispered.

Shotgun raised his head and growled.

Pistol cocked his ear to one side and waited.

Angel didn't even open her eyes.

Finn shook his head. "Old houses groan with the cold. The dogs are going back to sleep, and the cat didn't even wake up. Now where were we?"

She threw a leg over his lap, and his arms went around her as she rested her cheek on his chest. Hard muscles barely muffled the steady beat of his heart. She liked that about Finn O'Donnell. He was steady and true, kind and honest, and he took in strays, which testified to his kindness.

⌒⌒⌒

The window creaked when Martin raised it all the way to the top, letting in a blast of arctic air. "Y'all okay? I know it's cold, but we're lucky it ain't rainin' or sleetin'."

"It was scary and we heard coyotes and we're cold," Adam said.

"But we kept going until we saw your light." Olivia shivered.

"We done talked about y'all hidin' in the barn, but it's too cold. Give me your hand, Ricky, and I'll help you inside. There's plenty of beds in here and it's warm," Martin said.

"But what if your aunt finds us?"

"I've got an idea that will keep her out of my room," he said.

"Okay, anything to get warm. My feet are so cold, I can't feel them," Olivia said.

All three kids scrambled over the windowsill. Martin put a finger to his lips and tiptoed to the door, peeked out, and shook his head. "Granny Verdie's light is out, and if Callie had heard anything, she'd already be on the way, so she must be asleep, too. Take off your coats. What did you bring with you?"

"Nothing," Ricky said.

"Okay, then you guys can use some of my pajamas. Olivia, you got a problem sleeping in one of my shirts and my loungin' britches?"

She shook her head.

Martin opened up a drawer and handed out sleep clothing and then opened his closet door. "You can change in here, Olivia. And we'll hang up y'all's jeans so they'll be dry tomorrow mornin'. Anybody hungry?"

All three heads bobbed up and down.

"I snuck some peanut butter, bread, and jelly in here while nobody was lookin'. And I got some milk and some plastic cups."

"I hope they don't take you to jail for helpin' us," Olivia said.

"We can't let y'all get split up." Martin pulled the wooden thread spool at the end of a long cord, and the light came on in the closet. "I cleared out the whole floor, so anyone knocks on the door and I'm not here, you get in here and shut the door. It'll be your hiding place until we can figure out our next step."

It was well after midnight when all four bunks were filled.

"Martin?" Olivia whispered from the bunk above his.

"Yes?"

"Thank you. I get mad at my brothers, but I don't want to never see them again," she said.

He remembered how terrified he was when he was in foster care. "I'd just die if they took me away from Callie, so I know how you feel."

"They're already asleep. They were brave little guys, even when the coyotes howled." She yawned.

"Good night, Olivia," Martin said.

"This bed is so warm. I could just stay here forever."

—∿∿∿—

Callie awoke early and made her way to the kitchen, where Verdie was already sitting at the table with a mug of coffee in front of her.

"Good mornin'. Coffee is made and oven is heating up for biscuits. Thought we'd start off the day with sausage and eggs. Snow hasn't melted much, but the sun will take it down some today. Then it'll be muddy tomorrow, and on Monday we'll get a fresh layer on top of frozen mud. You and Finn still plannin' on runnin' in this shit?"

Callie poured a cup of coffee and sat down at the table. "This is Saturday. We take the weekends off, but I have to admit, it just makes Monday rougher. Did you sleep well?"

"Thought I heard a window squeak and then voices, but convinced myself I was dreaming. Pistol would have told us all about it if anyone came around the house," Verdie answered. "But for the most part I slept much better than I did down there at the funny farm. Home is where your heart is."

"Home is where your boots are, according to Finn." Callie smiled. "Thank you for letting Martin borrow Patrick's boots."

Verdie grinned. "He would have liked the idea of a kid wearing them."

"Verdie, I love your cooking and I love having you here at the ranch, but you don't have to make three meals a day around here. You can be our guest," Callie said.

"Got to stay busy at something, or my bones will think I've quit. If that happens, the damned old things will stop working altogether, and I'm not ready for that. If it makes you feel better, we'll work together. You get out the eggs, and I'll start making sausage patties."

"Good mornin', ladies." Finn's voice still had the morning gruff in it. He sported bedroom hair, and his blue eyes had that early-morning look in them that was so damn hot it took Callie's breath away. She stepped back and her shoulder touched his hard chest. She poured a cup of coffee with trembling hands and carefully handed it to him.

"Martin must be worn out. He's sleeping later than usual," Verdie said.

"Good mornin'." Martin yawned from the doorway. "Is that sausage I smell? And waffles? I could eat a horse. Y'all better make a lot."

"Not waffles. Just eggs and sausage and hot biscuits," Callie said.

"Did you hear from Polly yet?" Martin asked.

"She might call today," Verdie said. "How many biscuits does a boy who's hungry enough to eat a horse need?"

"A lot." Martin poured himself a glass of orange juice and plopped down in a kitchen chair. "I'm worried about my friends, Callie. Why can't they come here? If we can't afford it, I don't need nothing for Christmas now that Granny Verdie gave me some boots. I'll even wear them butt-ugly shoes to school when my black ones wear out."

"It's complicated," Finn said. "There are laws and things that have to be done for kids to be placed in foster care."

"'Complicated' is just a word big people made up to say no." He pouted.

Finn laid a hand on Martin's shoulder. "It's like this, son. There's lots of paperwork involved before folks can be foster parents, and they prefer the people who are going to be foster parents to be married. Even if we wanted to take the kids, the law probably wouldn't let us."

"Then the law needs to be changed. You and Callie

are the best parents in the world, we even got Verdie to be the grandma, and we got lots of beds for them."

"It would take a miracle," Verdie said.

"Well, then, I want a miracle for Christmas," Martin said.

Chapter 16

"WHAT DO YOU THINK, PARTNER? SHALL WE FEED cows or take care of the horses first thing this morning after breakfast? Or would you like to stay in and read and let me and Callie do the work?" Finn asked.

"Cows. They'll be hungry," Martin answered quickly.

"Smart move. That's what I would have said, too, because once the sun melts the snow, it's going to get muddy, and we could get stuck out there," Finn said.

"What are you going to do this morning, Callie?" Martin asked.

"There's always Saturday cleaning that has to be done," Callie said.

"Well, don't go in my room. I'm working on a Christmas present, and I don't want you to see it until Christmas day," he said.

"Oh, really?" she asked.

"Promise you'll stay out of my room," he said.

"I promise." She agreed, but she was a bundle of mixed emotions that morning. And the churning deep in her gut had a hell of a lot more to do with this new relationship with Finn than whatever Martin had in his room.

Ever since she had awakened, she'd felt like the other shoe was about to drop. Add that to the heat between her and Finn, and she had jitters that had nothing to do with black coffee that morning. Then there was Verdie, bless her heart. Callie had only known her for three days, but it felt like they'd been a part of each other's lives forever—as if she was the grandmother Callie never had. A hell of a lot of change going on, and it was unsettling.

"Oh no!" Martin pushed his chair back so quick that it fell on the floor with a thud. He took off for the bathroom with a hand over his mouth, and Callie followed right behind him.

"Open this door," she yelled when she heard the lock click.

"I'm not going to upchuck. It's going the other way. Would you take my place this morning with the feeding? I'll be better in a little while," he hollered.

"I can't leave you here alone if you're sick," she said.

"Granny Verdie is here," he said. "I'll be fine, but it would be awful if this happened out there in the pasture."

"Are you sure?" Callie asked.

"Finn needs your help," he called out.

"I'll have my phone. If you need me, you'll promise to call, right?" she asked.

"I promise. Just go help Finn, and tell him I'm sorry," Martin said.

She turned around to find Verdie right behind her. "Probably nerves over his little friends. We'll be fine. I'll give him a dose of that pink medicine. Raised my boys on it, and there's a brand-new bottle in the medicine cabinet."

"I'll take it," Martin yelled.

"And it will make you all better by noon. You'll probably be ready to build a snowman after dinner," Verdie shouted through the closed door.

Finn peeked down the hallway. "Hey, is my partner sick?"

"That one is. I'll be standing in this morning," Callie said.

"Does he need to go to the doctor?" Finn asked.

"I think it's a case of nerves," Verdie whispered. "He's so worried about those children that it's upset his stomach. He'll be fine."

Cassie dressed in jeans, a sweatshirt, and her new coat and met Finn in the living room. Shotgun got up slowly from the front of the fireplace, shook his fur, and ambled toward the door. Pistol looked up, shut his eyes, and went back to sleep.

"Pistol isn't much of a cow dog." Callie laughed.

Suddenly, as if he understood what she said, a low growl came from his throat, and he set up a yapping that would have raised the dead all the way down in Fort Worth. He ran to the door, hackles standing up like porcupine quills and carrying on until Angel trotted across the floor sideways, her fur puffed out like a dandelion to put the fear of a limping yellow kitten in whatever was on the porch.

Finn opened the door to find Sheriff Orville with his finger headed toward the doorbell.

"Good morning. Guess that noisy mutt announced my arrival." Orville sent a bright smile toward Callie.

"Can I help you?" Finn asked.

"We've got a call from the Laytons up the road from you. Their foster kids went missing last night. We're just checking the neighbors to see if anyone saw or heard anything," he said.

"Well, come on in where it's warm. We're just

getting ready to do chores, but those kids sure aren't here. You want a cup of coffee?" Finn asked.

"No, thank you. I got a cup in the car. Mr. Layton says that the kids have taken quite a likin' to the little boy who lives here. He was hoping the kid might have talked to them and would know where they might be headed or holed up. You didn't tell me you had a kid."

"That would be my nephew, not my child. His name is Martin. He is friends with the kids and is very upset about them going back into foster care. He's not feeling well, but I can ask him. Please come inside, Sheriff," Callie said, but she caught the sly wink from Finn and blushed.

He nodded and stepped into the living room. "I'd appreciate that, Callie."

Callie started to swing the door open but remembered that he'd asked that she not barge into his room, so she shouted through it. "Hey, Martin, the sheriff is out here. Your friends are missing, and Mr. Layton is worried. Have you talked to Olivia?"

"Hot damn! Joe wants a doughnut," Joe yelled.

The door opened immediately, and there was Martin, all the color drained from his face. "Oh, no! Did someone steal them? We should have taken them in, Callie. Now they're gone, and it's cold, and what if they freeze or starve? What's Joe hollerin' about? Did Verdie make doughnuts?"

"You just get to feeling better. The police will find them." She touched his forehead, but he wasn't feverish.

Evidently Joe could smell doughnuts, and that set him off. "Run, dog, run. Cops," he said loudly.

Orville raised an eyebrow and she shook her head.

"He's upset because he wanted us to take them, but we aren't approved foster parents. Sorry about the bird."

"Well, thank you. Call me if you hear anything. Small as Burnt Boot is, we'll find them."

"Now I'm really worried," Callie said as soon as the door closed. "I hope they're holed up in a warm barn. Maybe they've gotten into the school or the church. That's the two places they know won't be occupied on a Saturday."

Finn draped an arm around Callie's waist. "Let's get the chores done, and if they haven't found them by then, we'll help with the search. Just knowing we're out there will make Martin feel better."

"He'll throw a fit to go, even if he's not feeling better," she said.

"We'll take him with us, I promise."

Verdie waved from the kitchen table as they passed. "Don't worry about those kids. They're probably some-where warm and safe, and like the man said, this ain't a big town. Somebody saw them or is keeping them, and they'll be in touch with the Laytons right soon."

When they were in the truck with Shotgun right between them, Callie sighed loudly. "I'm sorry, Finn. It's just that he's never made friends before, and he's been so happy here."

The truck roared to life when he started the engine. "Don't worry. It'll all blow over in a week or two, and he'll make new friends. I wonder why Joe yelped about doughnuts."

"He probably could smell them on Orville." Callie laughed. "I bet if you kissed me right now, you could taste them. Kind of like the smell a smoker leaves behind when he's been in a room."

"Never accuse me of passing up an opportunity like that." Finn leaned over and let his tongue slip inside her mouth.

"So?" she asked when he moved away.

"No doughnut taste there, but it was right nice. Anytime you want me to check for doughnut breath, you just let me know."

"If you need me, I'll be in my room reading." Verdie knocked on Martin's door and raised her voice so he could hear it.

"Dammit, kid! Talk to Joe," the bird yelled.

He opened it just enough that he could step outside into the hallway with her. "I'll be fine. I'm feeling better. I'll go change out Joe's papers in a little while and read him a story."

"I promised I'd be honest with you, Martin. Tomorrow they're coming to take those kids away to Gainesville to a place where they'll stay until Monday. Then they are going to put them in three different homes," Verdie said.

Tears rolled down his cheeks. "I wouldn't never want anyone to put Callie in one place and me in another."

Verdie hugged him tightly. "I had a bunch of brothers and a sister, and I sure wouldn't have wanted to be torn away from them, either. But if you know anything about the kids, Martin, you need to tell me or Callie so we can let the Laytons know. They're real worried."

"Yes, ma'am." He nodded. "I'm hungry again. Reckon

it'd be all right if I stuffed some of them leftover eggs in a biscuit?"

"Guess that medicine worked pretty good." She smiled.

"I can do it myself and eat it while I work on Callie's Christmas present. I'll be real careful and not make a mess," he said.

"If you do, clean it up. We sure don't want any mice to scare Callie, do we?" She left her door open just a crack instead of shutting it all the way.

When she heard him coming back up the hallway, she peeked out to see him carrying a plate with half a dozen biscuits stuffed with leftover eggs and bacon in one hand and a quart jar of milk in the other.

The door to his bedroom closed, then immediately opened again and a little blond-haired girl tip-toed across to the bathroom. The process repeated twice more. A dark-haired boy was next and then a blond-haired one who looked a lot like the girl. When Martin's door closed the final time, she quickly crossed the hallway and laid her cheek on the door. They were laughing softly and talking as they devoured the leftover breakfast, then the tone changed as they talked about the police.

She went back to her room and made a big noisy show of shutting her door and then called out, "Martin, darlin', I've decided to make cookies. Can't keep my mind on my book. If you need me, I'll be in the kitchen."

"Cookies! Yes, yes, yes!" Joe said.

"Okay, Granny Verdie. I'm goin' to rest awhile now."

She went straight for the phone and called Polly, tapping her foot on the floor through five rings, and was just about to hang up when she heard Polly answer breathlessly.

"Hello."

"Polly, where in the hell were you?"

"Talking to Orville. The Laytons' kids ran away in the night, and they can't find them," Polly said.

"They're at Salt Draw. Martin has snuck them into his bedroom. Now what are we going to do? Can you pull any strings and let me have them at least until after the holidays? By then I'd be willing to bet that Finn and Callie will be able to foster them. Poor little things just want to stay together, and our boy over here on Salt Draw doesn't have a problem sharing. We've got lots of room," Verdie said.

"Shit, woman! You are eighty years old," Polly said.

"Well, you're the same age as I am and still runnin' a beer joint, so why can't I have some fake grandbabies for the holidays?" Verdie protested.

"Okay, okay, I'll see what I can do. Nobody wants to come out here in this kind of weather anyway, and I've still got some pull at the office, but I'm not making any promises. You sure about this, Verdie?"

"Never been more sure about anything in my life," Verdie answered. "How soon can you call me?"

"We'll have to bring in the law, since they ran away, and Finn and Callie will have to be willing. Finn most of all, since it's his ranch and all," Polly said.

"Bring the damn FBI and the CIA if you have to. Just don't take them, not when we've got a place for them right here. Half an hour?" Verdie asked.

"Good God, Verdie, that would take magic. Maybe by noon." Polly laughed.

"Then get off the phone and get to work. I'll start making cookies so I can have something to offer all those people you mentioned when they get here."

"Call you when I know something. And Verdie? I'm glad they're safe."

Chapter 17

THE FRONT YARD WAS FULL OF VEHICLES WHEN Callie and Finn returned from doing the feeding that morning. And right there in the midst of a very suspicious-looking van and two fairly new trucks was the sheriff's car.

Finn parked and then leaned over the console to kiss Callie on the cheek. "Whatever it is, missing kids or feudin', we'll get through it together. Besides, I'm sure Verdic has it under control."

Callie pulled the stocking hat off and shook out her dark hair. She didn't have her makeup kit from her purse, so whatever the problem was, she'd have to face it with a windblown face and most likely a few bits of straw in her hair.

"You are beautiful," Finn said.

"You weren't supposed to know that I was fretting about facing people looking like this," she told him.

"We were closer than twins, Callie. We can read each other's minds. That's what kept us alive," he reminded her.

"Then thank you for the compliment. Let's go see what Martin has done now." Thank God that he couldn't really read her mind or he'd be running for the hills.

"What makes you think it's Martin? Maybe it's Verdie. She might be having a town meeting to discuss the Christmas program at church tomorrow."

"And that would include Orville?" Callie asked.

Finn held her hand tightly in his. "You never know what she might have up her sleeves."

Guns weren't drawn, and the six people already around the table were laughing and telling stories when Finn and Callie went inside. Her eyes went from Orville to Verdie and back around the circle.

"Martin?" she mouthed to Verdie.

"In his room, but he's fine. He's not sick anymore."

Polly waved at Finn. He let go of Callie's hand and waved back.

"Hello, Polly. What brings you out to Salt Draw?"

"Tryin' to help Verdie out," Polly said.

"Y'all pull up a chair, and we'll get down to business," Verdie said.

"Hot damn! Joe wants a drink," the bird said.

"Don't mind the bird." Verdie laughed. "He's crazy as hell, but he entertains me. I hated him at first, but he grows on a person. I wish I'd gotten one like him years ago."

Finn seated Callie first and then sat down so close to her that their thighs were plastered together. "Verdie?" Callie asked.

"Okay, I'll introduce the bunch of you. I forget that everyone don't know everybody else. This here is Amanda. She's the lady from the social services in Gainesville. She's the one who handles the kids staying with the Laytons. That's Arlan Layton and his wife, Beth. Y'all know Orville. We've got ourselves a problem, and we can't go no further until I get your opinion, Finn."

Callie laid a hand on Finn's thigh and squeezed. She'd known that this group of people had nothing to do with a church program.

Finn covered her hand with his. "It's got to do with the kids, right, Verdie?"

"They are hiding out in Martin's room right now. Probably been there since last night. Amanda drove out here on slick roads so she could take them to the group home, but she's agreed to let the kids stay with us through the holidays if you are willing. It's your ranch, so it's your decision," Verdie said.

"And after the holidays?" Callie asked.

"Then they'd still go to separate homes unless a qualified one opens up that would be willin' to take in three kids," Amanda said. "This is a special arrangement that normally I wouldn't even consider, since you two haven't been vetted, but Polly vouches for Verdie, and she does the same for you all. Polly was my supervisor for years, and I'd trust her with my life, so her word is gold in my books."

"Could Callie and I talk about this in private for a few minutes?" Finn asked.

"Sure," Amanda answered.

His hand on the small of her back normally would have melted her into a boiling pot of desire, but she was so worried about those children that she was quivering inside. Poor little darlings had walked for more than a mile in freezing-cold weather. Had Martin even managed to get food into the room for them that morning?

Finn shut the door to his bedroom, sat down in an overstuffed rocker, and pulled her down in his lap.

"Wind call, Brewster," he said. "Give me the news fast because this is about to happen."

"Lots of dust blowing. Wind looks like a tornado

bearing down on us, and visibility is less than five feet, sir," she said.

"That mean we should call it off? Or can you see past it to the target?"

She laid her head on his chest. "I can feel the fear of four little kids in that room, Finn. We cannot turn them away. I'd worry the rest of my life if they were split up because we didn't do our best to keep them together. And Verdie has gone out on a limb for us, and…"

His lips found hers in a sweet kiss that stopped the words and eased some of the fear in her heart.

"Stop worrying, darlin'." He broke away and gazed deeply into her eyes. "We're going to take in three kids. Never was a doubt in my mind, but I would never make a decision like that without asking my partner."

"Martin needs to be punished for not coming to us. I know he told them to come here and he'd hide them. I'm not sure how, but he did it," she whispered.

"He will be. I had two brothers and a sister. He's going to have to share that room, share the bathroom, and put up with a sister. It won't be like playing with them at school. He'll be instantly thrown into a sibling situation."

"And after the holidays?" she asked.

"We'll start the process to get certified for foster care. If they're having trouble finding a suitable home, maybe they'll get the ball moving faster."

"You haven't even met those kids," she said.

"No, and I don't expect every day to be perfect. It wasn't where I grew up. But we'll do the best we can with what we've got to work with that day."

"You are amazing," she said.

"We're both guilty of taking in strays. And before you say a word, I know these kids aren't dogs and cats. We might have to beg Verdie to stick around to help us with the new crew, but something tells me she won't give us much sass about it," Finn said.

He tipped her chin up, and his blue eyes drifted shut as his lips found hers in a harder, more demanding kiss. One hand tangled itself into her black hair; the other found its way up under her sweatshirt, making long, lazy circles on her back. He moved from her lips to her eyelids and her earlobe, where he whispered, "You think we've made them wait long enough?"

She giggled. "You didn't bring me in here to talk, did you?"

"I knew what you'd say and what we'd agree on. I wanted to touch you and hold you, Callie, to reassure you that everything was going to be all right, and this was a perfect excuse."

Her sudden intake of breath sounded like a faint sneeze. "You are a rascal."

He stood up but kept his arms around her. "That would be the pot calling the kettle black for sure."

His words made her knees go weak. "Now we'll have four kids and Verdie in the house. You think we'll ever have a moment to ourselves?"

"Oh, honey, with what I've got planned and what I know right now, it's not going to be a problem at all. Matter of fact, I'm thinking I just got handed a special Christmas present." He grinned.

"Then let's go tell them we've made a decision," she said.

Conversation came to a screeching halt when Finn

and Callie were back in the kitchen. Six sets of eyes were on them when they sat down, and Amanda asked, "Have you made a decision?"

"We'd love to have the children here, but we do have a question. What would it take for us to become foster parents so they can stay past the holidays? We'll be attached to them by then, and it'll be even tougher to see them leave," Finn said.

"It would be unusual but not impossible. You'd have to be the primary foster parent, but with Callie as hired help and Verdie as a nanny figure, there's a good chance it could work," Amanda said. "We can take it a step at a time. The first is settling them in for the next three weeks. Would you be willing to keep them until after the New Year?"

"We are." Finn nodded.

"We thought Amanda would be taking them from here, so we brought their things," Beth said. "I've enjoyed having them, but since you are taking them, we are planning on leaving first thing in the morning. All we have to do is load up the truck. We sold our home as is, so we don't have to move furniture."

Callie laid her hand on Beth's. "We'll take good care of them, I promise."

"I know you will. Y'all have got your work cut out for you. We were their sixth home, so they don't trust too good."

"We'll give it our best," Callie said.

"I'll help you unload," Finn offered.

"Appreciate it." Arlan shoved his arms into the sleeves of his coat, which had been hanging on the back of his chair.

"Verdie, if you'll show me where the kids are hiding, I need to visit with them," Amanda said.

"So my services aren't needed anymore?" Orville asked.

"I guess not," Polly said. "Me and you can get on down the road about our business. These folks can finish up the process here."

"I'm glad it's turning out this way. A family doesn't need to be separated during the holidays. Finn O'Donnell, you are a good man, and, Callie, you are one of a kind." Orville shot another brilliant smile her way.

Finn grinned. "Thank you, Sheriff. Next time you come back to Salt Draw, maybe it won't be on official business."

"I hope not."

"Verdie, keep me posted on the news out here. I've got a feelin' you are going to be pretty busy with four kids underfoot." Polly laughed.

"Best Christmas present I've got yet. Just think of all the bossin' I get to do. Come on, Amanda, and, Callie, you and Finn best come along, too. We'll just get the introductions done all at once," Verdie said.

Verdie threw open the door to find a kid on each bed, books in hands and eyes bugging out as four adults paraded into the room with them.

"Don't put Martin in jail," Olivia said. "He was just helping me. I don't want to lose my brothers. They're all I have for family."

"And we don't want to lose Olivia. She takes care of us," Ricky said.

"Callie, I just couldn't let them go away in different homes, so please don't be mad at me," Martin said.

"It's okay, kids." Verdie pushed her way into the room. "We've made a deal, but you have to hear Amanda out before it's final. Don't cry, and, little dark-haired boy, don't you dare throw up on that pillow. You're going to have to sleep on it tonight."

The dark-haired boy nodded. "I'm Ricky and my brother is Adam and my sister is Olivia, and I do feel sick to my stomach."

"Ricky is going to sleep here tonight?" Olivia asked.

"Finn O'Donnell has agreed to let you kids stay here on Salt Draw Ranch until the holidays are over. He's asked about being your foster parent, but there's a lot of red tape we'll have to take care of. But right now, you get to stay in Burnt Boot if you promise me you will not run away again," Amanda said.

"For real?" Olivia asked.

"Yes, and you can thank this lady for making it happen."

Verdie nodded at Olivia. "Martin calls me Granny Verdie, so y'all can, too, if you want to."

"I can't believe it," Adam gasped.

Verdie went on, "This is Callie and Finn. We live here with Pistol and Shotgun the dogs and Angel the cat and Joe the bird. Any of y'all allergic to animals?"

"A bird? For real? Can I see it?" Olivia climbed down from the top bunk and hugged Verdie first and then Callie. "Thank you so much for not letting them put us in different places. We'll be good, we promise."

She gave Ricky and Adam a long stare. "Well?"

"We promise, too," they said in unison.

"What we want you to be is happy," Callie said around the lump in her throat.

"And to promise us as well as Amanda that you won't run away again," Finn said.

"We promise. We won't never ever run away from here," Olivia said.

Chapter 18

FINN HELD OUT A HAND TO THE LITTLE BOY ON THE bottom bunk. "Welcome to Salt Draw. Why don't the bunch of you come out to the dining room and tell the Laytons good-bye. And then we'll go over the house rules."

Ricky had a good firm grip for a little boy, and so did the kid on the top bunk. Olivia's hand was a bit shaky but then tears were flowing down her little cheeks.

"Mr. Finn, thank you for letting us stay here," she said.

"You are very welcome. When Martin came here last week, we didn't go over house rules because Callie took care of that part of his life. But I thought we'd get things straight before you unpack your things," Finn said.

"Our things?" Adam asked.

"That's right. The Laytons brought your stuff, and it's waiting for you in the living room," Finn answered. "Callie and I will show you the way. Did you come in by the front door?"

"No, sir, by the window," Ricky said.

"I see." Finn smiled.

Beth and Arlan Layton hugged the kids, but it wasn't a tearful parting. The Laytons had heavy hearts because of her illness. The kids felt awkward because they'd run away, so it was a quick good-bye, and then they were alone in the living room.

"That is the biggest, prettiest, awesomest tree I've ever seen." Olivia's eyes darted from tree to decorations and back to the tree.

"Do those dogs bite?" Ricky hid behind Martin.

"Naw, they're good dogs. Angel, that's the cat, climbs the tree, so we have to watch her, but the dogs are fun, especially Shotgun. Pistol, now he likes to lie by the fire and bark when strangers come around, but Shotgun will go out in the yard and play anytime you want to." Martin's voice was full of joy and pride.

"Shit, Verdie! Don't burn the cookies!" Joe pranced from one end of his perch to the other, saying every phrase he knew, then starting all over.

"That's a big bird. I was expecting a little bitty one like a canary. And he says dirty words," Olivia said with wide eyes.

"But he's so pretty," Adam said. "Does he ever fly around in the house?"

"Not anymore," Finn said.

"Okay, kids, all four of you can sit on the sofa and listen to Finn," Verdie said. "I expect his rules won't be hard to obey, but you need to hear them."

The kids sat down and looked up at Finn, three with big round blue eyes and Martin with his dark brown eyes.

Finn pushed the coffee table back and kneeled in front of them so his eyes would be on their level. "Rule number one is that you really have three bosses in this house, but we're all three pretty fair about things. Verdie is a grandma, nanny, mama, and babysitter, all rolled into one, and you have to obey her. Callie and I are like parents, so you have to mind us as well. Rule number two is that you have to make your own beds before school in the morning, remember to brush your teeth, and pick up after yourselves. You boys will bunk in with Martin. Showers begin at eight thirty every night. Bedtime is at nine, reading for thirty minutes, and lights out at nine thirty. Miz Olivia will have her own room right next door."

"Callie?" Verdie asked.

"Will be moving to the other wing so that the kids can be close together," Finn said.

Verdie smiled. "Why, thank you, Finn, for including me with the kids."

"Unless you want to move, then Olivia can have your room," he said.

"I can stay in the room with the boys. There are four beds in there, and me and the boys are used to sharing," Olivia said.

Verdie patted her on the shoulder. "Girls need their own space. I'd move you in with me, but I'm not turning out my lights at nine thirty. And I was very serious when I thanked Finn. I'm tickled to be on the wing with you kids. It'll be like it was when I was a child. You okay with the move, Callie?"

"Yes, ma'am. I could sure use some help from these big strapping boys getting my things out of that room and into my new one. Olivia, you'll have to put up with Angel coming in your room at night. She's been sleeping on the end of my bed," Callie said.

"Is that all?" Martin asked.

"That's the whole list of rules," Finn answered.

"It's sure a short list. You didn't say anything about doing homework when we get home or nothing about chores."

"Those things are your responsibility and don't fall under house rules," Finn said.

"Look, Olivia, mistletoe." Adam pointed toward a sprig hung in the archway between the living room and dining room.

"Well, I'm not kissing you, so don't go stand under it," Martin declared. "When I get big enough to kiss girls, it's going to be Sally." He blushed scarlet.

"Didn't intend for those words to come out, did you?" Finn chuckled.

Martin shook his head.

"Well, I wouldn't kiss you either. I'm going to fall in love with Harry when I'm sixteen. But not until then. Kissing you would be like kissing a brother." Olivia skewered up her face.

"Well, I'm real glad we got that settled," Callie said.

Finn took her hand and led her to the spot right under the mistletoe, picked her up until her feet were six inches off the floor, and kissed her right there in front of them all.

"Well, how about that?" Verdie grinned.

"It's like a movie," Olivia sighed.

"Didn't want to waste the chance." Finn grinned as he set Callie on her feet.

She tiptoed and kissed him on the chin. "Neither did I."

⸻

Finn had broken the ice by kissing her in front of them. The boys' noses were snarled up like they'd smelled something horrible. Olivia was wide eyed, and Verdie was still smiling. The awkward moment had passed.

"I like cats, but we never could have pets in the places we've lived," Olivia said shyly, changing the subject.

"I bet by the end of the day that Angel will let you hold her, and she'll probably sleep on your bed," Callie said.

"This all"—Olivia swept the whole room with her arms—"feels like a dream."

"I expect all four of you best get on in the bathroom and wash up for dinner. Since we had all this to settle this morning, we're having grilled cheese sandwiches and tomato soup, but supper will be fried chicken," Verdie said and quickly wiped away a tear.

"Y'all got any questions?" Finn asked.

"You sure those dogs won't bite us?" Ricky asked.

"I'm sure," Martin answered. "Let's go wash up. I'm starving, and I love cheese sandwiches."

"Hands. Bathroom," Verdie said.

Martin hugged Finn. "Thank you."

"You are very welcome, son," Finn said.

"Y'all come on. I'll show you where the bathroom is, and after dinner, us boys are going to help Finn clean up the barn if you think you're big enough," Martin said.

"Anything you can do, I can," Adam declared.

"Me too," Ricky said right behind them.

"Well, that's done," Callie whispered.

"Martin almost made me cry," Finn said.

"Big old mean soldier like you?" Callie asked.

"Big old mean soldier has a soft heart," Verdie said. "Y'all can help me get some food on the table. Them kids need something warm in their stomachs. I know Beth Layton was good to them, but I swear them boys look like they could use fattenin' up."

"Which brings us to the second question of the day," Callie said.

Verdie was behind the refrigerator door taking out butter, cheese, and milk. "Which is?" she asked.

Finn had started toward the pantry for tomato soup. "If it works out for us to keep these kids past the holidays, would you stay on as the nanny?"

Her head popped up over the door. "Hell no!"

"Hell no! Hell no!" Joe filled the house with several wolf whistles in between repeating what Verdie said.

"If you don't shut up, I'm getting out the tomato cage and the apron," Verdie threatened.

Callie stopped in her tracks. "Finn would pay you."

"It ain't money."

"Then what is it?" Finn asked.

"If I can't be the granny, I ain't stayin'. I want the title, not the damned old money. I got more of that than I can ever spend. You let me be the granny, and I'll tell the funny farm to give my room to someone else."

Callie let out a whoosh of air. "You scared me, Verdie McElroy."

"Just keepin' y'all on your toes. This is my home. I figured it out after I left it, and God has seen fit to give me a second chance at livin' here. I'll be glad to stay on and help you run this ranch, Finn. If you'd have told me you needed some help, I wouldn't have ever left," she said.

"Sure funny how a man's life can do a hundred-and-eighty-degree turn in a few days, ain't it?" he said.

"Patrick used to say that it was a good thing we didn't know what the next five minutes would bring in lots of cases."

Four little kids coming down the hall sounded like a herd of elephants. Martin led the line and held out his hands for inspection.

Callie looked at the tops, the palms, and then the nails. "Good job, soldier. Next?"

Adam held his out his hands and she did the same, all the way down the line to Olivia. The girl's hair was in need of a good shampooing and application of conditioner. It was thick and straight as a board, hung in her eyes, and needed a cut or a shaping. Callie took her small hands in hers and examined them like she had the boys.

"Good job, soldier. All four of you can sit at the table until we get the food ready."

Martin's smiles and the tone of his voice as the kids all talked at once was music to her ears. She'd never seen him that happy, not even when the social services lady told them that he wouldn't have to go to foster care while Callie got guardianship papers in order.

Callie's new room was one door down the hall from Finn's with the old nursery across the hallway. The linen closet and bathroom were on the same side as the nursery. The little boys carried what they could, but Finn brought in her clothing and hung everything in the new closet.

Olivia was like a little girl with unlimited money in a candy store over the room that Callie vacated. Her meager possessions were lined up on the dresser and her Bible was on the nightstand. Her clothing took up less than a foot of space in the closet, and the shoes on her feet were all that she had. Amanda had said social services would send a check each month, but Callie had money saved, and she was determined the child would have a few things before the money arrived.

The moon hung in the sky outside her window that night like an omen telling Callie that everything was working out in every aspect of her life. She wrapped her arms around herself and stared at the patterns the lacy curtains made on the walls and ceiling as the moon slowly rose and clouds shifted back and forth across it.

Her new bed was king-sized and felt like it covered an acre of ground. There was one of those tall chests in the corner like the one in Finn's room, a gold velvet rocker in the other corner, and a desk located where his fireplace was over in his room. Martin was all the way across the house from her. But he had Adam and Ricky in the bunkhouse, as they had started calling their room with him, Verdie across the hall, and Olivia right next door.

A soft knock on her door drew her attention away from the moon, and she wondered what Verdie needed. Then she remembered that she'd locked the door. She crawled out of bed and scolded herself. What if Martin needed her? What if he had one of those bad dreams and they had to relocate to the sofa for the rest of the night? He'd wake up the whole house beating on her door.

She had barely gotten her feet on the floor when the closet door opened and there was Finn, or his ghost. She wasn't sure which it was for a split second as her heart did triple time and the adrenaline rush threatened to put her into flight mode. He'd told her good night at the door half an hour ago, and she'd locked it when she came into the room.

"What the hell?" she asked.

"I knocked." He smiled.

She looked from bedroom door to the closet and back again.

"I discovered it while I was hanging up your clothing. Evidently one of the former owners in this place liked to keep separate rooms, but they didn't want anyone to know. There is a secret door connecting my closet to yours. This place is full of tricks." He sat down in the rocker and patted his leg.

She took two steps, and he pulled her down into his lap, wrapped both arms around her slim body, and kick-started the chair into motion. The movement and his steady heartbeat soothed her nerves more than a shot of Jack could.

"Did I tell you about the secret closet behind the bookcase?"

"What's in it?"

"Booze."

"It wouldn't be as intoxicating as this." His lips found hers, and every sane thought flew right out the window, headed for the moon. "I was so damned excited when I found that door, but I wanted to surprise you, and then I had to wait until the kids were asleep. And they were too wound up to go to sleep. I made three trips to the kitchen and checked on them before I found them passed out," he whispered.

"I'm glad I didn't know, or I'd have been crazy. You think Verdie knows about the closet?"

"Hell, she might be the very one who had it installed,

but I'm not saying a word about it or she might make me nail the connecting door shut." He smiled. "Now, I'm going back to my room. I just came for a good-night kiss. I'm sure that will keep the nightmares away."

He tipped her chin up with his fist and tangled his fingers in her long, dark hair. His lips covered hers in a steamy kiss that left her legs feeling like rubber and her heart racing. He picked her up and gently laid her on the bed, kissed her softly on the nose, and left her lying there wanting more.

He was halfway across the room when he turned around, an evil grin on his face. "I heard that you and Betsy had a little problem at the store. I understand she's gunnin' for you since you humiliated her."

"She'd best bring a lot of ammo." Callie yawned.

After Finn went into the closet, she snuggled down under the covers and shut her eyes. She was almost asleep when the dream started. There was a small, swarthy boy in ragged clothing right outside the base. His face was frozen in terror, and he was whining, looking down at his feet and the land mine beneath them.

She sat straight up in bed, sweat dripping from her jawbone onto her nightshirt. She rubbed her eyes to get the visual to go away, but the muffled whining continued, and it was coming from Finn's bedroom. She padded across the room, through the closet, pushing back clothing until she found the next door, and then worked her way through jeans and shirts.

Shotgun raised his head when she stepped into the room, but he didn't growl when she headed straight for the bed. She threw back the covers and crawled in the bed with Finn, cradling his head against her shoulder.

She recognized the strange noise coming from Finn immediately. It was the haunting nightmares again. She'd wakened herself many times moaning just like that.

"Shhh, it's the bad dreams. It's not real," she whispered.

His eyes opened slowly.

"Callie?"

"Closet door, remember? What was going on in the dream?"

"There was a little girl with blue eyes in the school. She ran out at the same time I fired, and I knew she was dead."

"I dreamed of a little boy outside the base on a land mine. It's the children being here that brought it on, I'm sure," she said.

He pulled her close to his side. "Will we ever be normal again?"

"Normal is just a word. For us, this might be normal," she said.

"Stay with me a little while. You're the nightmare whisperer." His face was pressed into her hair now.

"Maybe it takes both of us to chase them away," she said.

"Callie, my precious Callie." His voice was low and hoarse when he propped up on one elbow and lowered his mouth to hers.

He slowly undressed her, removing her shirt, socks, and underpants. She didn't even notice where he tossed the pieces of clothing, because hot sensual kisses on every part of her body had erased all thoughts of anything but wild abandonment in Finn's arms.

He traced the outline of a moon pattern on her face.

"You are gorgeous, Callie Brewster." He bent low and kissed the tip of her nose.

Every nerve ending in her body hummed with want. She pressed her body tighter against his and ran a hand inside the thermal knit shirt that covered a bed of soft dark hair. She cupped his face with her hands and kissed him with so much raw passion that she felt like she was burning up.

"You are driving me insane, Finn O'Donnell," she gasped.

"Must be that full moon, because you're doing the same thing to me," he said.

Taking time to kiss her from lips to belly button, he continued on down her body and even kissed the soles of her feet, making her squirm and moan. Who would have thought that knees and feet and inner thighs could be erotic zones? Everywhere he touched with his hands or his lips felt like a blowtorch next to her body. She wanted him to stop; she wanted him to never stop.

"You are making me bat-shit crazy!" She tugged his shirt up over his head and gave it a toss into the darkness. His pajama pants followed, and she stared at his nude body in awe.

"My God, you look like a Greek god in the moonlight," she whispered.

"Darlin', Greek gods do not have black hair. They're all blonds," he said.

"Darlin', I'm telling this story, and you are a Greek god in it." She pushed him back on the pillows and straddled his waist. She'd had a few relationships but never had she been so uninhibited, never had it felt so right as it did right then.

"Do Greek gods do this?" He rolled on top of her and with a powerful thrust began a rocking motion.

"In my dreams they do." She arched against him and nothing mattered but satisfying whatever it was that was between them. She dug her nails into his back, and he landed a hard kiss on her lips, his tongue probing her mouth, kisses turning him on as much as the ultra-hot sex. She reached first one climax and then two before he finally buried his face in her neck and said her name in a hoarse drawl.

"Oh. My. Sweet. Lord," she gasped.

"If every time gets more intense, we'll burn out the relationship," he said hoarsely.

"But what a way to go." She nestled down into the crook of his arm when he shifted his weight to one side. He kissed her eyelids, her forehead, and then her mouth, and they slept until the first rays of daylight drifted through the window.

She awoke to find Finn staring down at her, a smile on his face.

"I'm going to love having you this close every night."

"We won't be like a flash in the pan and fizzle out. Promise me we won't, Finn."

"I promise." He stretched out beside her. "We're in this for the long haul, darlin'. We've got four kids to raise."

"And a granny to take care of in her old age," Callie said.

"But right now, in this room, there is only the two of us."

She flipped her body over on top of him and guided him into her. "Now there's one of us," she whispered.

He rolled with her, and her legs went around him. Her hands looped around his neck and brought his lips to hers in a fierce kiss that held the promise of a future together as they made love like Callie had never known. It was more than sex, more than gratification, and words could never explain the warmth that penetrated her heart. She hoped it would never end and that this was just the beginning of a lifetime of memories.

"Oh. My. Blessed. Soul," she said when they reached satisfaction at the same time.

Finn collapsed for a few seconds then propped up on an elbow. Still gasping for air, he managed to kiss her passionately.

"I feel like I've defied gravity and I'm floating," she panted.

"I'm right there with you," he said.

"I'm going now, Finn. We've got four kids to get ready for church," she said.

He hugged her tighter. "You know I had a crush on you over there, but…"

"I didn't know. But I'll confess that I had one on you, too."

"What in the hell was the matter with us?" He grinned.

Chapter 19

POLLY, GLADYS, VERDIE, OLIVIA, RICKY, ADAM, MARTIN, Callie, and Finn—that's the way they were lined up down the church pew. Two weeks before that day Finn had been getting ready to move to Burnt Boot and was resigned to spending a winter alone with only Shotgun for company. He'd gone to church with his parents and his brothers' and sister's families that Sunday in Comfort, Texas. Last week, he had attended right there in Burnt Boot with Callie and Martin. This week he had the better part of a pew with him when he walked into the church that morning.

"If we grow by this much another week, I'll have to build another wing on the house," he leaned over and whispered in Callie's ear.

"Just don't move me out of my new room. I like that secret passage," she whispered back.

It was Finn's turn to blush, and there wasn't a damn thing he could do about the heat filling his neck and face. But he didn't have to suffer alone. He cupped his hand over Callie's ear and said, "I liked waking up to a buck-naked woman in my arms this morning."

Instant fire turned Callie crimson from her hair roots to her fingertips. The visual his comment put in her mind, his breath on her neck; holy hell, neither of those things belonged in church.

She smoothed her denim skirt down over her thighs and immediately thought of his hands on her body and the blush deepened to a deeper scarlet. Thank God the preacher finally took the pulpit and announced that they would sing a hymn, or her pretty red Christmas sweater might have started to smoke.

Even then, she had to keep focused on the words in the hymnal because her eyes kept straying to the hands holding it and thinking unholy thoughts about what she'd like them to be doing.

When the song ended, the preacher said, "This morning's special program is our version of the Hanging of the Green. I'm turning the program over to Quaid Brennan, who serves as the Sunday school teacher for our teenage group."

A small group filed from the back of the church, singing "Mary, Did You Know?" She looked down the line of four little kids and tried to imagine Martin, Adam, and Ricky with changing voices and scruff on their faces. There they sat—two little dark-haired boys and one blond who would change drastically in the next three years.

Then there was Olivia, looking pretty in her little denim skirt and braids. Thank goodness Verdie had decided to French braid her hair that morning. It tamed that wily mop of blond hair and made Olivia feel pretty at the same time.

Quaid stood behind the pulpit as the group took their places in the choir section behind him. He talked about the wreath that one of the kids came forward to hang on the front of the pulpit. It was round, signifying the unending love of God in sending his son to earth. *Love,*

Callie thought. Just thinking the word twisted her heart up until it looked like Olivia's braid. Love for Martin; that was one thing. But love as in *falling in* was a whole different matter. To have a crush, to be half a consenting adult couple with a secret passage between bedrooms, that was something different than love. Love meant trusting with the whole heart. Callie didn't know if she or Finn could ever do that with their past history.

"You look like you just saw a ghost," Finn whispered. "Are you sick?"

"No, just letting my mind go where it has no business visiting," she said.

During the last ten minutes of the service, Callie crossed and uncrossed her legs, tried not to think of that last cup of coffee she had that morning, and for damn sure didn't let her mind wander to running water. If Quaid didn't end the program soon, she would have to do the pee-pee dance all the way down the aisle with Betsy Gallagher staring at her. She'd already gotten so many drop-dead looks that it was a wonder her bladder hadn't dried up like a prune.

The second the old guy delivering the benediction on the back row said "Amen," she dashed off to the ladies' room, leaving Finn to fend for himself. Maybe Verdie and the kids could protect him from the feuding bitches until she returned.

She had finished and was washing her hands when Honey and Betsy pushed open the door.

"Well, well, well." Betsy leaned against the door, holding it secure with her back. "Here's the hired hand who likes to do kinky things with women. She's into biting the same sex."

"I understand church is neutral ground," Callie said.

Honey leaned in to the mirror and fiddled with her eyebrows. "Neutral in that the Gallaghers and the Brennans can't fight each other. Nothing in the rule book says we can't fight outsiders."

"You sure you're up to that?" Callie smiled into her part of the mirror and filled the palm of her hand with soap at the same time. "Did Betsy tell you that I haven't had my rabies shots this year?"

"I don't talk to Betsy. I got my information from another source. I don't need a damned Gallagher tellin' me anything." Honey drew her hand back to deliver an open-handed slap right to Callie's face.

Callie flicked soap in Honey's face and stepped to one side as Honey crumbled in a heap in the floor, clawing at her eyes and squealing like a piglet between a rock and a hard place.

Betsy opened the door for Callie. "I don't like you and never will, but that was damned beautiful. See you later, Honey."

―――

"I liked church this morning," Olivia said on the way home.

"Can we start going to Sunday school?" Adam asked. "I want to be a part of that program when I'm old enough. I liked the story about the wreath."

"I liked the part where they all took an ornament and put it on the tree, and when the preacher plugged in the lights and it all lit up. It reminded me of our big tree at home," Ricky said.

Home. Kids adapted so much quicker than adults.

The pickup was cramped and full that morning with the four kids in the backseat and Callie between Finn and Verdie in the front. When they got to the ranch, it looked like the truck exploded, spitting kids and adults out of all four doors.

Martin's stomach growled loudly at the aroma of roast beef when he slung open the back door. "That smells like heaven," he said.

Verdie patted him on the hair and said, "You young'uns go on to your rooms and get changed into play clothes, then you can help me put it all on the table."

"Yes, ma'am." Olivia beamed.

Callie and Verdie reached for bibbed aprons at the same time, tossed the neck strings over their heads in unison, and tied each other's waist strings.

Family. Home. One week and one day since she and Martin showed up. Less than a week since Verdie had moved in. Only twenty-four hours since the three kids had arrived. But it seemed like they'd all been connected forever. She'd heard that miracles happened in December. Hearing the kids' giggles, Finn's whistling, and, oh my God, what was that?

Finn yelled from the living room. "Looks like Angel crawled out on a limb that was too little to support her. She's hightailed it toward Olivia's room with Pistol right behind her. Poor old boy was sleeping when the tree went down on top of him. He must've thought the world had come to an end."

"Oh, no!" Olivia slapped her hands over her cheeks. "Our beautiful tree. Oh, Miz Verdie…I mean Granny… I'm so sorry."

"Kids and pets." Verdie laughed. "Never a boring moment."

"But your precious ornaments," Callie almost cried.

"That had been in the attic for ten years because I didn't have kids and pets. I'll take the loss of the whole lot of them to have kids in the house again," Verdie told her. "Come on, boys, help Finn set this thing up. Olivia, you get the paper towels so we can clean up the water that spilled from the pan. And would you look at this. Only one ornament is broken. Now that's a miracle for sure. Set it up easy now. That's good. I believe they're all going to hang just right. Did bust a string of cranberries." She wrapped the two ends around branches and stood back. "There, now it's perfect again. Finn, you might put some water in the pan. And Olivia, honey, throw those wet paper towels in the trash can."

"You are amazing," Callie said.

Verdie blew off the compliment with the wave of a hand. "We've got dinner to get on the table. Olivia, you and Martin get down seven plates. Adam, you and Ricky get seven forks, knives, and spoons and meet me at the table. Finn, you can slice the roast soon as Callie finishes using the electric knife for the bread."

The house phone rang, and Verdie reached around the doorjamb to grab it. She put her hand over the receiver and said, "It's Polly. Y'all go on and do what I told you. I'll just be a minute."

Verdie listened for a few minutes, then giggled. "Imagine that. Why don't y'all come visit sometime this week, and we'll see if we can straighten all this out before they go to settin' fire to things. Bye now."

Verdie patted Callie on the shoulder on her way back into the kitchen. "What was it that you did before you came to Salt Draw, Callie?"

"I worked in a gym and taught a class in self-protection to women. Lots of times it was battered women," she said.

"Well, I guess you showed Honey that you don't need a gun to protect yourself, didn't you?" Verdie laughed.

"What?" Finn asked.

"Later. I'll tell you about it after a while," Callie said with a wink.

Callie assigned seats around the table—Finn at the head with Callie to his right, Olivia between her and Verdie, the three boys across from them. The moment the kids sat down, they bowed their heads.

Finn looked at Callie, who looked at Verdie.

"This is your house, Finn. You'll either take care of grace or tell us who is saying it," she said.

"I'll give the blessing today," Finn said. He reached for Callie's hand and the gesture went around the table until they were one family circle. He bowed his head and blessed the food in a couple of short sentences.

"Wow!" Adam dropped his brother's hand and Martin's at the same time. "I like your blessing. Arlan prayed for hours, until we thought we'd starve plumb to death just sittin' there waitin'."

Verdie laughed. "Used to have a man like that in church. We all wanted to string him up by the damn rafters when the preacher asked him to do the benediction."

Callie took the platter of roast from Finn's hands. "Which one? The preacher for asking or the long-winded man?"

"Both of them," Verdie said. "And I can say *damn*, but you had better not let me hear you sayin' bad words, or you'll be doin' chores on Sunday afternoon rather than going outside to play." She punctuated each word with a fork toward a child.

"But, Granny, it's too muddy to go play outside," Ricky said.

"If it's muddy, can we cuss? And we're supposed to call her Granny Verdie." Martin had an impish expression on his face.

"Hell no!" Verdie said. "Since it's too muddy to go outside, I vote we get out the Monopoly game and the bunch of us play all afternoon. And Granny is just fine or Granny Verdie is just fine. Either one works."

"You mean it?" Olivia asked. "I love that game."

"I love roast and carrots," Ricky said. "And I love green beans with bacon in them just like this. Man, you are a good cook, Granny."

"Well, I love this bread," Adam piped up. "I ain't never eat bread this good. Did you make it, Granny, or did the angels in heaven send it down here for us?"

"He's a charmer, Callie. We'll have to watch him closely." Verdie smiled.

"I still think this is all a dream," Olivia said. "Oh, look, Angel is under the table and so is Pistol. They look hungry, Granny."

"Yuk! Joe needs a drink." The bird spit and sputtered while he sharpened his beak on the perch.

"We don't feed the animals at the table, and Joe is not getting a drink," Verdie said. "What we are going to do is start around the table, beginning with Finn, and we're going to say two things that we really want for Christmas, because tomorrow before the roads get any worse and while you kids are in school, me and Callie are going to town to do some shopping."

"Ah, shucks!" Martin said. "Payday was Friday, and we haven't got the money yet, but I know Finn is good for it, and I wanted to buy some presents, too."

"Payday?" Adam asked.

"Each kid who works on the ranch gets a paycheck on Friday. It's not a lot of money, and you have to put half of it, in savings, but the rest is yours to save up or spend however you want," Finn explained.

"Are you serious?" Adam asked.

"You can keep my money if you'll just let us live here," Ricky said. "I like that bunkhouse room and havin' my own bed and all them books in there and food like this."

Callie drank half a glass of tea, trying to get the lump in her throat to go down, but it was in vain. Finn laid a hand on her knee and finally spoke up, but his voice was hoarse with emotion. "Well, son, it's like this. Good ranch hands are hard to come by, so I pay twenty dollars a week and room and board. But ten has to go into your savings account, which Callie will set up for you. There's two Fridays between now and Christmas. I reckon that would give you about twenty dollars total to spend if you wanted to do some shopping the Monday before Christmas."

"I'll be a good ranch hand," Ricky said seriously. "But I could work for a lot less since you're throwin' in room and board."

"Me too," Adam said.

"Are girls ranch hands?" Olivia asked.

"Yes, they are," Verdie said. "Now pass me that bread, Ricky. And, Finn, send the butter down here. I'm itching to get into that game of Monopoly."

Callie touched Finn's knee under the table. "Are you going to play?"

"No, ma'am, I'm having my Sunday afternoon nap. How about you?"

"Sunday nap sounds wonderful." She smiled.

"Old people take naps," Martin piped up from Finn's left.

Verdie sent the bread on around the table. "Not this old person. She's going to whip four little whippersnappers at Monopoly and try to keep the cat from climbing the Christmas tree again. I've got some livin' to take care of."

Chapter 20

CALLIE REMOVED A QUILT FROM THE RACK UNDER THE window and curled up under it on the bed in her room. It wasn't long until her closet door opened and Finn padded barefoot across the floor. She held the quilt up for him, and he crawled in with her, pulled her into his arms, and kissed the top of her head.

"You smell wonderful, like fresh air and vanilla ice cream," he said.

"That would be because I stepped out on the front porch for a minute, and I wear warm vanilla sugar perfume," she said. "You smell like Stetson, and let me see..." She kissed him soundly on the lips, letting her tongue slide between his lips. "And sweet tea and roast with a little bit of chocolate cake thrown in for sexiness."

His blue eyes sparkled, and she realized that something was different.

"What?" he asked.

She raised an eyebrow.

"I can tell when something is on your mind," he said. "We didn't just meet a couple of weeks ago, Callie. We've known each other for years."

"Want me to speak freely, sir?"

"Yes, please, Brewster."

"The anger at Lala is gone."

Finn kissed her on the forehead. "I realized last night before I came through the secret door that I had moved on and the anger was gone. I couldn't stop smiling all day because I'm so damn happy."

She laid her head on his chest and ran her hands under his shirt. She'd never grow tired of feeling his skin under her hands, of kissing him and sinking into his blue eyes.

"Okay, now what?" she asked.

"I was thinking about a nap."

"Right now?"

He rolled on top of her and pinned her arms above her head with his fingers tangled in hers. He bent forward and claimed her lips in a hard kiss that answered her question without another word. He moved from her mouth to that soft spot in the curve of her neck. He damn sure knew his way around the female body, and she damn sure enjoyed every second of it.

"Got a house full of kids out there," she whispered.

"So we'll be quiet," he said. "Besides, they're in the kitchen, and they're making enough noise to raise the roof."

"Then what are you waiting for?"

"Might be easier if we weren't dressed," he answered.

She pushed him off, crawled out of bed, and hurriedly dropped all her clothing on the floor. His eyes never left her body during the undressing process. Combined with the heat from his hands on her body and the tingle of his fingers entwined with hers, her hands shook as she pushed her underpants down to the floor.

"You are beautiful in the moonlight, but you are absolutely breathtaking in the sunlight, Callie." He slid over the bed and quickly undressed.

Her arms went around his neck, and with a little hop, her legs were firmly wrapped around his waist. His big rough hands cupped her bottom as he sat down on the bed. In one swift roll, she was underneath him and he was already sinking inside her.

She buried her face in his shoulder and tasted the remnants of his shaving lotion and the delicious part that was just plain old Finn O'Donnell. "It's a good thing we didn't know each other like this over there."

"I know," he said softly. "We would have never gotten a single mission done."

Talk stopped.

The rhythm took over with every hormone in her body crying out for release. He took her to the top of a high cliff several times, but he didn't allow her to tumble over the side into that cool body of water waiting at the bottom. Her body was an electric heater, and he held the remote control. He'd switch it to hot, then back to warm, only to jack it up to scorching hot, and then finally she grabbed the imaginary remote, arched against him, tangled her hands in his thick dark hair, nipped his lip, and said his name in a muffled scream.

"God almighty, Callie." He collapsed on her.

They were both panting in a rasp when he rolled to one side and took her with him in a tight embrace. "My knees may never work again," he said hoarsely.

"Mine either," she said.

And then they slept that deep sleep reserved for babies and consenting adults who have worn their bodies out with hot sex.

Snow still lingered on the patches of ground in the deep shade, but for the most part it had melted. Finn and the boys changed the tire on the old truck, and he showed them how to put a piece of wood under the back tires so they wouldn't spin any farther down into the mud. Then he let them ride in the back of the truck back to the house, where they all gathered the eggs and then helped him muck out the stables.

"Isn't this a morning job?" Martin asked.

"Can be, but since my ranch hands have to go to school in the morning, I figured maybe we'd turn it into an evening job. We'll shovel out the stalls, put fresh hay in, groom the horses, and then saddle them up for a twenty-minute ride around this part of the ranch. They haven't been exercised every day like they should be. Pretty soon I'll turn them out to pasture, and they'll get plenty of running. Then you can rub them down and feed them," Finn said. "While you do that, I'll go out to the barn and take care of the milking."

"You mean we get to ride?" Adam said.

"And we get paid to do it?" Ricky said with wide eyes.

"I'll lead the horses out. A saddle is pretty heavy, so I'll help you get the horses rigged up to ride when I get done," he said.

"I only ever rode a horse one time," Adam admitted.

"It's okay. We'll all be learning how to ride. I ain't rode a real horse either, but I bet we'll do all right. We're cowboys," Martin said. "Come on. I'll show you where the shovels and the wheelbarrow are kept."

Finn had never seen three little boys clean faster or harder than those kids did. The stalls were spotless by the time he returned with the brushes from the tack room.

Martin set down a three-legged milking stool and be damned if Rebel stood still and let the kid brush his coat.

Adam balanced on the bottom rung of a stall and Glory's muscles rippled at every brush stroke.

Ricky found a five-gallon bucket, turned it upside down, and was using it to brush tangles from Miss Mary's mane. The tamest of all the horses, the old black mare looked like she'd fallen in love with the kid.

"Well, I'll be triple damned," he said. "They're all three naturals."

When he settled the boys in the saddle and gave them a few basic instructions about how to use the reins to guide them, he found out real quick that they might be naturals with a brush, but they needed some serious training in the saddle.

Martin was the first to slide right out of the saddle, landing in a mud puddle and soaking his whole upper body in icy water the color of chocolate milk. Finn sent him straight to the house.

Adam lasted five minutes longer, and when he tumbled off the horse, he landed in a pile of fresh cow crap. Straight to the house he went, too.

He tied Rebel to the barn door and slung a leg up in Glory's saddle. The big black horse recognized his rider and pranced around in the yard for twenty minutes, strutting in front of Rebel, who voiced his disapproval every two minutes.

Ricky didn't fall off, but he carefully kept Miss Mary moving in wide circles, letting her have the lead most of the time. He sat as straight as he could in the saddle while Finn exercised both of the other horses and then just sat there inside the barn while Finn unsaddled the other two.

"You can get down now, son," Finn said.

"I don't know how and it's a long way down and I don't want to fall," Ricky said honestly.

Finn strolled over to the boy, picked him off the horse like he was a feather pillow, and set him on the ground.

"My legs feel funny," Ricky said.

"They will every time you ride," Finn told him.

"Do yours?" Ricky asked.

"Oh, yeah, they do. You think you can rub Miss Mary down if I unsaddle her?"

"Yes, sir. I'll work 'til dark if you want me to."

"I reckon by the time we get these horses fed, we'll be done for the night."

"Finn, if we're still here in the summertime and I used my own money that I save up, do you reckon I could buy a lamb to show at the stock show? I always wanted to be in 4H, but I never could have an animal."

"I'm sure that would be possible. What would you think about showing a steer? We've already got lots of those on the ranch," Finn asked.

"I'd like that real good, but I'm not big like you. I don't think I could control one of them in the show ring, but I think I could train up a sheep and then when I got to be a big cowboy like you, I could show a steer," Ricky said.

"Sounds like a good plan to me," Finn said.

If he had to move heaven and earth and hock the ranch, he planned on keeping those kids at Salt Draw until he had them raised. In just two days, the whole bunch of them had flat-out stolen his heart.

But Callie was the biggest thief of all.

Olivia danced around the kitchen table. "I love my braids. Can I have them for school tomorrow?"

"You sure can. I was thinking maybe we'd take you to the beauty shop and have your hair trimmed and maybe thinned," Callie said.

Olivia stopped. "Please don't cut it off. I've wanted long hair all my life, but all the places where I lived didn't want to help me with it. If I could just have braids like this, it could grow long, and I'm learnin' how to brush it myself."

"I'll help her," Verdie said. "We might have to get up fifteen minutes early, but that ain't no big deal. Come on over here and get these bowls and set the table for supper."

"It does look pretty in braids, and when it's pulled back from your face, your eyes just shine," Callie said.

"Really? You think my eyes are pretty?" Olivia asked.

"Pretty, damn pretty." Joe's wolf whistle was long and drawn out.

"Of course. They're gorgeous." Callie hugged her. "Even Joe thinks so."

"I'm so mad, I could spit tacks." Martin threw himself on the sofa. He'd changed out of his wet clothes, taken a shower, washed the mud from his hair, and was now wearing pajamas. "I can't believe that Ricky stayed on that horse, and me and Adam both fell off."

Shotgun crawled up beside him and laid his head on Martin's lap. The boy stroked his fur from the tip of his nose down his backbone to his tail and then started all over again.

"At least you fell in mud. I'm glad I hadn't had my supper. It would have come right up the way I smelled.

That cow stuff is worse smelling than what we shoveled out of the stalls."

Martin scooted down to give Adam room to sit down. "You want something real bad? You ought to fall in pig crap."

Callie noticed that Adam's pajamas were faded and a couple of sizes too big. She started a mental list of things they needed before the Christmas holidays. Pajamas and shoes were at the top.

"Pigs." Olivia stopped in her tracks. "I want a pig to show in the stock show."

"How about a lamb?" Verdie asked.

Olivia shook her head. "I read *Charlotte's Web*, and I want a pig. Not a black one but a white one like Wilbur, so when it's all cleaned up, it almost looks pink."

"They stink. You remember when we went to that farmer's place on a field trip when we lived with the Crowder family? Remember how bad them pigs smelled?" Adam yelled from the living room.

"Animals stink. That's just the way of it, and I'm going to save my money for a pig," Olivia said.

Verdie patted Olivia on the back. "I bet you could train a pig to do tricks in the show ring, Olivia. We'll have to see if the Brennans will part with one of their Poland China piglets next spring, but Adam is right about the smell."

"Hey, where are you guys? Guess what! Finn says I can buy a lamb and keep it on the ranch, and someday when I'm big like he is, I can show a steer at the stock show." Ricky came through the kitchen more animated than Callie had seen him yet.

Finn slipped an arm around her waist and squeezed.

"We've got to keep them, Callie. I'm already attached to the critters."

"We talkin' about Angel and Pistol or the kids?"

"The whole lot of them. Verdie included. A ranch is just dirt without kids and animals, even if they knock over Christmas trees and fall in mud and cow shit. But it needs a good woman, too."

"You callin' me a good woman, or are you going to put an ad in the newspaper for one?" she asked.

"Open that closet door later on tonight, and we'll discuss that," he whispered.

Chapter 21

THE AIR WAS SO CRISP THAT IT MADE ITS WAY THROUGH THE heaviest coats to chill Callie to the bone. She worried that Verdie would freeze as they dashed from the truck into the Western-wear store not far from the outlet mall. Finn held the door for her and Verdie, and the familiar smell of leather, starched denim, and cedar paneling filled her nose. Christmas carols played through a couple of speakers attached to the wall above the boots, a green jar candle burned on the counter, and folks bustled around the racks. Martin would love this store. So would the other three kids. She could picture Olivia in a show ring all dolled up in that cute little pink shirt and that blinged-out pink belt with the rhinestone-studded buckle.

"This is my Christmas present." Verdie stopped beside a round display of purses, wallets, key rings, and belts.

"What? That fancy purse?" Callie asked.

"No, just getting to shop for presents. I haven't done this in years. Even before Patrick died, we got to where we just sent gift cards to the grandkids. We didn't know what they liked, what sizes they wore, or even what kind of music they listened to. And truth be told right here and now, Patrick said he wasn't buying that shit that sounded like a truckload of squealing hogs collided with a truckload of china dishes."

Finn chuckled. "That's what my grandpa says."

"Well, let's get to it," Verdie said. "I'm buying the kids boots. They all need a pair, and I checked their sizes before I left the house."

Callie could feel Finn's eyes on her.

She shrugged. "You can't fight city hall."

"What are you two fighting about?" Verdie asked.

"She wouldn't let me buy Martin a pair of boots," he answered.

Verdie stopped in her tracks. "Are you crazy, girl? Burnt Boot is country livin', and that means boots, jeans, and belts with silver lacin' and silver buckles for church. Old wore-out boots, faded jeans, and work belts for school."

"I didn't want him to be a cowboy," Callie said.

"Then you shouldn't have brought him to Burnt Boot, Texas. Both of y'all come on and help me pick out four pairs of kids' boots. I feel like I done died and went to heaven," Verdie said. "Oh, and Olivia needs some Sunday shoes, too, so we might have to go on down to Denton after lunch. I figured we'd eat dinner today at that Cracker Barrel right there beside the outlet mall. I do like their ham steaks, and we'll have worked up an appetite by then."

Callie pushed a strand of dark hair back behind her ear and looked up into Finn's blue eyes. "So what are you buying now that they'll have cowboy boots from Verdie?"

"Rubber boots they can use for work boots until they get those too worn in for church. Verdie will go for fancy. I'll go for tough, but they get their rubber boots today, not for Christmas," he said. "And you?"

"Belts. Might as well jump in the deep end if I'm going to swim in the water at all." She smiled. "And Olivia needs that pink pearl-snap shirt over there."

He dropped a kiss on the top of her head and said above the music and the noise of the conversation all around them, "We've got a convert, Verdie."

"Praise the Lord. What do you think of these for Martin?" She held up a pair of black cowboy boots with rounded toes and a walking heel.

"He will love them," Callie said.

"These are for Sunday," Verdie said. "It's a toss-up between this one and this one." The one in her other hand was black eel with a hand-stitched top and a price tag of over two hundred dollars.

Callie gasped. "Good Lord, Verdie. He'll outgrow them in no time, and that's too much money for a pair of boots for anyone."

"My thinkin' exactly. So we'll have three pair like this. They all wear different sizes with Ricky having the smallest foot and Martin having the biggest one. Way I figure it is when they outgrow them, they can be passed down for work boots."

A sales clerk appeared from the backside of a round rack and held out her hands. "I'd be glad to wrap those for you, ma'am. No charge for anything if you spend more than twenty dollars in the store."

Verdie loaded her down with three boxes. "Thank you. I'll have these three pair, and you come on back when you get that done, because we'll have some more picked out. What do you think of these for Olivia, Callie?" She held up a pair of brown boots with white tops and a brown cross cut into the leather. All the fancy stitching was done in pink and they had a thin leather pink insert around the top and down the sides.

"They are beautiful," Callie said. "And they match that shirt and belt I want to buy for her."

It took three trips for Finn to take all the packages to the truck, and the backseat was half-full when they left the store.

"Be right back," Finn said, and he went back into the store.

Callie watched him as long as she could. The way he walked—with that tight little strut, his arms straight at his sides rather than swinging, his shoulders squared, and his head held high—made her knees go weak, and she was sitting down, for God's sake.

In an attempt to corral her thoughts, she unfastened her seat belt and turned around to face Verdie, who barely had enough room to sit surrounded by all the brightly wrapped packages.

"How in the hell are we going to take them kids shopping?" Verdie asked.

"Same way we take them to church." Callie turned back to face the front and checked her reflection in the mirror behind the sun visor. Yep, she was pink, but at least the hives hadn't set in like they usually did when she spent too much money. It wasn't that she'd come to Burnt Boot broke, but she had a constant fear that the lack of start-over money would make her stay in a place when she wanted to leave.

"Think, Callie," Verdie said.

"Oh!"

"Yes. Oh! We're crammed in this thing with all of us, and I don't have the old work truck tagged or insured to take off the ranch property. We need a van," Verdie said.

Callie's hands started to sweat. She'd had a small car that was paid for, but since it was traceable, the government told her it would be best if she sold it. She got a mere two thousand dollars for it. It was in her cash bag at the ranch, but there wasn't a dependable van out there for that kind of money.

"Before we do anything else, we're going to that car dealership across the road and I'm buying a van. A brand-spanking-new one that will seat seven people and has a good amount of space in the rear end for Christmas packages," Verdie announced.

"But," Callie gasped.

"I've got more money right now than I could burn through in what's left of my life. I want a van and I'm having one, so I'll hear no arguments. I just hope that we can get it all done pretty quick. I've got lots more shopping to do, and the kids get home from school at four," Verdie said.

"That's impulsive," Callie said when she could catch her breath.

"No, it's necessary. That way you can drive me back down to Dallas to get my things when I move out of the funny farm. I'll still drive in Burnt Boot and Gainesville and even Denton, but I will not fight the damn Dallas traffic."

"What's necessary?" Finn tossed a pair of black rubber boots with bright pink hearts on them into Callie's lap. "They aren't cowboy boots, so don't hang me from the nearest scrub oak with a moldy old rope. They'll keep your feet dry when you help me with morning chores."

Hearts. They had hearts on them. That's one of those subliminal messages for sure.

"Thank you," she said. "I love them, Finn. I really do."

"Good. Now where to next?"

"Verdie says we're going across the street to the car dealership." Callie hugged the boots to her chest.

"I'm buying a van. Don't try to talk me out of it. I've got the money, and I want a red one. I don't give a shit if it's a Ford or a Cadillac as long as all my kids can ride comfortably in it and it's an automatic shift. I'm too damn old to drive a stick," she declared.

"Yes, ma'am," Finn said.

Callie shot a look at him across the console.

He reached across and patted her on the cheek. "Like you said, darlin'. You can't fight city hall."

Verdie couldn't find a red one, so she settled on a black one that had all the bells and whistles. While she completed the paperwork and Finn talked to one of the salesmen about a new truck he intended to buy before the end of the year, Callie wandered through the showroom.

"Can't a woman go anywhere without running into you?" Betsy asked from the other side of a brand-new red truck.

"It's a small world," Callie said.

"Well, shit! What are you doing here?" Honey said.

"Lookin' at vehicles," Callie said.

"I wasn't talking to you," Honey smarted off.

"Good," Callie said and kept walking.

"Where's Finn?" Honey asked.

"It's not my day to watch him," Callie threw over her shoulder.

Lord, love a freakin' duck! The feud followed her around worse than Pistol.

Honey's high-heeled boots made a clicking sound on the shiny tile floor when she spotted Finn outside. Not to be outdone, Betsy beat her to the door and was plastered up against Finn's side before Honey could get to him.

Callie leaned against the fender of a brand-new Caddy and wished she could read lips. She'd had a dustup, as Verdie called it, with each of those bitches. It was Finn's turn to put them in their place. He did a speedy good job, because in less than a minute, they were all up in each other's faces. The poor salesman tried to talk sense to them right up until Honey blackened his eye and then grabbed Betsy by the hair.

Someone must have called Orville, because he showed up pretty quick, and between him and the salesman, they dragged the two women apart. Honey was screaming something about burning Wild Horse down, and Betsy wasn't making any bones about what she intended to do to River Bend.

Verdie came out of the office with keys dangling from her hand and saw what was going on. "Where's Finn?"

"He was out there, and then he left. I reckon he's sitting in his truck waiting on us to plow through that bloody field," Callie said.

"You reckon you ought to teach them all a survival course before they do something other than pullin' hair and scratchin'?" Verdie laughed.

"How much you reckon they'd pay?" Callie hooked her arm through Verdie's, and they went out a side door, leaving Orville with the mess.

—w—

Three boys and one little blond-haired girl brought home worried expressions on their faces that afternoon. They went straight to their rooms without stopping, put their backpacks away, and filed out with big eyes. Martin was the first one to the kitchen, where Finn was sitting at the table and Callie was busy pouring hot chocolate into cups.

"They were wrong, weren't they, Callie?" His voice quivered and only his thick black lashes held the tears at bay. "They ain't goin' to let us keep the kids, are they? We done saw the van in the yard. Where are they, anyway?"

"That's my new van." Verdie brought a platter of homemade ginger cookies from the pantry. "I wanted a red one, but they said it would take four weeks to get it, and we needed it now, so I had to buy a black one."

The whooping, slapping each other on the back, and high fives went on for a solid minute before Verdie stuck her fingers in her mouth and whistled. "Cookie and hot chocolate time and then chores, supper, and homework. Lord, I'd hate to see what you kids would do if you saw presents under the Christmas tree."

They all whipped around at the same time. They stood like little concrete statues without even a whisper of breath escaping their lips. Presents were stacked behind the tree, on both sides as far as possible, and extended out into the living room by six feet.

Olivia was the first one to move; she ran to Verdie and hugged her tightly. "I can't believe it, Granny."

The boys followed her lead and Verdie shooed them back to the table. "It's Christmas for God's sake. That means presents. But Monday means chores. All y'all got a new pair of rubber boots lined up at the back door. You can thank Finn for buying them for you. I best not catch any of you outside in your shoes, getting your feet wet and catchin' cold," Verdie fussed.

———✺———

Finn's finger made lazy circles on Callie's shoulder that night while the fire crackled as it burned down to embers in the fireplace not far from his bed. "They were a happy bunch of kids at the supper table, weren't they?" he said.

"I think Verdie was even happier than they were."

"How about you, Callie? Are you happy? Or have you just settled into this?"

She thought about the questions for a few seconds before she answered. "I'm happy and I haven't just settled. It's like running away from something, Finn. Only instead of running away, you've run in a big circle and just made your way back to where you belonged the whole time." What she couldn't say was that her heart was so entangled with his that she'd never run again. If she did, she'd have to do it with half a heart, and she didn't think living like that was even possible.

"How about you, Finn? Are you happy? You've had a lot shoved at you in a short time."

"I'm happier than I thought I could ever be, Callie. You put into words what I was thinking. I ran and ran and finally came right back to where I belong. Changing the subject now. Your hair is so silky," he said.

"You are making me hot as hell touching my shoulder, not my hair," she said.

"Oh, really? Well, darlin', your hair is brushing against my cheek and making me just as hot," he told her.

She propped up on an elbow and bent to kiss him, her hair making a veil over their faces. His hands found their way under her nightshirt and massaged her back.

"I can't think when you do that," she whispered.

"Good, because I can't think when you are anywhere near me. But before we go another minute, I do need to ask you something. Do you have something to wear to a ranch party?"

"Why? Are we throwing one?"

"No, going to one. Quaid Brennan called while I was out there with the kids. We're invited to the River Bend Christmas party next Friday night. I said we'd be there, and now I wish I hadn't."

"Why?"

"Because of all the cowboys who will be trying to steal you away from me." He slipped her nightshirt up over her head.

"Are you asking me out on a date, Finn?" she panted.

"I guess I am at that. Pick you up at six?"

"I'll be ready," she said. "Is it polite to kill Honey at her own party?" She slid her hand down into his lounging pants. A quick intake of breath told her that he was just as hot as she was.

"Ahhh, darlin', the women won't even glance my way."

She squeezed. "If they do, they'll learn that I'm a damn good shot."

Chapter 22

Olivia held a hand over her heart, her big blue eyes sparkling as she gazed at Callie. "You look just like a princess."

"Thank you," Callie said. She only hoped that Finn thought the same thing if and when he ever came out of his bedroom. She and Verdie had driven the new van down to Denton the day before, and she'd bought a gorgeous red velvet dress that hugged her body and was slit up to her thigh on the right side. It came with a matching jacket, so she didn't have to buy a fancy coat that she'd probably never wear again. But she did have to buy shoes, so she'd opted for the matching red velvet pumps.

She'd spent extra time on her makeup and twisted her hair up into a crown of curls held with a rhinestone clasp that came with the bracelet on her arm. Now she waited, worrying her fool head off that she'd overdressed for the occasion. If she had, it was Verdie's fault. She'd told her that River Bend and Wild Horse competed to see who could put on the fanciest Christmas party, so she should buy something flamboyant for each party.

"Don't you think she's gorgeous?" Olivia asked Martin when he and the boys came out of their room.

"I like her better in jeans and a flannel shirt," Martin said.

"I like her better in that," Ricky whispered.

"Adam?" Verdie said from the kitchen.

"I just like Callie no matter what she's wearing. Matter of fact, I love Callie almost as much as I love you, Granny," he answered.

~~~

Finn had been to dozens and dozens of Christmas parties. His family had one every year since before he was even born in Comfort for all the hired hands, their spouses, the neighbors, and business associates. He was no stranger to how to dress for one, how to behave at one, or what to expect. So why in the hell did he feel like a sophomore taking the prettiest girl in class out on a first date? Why couldn't he get up out of the rocking chair and get his cowboy butt out there in the living room where she was waiting?

He'd heard her bedroom door close ten minutes ago. They'd been to bed together, they'd had steaming hot sex, not to mention the fact he couldn't keep his hands off her no matter where they were. So why was he still sitting there?

Shotgun went to the door and whined.

"It's time, isn't it, old boy?"

The dog ambled down the hallway and stopped at the archway into the living room, his tail thumping against the floor. Finn could hardly breathe, his chest was so tight. Was that his Callie? The woman he'd flat-out fallen in love with?

Love!

Did he just think that word? He'd never imagined that he could love anyone after Lala had let him think she was dead and then betrayed him even further when he found out she was a spy. How did a full-grown man know he was in love in just two weeks? It didn't make a bit of sense, but he didn't want to ever imagine not having her in his life.

She turned around and their eyes locked somewhere near the Christmas tree. Everything about her was purely exquisite. There were no words, no compliments in the human language to describe her in that red dress with all that dark hair piled up on her head. Her lips were the same color as the dress, and thinking about kissing her until all the lipstick was gone sent him into semi-arousal.

"Well, don't you look sharp for a rough old cowboy?" she said.

"I'm a wilted dead onion plant compared to a perfect spring rose when I stand next to you. I won't stand a chance of keeping you on Salt Draw after tonight. The cowboys will be lined up from here to Gainesville just to kiss your hand," he said.

She crossed the room and handed him her jacket. "That's the craziest line I've ever heard."

"I didn't buy you a corsage, but Verdie told me what color you were wearing." He pulled a long thin box from behind his back and held it out.

"This feels like a scene from *Pretty Woman*." She smiled up at him.

"That was just a movie. This is the real thing and, darlin', you are a hell of a lot prettier than any actress on the big screen," he said.

"And she smells better, too, huh?" Ricky said.

"What is it in the box?" Olivia asked. "This is like *Cinderella*. When I grow up and get invited to a ranch party, can I wear your dress, Callie?"

"That box ain't big enough to have a shoe in it," Ricky said.

"Are you going to open it?" Finn asked.

———✵———

Callie's hands shook as she reached out to touch the deep red velvet box. "You won't snap it shut and scare me, will you?"

"Why would he do that?" Martin asked.

Finn leaned forward just slightly and kissed Callie softly.

Olivia sighed, and all three boys shut their eyes.

Callie gently opened the box and gasped. "Oh, Finn, it's beautiful."

A dark red ruby dangled from the top of an open gold heart pendant surrounded by sparkling tiny diamonds.

"I figured it would be easier to put on than a corsage." He smiled.

She lifted it from the bed of red velvet and handed it to him. "A little help, please."

She couldn't cry. It would ruin her makeup, and he'd think she didn't like his present, but it took every bit of her willpower to keep the tears at bay. No one had ever given her anything like that. She only hoped that it was symbolic of him giving his heart as well.

"Well, now, that just flat-out sets off the whole outfit. Y'all get on out of here so me and these kids can make microwave popcorn and watch movies. We've got them all picked out, and we're staying up until midnight. If y'all get in after that, come in real quiet so you don't wake us up," Verdie said.

"Yes, ma'am." Finn helped Callie into her jacket.

"Good-night kisses." She bent down in front of Martin.

"I want one, and I want you to leave a lipstick kiss on my forehead. I'm not going to wash it off, so it will make me have dreams of princes and castles," Olivia said.

She gave them all a kiss and looped her arm into Finn's. When they reached the porch, he scooped her up and carried her through the new-fallen snow to his truck, settled her into the passenger's seat, and let his lips softly graze hers before he slammed the door shut.

"Oh, look how pretty the lights around the house are, and how the tree looks in the window. It's like a storybook," she said as they drove down the lane.

"Sometimes that scares me," Finn admitted.

"Storybooks?"

"No, that everything is going so well. I keep waiting for the other boot to drop or for something to fall apart. I even worry that someday you and I will get into a great big fight and you'll leave me. I don't think I could stand it," he said.

She laid a hand on his thigh. "This would seem too fast if we hadn't known each other so well before now. I'm not going anywhere, not until you give me a pink slip."

"That ain't damn likely." He grinned.

"Looks like this is our turnoff," she said. "Oh, my sweet Lord, look at all those lights. I thought we had enough to blow the electric company, but they're nothing compared to this."

"Verdie says that River Bend and Wild Horse compete with each other for the biggest and best in everything. Wonder what next week's will look like? I got a call from Tyrell Gallagher inviting us, but you were in your room getting dressed, and then I was so stunned that I forgot until now," he said.

"Does that mean you're askin' me out again before you even see if you get lucky tonight?" she teased.

"I'm already lucky. I get to walk into that place with you on my arm," he said.

"Now that, darlin', is a lovely pickup line." She giggled.

He pulled the truck under a covered portico, and two valets appeared from just inside the door. His door and Callie's opened at the same time. He handed his keys to the young man and hurried around the truck to Callie's side.

Tucking her arm into his, he whispered, "Dammit! I was hoping we'd have to park out in the pasture, so I could carry you inside. That would show those cowboys that you are mine."

"I already feel like a princess with you escorting me. And it ain't the cowboys I'm worried about. It's Honey and Betsy trying to seduce you that scares me."

Declan Brennan met them at the door and shook hands with Finn. "Merry Christmas, and welcome to River Bend. Please go right on in and visit until we're ready to sit down to dinner. Afterward there will be dancing, and may I say, Miss Callie, that you look absolutely ravishing tonight? Save me a dance or two or a dozen." He bent at the waist and kissed her hand.

"Thank you, and I will save you a dance," she said.

"I'd planned to monopolize your time and dance every dance with you," Finn said.

"We have to play nice with the host, Finn. While

I'm dancing with Declan, you should dance with Leah Brennan, but if I catch you with Honey, know that your luck has run out."

As if on cue, Leah Brennan crossed the room and picked up both of Callie's hands. "Thank you so much for coming, and thank you for what you are doing for the O'Malley kids. That is so sweet of you. I've had them in my Sunday school class since they moved here."

"It's a two-way street. They make us happy, too," Callie said.

"Come on. I'll introduce you to the ladies." She grabbed a tall, blond-haired, green-eyed cowboy and said, "Finn, this is Quaid. Quaid, Finn. Don't know if you've met before, but you have now. Quaid, honey, take charge of Finn and make him known to all the men-folk. Go talk cows and hay and bad weather while I steal Callie away for a while."

Callie was introduced to half a dozen women all with the last name of Brennan. She spotted Honey across the room, sidled up to a fellow in a three-piece suit, a hundred-dollar haircut, and a flashy ring on his finger that looked like a sports ring from where Callie stood.

A blond wearing hot-pink satin with sparkling diamond drops in her ears, a diamond choker around her neck, and high heels that probably cost more than Callie made in a month at her old job at the gym tapped her on the shoulder.

"I have a question. Are you and Finn an item, or is this just a Christmas date? We don't see a diamond on your finger or a wedding band either. So what's the deal over on Salt Draw? I heard that Verdie is back playing nanny to all those children. That true?"

"Verdie is definitely back, and we're so glad to have her. I'm Callie Brewster, and you are?"

"Kinsey Brennan."

"I thought Honey was the Brennan interested in Finn and Salt Draw," Callie said.

"She is, but I damn sure like the way he fills out those jeans." Kinsey smiled.

"No honor among thieves?" Callie asked.

"That's beside the point. Now about you and Finn?"

"We're not engaged, and we're not married," she said.

"And?" Kinsey asked.

"But?" Honey said right behind her.

"*But* I'm more than a hired hand, *and* if anyone tests me, I have a license to carry a concealed weapon, and I'm not afraid to use it to protect what is mine," she said.

Kinsey laughed so hard that Finn caught Callie's eye and raised an eyebrow. "Me and you could be friends, Callie Brewster. Let's go get some punch. Anyone want to go with us?"

"I wouldn't cross the floor with that…" Honey's mouth clamped shut.

"I still haven't had that rabies shot," Callie said.

Honey turned around and went back to her football feller who was sipping whiskey in the corner.

Kinsey looped her arm in Callie's. "Is your gun in that little red evening purse?"

"I wouldn't dream of taking Finn out in public without it, and before you ask, yes, it's loaded. What good is a pistol with no bullets?" she answered.

"Anyone tell you about the feuding history?" Kinsey changed the subject.

"I've heard a little bit, but refresh my memory while we walk. I assume we're going to the bar?"

"No, darlin'. This is the Brennan party. We only get a little champagne at the dinner toast. Back in the beginning days of Burnt Boot, old Grampa Brennan was a preacher man."

"And?" Callie turned the tables.

"And there's someone I have to talk to over there. I hate to leave you alone, but I have to go. We'll talk about the feud later," Kinsey said.

"I'll introduce her," Polly said right behind them. "Come on, let's get some punch, Callie."

"Yes, ma'am," Callie said.

"You can carry a pistol, but I carry a pint of high-grade Patrón. That tends to cut the sweet in that punch bowl and give it enough kick to get us through the evening," she whispered. "I will say this for the Brennans. They throw a decent party and they serve up a mean steak that will melt in your mouth. If you weren't involved with Finn, I'd tell you to make a play for Quaid Brennan or maybe Declan."

"Are you serious?"

"About the men or the tequila?"

"Both."

"Oh, yes. But you're involved with Finn. His eyes have been on you ever since Kinsey stole you away. And I'm very serious about the tequila. Don't you tell a living soul that I'm the one who brought in the liquor. Let them think it was a Gallagher who paid someone to bring it in. And if Mavis is serving ham tonight as well as steaks, be sure to partake of it. You can find a good steak anywhere between here and the coast, but Mavis grows her own hogs and has a couple of state-of-the-art smokehouses. Her ham is to die for."

Polly waited until no one was looking and dumped a whole bottle of tequila in the punch bowl. Then she dipped up two crystal cups full and handed one to Callie. She was right—it did cut the sweet and give the punch just enough kick.

—◦◦◦—

Finn was so damned glad when Declan picked up a small crystal bell and rang it that he could have shouted. He could move across the room to lace his fingers in Callie's instead of talking about cows, crops, and weather. The other cowboys in the room hadn't said a word about her, but they had sure enough stared their fill, and it was time they realized that she had come with him, and she'd damn sure be going home with him, too.

"We'd like to thank all of you for attending our party this year. River Bend is fortunate to have had the best year ever, and we are glad you are here to share the good times with us. Merry Christmas! And now dinner is served," he said.

Double doors opened into a massive room filled with round tables covered with snowy white cloths waiting for the guests. A poinsettia sat in the center of each table, and wall candles filled the room with soft light.

Several waiters lined the walls, and starting with Declan and his sister, Leah, they checked a chart in their hands and led the guests to their tables. Finn and Callie were seated near the middle at a table with Quaid Brennan and Kinsey, Polly and Gladys, and one other couple that Callie had never met.

Kinsey made introductions. "This is our foreman and his wife. They've been with us for years."

Callie leaned in close to Kinsey's ear and asked, "Why are you willing to sit at the table with me? You have to know about the thing with Honey."

"We invited Finn because he owns Salt Draw, and you are his plus one. And, honey, what you did to Betsy was far better than what you did to Honey," Kinsey answered.

Waiters came around with bottles of champagne and filled fluted stems so effortlessly that Callie didn't realize her glass was full until Declan rang the bell again and stood up. "We'll have our traditional Irish blessing to serve as grace tonight before the waiters bring our food. 'The light of the Christmas star to you, the warmth of home and hearth to you, the cheer and goodwill of friends to you, the hope of a childlike heart to you, the joy of a thousand angels to you, the love of the Son and God's peace to you.'"

"Amen," Gladys said loudly, and everyone in the room echoed it.

Dinner started with a lovely potato soup, followed by a crisp salad, and then the entrée, which was the best steak Callie had ever eaten. The small dessert carts rolled around the room held cheesecakes of every kind and description, pecan pie with or without vanilla bean ice cream, pumpkin cake, and chocolate mousse. After that, coffee was served in china cups with the River Bend logo imprinted in gold on the side.

Callie leaned over and whispered softly, "Think Wild Horse can outdo this?"

Finn smiled and kissed her on the cheek. "I'd really rather be home eating fried chicken with the kids."

"But Verdie said we have to socialize."

"And we can't argue with her. This reminds me of the officer's ball over there. Remember?"

"Honey, it wasn't nearly this fancy, and the steaks weren't this good either."

"Hey now. You wait until you taste my steak," Finn said.

"What makes it so special?"

He didn't give a damn if it was bad manners or not, he cupped his hand over her ear and said, "Because I will feed it to you with my fingers, and the only thing either of us will be wearing is a smile."

Crimson filled her cheeks, and he chuckled.

"What did he just say to you?" Kinsey asked.

"This place would catch on fire if I said the words out loud," Callie answered.

"Well, shit! I do like a cowboy who talks dirty. I might give you a run for your money even yet. I figure I can shoot as good as you can," Kinsey said.

"But can you outrun a bullet?" Callie asked.

"I'd love for you to be in the Brennan family with your attitude." Kinsey smiled. "Looks like it's time to move back into the cattle pens while they take out the tables and get this room ready for dancing."

Finn pushed back his chair and pulled Callie's back as she stood. Soft Christmas music played as he put his arm around her shoulders and hugged her tightly. "Good food. Beautiful woman by my side. Only thing that would make it better would be if we were alone and not in a crowd of people."

"Amen," she said.

The Brennans were efficient, because in fifteen minutes the big doors opened to a different room altogether. Small tables for four circled the room, leaving the shiny hardwood floor ready for dancing. Tables were covered in red-and-green plaid with a red jar candle flickering in the middle of each one. Longer tables had been set up on each side of the double doors with finger foods, cheese cubes, tiny bite-sized sweet tidbits, and a punch bowl on each. Polly winked when Callie caught her dumping another bottle of tequila in the punch bowl after it had been refilled.

Good grief! Callie thought. *Where is she hiding that much liquor anyway? She must have brought one hell of a big purse in here.*

The band's guitar player struck a chord. The lead singer stepped up to the microphone and, with only the guitar behind her, started singing "White Christmas."

Finn waited for the first Brennans to take the floor before he picked up Callie's hand and asked, "May I have this dance, Miz Callie?"

She stepped into his arms, and instant heat flowed through her veins as one hand possessively rested on her lower back and one loosely held her hand. The fabric of his black Western-cut jacket kept her from feeling the muscles in his shoulder, but his heart kept time with hers, and his eyes were glued to hers.

The candlelight flickered in his crystal-clear blue eyes rimmed by the blackest lashes she'd ever seen on a man. She was wallowing in them when suddenly he twirled her out and then brought her back in a move that sent her arms around his neck, and both of his hands came to rest a little lower than the small of her back.

"I'm wondering how this dress would hold up in a hayloft," she said.

"I'm glad I'm wearing a jacket, or everyone in this place would know I'm about to bust out my zipper," he whispered.

"We can't leave yet, can we?" she asked.

"Playdate isn't over until midnight," he said.

"Then we'd best dance with other people so we don't catch the place on fire."

"I don't want anyone else to dance with you."

"Jealous?" she asked.

"Hell yes."

Quaid Brennan tapped Finn on the shoulder and said, "May I cut in?"

The minute that Finn stepped back, Honey looped her arms around his neck, and just like that, they'd changed partners.

"You are beautiful tonight, Miz Callie. I'm going to cut to the chase without the flirting because this song is about to end. Can I take you to dinner tomorrow night?" Quaid was pretty with his blond hair, green eyes, and chiseled, ruggedly handsome face, but he wasn't Finn O'Donnell.

"Thank you but no thank you."

"Are you and Finn more than boss and hired hand?"

"You might say that."

"My ranch is bigger than his," Quaid teased.

"It's not the size of the ranch, darlin'. It's the heart that runs it," she answered.

The song ended and Quaid was quickly replaced by another cowboy. "May I have this dance, ma'am? I've been watching you from across the room, and you float like an angel with your feet not even touching the floor."

He pulled her in for a two-step as the male singer started a traditional tune from Alabama called "Christmas in Dixie."

He was Quaid's opposite with a crop of jet-black hair that looked like he'd just crawled out of bed, brown eyes rimmed with black lashes, and heavy brows. Put him in a three-piece suit and Hollywood could make him into a member of the Italian mob.

"I'm Cam Brennan, and I'd be honored if you'd come to dinner here at the ranch after church this Sunday," he said.

"Thank you, Cam, but I've got four kids at home that I'm responsible for. I don't think I've ever known a Cam before," she said.

"Mama liked Cameron, but Daddy shortened it," he said. "You sure I can't change your mind about dinner? How would it be if I challenge Finn to a duel and whoever is left standing gets to have your company on Sunday?" he said.

"Finn O'Donnell was a sniper for the army. That's classified, so don't go tellin' anyone. I only know because I was his spotter. We're both pretty good with firearms, so my advice, Mr. Cam Brennan, is that you don't mess with either of us." She smiled sweetly.

"I like a feisty woman. If you ever decide to get out of a puddle and go swimmin' in the ocean, come on over to River Bend. I'll give you a job doin' anything you want. Hell, you can just sit on the porch and look pretty, and I'll pay you double whatever Finn is giving you."

"I'll keep that in mind," Callie said as the song ended.

Chapter 23

THE CLOCK ON THE PICKUP DASHBOARD READ TWELVE ten when Callie buckled her seat belt. She was irritable because she'd seen far too many women staring up into Finn's pretty blue eyes all evening, and she had only gotten the first dance, the last one, and part of one in the middle of the evening with him.

"Tired?" He started the engine and drove down the long lane toward the road.

"To the bone. I'm glad the kids are home tomorrow. The boys can help you feed in the morning. And I'm damn glad that it's Saturday, so we don't have a workout. Are you aware that I haven't had any target practice since I got here, though?"

"Then we'll set up some targets in the barn tomorrow and do some shooting. You feelin' like you might need to shoot something?" Finn asked.

"A whole bunch of somethings. If I took out one of the families, then there couldn't be a feud, could there?"

"I was thinking that I'd stay in bed until about ten o'clock, you'd take care of chores, and then we could go play army until noon."

"You're the boss," she smarted off.

"Hey, I was teasing. What's got a burr under your saddle? I thought the evening went fine, except I didn't like all those cowboys dancing with you."

She crossed her arms over her chest, leaned back,

and shut her eyes. "Then why didn't you dance with me more?"

"It's called being polite. Shit!"

He hit the brakes, and the truck went into a long, greasy sideways slide.

"What?" She grabbed at the dashboard.

"Those fools. Don't they know that a pup will freeze in this kind of weather?"

"What are you talking about?"

"Someone just tossed a puppy out the door of a car and then drove away. I almost rear-ended their car before I could get stopped on that slick snow and ice," he said.

For a split second she could see the red taillights disappearing down the road, but then the new falling snow covered them completely.

"How far back?" she asked.

"It's snowing like hell, and I might have run over the dog before I even saw him."

"Then I'll walk back until I find him. I won't let a little puppy freeze to death," she said.

"In that getup? You'll ruin your shoes and your dress and catch pneumonia to boot," he said.

"We are going back to get that dog," she said. She'd have nightmares if she left a poor defenseless puppy out there in six inches of snow with the promise of another two inches before morning.

"Bossy after dancing with all those big important ranchers, aren't you?" He put the truck in reverse and backed up slowly. "If I run over that dog and kill it, I don't want a single tear or whimper out of you."

Her forefinger came up in a blur. "You kill that dog,

and I'll sling snot all over this truck and there won't be a damn thing you can do about it."

—◦◦◦—

If the pup hadn't had a black spot on its head and if it hadn't been huddled down close to the side of the road, Finn would have never seen it. He braked, slid a few feet, and opened the door to find not one but two bundles of white fur whimpering in the snow. He reached down without getting out of the truck, picked up one by the scruff of the neck, and set it down behind Callie's seat.

"See, that didn't kill you, did it?" Callie said.

He started for the second one and the critter ran. White dog. White snow. Woman who was turned around in the seat talking baby talk to the puppy hunkered down in the floorboard of the backseat. He could shut the door and go and no one would be the wiser, but he couldn't leave that puppy out there to freeze.

He engaged the parking brake and crawled out of the truck.

"What are you doing?" she asked.

"Keeping you from slinging snot," he said gruffly.

Stepping out in the blinding snow, he caught a movement to his right. He whistled and the pup whined but kept backing down into the ditch. The ground was uneven and slick with several inches of snow on top of a thick layer of ice. One second Finn was bending to catch the dog; the next he was sprawled out on his stomach, snow in his nose, his mouth, and down the front of his shirt. But, by damn, he had that critter by the leg.

"Finn! What is going on?" Callie yelled.

He came up with the wet dog and carefully carried it

back to the truck. "There were two of them, and this one is shy. I had to run her down."

"My God, Finn, are you all right?"

He put the whining pup on the back floorboard, crawled into the driver's seat, and started home. "Are you happy now?"

"Coming from the man who takes in strays more often than I do," she said.

"They are not living in the house. We will put them in the barn. They'll be big dogs, and we've got enough animals in the house." His focus was straight ahead. If he looked at her and she cried, he'd give in, and this was one fight he didn't intend to lose.

"Yes, sir, boss man. I was going to suggest the same thing. I believe they've got some Great Pyrenees in them, so they'll get big quick. But they'll be great cattle dogs," she said. "I can't wait until the kids see them. I'm glad there are two. One would be lonely."

Her tone had changed, but Finn wasn't ready to make up, not yet. He hadn't liked the way she'd flirted with all those Brennan cowboys, and he damn sure hadn't liked the way they had looked at her.

If he stopped outside the barn, she'd get out and ruin her shoes and possibly her dress. Then tomorrow that would be his fault, so he told her to stay in the truck while he opened the big doors and he drove right into the barn.

Just as he thought, she bailed out of the truck and went straight for the tack room to get a bowl of dry food for the new babies, who were both cowering behind a bale of hay. Finn made a dog pen by arranging eight bales of hay, tossed a horse blanket in the middle, and put food and water off to one end.

"They'll be fine. Now if Queen Callie says it's all right, I'd like to go to the house and get out of these wet clothes," he said.

She narrowed her eyes at him. "Don't make fun of me."

The puppies ignored the food and water and set up a whimper.

"Thank God you didn't demand that we take them in the house. They would have wakened everyone and kept us all up until morning." He sat down on one of the hay bales, jerked off his boots, and removed his socks.

"What are you doing?" she asked.

He rolled the socks into a ball and threw them in the pen. Both puppies sniffed them and then curled up in a ball with their noses close to the socks.

"Works every time." He put his boots back on. "Let's go get some sleep. Morning will come fast."

And Finn meant sleep.

———

Callie undressed, took her hair down, put on a night-shirt and a pair of underpants, and dived beneath the covers. She was absolutely chilled to the bone marrow. The velvet jacket and dress were not meant to provide warmth in an icy-cold barn, but she would have stood in front of a firing squad before she would have admitted she was cold. He was cold, wet, and mad at the whole world. Add that to a healthy dose of jealousy because she'd flirted with other cowboys, and it made for a miserable, lonely night.

She waited for the closet door to open. Hell, she'd even made sure her shoes were tucked under the rocker so he wouldn't trip over them on his way to her bed. She wanted to cuddle up beside him, to feel his hard, firm body next to hers, to draw warmth from him.

Fifteen minutes passed.

The door didn't open.

She was still shivering. Only now it wasn't related to weather but to anger.

She threw the covers off and stormed across the floor, slung open the closet door, pushed her clothing to one side and then his, and opened the door on the other side. Invited or uninvited, she wasn't through fighting, and if she couldn't sleep, neither was Finn.

Shotgun growled when the door opened, but when he realized who it was, he flopped his big yellow head back down on the rug and shut his eyes. She crawled right up in the middle of the bed, crossed her legs and her arms, and said, "What is your problem anyway, cowboy?"

He rolled over with his back to her. "I'm tired, Callie. Go back to your own bed and get some sleep. It's after one o'clock."

She stood up in the bed and threw off her nightshirt and then her bikini underwear. "The hell I will. I can't sleep, and we are going to settle this."

"There is nothing to settle. It's been a long night."

She crawled under the covers and hugged up to his back.

"I told you to sleep in your own bed," he growled.

"How long have you known me, Finn?"

"Long enough to know you never listen."

"I turned down a dozen dates tonight. One even said right out loud that his ranch was bigger than yours, and I don't think he was really talking about land and cattle.

Another one said when I got ready to get out of a mud puddle and swim in an ocean to give him a call. But none of them turned me on just by touching my fingertips or by a glance across the room. I've been in love with you since before I even knew I was in love with you. I've said my piece. You can lie there and pout if you want to, but I'm not going anywhere. Since you're too stubborn to come to my room, I'll sleep right here where I can feel your skin against mine," she said.

"Damn it all to hell!" He flipped over and brought her to his chest in a fierce hug. "I love you, too, Callie."

"Good. Now can we go to sleep? We have to get up in less than five hours, and I'm cranky when I don't get my sleep."

He chuckled, and all was right with her world.

Then he kissed her on the forehead and said, "Good night, darlin'."

And the clouds came close to parting.

"You kids put on them new rubber boots and bundle up real good. It's still spittin' snow out there, and I don't want a bunch of sick kids this close to Christmas. You bring the eggs in and then you can build a snowman. My rules say that you can stay out as long as you want. However, when you come inside, you are in for the rest of the day except for evening chores. There'll be no running in and out. Cold and then hot and then back again is what makes kids get sick," Verdie said.

As they hurried out into the backyard, the old work truck pulled up and Callie and Finn got out. Finn yelled at the kids that before they started a snowman, they might want to go out to the barn and have a look at what was there.

Like all kids, Martin and the O'Malley children weren't about to walk when they could run like the wind through half a foot of fresh snow.

He slipped his arm around Callie's waist. "No matter how much they beg, they cannot bring those things in the house."

"You are preaching to the choir."

"Just bein' sure that we're on the same page. Have you told Verdie yet?"

"Thought you might want to do that." She stomped through the snow, picking her feet up high to keep from throwing snow inside her new rubber boots.

"Tell me what?" Verdie opened the door for them.

"This woman was an old bear last night," Finn said.

"He was the one who acted like a rabid coyote with a sore tooth," Callie tattled.

"Did you make up before you went to sleep?" Verdie asked.

"Yes, ma'am," they said in unison.

"Here they come." Callie pointed.

"Looks to me like you brought home two polar bears from the party last night." Verdie laughed.

"Someone threw them out on the road right in front of us. Finn got his suit all wet rescuing the second one." Callie kicked off her boots, set them on the rug beside the door, and headed straight for the coffeepot.

"Bastards! It ought to be legal to shoot people who take puppies and kittens to the country and dump them out," Verdie huffed. "Look at those kids. Now if that ain't just what this old ranch needs. Kids and pups. You ain't plannin' on bringing them in the house, are you? You do know they'll be as big as a small calf when they're grown."

"I'm sure the kids will want to bring them inside, but we're going to stand our ground. Two dogs, a cat, and that talkin' parrot are enough for the house," Finn said.

"Well, I'm not staying in the house when there's snow on the ground and new puppies. I'm going to put my boots and coat on, and I'm going out to play with the kids," Verdie said. "Y'all going with me?"

Callie wrapped her arms around her waist and shook her head. "No, thank you. I've just spent the past two hours out in the snow. I've had enough of it today."

"I'm in the same boat with Callie. I'm tired of being outside," Finn said.

"Okay, but I'm not missin' a minute with the kids. And when we get too cold to stay out there anymore, we're making snow ice cream." Verdie's last words faded out on the way to her bedroom.

Finn poured a cup of coffee and carried it to the living room where he sunk down in the sofa and propped his cold feet on the coffee table. From the kitchen window, Callie could see the kids bounding through the snow with two furry bundles bouncing around like windup toys all around them. Their giggles, especially Martin's, was music to her ears. She couldn't remember a time that he'd been so open, carefree, and so much like a kid his age.

The sound of Verdie's boots on the floor passed behind her, leaving the faint smell of her perfume in the kitchen. The minute Verdie was off the back porch, she picked up a handful of snow and patted it into a ball, heaved it toward the kids, and hit Ricky on the shoulder. He squealed, and the fight was on.

Dogs running between the kids.

Verdie hiding behind a tree with Olivia joining her team, making it the girls against the boys.

"Hey, this fire is waiting on you," Finn called.

She found Shotgun curled up on Finn's left with Pistol right beside him and Angel lying across his shoulders like a blond fur collar. "Looks like they've only left me one option."

"The rocking chair or the rug?"

She straddled his lap and laid her head on his chest. "No, this one."

He put his feet on the floor, his hands on her butt, and pulled her close enough that neither light nor air could come between them. "I like this option." He buried his face in her hair.

"I smell snow and coconut. It's a hot combination," he whispered.

"It's not nearly as sexy as your shaving lotion and coffee mixed up together," she whispered.

"This feels right, Callie. You, the kids, Verdie, and the animals. It's the way a ranch is supposed to feel."

"It's the way life is supposed to feel, whether it's on a ranch or in the middle of a town the size of Dallas," she said.

His hands slid up under her shirt. "Your skin is so warm and feels like silk."

She shifted her position and brought a hand up to trace his jawline. "Are all the O'Donnell men as blistering hot as you?"

"Oh, no! I'm the ugly duckling of the bunch. Wait

until you meet the whole lot of them. The really handsome ones will try to steal you away from me, especially
Sawyer. He's got a thing for dark hair and pretty, aqua-
colored eyes." Finn chuckled.

"Like a wise man said last night, it ain't damn likely,"
she murmured just before she closed the space and her
lips met his.

"Is this makeup sex time?" he asked gruffly when the
kiss ended.

"Right here in front of the fire sounds exciting, but
we've got four kids and a granny who could bust through
the door any minute. Makeup sex will have to wait until
tonight." Her lips found his again.

Would there ever come a time when his touch didn't
make her melt into a pool of hot lava? Or his kisses
wouldn't turn her legs into useless sticks? She hoped
not, because for the first time ever, she felt like all was
right with her life and nothing could go wrong. Not with
Finn to protect not only her body, but her heart.

Chapter 24

CALLIE CHECKED ALL THE KIDS ONE MORE TIME AS they got out of the van in front of the church. Verdie had done Olivia's hair up in a crown braid, and she wore a new red corduroy skirt, a bright green sweater with red trim, and a matching Christmas bow at the back of the braid.

"Today is the senior citizens' program, so I'll be joining the old folks in the choir. You two are on your own with the kids. Polly and Gladys will be with me, so you'll have the whole pew to yourselves," Verdie said.

"Well, Verdie! Why didn't you tell us you were in the program? You haven't practiced," Callie said.

"I'll miss you sitting beside me," Olivia said.

"I'll miss you, too, but next week is your turn, and I'll have to sit by myself and miss you then," Verdie said. "And, Callie, we're so damned old and have done this program so many times that we know it by heart. We don't have to practice. We just have to show up."

"What's in the tote bag?" Ricky asked.

"It's my character props," Verdie answered.

"What's that?" Adam asked.

"It's what I put on so I'm not Granny Verdie but whoever I'm supposed to be in the program. Kind of like Olivia when she is Lucy in the Charlie Brown part of the play next week," Verdie answered.

"Shhh." Olivia touched a finger to her lips. "We're all going to surprise Callie and Finn."

Verdie winked over the tops of the kids' heads at Callie and Finn. "My lips are sealed. They won't get another tidbit of information from this old granny."

Callie made a mental note to ask if the kids needed anything for their play. And was it at school or at church or both?

Verdie circled around the sanctuary to the back of the church, through a door into what most likely led into Sunday school rooms, with Polly and Gladys right behind her. The pew looked empty without the three elderly ladies at the end and felt emptier yet with Callie at one end and four kids between her and Finn.

The preacher had a big smile on his face when he took his place behind the podium. "This morning the senior citizens of Burnt Boot will present the Christmas program. They say that laughter is good for the soul, and if the soul is happy, then all is right with the world. So with that said, I'll turn the program over to Polly Cleary."

Old quilts, some frayed at the edges, pinned to a rope line with clothespins, formed a barrier between the pulpit and the choir section. A red leg appeared from between two quilts, and Callie gasped. Surely they weren't going to do a burlesque in the church.

Then a walker decorated with gold garland and jingle bells came out of the curtains with Polly behind it. She wore a red sweat suit with a picture of Rudolph's head on the front, a flashing red nose, and antlers to match. She slowly pushed the walker to the podium and motioned for the preacher. "Take this back so Gladys and Verdie can join me. We ain't got but one, and we have to share.

Verdie is slow as well, Christmas, so I'll tell y'all a story while she's on her way out here."

Olivia poked Callie on the leg. "Is this really church?"

Callie nodded. "I think so, but I'm not sure."

Polly adjusted her antlers and said, "Back in the summer, Verdie McElroy put up her ranch, Salt Draw, for sale, and when the right buyer came along, she sold it. The new owner is Finn O'Donnell, sitting in the middle pew right there with his family. We're right glad to welcome them to Burnt Boot, but we was sure worried about our dear friend until a couple of weeks ago, when she decided to come on back home where she belongs. Trouble was—oh, here comes Gladys, bless her heart, she's older and slower than me, so forgive her for takin' so long to get here. She talks slower, too, so since y'all don't want to starve plumb to death, I'll do the talkin'. Now where was I? Oh, trouble was that poor old Verdie, here she comes, folks. Everyone give her a hand."

The applause came close to raising the roof a few inches when Verdie pushed the walker out from the back of the church. She wore a sweat suit that matched Polly's and Gladys's, but hers had a picture of Santa Claus on the front, and her Santa hat sat at a cocky angle.

"Is that Granny Verdie?" Ricky gasped.

"Looks like it," Finn answered.

"Thank you, thank you. As I was saying, trouble was she decided to come home right in the middle of all this weather, and she had to hire a sleigh to get her here because the snow was so deep, and right outside of town, you'll never believe…"

Verdie tried to wrestle the microphone from Polly, but she hung on, and pretty soon there was a make-believe fight going on right there behind the podium. When Verdie came up with the microphone, the walker had been turned over and the preacher had darted out from behind the curtains to settle the fight.

"Let go of me, preacher. She was infringing upon my rights to tell my story, and even if this is church, she's not going to steal my thunder," Verdie said.

"I like this kind of church," Olivia said.

Polly crossed her arms over Rudolph and pouted. Gladys threw an arm around her to console her, and music filtered out from the speakers at the back of the church.

"I thought we'd just sing what happened rather than tell the story, that is, if Polly can suck in that lip and help me," Gladys said.

"If I can hold the microphone, I won't pout," Polly said.

"Oh, okay, if you'll just stop acting like a sixty-year-old." Verdie winked at the congregation. And the three old ladies broke into their rendition of "Grandma Got Run Over by a Reindeer," substituting "Verdie" for "Grandma" in the lyrics.

When the song ended and they staggered off the stage with Verdie using the walker and the other two hanging on to the sides, everyone could see big hoofprints on the back of Verdie's shirt, and the whole congregation gave them a standing ovation.

The next group was three old guys, each wearing a hoodie with an initial on the front. It didn't take much imagination to know that they were the Chipmunks. Callie recognized the music as "Christmas Don't Be Late," and she was amazed at how much those fellers sounded like the original Chipmunks. When Alvin sang that he wanted a Hula-Hoop, one came rolling out from behind the curtains. Alvin did a great job of making it stay up as he sang the rest of the song, even when the preacher yelled "Alvin" just like on the recording.

Polly came back, this time pushing herself in a wheelchair, and picked up the microphone from the pulpit. "Sometimes you kids make a list for Christmas. Well, just because we're older than twenty…"

"Pol…llly." Gladys's head poked out from between two quilts.

"Okay, older than twenty-one…"

"Pol…llly." Verdie's head came out from the other end, and she was wearing the flashing Rudolph antlers.

"Oh, all right, you two ain't a bit of fun, and it's Christmas," Polly said. "Just because we are old enough"—she paused and looked over the audience— "to get senior citizens' discounts at Dairy Queen and the Pizza Hut, doesn't mean that we don't make a list. As for me, I was thinking maybe I'd wish for a white Christmas this year, but wait, we already got that. Well, then, I guess the next thing on our list will have to do."

The curtains parted and five old gals plus the same amount of gents filed out. The ladies had put tutus on over their sweat suits, and the guys wore striped vests and top hats.

Polly jumped up out of the wheelchair and yelled, "Hit it," and the music started for "All I Want for Christmas Is My Two Front Teeth." They had made a few adjustments to the lyrics: "All I want for Christmas is to find my dentures." They sang that if they could find their dentures they could whistle and say "sister Suzy sitting on a thistle."

When that ended, they entertained the congregation with "Jingle Bell Rock" and "I Saw Mommy Kissing Santa Claus," and then Polly wound up the half-hour show by asking everyone to pick up the hymnal from the back of the pew in front of them and open it.

"Like our preacher told us, laughter is good for the soul. So is music and singing. We've had a good time here this morning, and we're tickled to be here another year with all y'all. Here's hoping we can all ten be here again next year and that Verdie don't get in the way of a reindeer. Now Gladys is going to play the piano like she used to do when we really were too young to get those senior citizens' discounts, and we're all going to finish this morning's service by singing together. The song is right there inside the cover, and we want to hear your voices lift the roof," Polly said.

Verdie pushed her way to Polly's side. "Really we want you to sing loud because we're all hard of hearing."

Gladys hit the keys and Polly handed the microphone to Verdie, who led the whole group in "Joy to the World."

Callie could hear Finn's deep Texas twang over the sweet little voices of the children and wished she was standing beside him.

Callie steered clear of the ladies' room that morning and only caught a glimpse of Honey and Betsy shooting evil looks at each other. If only they'd both have to make a run to the bathroom, she'd gladly lock them inside.

—ww—

"Boy, I wish church was like that every week," Martin said on the way home.

"Not me," Finn whispered toward Callie. "I missed you sitting beside me."

"Sometimes I nearly fall asleep when the preacher starts talking about that old stuff, but I didn't this morning," Ricky said.

"I like the part when we all get to sing," Olivia said. "Someday I'm going to be a country music star and sing in Nashville. Maybe I'll even get asked up on the Grand Ole Opry stage when I get to be really famous."

"It was fun," Verdie said. "Never knew how much I missed the little things about Burnt Boot until the well run dry. I'm glad to be home, and I'm not leaving again. If y'all kick me off Salt Draw, I'll go live with Polly and be a barmaid at night."

"Verdie!" Callie exclaimed.

"I'd rather do that than go crazy on depression pills at the funny farm. Oh, I meant to tell y'all. My grandkids called last night. They can't come for the holidays this year, but they asked me what I wanted."

"What did you tell them?" Olivia asked.

"I said I wanted seven tickets to the Rainforest Café in Grapevine, Texas. I thought we might go have dinner there for New Year's Eve and then go ice-skating in Frisco at that big old mall they got down there," Verdie answered.

Olivia slapped a hand over her mouth. "Are you serious?"

"My Rainforest tickets will be here in my Christmas card sometime this week, but we'll have to clear it with Callie and Finn," Verdie said.

Finn reached across the distance between the two bucket seats in the front of the new van and laced his fingers into Callie's. "Fine by me, but now you got to convince Callie. She might have other ideas to bring in the New Year."

"Callie, please," Martin whispered right behind her.

"How could I ever say no to a deal like that? How many of you have ever ice-skated?"

No hands went up, but Finn squeezed her fingers.

"You?" she asked.

"Couple of times, ma'am. We were up in Montana for a rodeo one winter, and then we went to the finals in Las Vegas. One of the casinos has a rink on the bottom floor. I'll teach you," he answered.

"How about you, Verdie?" Olivia asked.

"When I was a girl, we had some real hard winters around these parts and the ponds froze over. We didn't have skates, but we put old socks over our shoes and had a big time. I'm willing to learn if you are," Verdie answered.

The buzz sounded like bees had been turned loose in the back of the van. It was still going on when they piled out of the vehicle at the house and tore off to their bedrooms to change clothes.

Verdie picked up an apron and looped it over her head. "I'm thinking that this afternoon we'll play board games and maybe I'll read them a book."

"I'm taking a long nap," Finn said.

Callie turned around for Finn to tie her apron strings. "Me too."

"Makeup, round two?" he whispered into her ear so softly that only she heard it.

She nodded.

"Stop whispering. It'll make me think something is going on between you two. Want to tell me what all this moony-eyed business is about?" Verdie teased.

"It's need-to-know," Finn said.

"What does need-to-know mean?" Martin asked. "I'll set the table. Adam and Ricky will be here in a minute to get the napkins."

"Need-to-know means it's information you only get when you need it," Finn said.

"And you don't need to know," Verdie said.

"Sounds like big people talk. I'm not ready for that," Martin said. "But I'm ready for dinner. I'm starving and I love chicken baked in the oven and potato casserole. And I couldn't hardly sing for thinkin' about that peach cobbler over there on the cabinet."

"And I couldn't hardly sing for thinking about session two," Finn whispered in Callie's ear.

Chapter 25

CALLIE'S HEART THREW IN AN EXTRA BEAT WHEN FINN dropped a kiss on her cheek and crawled in behind her. One arm went under her, one around her, and his face was buried in her hair. It was absolutely amazing that they could be wound up in a cocoon with five other people in the house and yet feel so very alone in her bedroom.

"Being in your arms feels so good," she said.

"Yes, it does," he agreed.

His hands traveled down her arms in a lazy fashion, taking his time until she shivered and flipped over to face him, body pressed against his, hearts thumping so loud that she was amazed the kids didn't come running to see what the noise was all about.

"I like the way our bodies fit together," he murmured.

She wanted to touch him, to feel that he was ready, and then she wanted to make wild love, not the kind where he built her into a frenzy then backed off with sweet little kisses to let the flames cool to embers. She wanted the fire and the heat all at once.

Carefully unzipping his jeans and slipping her hand inside, she let out a gasp. Nothing between naked flesh and his zipper pushed her desire to have him even higher. She sat up, unzipped his jeans, and tugged them all the way off. Then he pulled her shirt up over her head. Everything was going so fast, it was a blur. Then he slowed down, taking his time to unfasten her skirt, to pull it all the way off, and then gently lay it over the rocking chair.

"My God, Finn, I'm aching for you," she said.

His eyes were shut when he kissed her. His hands went under her bottom for leverage, and she grabbed the rungs of the headboard with both hands. His lips came down on hers with so much passion that it almost brought tears to her eyes.

She kept up with the rhythm, and her body responded even though her mind and soul nagged at her in worry. Something was out of sync between them.

"Callie," he said hoarsely.

"Oh. My. God," she whimpered and hung on to him, hoping she was wrong and when she opened her eyes, everything would be perfect again.

———⁓⁓⁓———

Finn rolled to one side, keeping her tightly in his arms and close to his side, so she wouldn't look at him with those big aqua eyes. He'd thought he'd gotten over his commitment issues, but there they were in living color, upsetting his world again, and she'd seen it. Even the wild, passionate sex hadn't completely erased it.

Why did doubts about Callie leaving him flash through his mind when he crawled between the sheets with her?

"It was fear of me being like her, of leaving you, wasn't it?" Callie propped up on an elbow. "Open your eyes, Finn O'Donnell."

If he did, she would know, and he'd fallen in love with Callie. He didn't want to hurt her, but she deserved so much more than a hard heart that could still conjure up doubts right in the middle of sex.

"I said to open your eyes," she demanded.

That was his Callie. The one who'd been his partner. Bossy as hell and twice as sassy. He opened his eyes.

"Now look at me. Look right into my eyes and don't blink. What do you see?"

"I see Callie."

"What do you feel?" She pressed tighter against him.

"I feel your naked body against mine," he said.

"What do you smell?"

He smiled. "How graphic do you want me to get?"

"Tell me."

"I smell your perfume, coconut in your hair, and the musk that is your scent and no one else's after we make love," he said.

"That's because I'm right here. Lala did you wrong, but that is all in the past. Shut the door on it. Slam the damn door on it. I'm not going anywhere. If you can help me to get over my commitment fears, then I'll help you with yours. They're going to pop up for both of us. There's nothing we can do about it but fight the hell out of it when it happens. It will happen less and less, trust me. I love you and that's the way it is. Now you can blink."

"I love you, Callie Brewster," he said softly.

"Remember something important. We were friends and partners a long time before we were lovers, so we know and understand each other. Now kiss me again." She pointed to a sprig of mistletoe that she'd hung on the bedpost right above her head.

He drew her down for a kiss, and all doubts faded.

There was only Callie, his old spotter, his best friend, his new lover.

"Please tell me those sirens I hear are in my head and not really getting closer and closer." Her voice was muffled against his chest.

"I believe they're real."

"Shit! I may buy two Stinger missiles and blow both those feuding families out into the Red River for messin' up my afternoon." She threw back the covers and grabbed the pair of jeans hanging on the back of a rocking chair. "I knew they were up to something this morning in church. The air was almost crackling with tension."

Finn shot out of bed. "I felt it, too. Wonder which one set fire to the other one's barn?"

"You're kiddin'. Would they take it that far?"

"I just hope Honey Brennan isn't so mad at you for the soap in her eyes that she set fire to our barn."

"The puppies," Callie said as she hurriedly jerked on socks and rubber boots.

Callie reached the kitchen first. Verdie was on the phone and the kids waited at the table for her to return to the board game they'd set up.

"It's a fire at the Brennans' place," she said.

Before Callie could answer, the doorbell rang.

"Get that door while I finish talking to Gladys."

Expecting to see Honey or Betsy, or maybe both, ready to crucify her for arson, she was shocked speechless to see the sheriff on the porch.

Orville held a big flat box with a dozen doughnuts in it. There was a fleck of chocolate and a red sprinkle in the corner of his mouth. "Afternoon. Thought I'd stop by and say hello on the way to the fire. They won't need me for a few minutes."

"Doughnuts! Doughnuts! Joe wants a doughnut," Joe yelled from his perch.

"Come inside out of the cold. What's going on? We heard the sirens," Callie said.

He handed off the doughnuts to her, and she took them to the kitchen with Orville right behind her.

"Doughnuts!" Martin squealed.

"Only one each and, yes, Joe can have a few bites but not a whole one. It would make him sick. Olivia, you can pour up milk to go with them," Verdie yelled from the utility room.

"It's the feud, I'm sure. One of the Gallaghers set fire to a big round bale of hay. There was about sixty bales lined up at the edge of a fence, and it's burned through at least ten of them by now. Throws a lot of smoke, but it's not a barn or a house. Trouble was when the Brennans went to put it out, every damn...oops, pardon my language, kids...danged one of their truck tires were flatter than pancakes. Not slashed or cut, just all the air let out of them," Orville said.

"Wow!" Adam said. "How many trucks was there?"

"A bunch," Orville said.

"Afternoon, Sheriff," Finn said. "Reckon they need help over there?"

"Naw, they can put out that fire, but I was hopin' maybe you or Miz Verdie would ride along with me to kinda help me buffer," he said. "You want to go, too, Callie?"

"Let me get my coat," Verdie said. "Finn, you'd best come along with us."

"I'll stay here with the kids," Callie said. She'd had her fill of the feud, and she didn't want to encourage Orville one bit.

The roads were slick and Orville didn't seem to be in any hurry to get to the site of the burning hay, so what should have taken five minutes took fifteen.

"Is he afraid to drive on ice and snow?" Finn griped.

"He's got his reasons. Stunt like this means the Brennans will load their guns. Last time they did that, Orville got shot. Nowadays when a call comes from Burnt Boot, he goes by the doughnut shop, eats a couple, and gee-haws with the ladies who run it before he drives out here. And he always takes his time," Verdie explained.

The bales were smoldering and the firemen were putting the last of their equipment away when Orville drove over a cattle guard and onto River Bend Ranch. He parked beside the fire truck and was instantly surrounded by Brennans.

Most of them, women included, had pistols or rifles in their hands. A sawed-off shotgun was tucked up under Honey's arm, and Kinsey had a Glock strapped to her leg. Verdie hopped out of the truck and pushed her way into the middle of the crowd. Finn approached with caution.

Questions were flying like ducks going south for the winter. Poor old Orville kept one hand on his pistol, still in the holster with the safety on, and the other held up trying to fend off angry comments.

"Now, y'all just wait a minute. You don't know the

Gallaghers did this. Did you see them? Do you have evidence that they're behind it?"

"We're in the middle of a damned feud. Who else would do something like this?" Honey yelled, and then she spotted Finn. "Unless it was that hired hand over on Salt Draw. She's had it in for me ever since she got here. Maybe we're blaming the wrong party."

"Honey, you'd best watch who you are accusing," Verdie said loudly. "Callie Brewster has been in my presence all day. There's no way she set that fire or let the air out of a bunch of tires."

Finn bit back a smile. As hot as things had gotten in the bedroom that afternoon, maybe a spark bounced out the window, down the road, and jumped onto the hay. The tires, now, that had to be Gallaghers for sure.

"Callie doesn't go behind people's backs to speak her mind. She's up front and honest," Orville said.

"So what are you going to do about it?" Quaid asked.

"You bring me solid evidence, and I'll lock someone up. Your suspicions won't carry weight in court," Orville told them.

The feud had gone beyond the women fighting in the bathroom and at the dealership. Now it was getting down to business. Finn was determined to stay out of it as much as he could, but he'd keep a close watch on his property. Thank God the kids were enrolled in public school and wouldn't get caught in the middle of it.

"I'd advise the bunch of you to bury this thing once and for all," Verdie said. "It's gone on long enough. Most of you weren't even born when it started."

"That won't happen any time soon," Honey said.

"Since the sheriff is in the Gallaghers' pocket and won't do anything about it, we'll take care of it ourselves."

"I'm not in anybody's pocket." Orville blushed.

"I heard Ilene Gallagher was chasin' after you," Kinsey said.

"I'm warnin' the bunch of you. If y'all start something that winds up with someone hurt or killed or severe property damage that can come back on you, I'll haul your asses to jail." Orville headed for his car with Verdie and Finn behind him.

"Dammit!" he fumed. "Where'd they get that shit about Ilene Gallagher?"

"She's liked you since high school, Orville. On that part, there is evidence." Verdie laughed.

"Well, I'll be damned." He chuckled as he crawled into his car and slowly turned around.

Chapter 26

THE ATMOSPHERE IN BURNT BOOT WAS TENSE, AS IF everyone was sitting on a keg of gunpowder with a stick of dynamite duct-taped to the side of it. The Brennans would retaliate, and the longer they waited, the worse it could be.

But the feud was the last thing on Finn's mind that night as he tucked Callie's arm into his and escorted her through the doors of the Gallagher ranch mansion. "Have I told you that you are stunning in that green dress? I like it even better than the one you wore last week."

To call it a ranch house would be like calling a palace a cabin. It was built like an old plantation house with lights shining out from three floors. The entryway led to a ballroom with crystal chandeliers throwing enough light to illuminate half of Texas. Tables were covered in what must be the Gallagher plaid, a rich woven pink and green with green napkins and gorgeous pink poinsettias in the middle of each table.

A lady in black slacks, a white shirt, and a cummerbund of the Gallagher plaid took Callie's wrap.

"Well, has the cat got your tongue?" Finn held her hand as they made their way into what could only be described as a ballroom.

"No, but all this has," she answered.

"And to think, this, instead of Salt Draw, could be yours." He chuckled.

"I'd live every day in fear I'd do something wrong."

Tyrell was the first Gallagher to greet them, shaking hands with Finn and then bowing low to kiss Callie's fingertips. "You wore our shade of green tonight. The Gallagher family suffered a severe loss when you stopped at Salt Draw instead of crossing the road to Wild Horse. Someone as lovely as you would wear our plaid so well."

"Thank you for that compliment, but I was actually trying to match the green of the O'Donnell and the Brewster plaids when I bought this dress. They are bold and very similar." She smiled.

"Ah, Finn, you've got yourself a spitfire Irish lass, I see." Tanner laughed.

"She can hold her own," Finn said.

Betsy swept across the floor in a lovely green velvet dress that hugged her curves like a glove. The glow of the chandeliers, the dress, and pure mischief put a sparkle in her dark green eyes. Her red hair was swept up in a nest of curls behind a diamond tiara.

"Hello, Finn. Save me a dance." She ignored Callie and smiled at him before she moved on to the next guests.

Gladys touched Finn on the shoulder, and he whipped around. "Open bar here at this party. I'll take Callie to get a drink, and you can talk to the menfolk." She tucked Callie's arm into hers and led her through the maze of people to the bar.

"You need to meet Naomi Gallagher, Callie. She's the grand matron of the ranch, and she runs Wild Horse with an iron hand. Nothing gets past her," Gladys said.

"Not even the feud stuff?"

"Not one thing. She probably instigates ninety percent of it. She married into the family more than fifty years ago. She dated a Brennan first back in the day, and they had a big fight. She went for a Gallagher next and, believe me, she's made the Brennans pay and pay and pay. She might look like a prissy little old lady with dyed red hair, but believe me, there's horns under that ratted hair," Gladys whispered.

A bar stool served as Naomi's throne. Her cowboy boots with lots of flashy rhinestones didn't reach the first rungs. The brilliant diamonds on several of her fingers sparkled even brighter than the enormous crystal chandelier hanging from the vaulted ceiling. Even though she was a small woman, her dark green eyes left no doubt that she was the boss and everyone in the room would do well to respect that.

Her Southern voice was soft but demanded attention. "You'll be Callie Brewster from Salt Draw. I've heard about you. I'm Naomi Gallagher. I understand Verdie has come back home to roost. I'm glad. She should have never left, but life takes us on some strange trips. What are you ladies drinking tonight?"

"I'm pleased to meet you, Miz Naomi," Callie said.

"A Guinness and a shot of Jameson," Gladys told the bartender.

Callie nodded.

"Looks like you've been raised right." Naomi laughed. "I'm sorry to leave good Irish company, but I have to go mingle. Tell Verdie I missed her tonight and I envy her getting to stay home to play with the grandchildren."

Gladys propped a hip on a bar stool and drank deeply of the dark beer. "Let's take a case of this and run away to the barn with a couple of scorchin' hot cowboys for an orgy."

Callie had just tipped up the shot glass and had to swallow quickly to keep from spewing it all over the bar, the bartender, and Gladys. "Gladys!"

"I'm old, darlin', but I'm not dead, and I still remember how to do it." She laughed.

"Changing the subject on that note." Callie blushed. "Is there a Brennan queen?"

"Oh, hell yeah. Didn't you meet her? Mavis married the very Brennan who Naomi lost. About those cowboys?"

"Please tell me you were teasing." Callie smiled.

"Maybe. Maybe not. I don't imagine you'd be willing to share a single inch of Finn with anyone, since you've already put Betsy and Honey in their places over him."

A short brunette, wearing a crimson red satin dress that flowed from the waist down in a sweeping antebellum-type skirt, pulled out a bar stool. "Mind if I join you ladies? Lovely dress, Gladys."

"Why, thank you, Ilene. You look like you belong in *Gone with the Wind*."

"Thank you. I wanted that look. White wine, please," she told the bartender. "And there he is. I'd hoped he would be here tonight. Give me white zinfandel, please. That's the only kind he drinks."

She picked up the two glasses of wine and carried them across the floor.

"Well, hot damn!" Gladys said.

"What?"

"Look." She nodded.

Callie hadn't recognized Orville out of uniform. He wore a black Western-cut suit, boots, and a big silver belt buckle. When Ilene handed him the glass of wine, he smiled and said something that lit up her face brighter than the enormous Christmas tree in the corner.

"I didn't recognize him without a box of doughnuts," Callie whispered.

Gladys cackled and motioned for the bartender to bring her another shot. "Guess he just needed a wake-up call. Lord, the Brennans are going to shit little green apples. If the Gallaghers have the sheriff in their pocket, there's no tellin' what Naomi will try."

Tyrell claimed the bar stool next to her and said, "I heard you and Finn were together in the army."

"I was his spotter."

Tyrell pointed toward a longneck bottle of beer and the bartender set it in front of him. "I didn't know they let girls do that job."

"They can do it if they outdo the smart little boys," she said.

"Guess nobody much tangles with you, do they?"

"Not too many times," Callie said.

The dinner bell rang.

"There's my cue. Time to go. Nice visitin' with you, Callie," he said.

"That means we go rescue Finn from that group of men and find our seats. I already switched place cards. I'm sitting with y'all. If the Brennans decide to retaliate tonight, and I'm not sayin' they are, then I want to be by the exit out of this place," Gladys said.

"And they've put me and Finn out on the edge by the door?" Callie asked.

"Exactly," Gladys answered.

"Why?"

"You haven't been accepted. You are here because of Verdie. There's an order to the seating. The head table where Naomi will reign like a queen is all the way to the back of the room beside that enormous wall of glass lookin' out over River Bend. Importance starts there and ends up at the back table where we are sitting."

Callie smiled. "Strangely enough, I like that idea."

"Far away from Betsy as possible, right?" Gladys said. "She'll be up there at the head table."

"Where were you supposed to sit?" Callie asked.

"About middle of the room with Polly, but I've got a feelin' she's been spyin' for the Gallaghers. She's my friend and my sister-in-law, so I'd never ask, but still, they know things from the Brennan camp too quick sometimes," Gladys said. "I just switched places with a hired hand. He'll go home happy thinkin' he's the ranch glory child because he got to sit closer to the head table than the foreman."

When they were seated, Tyrell gave the welcoming speech and the waiters started moving through the crowd with carts. Warming dishes held steaks, baked potatoes, fried sweet potatoes, and green beans. Salads were already on the table along with fancy crystal plates filled with stuffed olives, mushrooms, celery sticks, and radishes.

Callie heard the noise above the buzz of conversation, but surely to goodness there wasn't a helicopter right above the ranch. Why would there be? Finn had his head cocked to one side, which meant he'd heard it, too.

"Is that what I think it is?" She squeezed Finn's thigh under the table, more in fear than in flirtation.

"Sounds like it. Maybe it's a medical chopper headed to Dallas, but it's definitely a helicopter," he said.

"It's hovering right outside the house," Callie whispered and noticed two of the waiters quietly slip through the big double doors and run outside.

One second it was warm and everyone was bragging on steaks. The next, the big glass window was gone. It didn't shatter to the inside or the out. Callie watched it rise up into the sky and fly off into the darkness. The room felt like the eye of a tornado and then the north wind shot through the open space, bringing cold, sleet, and snow with it.

"There's going to be dead Brennans floating in the Red River come morning," Naomi screamed above the din of people leaving food on the tables and trying to get out of the room.

Panic didn't set in until the cattle arrived. An old bull led the stampede into the room, crushing the head table and knocking Ilene into Orville, both of them landing on the floor at the same time. Then he plowed his way into the room like he was hunting for a big green pasture right there in the middle of winter.

There were about twenty cows behind him, and the whole crowd started running when they jumped over the short wall that had held the glass window and plowed right into the ballroom. Callie figured the best she could do was get out of the way, especially when the old bull came at her with what looked like a medium rare steak hooked in his left horn. She backed up into a corner, and the bull ran past her. His eyes were wild as he threw back his head and bawled at the big crystal chandelier, pawed a couple of times, and charged the Christmas tree in the center of the room.

Trying to help the people would be like herding feral cats. Betsy, bless her heart, was doing her damnedest to get them all gathered up and out of the room right up until she slipped in a nice warm pile of bullshit right there on the carpet and fell backward. The table she hit on her way down dumped green beans and corn into her pretty red hair, and a heifer raised her tail high and pissed in her lap.

Callie couldn't move from the corner. It all happened so fast and yet in slow motion at the same time. Betsy was screaming. Cows' eyes were rolling in their heads like billiard balls on a pool table. Naomi's cussing would have put blushes on sailors' faces. Gladys finally grabbed Callie by the hand and pulled her out of the corner.

"Time to get out of here before things get really bad. Looks like the steaks on the hoof have ruined steaks on the fine china plates." She slapped a cow on the flank to make room for them to escape through the doors.

"Where is Finn?" Callie yelled.

"I'm right here behind you, Callie. A cow got between us, but I was on the way to rescue you." His big hand closed over hers.

"I should have strapped my gun to my leg under this dress. There would be a bunch of dead cattle if I'd had it with me," she said.

"I knew I was right about not sitting up there at the front of the room," Gladys yelled. "See y'all later."

Polly passed Finn and Callie on the way to the pasture

to get their truck. "Y'all might as well come on down to the bar. I reckon that's where most folks will go now."

"So?" Finn asked.

"I'll be more comfortable there than here. Hell, they'll probably blame us first because we've been in the military. I wonder how they did that," Callie said.

Polly yelled over her shoulder. "Don't know how, but it was slick. The Brennans had better watch their backs now. To leave Santa with shit on him is one thing, but Naomi will be out for blood now."

"Want to stop by her bar for a couple of plain old Coors beers on the way home?" Finn asked Callie.

"Will you dance with just me? We won't be at a to-do, so we don't have to share each other. And please tell me we don't have to go to these parties every year, Finn."

"I hope to hell not," he said.

"I'm going to make a deal with Verdie. We'll take turns. She has to go every other year. She should have to get dressed up at least every two years," Callie said.

He drove back to the main road and turned north. In a few minutes he nosed the truck into one of the few remaining parking places in front of an old weathered building that looked as if it had never seen a coat of paint. A hand-painted sign swinging from chains on the porch had once said Burnt Boot Bar, but the letters in the last word were faded.

"We had a hamburger here that one time, but I never noticed the sign. I thought this was Polly's Place," she said.

"That's what everyone in town calls it. Her husband built it and ran it. She worked in Gainesville for the state department until he died, and then she retired and kept the bar. That's what Verdie told me," Finn said.

They'd just claimed two stools and ordered a couple of beers in Polly's bar when Amanda, the caseworker for the kids, touched Callie on the shoulder. "We have a family who is willing to take all three of the O'Malley kids, but they won't be able to take them until January tenth. This is a married couple over in Amarillo."

Callie's heart dropped to her knees. "Are they going to adopt the kids?"

"No, just foster them. If someone wanted to adopt them, then that would take precedence. Of course, it would have to be a couple. We seldom ever adopt kids out to single parents. And there's no one willing to take on three kids their age. Just thought I'd give you the heads-up so you'd be aware of what's going to happen." Amanda turned and started back to the table where her friends waited.

"Did you hear that?" Callie asked Finn.

"Marry me," he said.

Callie was stunned into silence. "What did you say?"

"I asked you to marry me."

"Are you drunk?"

"No, but I figure if you marry me, I might save you from a life of alcoholism," he said.

"Finn, you can't tease me out of this. I'm going to drink until you have to carry me into the house tonight like you did that New Year's Eve over there in the war when we put away all that whiskey your cousin sent to us in mouthwash bottles. And I'm going to make you tell the kids, because I can't tell, but you aren't doing it until after their trip with Verdie. She's liable to have a heart attack or else run away with the whole lot of them, and she's got the money to stay gone until they're all grown," Callie said.

"Marry me, and we'll adopt them, and Verdie will be safe, and the kids will have a home," he said.

"I'm not sure that's a good reason to get married," she said. "But it is tempting."

"We wouldn't have to tell anyone we're married. As long as it's legal on paper, then Amanda can't turn us down. She said that a married couple wanting to adopt took precedence over foster care, didn't she?"

Callie's heart did a backward flip. He would be marrying her just for the kids, not out of love and commitment. He did say that one time that he loved her, and they did have a pretty damn good relationship in and out of the bedroom, but still, she wanted the whole thing. A wedding with the dress and flowers in a church, not a twenty-minute trip to the courthouse in Gainesville to be kept a secret. She wanted to stand on the front lawn with Christmas lights all around her and yell that Finn O'Donnell was her new husband.

"Why do we have to keep it a secret?" she asked.

"I thought you might want to keep it under wraps, since we've only been together three weeks."

"When I marry, the only thing that'll be a secret will be what goes on in our bedroom."

"So will you think about it?" he asked. "I've kind of grown attached to that old gal and those kids being underfoot. And I don't imagine those new people will let them bring all the animals with them, either, so there's that to think about."

It was a piss-poor reason to get married.

"Don't give me an answer right now. Just think about

it until after the New Year, and then we'll decide," Finn said. "And, Callie, you're not like your sister. You are probably like your father. What was his name?"

"Tommy Jones." The words came out in a hoarse whisper. "He and Mama weren't married, so I got her maiden name, just like Lacy did, because Mama didn't marry her daddy either."

"A cowboy, I take it."

"Yes, he was a cowboy. Grew up on a ranch in the little town where they both lived in east Texas. Place called Jefferson right on the Louisiana border. With my background, you should be runnin' from me, not proposin' to me," Callie said.

"My offer still stands. Secret. No secret. Any way you want to call it," Finn said.

"I need a beer or two or ten after this night, and I need time to think about callin' it." She kicked the shoes off and yelled, "Hey, Polly, I'll have a Coors."

"Make that two," Finn said.

"Two Coors comin' right up. A helicopter took that glass, didn't it? I heard a whirring noise but didn't pay any mind to it. Figured it was one of them medical things and hoped no one in Burnt Boot needed it. Brennans were behind it. Everyone knows it, but they won't be able to prove it. I'm just wonderin' how in the hell they ripped it out so clean." She asked as she set the mugs in front of Callie and Finn.

"Someone cut the glass and put heavy-duty suction cups on it," Finn said.

"They'll find it floatin' in the Red River most likely," Callie said.

"Sounds like something out of a military movie to

me," Polly said. "There's Gladys. I called her to come on down here and help me tonight. With this kind of news, everyone will be coming to the bar to talk about it. Y'all need some change for the jukebox? It still plays three songs for a quarter if you like Merle Haggard and George Jones. I've got a new one ordered all digital and costing more. This one ain't got no Christmas music on it."

"Yes, please. Finn promised to dance with me." Callie fished out a five-dollar bill from her purse and handed it across the bar.

Polly gave her three dollars and eight quarters. "That should be enough to dance some leather off his fancy boots."

Finn ran a finger up under Callie's shawl from elbow to shoulder. "You were, hands down, the prettiest girl at the party."

"And you were, hands down, the best-lookin' cowboy. I don't want to talk about Gallaghers or Brennans the rest of the night. Go put some quarters in that jukebox and let's dance." She filled his hand with quarters.

"Any particular song?" he asked.

"You choose. I'll dance."

He plugged in two quarters and motioned for her to join him. She slid off the bar stool and padded across the wooden floor in her bare feet. Surprisingly enough it wasn't cold. That old potbellied stove over there beside a life-sized Santa was doing its job in keeping the place warm.

"I've picked out my three. It's your turn," Finn said.

She scanned down through the listing and picked out her quarter's worth, then turned around and put her arms around his neck. Brad Paisley started off the six songs with "Good Morning Beautiful."

"I thought this was all old songs by old artists," she said.

"Verdie told me that if Polly likes a song, she figures out a way to get it on a 45 so it'll go in the jukebox, and this is my song to you, Callie Brewster," he breathed into her ear.

The lyrics said that he never worried if it was raining outside because inside with her the sun always shined and his night was wonderful with her by his side—that when he opened his eyes to see her beside him, it was a good morning, beautiful day.

He twirled her and brought her back to his chest as the song ended.

"Well, this one is my song to you," she said as Sammi Smith sang "Help Me Make It Through the Night."

The first lyrics said for him to take the ribbons from her hair, to shake it loose and let it fall, to lay it soft against his skin like the shadows on the wall. She asked him to lie down by her side until the early morning light and to help her make it through the night. She said that it was sad to be alone, and Callie could relate to that. She didn't want to be alone, but Finn deserved so much more than she was or could give.

Finn tipped her chin up for a soft kiss. "I'm here, Callie, forever, amen, and I would have played that one, but it's not on the jukebox. I recognize this tune. I'm just a plain old country bumpkin. I don't wear three-piece suits, but this could be our song if you want it to be."

Cal Smith's "Country Bumpkin" told the tale of a couple's life from the time that a cowboy came into the bar and parked his lanky frame upon a tall bar stool. The barroom girl with knowing eyes looked him up and down and wondered how a country bumpkin like that even found his way to town. By the time the song got to the part about them bringing their first son into the world, tears were flowing down Callie's cheeks and leaving marks on Finn's white shirt. It went on to forty years later when she was on her deathbed knowing her race was almost done, and she looked into the eyes of her son and husband and told her country bumpkins good-bye. And Callie wept even harder.

"It's us if you want it to be," Finn said.

"Forty years isn't enough, Finn. And I could never leave you," Callie said.

"Then think hard about making this thing permanent," he said. "Oh, the next one is my last song. It's my story, in a way, but it brought you into my life, Callie. If I'd have been satisfied where I was on the ranch, if I hadn't wanted something more than cows and corn, I would have never met you. I thought of this song a lot and played it often, both by Waylon and Travis, when we were over there. It almost happened just like this with me and Daddy sitting on the porch and him not wanting me to go to the army but to stay in Texas and be a rancher."

The twang of the guitar started the song, and then Waylon began to sing that he wanted a life where corn don't grow. More tears dammed up behind her lashes as she thought of Finn telling his daddy that he wanted to leave the ranch. She could feel the emotion in Finn's body when the lyrics said that the weeds were high in the land where corn don't grow. It said that hard times were real and dusty fields were there no matter where you go.

"It was dusty, and corn damn sure didn't grow over there in Afghanistan," she said.

"Our kids might want to get away from it, Callie, but if we give them a good foundation, they'll come back," he said.

"I don't think Martin will ever leave the ranch. He's seen the world where corn don't grow, and he didn't like it," she said. "And this one is definitely for both of us."

Merle Haggard's "That's the Way Love Goes" started, and she looped both her arms around Finn's neck.

Haggard sang that he'd spent his whole life searching for that four-leaf clover, that she'd run with him chasing that rainbow, and that's the music God made for the world to sing.

"I do love you, Finn," she said.

"That's enough for tonight. Let's drink the rest of our beer before it goes flat and gets warm." He led her back to the bar.

A tall cowboy went to the jukebox and put in his quarter, and several other cowboys and cowgirls joined him on the dance floor as they did a line dance to Elvis Presley's "Burning Love."

"Guess they're ready to shake it up a little, but y'all sure looked cute out there making love with your eyes," Polly said. "And here come the Brennans. Okay, folks, let's get something straight. This is neutral ground. One nasty little trick, and me and my shotgun will take care of it," Polly yelled.

Gallaghers, some still dressed in fancy clothing, plowed in behind them.

"That goes for the whole lot of you. Be civil or get the hell out of my bar," Polly said. "Now where were we? Oh, I was sayin' that y'all looked cute out there. I bet you could do some fancy fast dancin', too."

The Brennans claimed the south end of the bar, and the Gallaghers took the north end. Wicked looks went back and forth, and for damn sure, they did not dance with one another, but no one started anything. Evidently Polly and her shotgun were a formidable couple.

"Okay, woman, let's show them how it's done," Finn said. "We're not going to let them ruin our night. Besides, Honey and Betsy are both here, and I want them to know that I'm taken so they'll stop this shit."

He and Callie took the floor in a fast swing dance where he twirled her out and brought her back, and she flirted with him with her eyes through the whole dance. When it finished, the tall cowboy sitting beside the juke-box said, "Don't leave yet. We've got more on the way."

The first sounds of "Jailhouse Rock" started, and Callie and Finn danced so fast that she was panting worse than she did during wild sex. Finn's cowboy boots were a blur, but she'd be damned if she let him get ahead of her even if she got blisters on her feet.

"One more," the cowboy hollered. "Y'all are really good. You must dance a lot together. Let's see what y'all can do with 'Cotton-Eyed Joe.'"

Finn wiped sweat from his forehead with a white handkerchief he took from his hip pocket and held his hand out to Callie. "You ever done any clogging?"

"Little bit," she said.

"Well, give it all you got," he said.

When the song ended, the whole bar was whistling,

clapping, and yelling for more, but Finn and Callie staggered to the bar, downed their beers, and asked for another.

"That was fun to watch. Y'all two are going to do just fine back here in the boonies." Polly laughed. "Me and Thomas used to cut a rug like that back when we first opened the bar. He taught me to dance Irish style. Looks like you two already know it."

Finn clicked his mug against Callie's. "To the Irish."

"To us," she said.

They closed down the bar at two o'clock in the morning, and Finn drove very slowly all the way to Salt Draw. They left clothing all over her bedroom floor, fell into bed, and he made such sweet love to her that she almost cried again. He went to sleep right afterward, and she propped up on an elbow to look her fill of the first man who'd ever proposed to her.

God almighty, but those long lashes fanned out on his cheekbones, and that full mouth knew how to turn her on. Could she trust herself to say yes? It wasn't Finn or even his doubts that bothered her but her own genetics.

Have you looked at another man since you've been in Burnt Boot? You are surrounded with good-looking cowboys who have done everything but kidnap you, and you've turned your back on them. Wake up, girl, and smell the coffee. This is the man for you, and you'll never leave him. You wallowed in your daddy's DNA, not your mother's.

She flopped back down on the pillow. Her inner voice had never steered her wrong, not one time, but still she had to think about it. They made sweet love. They made passionate love. They made wild love. They danced well together. They could take out a target together. She loved him, but saying yes meant a lifetime commitment, and she wanted to be sure.

"I'm not rushing. I've got a couple of weeks before the kids have to leave. I want to be damn sure that we can live together forever when I tell him I'll marry him," she whispered.

A pulsing pain hit her between the eyes. Lord, she was going to have a hellacious hangover come morning, which was only three hours from that minute. Verdie would be up rattling pots and pans, and the kids would be loud, and she'd feel like she had a marching band in her head.

She smiled, shut her eyes, and snuggled up against Finn's back.

"It's worth every single throb," she said.

Chapter 27

TWO GLASSES OF TOMATO JUICE SAT ON THE BAR THE next morning when Callie made it to the kitchen. Verdie pointed at them and said, "They are both just alike. Down one without coming up for air and by the time breakfast is done, you'll be ready for it. It's Patrick's special brew for a hangover."

Callie pushed her hair back and smelled the concoction. "How'd you know?"

"Well, Verdie, hot damn!" Joe squawked.

"I may fry that damn bird and tell the kids they're eatin' chicken. He was cute for a little while, but since he learned my name, he's a pest," Verdie said. "Back to the hangover and last night. Polly called me between customers. The Brennans best have a twenty-four-hour guard set up after that stunt. Naomi is out for blood. I heard Orville was there with Ilene. Looks like you've done lost your supply of doughnuts. And believe me, Naomi will sure enough be supporting Ilene in her relationship with Orville so they'll have the sheriff in their pocket over on Wild Horse. They found that big window without a crack in it this morning. It was settin' right in front of the Gallaghers' schoolhouse," Verdie said.

Callie held up the glass. "How'd you know I needed this?"

"If you'd have been giggling any louder, you would have wakened up the kids, and poor little things need their sleep, especially Martin with the news you are springing on him today. He's going to be so excited, he might not sleep for a week," Verdie said.

"What news?" Callie picked up the glass, tipped it back, and drank it down even though her eyes watered after the first sip. She shivered from black hair to toenails when she set the empty glass down with a thud. "Shit, Verdie, was that pure vodka?"

"It had some tomato juice and Louisiana hot sauce in it, plus one well-beaten raw egg. Never failed one time for Patrick," she said. "Now tell me why you aren't going to tell him."

"Tell Martin what news? What are you talking about?" Callie's whole body quivered like a dog shaking water one more time.

"Polly heard Finn propose to you last night. Didn't you say yes?"

Callie fanned her mouth until it cooled enough that she could speak. "I did not! My mama had two girls by two different cowboys and never married either of them. She died when I was sixteen, and I lived with my sister, who followed in her footsteps. It's in my genes, Verdie. Finn deserves better than that."

"You aren't your mother or your sister, girl," Verdie said sternly. "If you were, you wouldn't be doing the work of five hired hands, raisin' four kids who aren't yours, and puttin' up with a bitchy old woman like me. Any one of those things would have already put you on the run. Trust me. You've got roots and you are a settler, not a runner," she said.

"That's what Finn says. I want to believe him," Callie said.

"We don't get a whole lifetime of days, Callie. We get them doled out to us one at a time. At my age, I open my eyes in the morning and just tell the big man thank you. And if I'm still breathing come night, I have a drink of Jack, and I hope I get to start all over tomorrow, because I'm happier than I've been since my boys were little kids. Don't question. Just follow your heart, girl. It won't lead you down the daisy path."

"How do I know that?"

"You don't. That's where faith comes in," Verdie answered. "You're in love with Finn. You wouldn't love him if you couldn't trust him or believe him."

Callie hugged Verdie tightly. "Thank you."

"Who's in love with who?" Finn stumbled into the kitchen, took one look at the tomato concoction, and downed it in four big gulps. "Tastes just like what Grandpa used to mix up. Hell in a glass, but it works." He kissed Callie on the forehead.

Callie was glad that the kids came out of their bedrooms in a whirlwind. Olivia's hair hadn't been braided and hung in strings down in her face; the boys were still in their pajamas and clamoring for breakfast.

"We're starving," Adam and Ricky said at the same time.

"What's in that? Do we have to drink tomato juice for breakfast? I really don't like it too good. It's too thick," Olivia said.

"No, it was just for Callie and Finn. They had headaches after the party last night," Verdie said.

"And next year, Verdie is going to the party and we're keeping the kids," Callie announced.

"Not me. I'm too old for parties. I'm the granny, and the granny gets to call all babysitting duties and decisions about parties," Verdie said. "Bacon, eggs, and biscuits for breakfast. Olivia, it's your turn to set the table. You boys go get dressed for chores. Finn is going to need lots of help this morning."

"Why don't you kids watch cartoons this morning? I'll do the chores," Callie said.

"You serious? We can't let you do that. We need to make the money for our Christmas shopping on Monday," Martin said. "We done been talkin' about the things we want to buy."

"Okay, then." Callie smiled. "Who's going to the barn today and who's helping with housework and laundry?"

Olivia raised her hand. "I'll be staying in the house with Granny. Can I please dust? I'd rather do that than fold clothes. And I love to dust off the pretty Christmas things."

"Well, that's a good thing, because I hate to dust," Verdie said. "Now let's have some breakfast so the whole bunch of you can get your work done. You know what I want for Christmas? I want some new hot pads. Mine are looking like they should go to the ragbag, and I have to use two just to keep from burning my fingers."

Callie would have pasted a gold star on Verdie's forehead if she'd had one. She had just provided the kids with something useful and inexpensive that would thrill her for Christmas. Callie decided to use the opening and do the same.

"Well, I need some good warm socks. And I would really like a stocking hat so I don't have to borrow one of Martin's. And I just bet you that Finn would like some new work gloves, those brown kind that he uses out in the barn. He's constantly putting them down and the puppies chew holes in them." She laughed.

The kids' minds were working like gears in the backside of an old wristwatch. Bless Verdie's heart. She was a genius…or maybe a Christmas angel.

~~~

Finn nodded and added two or three things to his list when he caught on to what Verdie and Callie were doing. But his mind wasn't on presents or kids that morning.

He'd been serious when he asked Callie to marry him the night before. She might think it was just so they could adopt those kids, but it was because he'd fallen head over heels in love with the woman. And that little conversation just proved why. She'd make a wonderful mother whether she'd birthed the children or not.

Oh. My. Sweet. Jesus.

His mother's words when she was worried shot through his mind. Children! They'd been going at it hot and heavy, sleeping together in every sense of the word, and he hadn't even asked her about birth control. Surely to God, she would have said something if he'd needed to provide protection.

"Hey, it's the boss's day to give the kids a day off, with pay of course. If all you guys will help Verdie and Olivia with the inside chores until Callie and I get the feeding done, then all four of you can come out to the barn to help with the horses. I might even throw in five dollars extra for each of you for your Christmas shopping money on Monday if you'd consider that," Finn said.

"We'd sure earn it, 'cause I don't like to fold clothes either and I hate to make up beds," Martin said.

"Not me. I'll do it," Ricky said. "I don't mind making up beds or even mopping if I can have more Christmas money."

"I'm not just giving you the money. You'll have to do whatever Verdie tells you to do, and she's one tough boss when it comes to Saturday morning chores," Finn said. "But if you think you're not big enough to do what Olivia can do, well, then you can go with me, and Callie will do the tough stuff."

Adam puffed out his chest. "I can do anything Olivia can do, and I'm tough enough to do whatever Granny tells me to do. I'll stay in the house. Pass me the bacon. I need lots of bacon for energy."

"Well, Verdie!" the bird yelled.

Everyone's heads jerked around to look at the cage.

"Dammit, Verdie, Joe needs a drink," he said loudly.

"Where did he learn to ask for a drink?" Finn asked.

"Who in the hell knows?" Verdie said.

"Who in the hell knows?" Joe quipped.

"Guess I'd better watch what I say." Verdie laughed. "It appears he's broadening his vocabulary daily."

"Well, hot damn, Verdie." Joe pranced from one end of the cage to the other, then he stopped abruptly, tucked his head under his wing, and went to sleep.

"Think we could teach him some new things to say?" Adam asked.

"I guess he's upset because we play with the cat and the dogs more than we do him," Olivia answered.

"I think he's plumb took up with Verdie. He can be her pet," Martin said.

Finn laughed. "Well, Verdie!"

Verdie shook a pot holder at him. "That'll be enough

out of you. Woman can't have a damn secret in the world with that tattletale watchin' her every move."

She might be scolding him, but the twinkle in her eyes said that she liked the parrot, and Finn would be surprised if he didn't learn even more new phrases in the next few weeks.

He and Callie both finished breakfast at the same time. She pulled her hair up into a messy-looking pony-tail on her way to their wing of the house with him right behind her. He wore a red flannel shirt over his thermal knit shirt, put on two pair of socks and his old worn work boots, and whistled for Shotgun on his way back through the house. The big yellow dog bounded out the back door and into the snow, kicking up a cloud of it in his wake.

Callie stomped her way to the old work truck and let herself inside, slammed the door, and then grabbed her head.

"The cure didn't work?" he asked.

"Not so good."

"But you weren't going to tell Verdie for fear she'd make you drink another one, right?"

"You got it. Now why am I doing chores?"

"Thought we'd have some hayloft sex after we got done feeding," he teased.

"Hell, no! My poor old head would explode like a ripe watermelon."

"Well, damn! Some Saturdays just start off bad and get worse. You sit in here with your eyes closed, and I'll load the feed. Deal?"

She nodded without opening her eyes. "Deal."

He waited until she was behind the wheel after

the first cattle feeder had been filled before he asked, "Callie, I'm not sure how to approach this question."

"You want to take back the proposal, right? You've decided you were drunk and you don't want to take on a wife and four kids," she said.

He chuckled. "No, the proposal still stands, as informal and unromantic as it was. And I'm not marrying you because I want four kids. I'm asking you to marry me because I love you, and for the first time in my life, I'm happy. I didn't realize it, but I've always been looking at the grass on the other side of the fence, and now I'm happy inside my own pasture. That's because you're here with me and I love you."

"You calling me a cow?"

He laughed harder. "Not today when you have a headache, but sometimes my grandpa calls my granny an old heifer when she's being stubborn."

"I think that's sweet," she said.

"Are you serious?"

"As a hangover after a night at Polly's. Now what's this sensitive matter?"

"Birth control," he said.

She gripped the steering wheel until her fingers turned white. "Oh, my Lord! I didn't even think of birth control. My prescription for them ran out six months ago. I should have thought about it."

"It's been a long time for me, too, but I should have been more careful," he said.

"Shit! What is today?"

"December twentieth."

"I'm regular as clockwork, Finn, and I'm late."

"You're worried that I want to marry you just for the

kids. Now I'm worried you'll say yes so you won't have a child who has to grow up like you did with no father."

"I love you too much to do that to you, Finn. It's probably because of all this stress. Constant feud. Kids. Parties. Changing and accepting that I do like farming. I can't be pregnant."

"You like ranchin'?" he teased.

"Yes, I do. It's different now than it was when I was a kid."

"Callie, I would love it if you were pregnant," he whispered.

"Are you sure, Finn? You wouldn't just be offering to marry me because I might be pregnant."

"Darlin', I'd be okay with a dozen kids on Salt Draw. And I want to marry you."

"I'm going to marry you, Finn, whether I'm pregnant or not and whether we adopt kids or not. You know that already, don't you? And that's about as romantic as your proposal," she said.

He moved across the wide bench seat and kissed her soundly on the cheek. "I'll take that as a yes. How about three days after Christmas? That's on Sunday, and we can have it at the church. And we won't even know for sure if you are pregnant, so you won't feel like I'm marrying you because I'm responsible," he said.

She braked and stopped the truck close to the feeding trough of the second pasture full of black cows. "Sometimes being your best friend is tough."

He turned her cheek around and kissed her on the lips. "I love you. You set the date and I'll abide by it, but I'm calling Amanda on Monday and telling her to start the adoption proceedings. And, Callie, I don't feel like you're my best friend when I come through that closet door."

"Oh, yeah, cowboy? What am I at that time?"

"The woman I intend to marry and grow old with. The amazing lady who just said yes to this country bumpkin. When are we going to buy rings?"

"Rings? I don't want rings. I want a gold band. Diamonds aren't for feeding cattle and rounding up stray puppies."

He kissed her again, this time with more heat and passion. "I really, really love you, Callie. You tell me when and where, and I'll be there, but I'm still calling Amanda."

And now he had to go home and call his mother. He hoped his dad had the roof nailed on real good, because it could shoot right off the house when he told her he was getting married, adopting three orphans plus his new wife's nephew, and the lady who owned the ranch before had moved back in with him.

Maybe she'd think it was a Christmas miracle and not fuss at him too much.

Chapter 28

THE FOUR KIDS MARCHED SINGLE FILE THROUGH THE doors behind the choir section of the church. It was their day to shine, and the pew seemed empty with only Polly, Gladys, Verdie, Finn, and Callie and no fidgeting children.

The preacher took his place behind the pulpit, but the buzz didn't die down until he cleared his throat the second time. "And y'all blame the pre-service noise on the children." He smiled. "Must be the excitement of the holidays upon us, but I do believe y'all are louder than the kids. Today's program ends our month of Christmas and is put on by the youngsters who are twelve and under. For you newcomers, we used to have a school program and a church program, but with the busy time of year, we decided a long time ago to combine them. Shhh." He put his finger to his lips. "Don't tell the FBI or whoever thinks we should separate church and state. Up here in Burnt Boot, we kind of do things our own way. Now I'll turn this over to Tamara Johnson, the secretary at our public school, and she'll narrate today's program. Merry Christmas to each and every one of you, and may the Lord bless and keep you in the New Year."

Finn laced his fingers in Callie's hand and whispered, "I called my folks last night. After the first initial shock, they are excited. You just have to set the date."

She cupped her hand over his ear and said, "I was just late, not pregnant. You don't have to do this."

He squeezed her hand. "Look, our kids are the first ones. Martin is Charlie Brown and Olivia is Lucy. They're doing Charlie Brown's Christmas. Look at their smiles. And, darlin', I'm disappointed, but there's always next month."

The children lined up and sang "Christmas Time Is Here." Callie's heart swelled with pride when all four children delivered their lines perfectly in between verses of the song.

"It's Beginning to Look a Lot Like Christmas" was their next song, and Snoopy popped up from the choir loft to sing with them.

"It's Ricky," Finn said proudly. "Guess those dogs taught him how to walk on all four legs."

Then Snoopy picked up a cardboard guitar. Adam, who was playing Schroeder, scooted a tiny toy piano to center stage from behind the Christmas tree, sat down in front of it, and popped his knuckles. The music started for "Rockin' Around the Christmas Tree," and all the kids started doing their version of the Christmas dance. Adam played a mean piano, and Ricky got down with a rock guitar. Charlie Brown and Lucy both had some fine dance moves.

Polly leaned forward and asked, "Wonder where they learned how to do swing dancin'."

Finn laughed hard but not as loud as the three old women on the other end of the pew. Verdie didn't care who heard her when she said, "Those are my grandkids."

"Please tell me that you'll tell her no when she wants to put a real piano in the living room and buy a guitar," Callie said.

"No need to buy a guitar. I own three and play them all. I can teach Snoopy how to play if he really wants to." He grinned.

She rolled her eyes toward the ceiling. Finn really would make a wonderful father, and all four of those kids needed him, so why was there still a tiny doubt in her mind?

It's not about Finn. It's about me, she argued with the voice in her head.

"Did we do good, huh, huh, huh?" Martin bounced around in the van like a puppet on a broken string. "Did we surprise you? Did you see that I got to be Charlie Brown? I never got to play the big part before we moved to Burnt Boot."

"And I was Lucy," Olivia said.

"Well, I was Snoopy and we decided this morning to name the new puppies Snoopy and…" Ricky stopped for a breath of air.

Adam picked up where he left off, "Snoopy and Linus. We was going to name them Snoopy and Schroeder, but Linus is easier to spell. Granny, I saw you clapping for us. Did you like the play?"

Verdie held up a palm to quiet them. "It was the best one of the whole season. And y'all did so good, I think we should celebrate. Finn, you think this van can get us all the way to the McDonald's place in Gainesville? And maybe afterward we could go do some shopping at the Dollar Tree. I heard that's a real good place to do some serious present buying."

"I bet if the kids would sing their songs one more time, this brand-new van might go that far," Finn said.

"But we left our money at home," Olivia groaned.

"I'll pay for your presents, and you can pay me back when we get home," Verdie said.

Verdie nodded at Ricky. "Okay, Snoopy, you get to lead us in the first song y'all did this morning."

The song started kind of shy-like, but by the time they got into the second song, the van was filled with loud singing, and Verdie was singing right along with them. Finn kept time with his thumb on the steering wheel and shot an occasional wink toward Callie.

"You like this, don't you?" Callie asked.

"Love it, darlin'. Reminds me of when we used to get out the stringed instruments and sing under the shade tree on Sunday. Us kids got to sing right along with the adults, and soon as we could play an instrument, we got to relieve them when they needed a break. You're going to love the O'Donnell family."

"But are they going to love me?" she said softly.

Finn reached across the distance separating the two bucket seats and patted her on the knee. "Yes, they are. It's the season of love, darlin'."

"Did I hear that your family is coming for Christmas?" Verdie yelled above the singing from the seat right behind Finn.

"Maybe after Christmas. Callie and I are still working out the details," he said.

"Won't that be fun? If they've got travel trailers, we'll line 'em up in the backyard. If they don't, we'll put the kids in the living room in sleeping bags and give them the bedrooms, right, kids? We could put a bunch of them in the old bunkhouse if y'all will shift all your gym stuff to the side. It sleeps about twenty, or double that if they bring sleeping bags and line 'em up on the big living area floor." Verdie had already started making plans.

Olivia stopped singing. "Do they have kids?"

"Oh, honey, the O'Donnells bring a whole bunch of kids," Finn answered.

"Then Christmas won't be the end but the beginning," Martin said.

"You got that right," Finn told him, but he was staring into Callie's eyes when he said it.

Shopping with the kids was a whole new experience. Since the store was so small, Verdie organized the whole affair. Finn and Callie would take all but one kid to Walmart to buy dog and cat food for the animals while she shopped with Olivia. When they returned, she swapped out kids until each one had time to do their shopping. At the end, they sent Verdie and Finn across the street to get a cup of coffee, and Callie took all four of the children into the store to shop for Verdie.

It took a couple of hours, but when they were finished, the back of the van was full of bags. Verdie had bought a box of labels at the Dollar Tree and slapped a sticker on each bag so the kids could identify them when they got home.

"And now," Finn said when they were all back in the van, "is this wagon train ready to go home, or would we like to go to the Braum's store for an ice cream cone? You kids probably won't be coming back to town before Christmas, since Granny Verdie decided to shop today instead of next week. So…" He paused and winked at Callie. "If you have any idea you might get hungry for one of those big old waffle cones filled up with soft ice cream, you'd better let me hear something from the backseat."

"Ice cream, ice cream," Verdie started the chant.

"Do we have four kids or five?" Callie asked.

"Right now I think it's four, but maybe we can make that number grow in a couple of years." Finn laughed.

She slapped him on the arm, and Verdie leaned up as far as her seat belt allowed. "Did I hear something about adopting more kids, or was that more cats and dogs? I'd rather have more kids if my two cents means anything."

"I think those four are keeping you busy enough," Finn answered. "But if you want us to go over to the Walmart parking lot and see if anyone has tossed out any kittens or puppies or maybe a kid or two, we could go back," Finn said.

"Don't you be sassy with me." Verdie grinned.

They were pulling off the road and into the lane at Salt Draw when Finn heard a gasp from the backseat.

"We've got company. I wonder who it could be," Verdie said.

"You won't let Amanda take us away before we get our presents wrapped, will you?" Olivia asked.

Verdie patted her on the leg. "Honey, nobody is taking you anywhere. We'll see who gets out of the truck, and if we don't like his looks, we'll send him or her on their way."

Finn parked and waited for someone to crawl out, but no one did. He raised the hatchback on the van so the kids could unload their bags and then opened the truck's passenger door to see a backseat full of suitcases, boots, and a very familiar saddle.

COWBOY BOOTS FOR CHRISTMAS

"Sawyer O'Donnell," Finn said.

A tall cowboy rounded the end of the house with Snoopy and Linus at his feet. "In the flesh. I checked out the bunkhouse. Good-looking gym you got in there. But there's plenty of room for a tired old cowboy to rest his achin' bones."

"We've got a spare room in the house," Finn said as the two cousins bypassed the handshakes and did a man-hug right there in front of four gaping kids and two women.

"Everyone, this is my cousin Sawyer. Sawyer, this is Verdie, Martin, Olivia, Adam, and Ricky, and this right here is Callie. Remember me talking about her when we did the cattle run last year?"

"I do, and I'm right pleased to meet the whole bunch of you."

Verdie stepped forward first and opened the front door. "Ain't no use in standin' out here in the cold. I bet you'd love a cup of decent coffee and some cookies. Then you can unload your things. You'll have a choice of the old nursery. It's got a twin-sized bed in it, or there's one spare bunk bed in the boy's room. But for now you bring your gear inside, and we'll get all this Christmas shopping unloaded, and then we'll sit down and get acquainted."

The kids all raced inside with Callie right behind them, directing traffic to separate rooms to wrap their presents. Olivia would be in her own room. Martin could have the bunk room, Adam would be in the living room, and Verdie offered her room to Ricky. Callie was glad she didn't have to give her bedroom to anyone, because she wasn't sure that Finn had taken all his clothing with him that morning when he left.

Sawyer was as tall as Finn, but a slightly toasted look to his skin said there was probably some American Indian or some Latino blood in there somewhere. His eyes were deep dark brown, and his hair so black that it had a blue cast in the sunlight.

"Looks like you've been a busy man." Sawyer followed Finn down the hallway to the old nursery.

"Little bit." Finn set the boot bag inside the bedroom door. "Mama sent you, didn't she?"

"Oh, yeah, she did." Sawyer grinned. "And I'm to report back to her by Christmas morning. Done your shoppin' yet?"

"Just got a little left to do. Why?"

"Well, since I'm going to be here until after Christmas, I guess maybe I should do some shopping for the folks in the house, and you're going to help me," Sawyer said.

Finn crossed his arms over his chest. "What makes you think I'm helping you? You didn't even tell me you were coming to visit."

"You are happy, Finn O'Donnell. I swear to God, you are happy. Never thought I'd see you like this again after what happened in Afghanistan. It's written all over your face. To answer your question, you're going to help me shop because I'm the one who's talkin' to your mama every evening. I already called her and told her that there are two big old pups in the barn, that the horses look great, that you've got a damn fine gym and a shitty shootin' range that I'll have to help you build up, and that Shotgun is happy. I didn't know about the cat and the rat-dog in the living room, or I would have reported on them as well. Tonight I'm telling her about Callie and the kids and Verdie. She reminds me of Grandma O'Donnell."

"Callie?" Finn asked.

"No, Verdie reminds me of Grandma. I can't believe that little bitty beautiful woman was your spotter. Lord, I expected a woman who was at least six feet tall and maybe weighed in at two hundred pounds, not one who looks like Jennifer Lopez's sister or cousin."

Finn chuckled. "I guess I forgot to tell Mama what she looks like. I could send a few pictures of Callie, Verdie, and the kids."

"It might be a good idea. It would put your mama's mind at ease," Sawyer said.

"So you're really staying until after Christmas?" Finn asked.

"Is there a problem with that? Truth is, my old girl-friend is back in town, and I don't want to deal with her, not after the stunt she pulled, breaking up with me and marrying someone else when we were on that cattle run." Sawyer removed his black felt hat and ran a hand through his jet-black hair.

"No problem at all. You're welcome to stay as long as you like. You interested in relocating permanently?" Finn sat down in a rocking chair and set it in motion.

"You offering me a job?"

Finn shook his head. "I got a crew that's working out pretty good right now. But Gladys Cleary has a nice little spread and the general store here in Burnt Boot. I heard she was looking for a foreman, but I got to warn you, there's a feud goin' on here, and believe me, right now it's hot as hell between the families." He went on to tell Sawyer what had happened in the last few weeks.

"The Gallaghers and the Brennans pretty much own the land in Burnt Boot. Only other three folks who have any property to speak of is Gladys, who has Fiddle Creek Ranch, and her sister-in-law Polly, who has the bar and runs a few cattle on her small acreage."

"A feud, huh? Got any good-lookin' women in this Hatfield and McCoy mix?" Sawyer asked.

"Dozens of them. And both sides want Fiddle Creek to get at the water rights, but I don't reckon that would have to worry you none. You'd be working for Gladys if she hired you."

"It's something to think about. I'll talk to her this week," Sawyer said. "You like it here for real? Be honest with me."

"Love it, and it would be nice to have an ornery old spy cousin around," Finn said.

"Well, I have been lookin' for a place to light for a while, and feuds don't scare me none. They can fight, and I'll stay out of it. Now tell me just how serious is it between you and Callie? Your mama said you mentioned marrying her. Is that true?"

Finn nodded. "It's not like we just met, Sawyer. We've known each other for years."

Martin poked his head into the room. "Granny Verdie sent me to tell y'all that there's coffee made and cookies on the table and to ask if Sawyer has had dinner so she'll know whether to stir up some real food."

"Cookies and coffee is plenty," Sawyer said. "And are you Ricky or Martin?"

"I'm Martin, but me and Ricky both have dark hair. Adam and Olivia are the blonds," he said.

"I'll have it all straight by tomorrow. You've got

brown eyes like me and the rest of the kids have blue eyes. That's one way to remember," Sawyer said. "Now, if you'll lead the way to those cookies, cowboy, I'd be obliged."

"Yes, sir," Martin said.

—⟶⟵—

Verdie grabbed Callie by the arm and hauled her into the kitchen. "I heard something in church this morning that I ain't had time to tell you. Naomi Gallagher is pissed about the window stunt, and she's declared full-fledged war on the Brennans. No more mice in the punch bowl or bullshit on Santa Claus."

"Please tell me we're not in the middle of it," Callie whispered.

"Not if I can keep us away from it, but it's fixin' to get rough around here. Naomi ain't been this mad since the Brennans rustled about a hundred head of cattle back in the fifties right after she married into the Gallaghers," Verdie said. "But right now we got to make that handsome cowboy welcome."

Finn and Sawyer pushed their way into the kitchen before Callie could say another word. It wasn't hard to see the family resemblance between Sawyer and Finn. They had the same tall, muscular build, the same square jaw and full mouth, and they even had the same swagger. But Sawyer's mother had to have some Latino in her for his skin to have that pretty permanent tan and those deep, dark brooding eyes. Or maybe he came from gypsy blood; whatever it was, it made for a damn fine-looking cowboy.

In Callie's eyes, he wasn't nearly as good-looking

as Finn, and it didn't take a genius to know that Sawyer had been sent to Burnt Boot to check her out. It was in his eyes when he scanned her out by the truck and again when he sat down at the kitchen table and the whole family gathered around it for a visit.

"Are you one of Finn's cousins who went on the trail ride with him?" Martin asked. "He told us a little about it when we was cleaning horse stables."

"Yes, I am. We went from north Texas all the way up across the whole state of Oklahoma and into Kansas to Dodge City. It was a real fun trip," Sawyer said.

"Man, I wish I could do that someday, just sleep out under the stars and ride a horse all day," Martin said wistfully.

"Horses! Get the rope. Hang the bastard," Joe hollered.

Verdie pushed the platter of cookies toward Sawyer. "Meet Joe, our crazy parrot. We never know what's going to come out of his mouth. What is it they say in Mexico— welcome to our crazy world? Well, this place is even crazier than what they've got south of the border. These kids are waiting for you to take the first cookie, but if I was you, I'd go ahead and get two. They've been shopping all afternoon, and even though they had ice cream on the way home, they're probably starving again."

Sawyer picked up two cookies and slid the platter back to the middle of the table. Four little sets of hands reached toward it.

"So you were Finn's spotter. He talked about you on the trail drive." Sawyer looked over at Callie.

"I was." She nodded. "We planned to start target practice once a week, but we've been pretty busy here lately. Maybe after the holidays and the kids get back in school, we'll get a schedule worked out for it. My spotter skills are rusty, but my aim is still pretty good with a pistol."

Finn slipped his hand under the tablecloth and rested it on her knee. "She's now my right hand again. Turns out she can tear down a tractor and put it back together just as well as she can spot for me in the desert. And I have to work to keep up with her on the morning workout."

"Good God almighty! You don't expect me to run and work out every morning, do you?"

"Good God almighty! Joe needs bourbon," the bird yelled.

"Does he mimic everything?" Sawyer asked.

"Yes, and he's smart enough to know how to use it," Verdie said.

Martin picked up another cookie. "Us hired hands don't have to work out. They won't even let us target practice, but next year I'm askin' Santa Claus for a BB gun, and I'm going to be as good of a shot as Callie when I grow up."

"Gun. Run, dog!" Joe squawked.

"Wait until your mama hears about Joe the parrot." Sawyer grinned.

"You better watch what you say. Like I said, he'll repeat anything," Verdie warned.

"Thanks for warnin' me, Miz Verdie. And if you get tired of Salt Draw, my mama would hire you as a cook on my word about these cookies." Sawyer turned up the charm.

"Only way I'm leaving Salt Draw again is feetfirst as they carry me out the door and put me in a hearse," Verdie said seriously.

"And that won't be for a very long time," Callie said quickly when Olivia's chin started to quiver.

"I dang sure hope not, now that I've found these cookies," Sawyer said. "Y'all sure got this place all prettied up for Christmas. That tree is just plain beautiful."

Callie could have kissed him for changing the subject. Olivia's little blue eyes went from misty to sparkly in seconds.

"It's the prettiest tree in the whole world. It's even prettier than the ones down on Main Street that the Gallaghers and the Brennans put up for the town of Burnt Boot. And did you see all the presents under it? And guess what, after chores tonight, we get to finish our wrapping, and there'll be even more. We ain't never ever had so many presents under the tree with our names on them. This is the best Christmas ever," Olivia said.

"It looks like it just might be," Sawyer said.

"Oh no!" Adam slapped his forehead and whispered to Verdie.

She winked at Adam. "We'll be needing to go do some more shopping tomorrow, Callie."

Callie read Adam's mind. There were no presents for Sawyer under their tree, and even the dogs, cat, and Joe had presents. "I was planning to go to Gainesville myself. Maybe we could all make one more trip before Thursday."

"Can I go, too? I'll help with the chores this evening and in the morning if you kids will let me go with you," Sawyer said.

"Yes, sir," Ricky said. "We go everywhere as a family, and if you're going to live here, then you're family, too."

Callie had barely gotten into bed that night when the closet door opened and Finn crawled in beside her. She snuggled up to his side and his arm went around her, drawing her so close that her body was plastered against his.

"I like Sawyer, and Verdie has already called Gladys. She says that if he's anything like you, she wants to talk to him on Tuesday," she said.

"He's not really like me. He's a lot more outgoing and a hell of a lot better-lookin'. The Gallagher and Brennan women are likely to fire up the feud even more because of him."

"Good. It'll take the pressure off me and you." Callie laughed.

Finn's fingertips moved up and down her bare upper arm, thoughtlessly, softly, driving her crazy. "I'd like it if he moved to Burnt Boot. His girlfriend ditched him while we were on the cattle drive and married someone else. Now she's back around Comfort. He needs a new start."

"Hire him on Salt Draw if he doesn't like Fiddle Creek. We'll need more help come spring," she said. "But right now I've got something to say, Finn. Before he calls your mama and before she calls you. I want to marry you and I want to adopt those kids, and even more, I want you to adopt Martin so that we'll all have the same last name. I don't imagine Verdie would let you adopt her, though."

"Okay," Finn said softly.

"To all of it?"

"Yes, ma'am. I was going to suggest it myself, but I

was going to take a step at a time so I didn't spook you so bad you'd leave me. I'd die without you, Callie. My heart would just flat stop beating."

"Next Sunday then. Call all your family, and Verdie can put out the word in Burnt Boot. We'll have a five o'clock wedding and a big potluck dinner in the fellowship hall for our reception."

She looked up into Finn's clear blue eyes and saw a solid future in them. One that included more than four kids and that would always be rooted right there on Salt Draw.

Finn pushed back the covers and went back through the closet doors to his bedroom. Lord, what had she done? Scared him away by agreeing to marry him in one week?

She was stunned into silence until the door opened again and he was crossing the room. "You scared the shit out of me. I thought you were running away just when I'd decided that you were right about me having roots."

He dropped on one knee in front of the bed, took her hand in his, and said, "Callie Brewster, my heart loved you long ago, but I wouldn't listen to it. But now that we have found each other, I never want to be apart from you again. I want to live the rest of my life knowing that you are my wife and soul mate. So will you marry me?" He popped open a small red velvet ring box with a set of gold bands inside. "I didn't buy an engagement ring, because you told me not to, so we'll have to wait to put these on each other until next Sunday."

"Yes, yes, yes!"

He cupped her cheeks in his hands, and it seemed like an eternity passed before his lips found hers.

"I love you, Callie."

Her arms slid around his neck as she whispered hoarsely around the lump in her throat, "I love you, Finn. And that wedding band is exactly what I wanted. And I want all those things you said, and I want to have them with you. Now will you please get into this bed with me?"

Chapter 29

ANGEL MADE A GAME OF RUNNING THROUGH wrapping paper and chasing ribbons, but the kids were so enthralled with their new boots and toys that they scarcely even noticed the animals on Christmas morning.

"Is this the Christmas you'd planned when you moved to Salt Draw?" Callie asked Finn over the noise and confusion of eight people talking at once.

"This is the Christmas I've always dreamed about, but I damn sure didn't think it was possible in such a short time." He leaned over a stack of boot boxes and kissed her.

Verdie held up her hand and whistled.

The only noise in the house was that of Pistol snoring beside the fireplace and the rustling of paper when Angel poked her head out to see why things had gotten so quiet.

"What is it, Granny Verdie?" Olivia asked.

"I found another present hiding back behind the tree. It's got Callie's name on it, so I thought maybe she should open it."

Verdie pulled out a big box and handed it to Sawyer, who'd claimed the recliner that morning. He handed it off to Finn, who passed it on to Callie with a twinkle in his blue eyes.

"Open it, Callie," Martin said.

"Is it from you?" she asked.

"No, you already opened up my gloves and stocking hat, remember?" Martin said.

"Yes, I remember, but I thought maybe you'd drawn a picture for me."

"I did, but I couldn't get Shotgun and Pistol to look like dogs. They looked more like sheep," Martin said.

Callie looked at all four children, who had put on their new boots from Verdie the minute they opened them. She'd taken a picture of them in their pajamas, hair uncombed, little faces smiling so brightly that it dimmed the bright sun just rising over the horizon.

"Well," Sawyer said, "if you don't open that last present, Verdie won't let us at those homemade cinnamon rolls she made special for Christmas morning, and the kids and I won't get to go out and build a snowman before dinnertime. We are all itchin' to get to wear our new hats and gloves and scarves."

She looked at Finn, who shrugged. "You have to open it to see who it's from."

"But it's too pretty to open." She ran her hands over the shiny red paper and gently touched the big gold bow.

"I'll open it for you," Martin said.

"I'll do it." Callie slipped the bow off the end and carefully removed the paper, only tearing the places where the tape stuck tightly.

She opened the box to find a gorgeous pair of cowboy boots, the very ones she'd looked at in the Western-wear store and gasped when she saw the price tag. They were black leather with aqua stitching around the phoenix cut into the front.

"Black for your hair. Aqua for your eyes. A phoenix

for what has risen out of the ashes," Finn said. "Let me help you put them on."

Callie shoved her right foot into the boot and then pulled it back out. Had the salespeople left cardboard down inside the boot? She reached in, wrapped her hand around a little velvet box, and brought it out as she locked eyes with Finn.

"We waited until today to tell y'all," Finn said as she popped it open.

"Tell us what? What have you got? Oh, that's a pretty box." Olivia pushed closer to Callie.

Callie held up the box. "It holds wedding bands."

Joe made his kissing sounds and then let out one of his loud wolf whistles. Then he yelled, "Bring out the bourbon."

Verdie laughed so hard that she had to wipe tears with the tail of her apron. Callie threatened to shoot the bird, and the kids all squealed that she couldn't harm a feather on Joe's body.

Finn draped an arm around her shoulders and kissed her on the forehead. "Don't you love it all?"

When the noise died down, Finn announced, "We'll be getting married Sunday night. On Saturday the families will start arriving. Now, Callie, you can tell the rest of the story."

"What? That Sawyer is moving over to Fiddle Creek because he got the job as foreman for Gladys Cleary?" she teased.

"Well, there is that," Finn said.

"Oh, man! We like having you here with us," Ricky said.

Sawyer patted him on the head. "Grow up, and I'll steal you away from Salt Draw to come work for me."

"No, sir. My home is right here on Salt Draw," Ricky said.

"Is there more?" Martin asked.

"Yes, but it only involves you, Martin. The man who is in prison for shooting that guy…" She paused. The other kids didn't know about it, but they were going to be family, so maybe there shouldn't be secrets.

Martin picked it up from there and told the story in only a few short sentences. "Do they want me to come sit by the judge yet?" he asked.

"No, that's the news I got just a few minutes ago. The prosecutor called even though it's Christmas. They worked out what's called a plea bargain. The man pleaded guilty to avoid the death sentence. He will be serving life without parole in prison, so you don't have to testify, and it's all over. At his age, there's no way he'll ever get out," Callie said.

Martin pumped his arm up and down. "Yes! Yes, yes, yes!"

Callie nodded. "And now for the rest of the news. We've been working with Amanda all week. It will take a while to get the papers in order and make it official, but we are adopting Olivia, Ricky, and Adam, and Finn is adopting you, Martin. So unless you kids want to keep your birth names, you will all be O'Donnells in a few weeks."

Verdie wiped tears away with the tail of her Christmas apron. "I just knew selling Finn this ranch was the best thing for me to do. This is our real Christmas miracle."

All four of them sat in stunned silence for several seconds before Martin finally said, "We'll be like brothers and sister?"

"I love you!" Olivia almost bowled Finn and Callie over when she clomped across the room in her new cowboy boots and hugged them at the same time.

Later that evening, when everyone was in bed, Callie snuggled up close to Finn and said, "I love my new boots, and I don't have any doubts about them anymore or the cowboy I'm about to marry. And Finn, darlin', you were right. I'm a settler, not a runner. I know it from the top of my head to the toes of my new boots."

"You'll get a new pair every single year from now on. I may write it in my wedding vows. I promise to love, honor, and buy cowboy boots for Callie every Christmas until death parts us."

"The story of our life together can be told by lining up all my boots...but this pair will be worn on Sunday night when I say my vows to you."

Dear Reader,

Merry Christmas and welcome to Burnt Boot, Texas!

It's always exciting to begin a new series, to introduce a whole new cast of characters, but even more so for the Burnt Boot Series. Finn O'Donnell of the Ringgold O'Donnells, whom you all met in the Spikes & Spurs series, is back to kick off the series for me.

You readers asked for more O'Donnells, so Finn and Sawyer have come back to star in their own books. Set in a fictional town where there's a major feud going on between the Gallaghers and the Brennans, *Cowboy Boots for Christmas* debuts the series.

As I finish writing this book, the weather is cooling down in southern Oklahoma, and fall is threatening to push summer into the history books. The stores are decorated for Christmas, and this week I got out the Christmas list. With a family the size of ours, I have to keep track of what goes in which of the gift bags lined up across the spare bedroom floor. But one thing for sure in this family: we all agree that home is where your boots are, just like Callie and Finn find out when they let go of the emotional baggage holding them down.

Here's wishing you all happy holidays and that you fall in love with Finn and Callie's story of finding love in the magic of Christmas.

Thank you to all my readers for continuing to read my books, share them, and talk about them. Big thanks to Sourcebooks for continuing to believe in me and to my wonderful agent, Erin Niumata, of Folio Literary

Management for all she does. And mere words can't express my gratitude to my editor, Deb Werksman, for her wonderful icing recipes. I make the muffin (the story) and together we put the icing on it, and believe me, she has some fantastic recipes. And as always, thank you to my own cowboy who has stayed with me through thick and thin for forty-eight years. He can sure enough testify that it takes a special person to live with an author, and I can testify that I appreciate him for all he does to make my world a better place.

Until January when Sawyer gets to tell his story, may your lights all burn brightly and may love surround you.

Carolyn Brown

Welcome to Fiddle Creek Ranch.
Have you met foreman Sawyer O'Donnell?

"That's pretty bold of you, Jill Cleary." His eyes sparkled when he teased. "We've only known each other a few hours, and a foot massage doesn't mean we are in a relationship."

"Honey, we've been through more in those few hours than most folks go through in a month. Believe me, I'm not ready for a relationship with anyone, so you don't have to worry about that, and, yes, I will take a foot massage anytime you want to give me one," she said.

"Just so we're clear," he said. "Now, I'm going to clean my quarters. Last chance—do you want that side of the bunkhouse?"

She shook her head, red hair flying. "I do not. I can be very happy right here with my two rooms."

Faded jeans hugged his muscular thighs and butt. His dark brown eyes were kind, mischievous, and full of excitement. Tiny little crow's-feet at the sides of his eyes said that he wasn't a teenager and that he had a sense of humor. His biceps stretched at the seams of the blue chambray work shirt. Two buttons were undone, showing a bed of soft black hair peeking out. She wished that he'd left all the buttons undone and that she could run her fingers across the hard muscles under the shirt.

Lord, she needed to get a grip!

The Trouble with Texas Cowboys

Coming soon from Sourcebooks Casablanca

About the Author

Carolyn Brown is a *New York Times* and *USA Today* bestselling author, and *Cowboy Boots for Christmas (Cowboy Not Included)* is her seventieth published book. She credits her eclectic family for her humor and writing ideas. Her books include the Lucky trilogy: *Lucky in Love*, *One Lucky Cowboy*, and *Getting Lucky*; the Honky Tonk series: *I Love This Bar*, *Hell Yeah*, *Honky Tonk Christmas*, and *My Give a Damn's Busted*; the Spikes & Spurs series: *Love Drunk Cowboy*, *Red's Hot Cowboy*, *Darn Good Cowboy Christmas*, *One Hot Cowboy Wedding*, *Mistletoe Cowboy*, *Just a Cowboy and His Baby,* and *Cowboy Seeks Bride*; and her bestselling Cowboys & Brides series: *Billion Dollar Cowboy*, *The Cowboy's Christmas Baby*, *The Cowboy's Mail Order Bride*, and *How to Marry a Cowboy*. Carolyn has launched into women's fiction with *The Blue-Ribbon Jalapeño Society Jubilee* and *The Red-Hot Chili Cook-Off*. Now she's having fun with her new Burnt Boot series, beginning with *Cowboy Boots for Christmas*. She was born in Texas but grew up in southern Oklahoma, where she and her husband, Charles, a retired English teacher, make their home. They have three grown children and enough grandchildren to keep them young.